The Sunlit

Field

A NOVEL BY

LUCY KENNEDY

NEW YORK

CROWN PUBLISHERS

For my *Mother*
and *Father*

*Except for Walt, all characters in this book are ficti-
tious and bear no reference to any persons, living or
dead. However, there is considerable fact in this fiction
—but it is fiction, and therefore the storyteller felt free
to bend a few dates and events to make her story.*

Chapter One

Po STOOD irresolute amid the confusion and bustle of the New Bedford wharf. A schooner down from Maine discharged lumber and took aboard crates of cackling geese; a whaler stowed biscuits and tea and harpoons. And beyond—the packet made ready to sail.

Ordinarily, Po would have enjoyed not only the smell of drying codfish and whale oil, but all the push and hustle under the blue spring sky, but now she balanced from one foot to the other indecisively. Then, through the rows of casks of whale oil, she walked back to stare again at the sign in front of the ticket office. It still read:

Spring Arrangement, beginning March 1, 1857
Packet for Brooklyn daily at noon
Fare four dollars.

She touched the place where, under her bodice, she'd hidden the two dollars. Of the four hoarded for her escape, two had gone for the stagecoach from Fall River to here. The line deepened between her brows. Then she recalled there had been steerage in the ship when she and her Da had crossed the ocean sea, and wondered if there might be on this packet.

It embarrassed her that, even at sixteen, in order to see the purser behind the high ticket window, she had to stand on tiptoe.

"That's the lovely ship you have beyond there, mister honey, and would it have a steerage now, for those not weighty with gold?"

"Nup!" You had to get used to the hard speech on them the way you could think words cost them money. "And don't try to stow away, nuther!"

She turned away then, and in a few minutes, the packet, its paddle wheels churning unconcernedly, pulled away from the wharf. In worried thought, she nearly stumbled over a coil of rope as she moved along the dock. Well, she could turn back. The two dollars would pay the stage to Fall River—and Cousin Frank. But certain ugly memories came into her mind's eye.

Threading her way through piles of crates of chickens, she glanced up at the prim white houses overlooking the harbor, then into the forbidding faces of hurrying business agents and whalers. How would you go about staying in a town like this?

With uncertainty, she stopped beside a damp mossy green mooring post. It nearly hid her, for she was slender as well as not tall. She sighed. If it had been she and her Da, now, they'd have *walked* to Brooklyn. She wasn't sure how far it was, but they'd have gotten there all right. But then, if her Da were alive, she'd not be running. Quickly, she numbed herself against that hovering sting. She was alone. She must pick the road fork herself.

A sailor, olive-skinned, with gold ear loops swinging, came along bent under his heavy sea bag. Just as he passed Po, he accosted a roustabout. His guttural question sounded like "—Brooklyn?" as he motioned to a ship in front of them. The roustabout nodded and went on. The sailor, tugging at his sea bag, went up a rope ladder to the deck above.

Its masts towered, but Po could see it was no marvel of the world, this ship. The black paint was peeling from its wormy-looking planks. The sails looked cobwebby, as if it was long since the sea had washed them.

It must have been the purser telling her not to, made the notion come into her mind. When she and her Da had come from Ireland there had been stowaways. They had not been shot or hung, either, only put in something called the brig. But what had happened to them when they reached Boston? Sent back? Put in prison? She wished she knew. On the other hand, they might not have been found at all!

She wished she could be sure she'd heard that sailor's question rightly.

In front of her, two seamen—one burly, the other small and brown —stopped, looking up at the ship.

"So the old *Red Tanager's* moving!" said the brown one.

"Who bought that floatin' coffin?"

"Someone in Brooklyn. Paid cash!"

"Huh! Good for about one more voyage, I'd say!" And he spat disgustedly far out into the oily green water slapping the stone wharf.

"Anyhow, no use trying to sign on! Principal's got his own crew, I hear!"

The burly one squinted through the afternoon sun up at the ship's deck. A swarthy sailor leaned morosely on the rail above. "Portugee, looks like!"

They were moving off when Po stepped quickly from behind the mooring post. In her excitement, she asked almost fiercely, "Is that ship for Brooklyn? Is it, sir?"

The seaman gave a half-amazed laugh, as if startled at the intensity of the dark blue eyes blazing up at him from the delicately oval face, behind the hood of shawl.

"Whatcha want to know fer?" He winked at the other. "You thinkin' of signin' on?" They both roared with laughter then as they passed on along the dock.

Po sighed, but, at the same time, knew there was one thing she could be glad of. They took her for a child. Her blue wool skirt, without hoops, came to her ankles, above the rough brogans. Her shawl muffled her from head to knees. She knew, in her present situation, her smallness was her great good luck.

For—she could go on to Brooklyn, and her cousin Brian—if she dared.

Uneasy, she watched a large gray rat run down the anchor chain from the hold of the ship. But she knew it wasn't rats, or cold, or heat, or hunger, or anything you endured with your skin or stomach, then forgot—that made her wonder if she dared.

It was a lurking thing you had to face. There was evil walking on two feet in the world—not like when someone killed someone else in a fit of hate or love, because they wanted love so much. The lurking ones were quite different. Po had come to call them . . . the Eaters.

If she was but sixteen, she had been around and about a great deal. Because her mother died when she was young, her father had taken her with him as he went about collecting songs. The Eaters were many places, she knew; you might meet one anywhere. Hadn't one of them devoured that young girl from the County Kerry who had been in the steerage with them from Cork?

They had all been jumbled together for over a month, and he had been one of the ship's crew. When the girl from Kerry, traveling alone to make her fine fresh start in a new world, arrived, it was no good. The Eater had used her.

And there had been the girl, fifteen, who had come, green, from some rocky town in Vermont, to the spinning mill in Fall River; and the older woman, an overseer, who devoured her.

The stone wharf had been built far out in the water to take large ships. The ship's prows jutted in over it. She found herself staring at a strange carved wooden head.

It was the *Red Tanager's* figurehead, and it had two faces. Ah, she knew that boy-o from her history book! It was Janus. He was framed between two fish nets, hanging to dry on tall net racks. One net floated, silvery gray, dry, like a pleasant light mysterious mist. The other hung dank, cold, wet, slimy.

Now she became aware of a man, who though he wore no uniform, as a ship's officer might, seemed to be connected with the *Red Tanager*, for he began snarling orders to the loading stevedores.

His legs were thin, like a toad's legs, and they supported a fat bloated body in a tight blue tail coat. A soiled neckcloth surrounded a puffy face. He took off the mangy beaver from his bullet head a moment, watching the stevedore, as, his back bent under a great bag of rice, he staggered across the short gangplank into the hold. A part of the hold had been opened for the loading, but the ship still rode high.

Coming crisply toward the *Red Tanager*, Po saw an official-looking man in dark blue uniform and peaked cap with gold lettering. His icy blue eyes in a wind-burned face scanned the ship and her decks and came to rest on the man in the beaver hat, who stared back stonily.

"I'm Port Officer Kerdy." His words were clipped so short, his lantern jaw scarcely moved. "You applied for clearance papers. Is your owner aboard?"

"I act fer him! I'm supercargo."

Kerdy stared suspiciously at the cask a stevedore was rolling up the gangplank. It sounded empty! "I'd like to see your principal." He was curt.

The supercargo stared back, stony. "Whatcha want him fer?"

Kerdy's voice whipped out. "I'd like to know what business you're engaged in!"

"We're takin' a load of hummin' birds' tongues to market."

"You won't take anything anywhere without clearance papers!" Kerdy's lantern jaw looked even longer.

"Why'nt you go in the hold and take a look around?" The supercargo half turned away, as if he did not care. Kerdy glowered at him a moment, then stepped briskly up the short gangplank, and peered around a few minutes. When he returned, he was still glowering, but he looked baffled.

"We don't like strange doings here!" His eyes fastened on the piece of light finished lumber a stevedore was carrying into the hold.

"Look here! I'm supercargo of this bark. I can act fer my principal! That's legal, and you know it! You seen the cargo. Gimme the clearance papers. We wanta move with the tide!"

Kerdy glared with baffled anger, then wrote rapidly on a pad. "Destination—Brooklyn?"

"Right!"

Po hardly heard the rest. So, the *Red Tanager* was for Brooklyn! And soon! She had to make a decision quickly.

4

Kerdy tore off the sheet, and laid it disdainfully on top of a keg. Then, as if fulfilling an official task, he consulted a large silver watch. "Tide's in twenty-three minutes," he said grudgingly, and walked away.

The stevedores had finished. Now the supercargo, frowning up the street into the town, examined his watch. He seemed to be expecting somone who was late. Finally, with puffings, he slowly hoisted his fat body up the rope ladder and disappeared on the deck above. Po had the feeling that in a few minutes the sailors would lift the gangplank and close the hold.

It was hard work making up your mind. She was staring at the figurehead. And would you look at that ass Janus, still trying to look both ways and in the middle! A great help was that boy-o! She took a long breath, and slipped up the gangplank and into the dark hold.

Inside, a sort of deck stretched across the bottom of the hull, but the planks were four or five inches apart, so that you had to place your feet carefully to keep from stepping between them. Through the decaying boards, she could see something slithering. Then she smelled the bilge, and knew it was only water moving oilily under the decking.

Arching dimly upward, so that she felt as if enclosed in the rib case of a giant skeleton, were the bones of the ship; and holding them together, as though with fatigue, were the siding planks.

The empty casks, carrying nothing—some sixty or seventy of them —stood in two long rows, one on either side of the hold. At the far end, where dimness passed into obscurity, the lumber of the cargo had been thrown down every which way. Above its confused tangle, a piece of thin white pine thrust upward, like an arm imploring aid. And there were the grain sacks, laid, row on row, like plague victims waiting burial.

Po knew she must find a hiding place quickly. She tried to tiptoe across the shaky decking, which seemed afloat over the crawling water. But her brogans set up echoes. When she stowed herself behind a good-sized cask, pulling in her skirts carefully, she found the planking she squatted on dry, but gritty with dust. Then she realized that it was from the empty cask in front of her she could smell the sour-sick smell of departed molasses.

The rafters of the deck above were in gloom, but she could hear the pound of heavy feet, hoarse voices calling, objects dragged. Then, the gangplank was lifted, and the hold closed up.

At first she felt suffocated in a deep well of black ink. Nothing had warned her of the lightlessness. It was like a nightmare of being lost in a cave that went on, and drearily on, into the bowels of the world. Then, suddenly, she saw the strange sulphurous light.

5

It hovered uncertainly over the bilge at the far end of the hull. She gripped the edge of the cask, and its gnarled splintery wood comforted her with its feeling of being real. The light seemed to move slightly. Then she realized it must be a phosphoric glow from some decaying matter in the bilge. But the knowledge did not seem to lessen her sense of oppression. She envisioned the corpse of some stowaway, dead of suffocation or hunger. And when she heard the slight rustling, like a mischievous whisper, that did not ease her, either. Perhaps it was rats. Would they gnaw at a dead body if they found it here?

With the hold closed, it had become warmer, and gradually, as though an anemic languor were stealing over her, she became aware of the smell. It was the shut-in bilge. It seemed the essence of the used-up, the spent, too stagnant and rotten to attack openly. It must creep up on you with stale feet, and wilt your spirit. She suddenly thought of Bethel Court, in Dublin, a tenement where she and her Da had to live for a time. The antique filth crept up on you just as stealthily, and could make you limp and fight-less before you knew it.

Well, in a place like this, you did the best you could. But being down here was too much like the dreams Po had had since she'd been alone. The insecure deck, the lost blackness, the unknown menace. Everything in America had, for them, been so blankly other than they'd pictured it. From her father, Po had come to dream of it as a great open sunny field, sparkling wet with dew, unused, unspent, still with the early morning shine on it. But instead, she had found . . . the *Red Tanager*.

She was startled by a noise. A hatch had been thrown open on the deck above. A square of sunlight fell into the murk, about the center of the hold. Then, a full sack, perhaps of grain, was flung down onto the pile. It landed in a grotesque heap. But the hatch stayed open.

Po concentrated on the square of light, where beams of dust danced. It cheered her. She had watched it for quite a long time, when, through the hatch, someone jumped below. He landed lightly, athwart the grain bag, and yet, Po saw, he was the biggest young man she had ever seen.

He towered like Gulliver astride a Lilliput mountain, as his huge legs straddled the grain sack. To Po, crouched down behind her cask, he seemed to soar up, a powerful giant—a giant with a thatch of uncombed red-gold curly hair, and a look as if he were about to burst out laughing.

As his sparky gray eyes glanced about, trying to pierce the gloom, it came to Po that he had come down to stow away, too. Not that he seemed hurried, or concerned, for he stood, careless, easy. And looking at the hang of his shoulders, heavy as a young bull's, at the immense fists, Po thought, "And why should he not be easy?"

6

She couldn't tell what kind he was, from his clothes. They puzzled her. Certainly, the brown wool pantaloons rammed carelessly into the tops of half-high boots, were not like a mill operative's. But still . . . even though his shirt was linen and white . . . he wore no neckcloth, and she could see his throat rise out of the open collar. And his coat wasn't broadcloth with tails and gilt buttons, but short and brown and unbuttoned. Well, one thing she was sure of . . . he'd not been traveling long in this cruel world. He could not have looked so fresh and new and unused.

Then she knew why she gazed at him, thranced. There was none of the stunted men of the Fall River mills about this buckeen! In all the gloomy months, he was the first she'd seen with such a look of size and wildness and youth with the shine on it!

He moved out of the light and came along the decking. In spite of his bigness, he sent up no clumsy echoes as Po had done, but moved lightly between the two rows of casks. Opposite Po, a few casks down, he picked the biggest, and dropped behind it, carelessly. But Po could see at once it was not big enough. Bits of him stuck out. And his hair! It blazed out over the top like fire on a mountain.

She guessed her eyes were more accustomed to the gloom, and eventually, he, too, would realize he was not hidden. But in the meantime! What if someone, in the next few minutes, came down the ladder?

"Psst!" she said softly.

"Who's there!" He sounded startled.

"It's me it is, plunged down behind the second cask!"

"A girl!" He seemed slightly indignant, as though she had been caught in the room reserved for gentlemen.

"And he," she said to herself, "thinking himself the swashing boy-o, stowing away. It kills the pleasure for him to think of a mere girl doing the identical."

"Squinge down!" she ordered fiercely. "Your hair can be seen for miles."

"A girl!" He did not sound so indignant now.

"Likewise your big awkward foot!"

He got his leg and foot back, but the bright hair still gleamed like sunrise coming up over the rim of the world.

She would have to give him her dark shawl to cover it. Her shawl! She'd do no such thing! Why, that shawl was woven by hand by the women of Ballyhouna, lovingly, in honor of her father. She wasn't going to fling it about at some towering stranger!

"Here's my shawl! Cover your head with it, leastways until we get moving!" she heard herself say. She took it off, still warm from her.

"Your shawl!" She couldn't see his face, but from the voice, she

7

guessed he had that look of bursting out laughing, and Po could tell the entire beauty of the situation had come to him. With all this blather he'd be caught. She stepped out a moment toward the square of light to toss him the shawl.

He sounded as if he'd been given the smallest piece of candy. "Why, you're just a child!"

Po knew she should be glad he thought so. But, obscurely angry, she tossed the shawl at him and sped back behind her cask.

He caught the dark soft woolen thing neatly and said, "Here, youngster, keep your blanket." He gave it back. "Might get cold when we're under way. Nice of you to take care of me!" Now he was standing up, and she could see from his face he thought it comic.

Then, as if they were two down feathers from the underbelly of a goose, he picked up a couple of casks and made a pyramid with a third, and dropped behind it.

Heavy feet pounded along the deck above and the hatch banged shut, making a smell of dust. There was rattling, clatter, and sails squeaking. And then, something began tapping at the sides of the hold. It was waves! They were leaving New Bedford, Massachusetts, and they had not been found!

The hold was dark again now, but she was not alone. In spite of the cramping, and the smell, for the first time in many months, she felt relaxed, and as if she could drift off into a delicious sleep. Then she heard him whisper, "Hey, youngster! My name's Larry! What's yours?"

She'd known uneasily this moment would come. "O'Reilly, Po."

"That's a funny one. What's it stand for?"

She hesitated. " 'Tis a nickname."

"Ha! Bet your family stuck you with some screamer, too! Know what my name is? Larcom Wainwright! Wouldn't that frizz your eyelashes? But I'd like to hear someone call me Larcom!" Po thought, with fists like good-sized rocks, how easy life must be.

Steps clumped near the hatch above and stopped, as if someone had an ear out, listening. They were quiet a long time, then he whispered, "Sure is an old ark, isn't it? I tried to sign on, but they wouldn't take me. I didn't want to hang around New Bedford until tomorrow waiting for the packet. Did you know we're going to Brooklyn?"

"That's where I want to go!"

"Why? You know someone?"

"A cousin of my dead mother's. He owns a grand thing called a saloon"—she tried to keep her voice modest—"at Fulton and Pineapple Streets. You know anyone?"

"No-o." He sounded vague and uncertain. "I just want to go there!"

8

There was a pause, and after a while he went on. "Did you ever hear of a certain game of ball called—base?"

"I did not."

He sighed then, as if it were hopeless to talk to her. But, after a bit, he whispered, "Someone told me you could live there, in Brooklyn, and do nothing else."

"Are you daft? What kind of a town would that be?"

"I guess it couldn't be true. A peddler selling Ma a clock told me." Larry sighed again. "Maybe I'll go on to the Ohio Country then, or California."

There was a long silence, though, before he continued, and when he did, it seemed as if all the swell was gone out of him. She sensed, a little sadly, he thought her a child he could throw words at without thinking; that he was really arguing with someone else, out of some guilty feeling he had.

"What I say is"—his whisper was belligerent—"if I don't want to, why should I have to go to Bowdoin?" He was working himself up into a rare argument.

"What's a Bowdoin?" asked Po.

"Oh, you wouldn't know. It's a college."

Suddenly, as if in clear amber sunlight, Po saw Dublin, and Trinity College. She saw the young men in scholars' gowns, listening dreamily, head on hand, as her father sang ancient Gaelic songs, ballads of heroes and battles and great angers.

But Larry grumbled on, "What I say is—"

"Ssh!" Po warned him.

A coil of rope or some light object fell with a hollow thump on the deck above. He was silent for a while, but then he broke out bitterly, "Let my uncles be doctors and lawyers if they want! I hate Latin!"

She understood him. In the nun's school in Dublin, she'd loved the Latin and Greek, but hated mathematics. And once, Sister Xavier tried to teach her embroidery. Po flared into tantrums and stunned the sister with a good hair-raising curse. How to express herself usefully had been one of the things she had learned when she and her Da stayed with Dermod the Tinker, to note his songs.

But Larry was still having this grand old argument with someone. "Why can't I do what I'm good at?"

"Why?" echoed Po, her voice drugged with fatigue.

He was suddenly gentle. "Go to sleep, youngster! I'll watch out for you." Po felt as if a warm strong arm had been placed around her shoulders. Half-gone with sleep, she thought it was the first time she'd had that safe feeling since her father died.

She took off her jerkin, the tight sleeveless vest that fitted over

9

her white linen bodice. The jerkin, rolled, made a fine pillow, and her shawl covered her. Po fell asleep.

She woke with a sound echoing in her ears. The hatch had banged open. A lantern flashed below. She must have slept a long time. A thin pair of legs in snuff-colored pantaloons was coming down the ladder. She saw the tails of a blue coat swinging behind a body, fat as a toad's—then the lantern shone on dirty linen around a fat neck, a face bloated and puffy, then a high beaver hat.

From somewhere above, a voice snarled down, "Where's that supercargo? Damn you, Rimshaw! How many times have I told you to search before we leave! One mouth's blabbing is too much! And git back up here and take some of those big Portugees down with you!" The voice was strange, phlegmy, yet gratingly flat and without timbre. It was a voice Po remembered long after.

Supercargo Rimshaw got back up, quickly, but left the hatch open. Almost without knowing what she did, Po moved back, slipping from cask to cask before he could return. Then she bumped into someone.

Someone had been hiding there in the dark beyond them, saying nothing! Po jumped away, heart pounding, mouth dry. The supercargo was back now, with a Portuguese sailor who began to kick the casks aside. One by one, they went over. There was no place to hide. Then, as a cask echoed on the hold, she heard the supercargo exclaim: "A nigger!"

With a hollow roll, the casks kept falling. They were at the cask next hers. Then, as her heart pounded wildly, hers went over.

Po felt the blood leave her face, and her hands and feet get cold, not so much because she had been discovered, but at what she saw. A slow vicious smile raised the corners of the supercargo's mouth. She knew, with a tight constriction in her stomach, that, without her shawl and jerkin, he had not been fooled as Larry had. "A gal!" he said, as if he'd found a coin in the street and would naturally be a fool if he didn't pick it up and use it.

The Portuguese sailor had discovered Larry, who came out, a careless look on him, as if he'd always gotten out of scrapes before.

"Put 'em in the storeroom for now," the supercargo said in a low voice. "No need for the big one to know we found 'em!" The sailor nodded, his gold earrings glinting in the lantern light.

The sailor led the way with Larry and the Negro. The flesh of Po's arm seemed to creep away as the supercargo grasped it.

Silently, they came on deck. She took a long breath of clean salt air and looked up into a vast dark sky. Then her heart gave a little leap, for twinkling at her, dark blue, brilliant, that way you could think it was saying "Courage!" was that great fling of stars, friendly stars, Irish stars, the constellation O'Ryan!

The supercargo's hand moved down her arm, and she felt as if a toad were touching her. "Don't be skeered, deary. You'll git likin' me. Next to the captain, I'm boss!" His hand moved on down her arm.

It seemed to Po she had often noticed how God made his world wondrously beautiful, just when one of his children was about to do something black mean. "Big one's gittin' off soon, in the small boat. After that, I'll be back for you!" Then she was thrust into a long narrow room, lit by a swaying whale oil lamp, and the door bolted.

Chapter Two

WHEN the lamp swung forward, it lit the face of the African to a tawny bronze, and glinted across his bright eyes, watching, wary. Young, about twenty-five, the cords of his throat were tense above the knotted red kerchief, and his bony shoulders hunched forward under a faded blue shirt. He squatted on the floor, chin on folded lean arms. The lamp lit Larry's red-gold thatch a moment, then swung back, leaving them in murk as dark as Po's fears.

Trembly, sick, she sank down on a box. She could still feel the supercargo's fingers on her arm. She rubbed frantically, trying to blot them away. If Larry knew, would he help her? She thought of him as he'd jumped below, big and wild and easy. "And isn't he the one with fists on him the like of which he'd think nothing of helping a girl with?" The thumping in her chest quieted a little. She was about to speak out to him, when she stopped, bewildered.

Larry had taken a ball out of his back pantaloon pocket, and was throwing it from one hand to the other, absorbed, like a child.

The lamp swung back and she saw the Negro watching her as if he sensed her danger. Then he glanced away, and she saw a look in his face that made her forget herself. It was a look she'd seen before, once on the face of a little girl whose father had just died of drink in Bethel Court. She'd seen it again on the face of an old English Jew in the steerage. It seemed to say, "I am still fighting—but there is no hope." Po said to herself, "We got troubles, this African and me."

Larry walked to the end of the storeroom where he had more

space. Then, as if no one in the world were afraid, or sick at heart, he began to throw the ball. Standing there, easy-like, placing his fingers just so, tossing it, with a whip of his wrist into the air, and then catching it, sometimes behind his back, and looking immensely pleased. Again and again he did this. His eyes could see nothing else. Po turned away from him to the Negro. "What's your name?"

"Juba." His voice, like a priest's intoning Latin, was deep and resonant. "I gotta git to Brooklyn! Gotta!"

"Why?"

He glanced, wary, at the ball player. Larry kept throwing the ball, but said over his shoulder, "Don't be scared to talk. My old lady's chief engineer on the underground in South Rockville."

Juba glanced at him again, wary, but finally, he went on. "Come up on de underground. Got lost from my woman and baby. Some say they landed them in Brooklyn. Gotta find them. Gotta git to Brooklyn!"

Larry caught the ball neatly, with satisfaction, and said, carefree, "Oh, you'll get there all right!" Po thought, "He always seems so sure everything's going to turn out blooming!" Then Larry turned, ball in hand, and said over his shoulder, "Something queer about this ship! That crew! And when I tried to sign on, they wouldn't have me!"

"And it's the queer old load they carry!" Po said thoughtfully. "Empty barrels."

"And why'd they put us in a storeroom instead of a brig? Know what I think? I think they *want* us to get away!"

Juba's eyes seemed to burn like fire for a moment.

"We're still too far from shore, though." Larry tossed the ball again, expertly. "Be suicide to jump for it now."

Juba dropped his head on his arms again.

In the close narrow room, smelling of old burlap bags and ancient dust, Po sat with a cold lump weighting down her brain. But, she must think, must do something! She looked at Larry, still tossing the ball. He seemed callous and unaware as a child. She was trying to find the words to tell Larry quickly that she was not a child but a sixteen-year-old girl, when Juba began to sing. Low and sad, at first, like he knew all the answers, and what else was there but to sing, but gradually losing himself, and becoming warm, dark and full of memory. His rich black velvet voice wrapped around her.

> "Come, brothers, to de river steal,
> Away, away, away, ah!
> While de night am dark as Dinah's heart,
> Away, away, away, ah,

> Ya hoo, so spryly, while de stars am peeping,
> We'll grab de eels while de fish am sleeping. . . ."

It seemed to Po she could see the moonrise over dark trees. She could feel the happiness of the eel-fishers, lost in what they were doing.

> "Come wid your bobs, and eeltubs, too,
> Away, away, away, ah!
> And jump into your log canoe,
> Away, away, away, ah!"

Ah, and didn't Po understand what Juba meant? Standing in the cramped gray room at Fall River, hadn't she sung often, "Bright Red is the Sun on the Waves of Lough Sheelin"? Po knew three hundred songs, absorbed from the very air around her Da, and she thought, now, shut up in the dark storeroom, listening to the black velvet voice, a strange thing. Most of them seemed to be about a green world, or a moonlit one, or a world where someone loved. That was because everything was so different. You sang to make it true.

> "We'll fish by de light of de firefly,
> That wink his wing like Dinah's eye,
> So sprightly we'll haul de sarpents up,
> And then so spryly fry de gals a supper. . . ."

But Larry had stopped throwing the ball, and was looking over at them, frowning.

"Say, I guess you better stop. Might bring them down on us!"

Juba looked at him a long moment, in thwarted silence. Then his chin dropped toward his chest, his lips stopped up by Larry's caution, and he stared ahead, dumbly.

Maybe Larry was right, but for some reason, Po was angry at him. She could hear her father say, "Nothing takes the bruise out of a thing like a song!" Didn't this Larry know, didn't he understand anything? Then she looked at the enormous carefree shoulders tossing the ball. "And how could he? Is it ever hungry or hopeless he's been? Or despised? Has he ever in his life felt the cruel and crying need to sing?"

Well, then, next best to a song for the easing of the mind was a story. Not quite so good, but a story, too, could uncrimp the tight claws in the brain. And if she spoke low enough, Larry could not stop them from that by warning about noise.

After a bit, as Larry kept throwing the ball, Po began to make up

13

a story, just off the top of her head, the way the Irish do, almost not knowing what was coming next. She began in a whisper. The tale was not meant for that giant with the ball. He wouldn't understand.

"In the old days, an ancestor of mine, a King he was, King Hugh, lived with his daughter Roseen on Killeney Bay. But the castle thatch was leaky, the black cow died, and they decided to leave off from there and travel to a great place they are hearing of where the air is shiny with the light alone from the faces of all there being that happy."

Larry stopped throwing the ball, and came closer.

"So King Hugh and Roseen sailed from the edge of the western waters. But when they got to this land, himself is captured by black monsters the like they had not been hearing of. Soon, King Hugh, being but a slender man at all, goes along with Death from that place. And Roseen went walking on from there to find the land she had been hearing of where the air has the shine on it."

Larry came closer and squatted down, listening.

"But along the way she falls into the traps of a thundering ruffian, a blowsey by the name of Toadagh. He flings her and a friend she has made, a Moorish African, into a stinking dungeon the like would shame the blackest demon in hell.

"Walking the world that way, Roseen had met a buck-o by the name of Chief Leary, who was that big he could pass for Croagh Patrick in a light mist."

Larry sat down more comfortably, as if to enjoy himself.

"But for all he is that big, he hasn't the wit on him, for the gossip goes his mother, Queen Muira, had dropped him, and he a baby, from the top of a six-story castle accidentally."

Larry sat up straight, shot a quick look at her, and frowned.

"But, Roseen thinks, maybe he would aid her from that place if she could but reach him the word. It was at that moment she remembered a charm her aunt, Queen Klonakilty, has taught her, and she dying. Roseen says over the Klonakilty charm and makes a wish this Leary with the mountain-size on him, be sent to help."

Larry leaned back now and folded his arms, and looked noble.

"But at that minute of the day, this Leary is making ready to go forth and play hurley. He hears a voice telling him to quit off from there and follow where the voice will lead. 'Leave off trouncing the King of Munster at hurley, is it?' says Leary. 'Come again Wednesday the week and maybe I'll go with you! Not now!'"

Larry put his hands on his hips and scowled at her, but Po went on. "Roseen waited, but Leary did not come. Then she heard this blowsey Toadagh coming to get her, and quick-like she says the

Klonakilty charm, but this time she is not asking for this ox Leary. 'Come yourselves this time, People, dears!' "

Larry jerked back, looking at her, annoyed.

"And right before their eyes, through a chink in the stone dungeon no bigger than a dog's flea, came a full baker's dozen of the Little People."

The tight cords on Juba's neck had softened, and now he swallowed with deep satisfaction. "Ha'nt's!" he said, leaning back, as if everything was all right now.

But Larry had drawn back, looking disgusted and indignant.

Po went on. "Themselves ask, civil-like, what can they do for those present? Roseen says they are finding the dungeon unconvenient and downright dull, and quick as a flash of sun on the river Liffey, they find themselves floating up and up, directly through the earth, and right up into the bright sunlight!"

Larry was staring at her now, with a face carefully expressionless. Then he let go a long breath. His eyes narrowed. "Now, let me tell one!" he said.

Po and Juba listened politely. "Once in the old days, one of *my* ancestors, he was sort of a king too . . . he was mayor of Rockville . . . was one of nine brothers, just enough for a baseball team. Every brother was seven feet tall, but so light on their feet when they ran the bases, folks thought it was comets whizzing by. They used a middling-sized oak tree for a bat, and when they larruped the ball, it often went clear to Taunton. But right across the street lived a family of just nine brothers, too, all twelve feet tall. And you know what they used for a bat? The mainmast of a schooner!"

Po's face flushed. "What do you take us for? Pulling our leg like that!"

"I suppose that stuff you were passing out was Gospel, eh?"

She felt her face redden with helplessness at his stupidity. "That . . . that . . . was . . . poetry!"

But, suddenly, Po had much more to worry about than poetry or lies. She heard a hurry-scurry on deck, a windlass creaking, orders bawled. The small boat must be going off. For a few minutes, the story-telling had helped, but now cold fear crept up on scratchy feet and settled black inside her.

At that moment, she even wished she'd stayed in Fall River. "Larry . . ." she began. But Juba had been edging to the door. Suddenly, he was gone. He must have been watching to get away in the to-do of the boat lowering. Po and Larry waited, breathless, to hear if he would be caught. The windlass creaked, the boat banged against the side, then a yell, feet running. Someone must have seen him.

After that, even though they strained, they could make nothing of all the mixed-up sounds. Then there was quiet.

Po plucked Larry by the sleeve, frantic now. She had to look far up at him. "You've got to help me!"

He just laughed reassuringly, and sat down on a box. "They won't do anything to you, youngster. Take you to the officials, probably, and they'll make a fuss over you and send you back to your parents."

"It's worse than you think. . . ." But just then the storeroom door was kicked open, and the supercargo, looking cruelly pleased, came in. The coarse lips smiled as he said, "That nigger'll never make it!" Then he came straight to Po, put a hand on her shoulder and left it there. Po saw Larry get to his feet. "Come on, dearie!" His voice was oily. Larry stood there, looking from Po to the supercargo with a puzzled frown. Po thought impatiently, "Oh, what's the use of waiting for anyone to help, who doesn't even know the difference between poetry and lies!" Her heart thumped like a bird in a box when the supercargo's hand shifted to her arm and clutched it with frightening firmness.

Suddenly, Po put her hand to her head. "Oh, I'm sick!" she moaned. "It's that sick I am I could die!" She was so frightened it wasn't hard to start shivering. Then she turned it into real shaking. "Don't tell them about me . . ." she cried wildly. "Please!" And she shivered and shook.

He looked at her, suspicious, but kept hold of her arm. "What's the matter with yuh?"

"Oh, I'll be . . . all right." She kept shaking and moaning. "I'm freezing, then I'm burning!" She put her hand to her head again distractedly. "Don't let them put me in the pest house! Oh, please! I'll die there just like they did!"

"Pest house!" He drew away a little, but didn't let go of her arm. "Who died?"

Po became almost incoherent. "Oh, I'll die. . .! And it taking me just like it did them! The doctor wanted to put me in the pest house when my mother and sister died. And me running from him! Don't let them get me!"

He jerked her around savagely, and looked at her. Po shivered and shook and moaned. "Listen to me, gal. What'd your Ma die of?"

"I won't tell you," Po screamed. "You'll let them get me and it's me they'll be putting in the pest house!" Then she clutched her head again. "Oh, I'm that sick. I'll die surely!"

Larry just stood there, stupidly agape.

"Listen to me! Tell me what you got?"

"Do you pass your promise not to let them put me away?"

"All right, all right! But what you got? What did they die of?"

16

"Yellow fever!"

He stepped away from her as if she were a hot coal. She shivered and shook and cried bitterly. His toad eyes squinted at her, angry, and a little suspicious, but afraid to take a chance. "A slut's always a liar," he grunted. He turned at the door, and Po moaned. "You promised not to let them put me in the pest house."

As he closed the door he said, "Time we git to Brooklyn, I can tell! I'll see you then."

Po knew she had to get away before morning.

Larry still stood, agape.

"What a liar you are!"

"And you standing there like a yob, with your mouth open! At least you could have thrown him a few bits to curdle his liver. How I was out of my head in the night, or threatened you with a knife!"

"I haven't got the gift for it, like you."

"I wasn't bad, was I?" Po was surprised at where it had all come from. But then, back in Ballyhouna, she knew she was as ready and fast a liar as anyone around the hearth, though apt to leave a raveling or two loose.

Larry was staring at her, eyes narrowed. "Say . . . how old are you, anyway?"

"Well, if it's sense you're counting, I'm old enough to be your grandmother."

"Hmmmmmm . . ." He sank down on a box, arms hanging between his knees, disturbed. "This makes everything awful complicated. All along, I been planning to go over the side when we got in close to Brooklyn—"

"Well, go ahead, then!"

"I figured they'd take care of you, a youngster. But now"—he looked at her, bothered—"I don't know. I don't know." It seemed to Po she could hear the supercargo's word "slut" echoing through the storeroom. "I'm all mixed up about you."

"Go on and leave me. It's me must get away from here, that much I know!"

"Well, look." Larry was frowning as he talked, slow and stubborn. "I don't care if you're—what you are. If you need help, I won't leave you. And as to that"—he made a fist and rubbed his knuckles with satisfaction—"I'll take care of him!" Po suddenly felt warm about Larry again, as she had when she first glimpsed him.

But he was frowning, puzzled. "I'll bet now that we're in close, they won't want us to get ashore. They'll lock that door!"

"All right, then. Isn't it now we must go before it's locked?"

"Yuh? Only trouble is, I know I can swim it, but can I tow you that far?"

17

"That you need not do. It's me can swim it!"

He let his breath out with impatient scorn. "You can't swim that far! No girl could!"

"I can. Many's the time I've swum from the Isle of Glen to Heg."

"More poetry, huh?"

Po peered out the small porthole into a dense fog, now turning from black to bluish gray. The fog wavered, as though a light breeze had sprung up, and as she peered, it seemed to her she saw a bit of shore line.

"We better go now," she said in sudden panic.

"You can't go," he said impatiently, "you'll drown!"

Po put one small hand, knuckles in, to her hip, arm akimbo, and her dark blue eyes sparkled at him with exasperation. "I'm going!"

"But"—he looked annoyed—"I can't let you go!"

"Let me go!" The sparkle in her eyes flared up to a blaze. "*Let* me go! And me with more sense in me when I was but a flower in my mother's hair, then you have now, grown to a giant though you be!"

"Well"—he looked stubborn and bothered—"I don't think you ought to try it!"

"Think! Ha!" Her dark blue eyes shot scornful sparks. "And up to this second of God's time have you displayed the intilligence of a traveling bear at a fair? Then will you leave to them that have been assaulted with trouble and understand its gineral management, to decide what they'll do?"

Larry looked a little confused at all the words spilling out at him so furiously. "It's not a good idea!" he said, stubbornly.

They both were quiet, suddenly. It sounded as if someone were coming along the deck.

The supercargo's bloated face flashed into her mind. She didn't know what legal power he had over them as stowaways. He could probably put them in prison. But it was not that which galvanized her now. She saw his puffy face, toad eyes darting out of it. He was one of the Eaters, she knew. She let out a short exasperated sigh.

"Will you go now," she said fiercely, "and go on over the rail? Or must I shame myself by getting ready in front of you?"

She started to slip out of her skirt, and he turned away from her. But he seemed annoyed, like a bear, teased and frustrated by some small thing he can't reach, but as if he had a good notion to clout out with his great paw anyway. Then he said, scornfully and bitterly, "You a youngster! Ha! You certainly beat a man down same as a grown woman!"

But quickly, Po unhooked her full blue woolen skirt, and slipped out of her jerkin. She wore no petticoats. She stood now, in her white linen blouse, gathered up at the throat and with wide full sleeves,

18

and her long linen drawers. She took off her brogans. Now she wrapped the shoes and skirt and jerkin in a tight bundle in her shawl, leaving two ends of the shawl loose. Then she fastened the bundle on her head, tieing the ends of the shawl securely under her chin, a way she had done many a time when she wanted to go to the Fair at Heg and there were no boats to take her.

Yes, steps were coming along the deck to the storeroom. Po knew the flapping shuffle was the supercargo, and her heart pounded. What if he had a Portugee with him? What if . . . But just then, he opened the door and stepped inside, and locked it after him.

"Now," he said, "we'll see what's what!" Then he turned and looked from Po to Larry. "I knew it!" He had the slow vicious smile. "I knew she was a slut! I knew she was lying. Thought you'd get there before me, eh?" His coarse lips sneered at Larry.

Larry lunged toward him, and the supercargo leaped back to the door. Larry's fist swung, and even in her fear, Po heard the crack as it struck the jaw with a horrible joy. It seemed as though she herself had smashed home the blow.

The two men were struggling, and then Po saw Larry was trying to get the key. He got it. He threw it toward her. It fell to the deck with a little ring. Po ran, picked it up, struggled a moment to open the door. Finally, she got it open.

Without even looking back, she ran to the rail. The mist was lighter gray, but dense. How far down? It didn't matter. She had to jump.

The water struck her with cold shock, then she swam away fast for a few minutes. When she looked back, the ship was lost in the heavy mist. She knew she should keep going, but she treaded water, and waited. After a while, she thought she heard a splash, then, through the mist, the sounds of shouts from the ship. Larry must have made it.

She swam for a long time then, her bundle lashed to her head. The water was smooth, and the tide in. It seemed longer, though, than to the Isle of Glen. After a while, when she was thoroughly chilled and tired, the mist thinned a little. She thought she could see sand dunes ahead. She put her feet down, and touched land. It was the beginning of a new life, but she felt tired and cold and lost. Larry was nowhere to be seen.

Chapter Three

AS SHE STUMBLED up on the cold shore, Po's breath came in trembling gasps. A log, watery black like charcoal, thrust up out of the beach. Exhausted, she sank down on it. Sand particles stung her legs, as with numb fingers she untied her bundle. But her skirt, when she put it on, flapped icily against the goose pimples on her legs. Her hair, unbraided now, hung lank as a shroud. Nose and eyes dripping, she peered into the gray mist. Shells, dead fish and seaweed littered the shore, but no footprints but her own marked the gray sand.

Except for the shuddering shrr . . . shll . . . as the swells slipped along the sand—silence. Just then, great gray gulls flapped over her head, crying strangely. She started up. Maybe they'd seen Larry's body washed ashore!

Hair streaming, skirt billowing, she ran along the shore. The gulls cried now like banshees, and into her mind flashed an Irish tale of a giant, killed by a god jealous of his size, and left to rot on a strand. Then . . . her heart gave a leap.

Striding through the mist, his legs like two oaks, came Larry. They began to run, glad to see each other alive. She ran right into his outstretched arms. He picked her up, crying, "You made it!" He held her still higher as if in triumph. "You swam it after all!"

Then, glancing at the ocean, he set her down suddenly. "We better clear out of here."

The mist still curled dense over the water, but, hanging like a mirage in space, the top of the schooner's masts had come into sight. Breathless, she forced her feet into her shoes. He took her by the hand, and swiftly, their feet crunching into wet sand, they moved away from the ocean. His hand was big and hard. Po thought, "Sure, it's like running across America with a giant!"

Sun began to flood through the mist. At the head of the wide beach, they paused. The sand sparkled now with scattered diamond dust, blue oyster shells glistened like sapphires. He turned suddenly and looked down at her. But instead of glancing away, he kept looking at her, with surprise. "You know," he said after a long moment, "your eyes are awful blue!"

They went on, crossing low sand dunes. Po's breath began to come hard, but she kept up with him.

"Mist's cleared!" he said, after a glance back. "See the ship? We better hide!"

Ahead, some large rocks jutted out of the sand. They dropped behind them. Po sat, breathing fast. Larry crouched, peering between the rocks. "If they lower a boat, we'll have to move!"

The world was warming. Larry sat now, his back against a rock. For some reason, she thought of her father. Strange! Her father had been small and slender as she was, as dark-haired. Then in some flash of thought, she saw why the two kept crossing in her mind. Larry was mixed up in her mind with the bright giants of the old ballads her father sang. "Now how in hivven did a thing like that happen?" she wondered.

He was staring at her with a puzzled frown.

"How long you been leading this life?" Po seemed to hear the supercargo's word "slut" echo. "Uh—er—traveling around like this?"

"I traveled all over Ireland since I was small. And a grand life we had, my father and I, with never a house or cow to keep!"

"What was he, then? A peddler?"

Po reared herself up. "He was a poet, a singer. A harper, they called it in the old days . . . like his father before him!"

"You mean . . . he just traveled around, and . . . sang? Never worked or anything?"

Po fixed him with a scornful eye. "In Ireland, let me tell you, a poet is honored. Even the stupidest gossoon knows when you're sick or sorry, a song can move the pain from your head out into the gineral sky!"

"Aw . . . what's that mean?"

"May God send you sense! You'd never deny, when you're happy, a song makes it keener?" She was proud and scornful. "Why, wherever we went, if something sad or gay had happened, he could make up a ballad. Is it a wonder they loved him? Wherever we went, the best linen was laid. Respect met us—" Her eyes wandered out to the horizon, on and on, across the sea.

Suddenly, he jerked his head up. "They've lowered a boat!" They could see tiny figures in the boat as it tossed up and down in the swell. "It's headed down shore. We better move! Keep as low as you can!"

They'd scurry ahead, then drop down behind a dune to look back. They came to a great sea meadow and crossed it. Beyond rose a small grassy hillock, crowned with stunted pines and high bayberry bushes. They climbed it.

"We can watch all around from here. Ought to be safe, if we keep down, to rest awhile."

They threw themselves on the grass, spent. Perspiration and grass stained his shirt, and he flung it off and stretched out, sun beating on his bare back. She saw the brown mole on his neck, and could have reached out and touched the bronzed skin on his arm.

The sun covered them like a blanket. Stretched out in the grass, its heat bore through her white linen bodice. She could smell growing things, roots sunk lovingly in fertile sticky soil. Insects, strange to her, crawled. Some flowers with furled white buds bloomed in the grass in front of them. She'd never seen them before. A bee assaulted one, lighting again and again on the tightly curled bud. The flower swung on its stalk. After a while, it unfurled a little and the bee squeezed its fat black body in.

Larry turned over and looked at her lazily with a half smile. She felt his eyes on her bodice, on the hips curving out under her skirt. He reached out and touched her skirt, then took hold of a fold of it, the way a little boy would his mother's. "Oh, he knows how to tear the heart out of you, does this one!" she thought, and noticed, half-angrily, her bodice pulsing up and down too fast.

"Did you leave your family?" That was safe, she thought.

He sat up and frowned. "Families!" He pulled up a tuft of grass by the roots, and stared at it moodily. Then he suddenly tore the tuft apart savagely.

"How come you left New Bedford?" he said after a bit. "That where you lived?"

"No. Fall River."

"Fall River . . . that's a mill town. . . ." He reached out and took hold of the tangle of her black hair and tugged it playfully toward him. Po felt strange. She could not shut out the feel of his hand searching through her hair. "Then why in God's name don't I tell him to leave off?" she thought. "I haven't the will power and that's the truth!" She began to talk fast.

"We came to Fall River because my father's cousin lived there. But it was November, skies were gray, the streets narrow, dark and lined with gloomy square buildings." But she could still feel his hand in her hair. She went on, rapidly. "Like monsters, they were . . . those buildings. In the dirty cold mornings, sure they'd open their jaws and swallow the entire population, men, women and children. At night, spit them out, used up, no good. The men weren't tall, and walking with big strides, like my father had dreamed. They were thin and stunted. Many had the maimed hands and arms on them. Some were coughing. Thread mills they were, and I thought I should die if ever I had to go in one."

"Well, who would make you?" He tugged her hair gently toward him.

"No one had time to listen to my father's songs. So . . . he had to go in the mill. Soon, I did too." Po stood up then, restlessly. She stared off across the sea meadow.

"In five months, my father—may bright angels with sweet harps sing with him now—was dead. The cousin was—" She stopped. Then she looked at Larry. "I ran away."

Larry rose then. He took her hand, warm and firm, as if to comfort her.

He was silent a moment. "Maybe," he spoke as if realizing something, "I ran away too!"

They stood then, looking inland, where a light shimmer of mist still partly obscured the land. All America was on beyond the sea meadow. It was enough to make your heart quail.

That's the way it was! You escaped one danger and landed on a shore, but you immediately fronted new problems.

"What's beyond?" Po wondered. "Is it like Fall River it will be?" But what if, instead, it were like her father dreamed?

She had no visible trunk, but in a shadowy bundle over her shoulder were all the scary, bad, hungry times of her life. You could start out more brash and roaring, she thought, if you had no such bundle.

Whisht! She was not going to be afraid. She was going to think maybe she had some peculiar little thing just hers because she'd been born in a certain place or seen a certain thing, and she was bringing it with her to give. That way, you came with shiny eyes instead of a bowed-down heart.

She looked up at Larry then. He was not looking inland now, but off north up the coast from where they had come.

That big he was you could think he'd never have a fear or a trouble—but she remembered how he looked when he tore the grass tuft apart as he spoke of families. He could have a bundle, too, maybe, of a different kind. "For isn't it like he wanted to leave something back there, but it came with him anyhow?"

But he looked down at her just then and smiled, and she looked up at him, radiant. Wouldn't it be wonderful, instead of walking the glowering world alone, if you walked touching another by the hand?

Suddenly, he pulled his hand away and frowned a little, and looked inland again. "I'm going to move around free now! Not get tangled up! See things! Have fun!"

Po felt scarlet flood her face that way you'd think he'd seen into her eyes too far.

Then in some strange flash, she saw he looked across the meadows, just as she did. " 'Tis maybe about different things, but he's got the same hope on him, shot through with the same quiggles of fear!"

"Well," Po said then. "There's no use shilly-dallying! We may as well commince!"

They started off then across the land, still hidden in mist.

Chapter Four

LARRY walked first, treading wary, alert, on the sand path. Before they had come into these scrub pines, they could still see the *Red Tanager,* hanging, threatening, on the horizon, and they spoke little.

Then ahead, in a tangle of tall bayberry and briars, a shed, grayed with salt wind, stood off from the path, and about a hundred feet beyond, Po saw a house.

"Ha! There we are!" Larry sounded as relieved as if all their troubles were over.

Small, brown-shingled, the house was set on piles near an inlet. There was no sign of life. Po could see a blank white door. How could you tell what was behind it?

"I'll go up and knock!" he said.

Po clutched his jacket sleeve and hung on.

"You'll bang on no doors till we see the lay of the land!" Po was so much smaller, she had to make herself sound fierce.

"Think I don't know oyster tongs when I see them?" he laughed, shaking her off. He gestured toward the dooryard, where a skiff, with gear strange to Po, was pulled up in the sand. "It's an oysterman's house!"

She hung on. "Wait now! And if 'tis the house of some local bailiff? And he a questioning man? Sure we but get from one hot pan till you put your big foot in another!"

"You like to run things, don't you"—he looked at her coolly—"Miss O'Reilly!"

Suddenly, a jangle of angry voices rose inside the house. The door flung open, a tall thin man jumped down the steps, ran to the shed, backed out a cart, and began hitching a shaggy horse to it. Sun-bleached hair jutting through a hole in his blue knitted cap, bronzed skin above his dark blue jersey, gave him a faintly seafaring look. He slapped his pocket, cursed, then went swiftly but cautiously to the house.

"The straw in back of the cart!" Larry exclaimed, exultant, to Po, but she already had the idea.

"Come on!" She stood up.

Just then, the basement door of the house opened. An old man, panting and stumbling among the bushel baskets and littered oyster shucks of the dooryard, ran to the cart and burrowed into the straw.

The first man came out now, sprinting toward the cart. A piece of crockery flew after him, shattering with a ping against the skiff. A woman, black hair in a tight knot, arms akimbo over a voluminous blue skirt and gingham apron, screamed in the door, "Heathen! That's what you are, Restored Jones! Going to one of them games, and it Sunday!" Restored was scrambling up into the cart. "And where's grandpappy? Don't you durst let him go!" Her voice had a sort of caw, and as she flapped her arms, she reminded Po of an angry blue jay. "An old man like that, a runnin' to a game!"

At that, Restored cursed, jumped down, ran around to the back of the cart, poked in the straw, and pulled the old man out. Dark-red crabapple cheeks glowed through wisps of straw. "Aw now Restored, you sure ain't goin' to let your granddaddy miss that game!"

"Now, Grandpappy"—Restored was annoyed—"you know Ar'minta don't want you to go to Sunday games! Git down!"

The old man's rheumy eyes looked crafty. "Ar'minta don't want you to go to no bawdy house in Brooklyn, nuther, and if you don't lemme go to the game," he burst out defiantly, "I'm goin' to tell her you was to one!"

Ar'minta was flapping down the steps, excited, angry. "And another thing," she cawed, "who's going to sort them oysters?"

Restored jumped back up on the cart, grabbed the reins, lashed the shaggy horse, and the cart started with a jerk.

Grandpappy, sitting in the straw in back, waved happily to Ar'minta as the cart rolled away. She stood, breathing hard, then went in the house and slammed the door.

Larry stared after them ruefully. "And I'll bet they're going to Brooklyn! Say! He's going toward the ocean! There's a little bridge down there over the inlet. He'll turn and come back this way, but on the other side of the inlet. Come on! Maybe we can get a ride yet."

They waded the inlet hastily, then threaded a strip of pines. Yes, here was the sand road! Already they could hear the screech of the cart, the blump of the hooves in the sand. They stood in the road and waved. Restored, lashing at the horse, did not slacken.

"Give us a lift!" Larry yelled after him.

"No time, son!" Grandpappy yelled back. "We gotta git to Brooklyn. Late now!" And the cart careened down the road.

"At least we know if we follow their tracks, we'll get there," Larry sighed, as they started walking.

But a mile down the road where the sand trail joined the highway, they met the cart again. Restored, with Grandpappy cackling advice, was trying to pull the cart out of a deep ditch. Larry seemed not to remember they'd refused him a lift. He was shoving Grandpappy aside—a heavy shoulder under the cart, three or four grunts and the cart was up. Restored's jaw, moving constantly in a steady rhythm of chewing. dropped open. He spat a long arc of brown juice. "Guess we can ride ye. Git in!"

Grandpappy's voice was high pitched above the cart wheels. "Come fer?"

"Oh—" Larry swallowed, glancing at Po. "Up the island apiece."

"Thought mebbe"—Restored glanced back over his shoulder, voice dry—"you mighta jumped ship from that bark out there!"

Grandpappy was cackling out boastfully, stroking his old coat, proudly, "This here's my sojer coat. On'y wear it fer big times like today! I fought with Washin'ton! Drummer boy! Right here on the Island!" His beard, long and beautiful as a saint's, was stained with tobacco juice and reeked of brandy. "You folks goin' in fer the Atlantic game, ain't you?"

Larry sat up. "Baseball?" His voice was tense, alert.

Grandpappy burst out, "Restored plays with the Atlantics. Best goddam first baseman on Long Island!"

Po felt Larry's tension in the straw beside her. "Got any good teams around here?"

"Any good teams?" Grandpappy snorted. "Where you been all your puny little life? Ain't you never heard of the Eckfords of Greenpoint? Or the Stars of South Brooklyn, or the Enterprises of Bedford? Ner the Putnams of Williamsburg?"

Larry's eyes glistened, and he seemed to strain forward. "This is a big game today, eh?"

He seemed to have forgotten the *Red Tanager*. Po hadn't. She kept wondering what had happened to that small boat. Had someone landed? Were they bowling along this road into Brooklyn too?

"Son, today you will get to see"—and Po thought it sounded as if he were talking of holy saints—"the Atlantics play the Putnams!"

Restored threw back, "The winner to play off with the Excelsiors!"

"And who are they, for the love of God, these Excelsiors?" Po wondered. "The archangels?"

Now Restored turned full around and stopped chewing, a rapt look on his face. "And whoever beats the Excelsiors will be the team that gits at the Knickerbockers!"

Larry stood up in the straw excitedly. "The Knickerbockers! The old Knickerbockers? In New York?"

Then Po saw a look on Restored's face she was to see on many other faces—cold, earnest, solemn. "The same. And goddam their fat stockbroking asses!"

"They won't even admit," said Grandpappy, "there is such a thing as a ball club in Brooklyn!"

"Why don't you challenge 'em?" Larry demanded, excited.

"They don't pay no attention!"

If a boat landed, Po thought worriedly, it would have been closer in to Brooklyn, perhaps about here. And someone from that boat— what if it were the supercargo?—might be coming into this highway from one of the side roads they kept passing. Po began to watch each sand trail apprehensively. Someone had to worry, for that Larry was as intent on this gabble about some child's game as if it really mattered.

"Bet you if I was playing on one of your teams, I'd get 'em to answer!" Larry threw out.

"You play, eh?"

Now they were passing another sand trail. Po stared down its avenue of pines as the cart rattled past.

"I'm a pitcher!"

"Eeayah? I heard lots of boys claim they was pitchers!"

But Po had jumped down into the straw. Coming up the side road, about to turn into the highway, Po glimpsed a black buggy. In it was the supercargo and one of the more vicious-looking Portuguese. Po tugged at Larry's arm frantically.

He pulled away impatiently, intent on Restored's words.

"If you want to join a club," Restored said, "I can tell you which one's best!"

The buggy had turned into the highway. "Larry!" Po whispered, tense. "Look back!"

But Larry, eyes aglow, was listening to Restored. "Whatever you do," Restored started to say, as Po, afraid to look back now, pulled fiercely at Larry, "don't join the Excelsiors! They're a bunch of slobs!"

"Larry! The supercargo!" Larry looked back. He got down in the straw fast enough then, pulling Po with him. He picked up great handfuls and covered her quickly. In her fear, the dry straw scratching her face, covering her, felt wonderful.

It was a little time before she heard the supercargo's voice, evidently pulled up beside their slower cart. She felt sure Larry had had time to burrow down, and she hoped there was straw enough to cover his bigness.

"Ain't happened to see anything of my nephew, big young fellow, kinda blond reddish hair?" The supercargo's voice was smooth, placating. Somehow this frightened Po much more than if he had been openly demanding. "Had a little dark-haired gal with him!"

They moved along then for quite a while, and Po guessed Restored was chewing, and maybe reflectively taking a long spit, and considering their sudden dive into the straw.

"I was expecting to meet him along here somewhere!" The supercargo's voice was so silky, it must mean he was not going to put the peelers on them. He and the sailor meant to find them themselves. Clearly, he wanted no one going into Brooklyn with tales of the *Red Tanager*.

Finally Po heard Restored's dry noncommittal voice, and thought, "Arrah now, isn't it the decent men you could meet, on any road in the world, as well as the others?" For she heard Restored say one word, "Naw!"

Po waited for a long time, afraid to show herself. The cart rolled down the road for quite a while, before she heard Larry say, "He's gone!"

Restored and his granddaddy looked at them, then, but just blinked their eyes, and said nothing. Larry did not offer any explanation, only looked back at Restored, and said, "Thanks!"

Restored chewed a moment, as if studying Larry's big shoulders and arms speculatively. Finally, he said, "You going to live in Brooklyn, ain't you? Well—just remember—the Atlantics is best!"

They drove on. Soon Larry was as absorbed in a lot of gibberish about maple clubs or ash as if he'd never seen the supercargo.

The horse drank from a trough under a sign "Two Mile House," and Po, through the door of the long low stone inn, smelled fragrant cooking.

"For the love of hivven," she cried, for the smell made her faint, "can't we stop a minute for food?"

The three of them looked as if she were a bothersome child, but went inside. A fat German in a white apron brought bowls of soup. It was delicate orange with bits of red and green floating, and when she asked, the man said it was "klem jowder."

Po tried to dawdle, hoping the supercargo would get far ahead, but they gulped down their soup, tossed out a coin, and were at the door, impatient to be away.

The soup made her feel better. It brought her spirit back.

They were turning into a wide road now. The houses were fairly close together, some joined like pans of hot cross buns. Carts, wagons, phaetons, buggies, men on horseback and on foot, all traveled in one direction. Po watched, apprehensive, for the supercargo. Then she heard a bell tolling, and remembered it was Sunday. She thought how interesting it was to see the populace all rolling off to church for themselves with such a keen look on them. The men on the road began jawing back and forth, some calling to Restored, "Who's to pitch?" or "We'll wallop the woolen drawers off you today!" Then it dawned on her they were not going to any holy services but to this game.

Suddenly her heart missed a beat. There it was, on an arched gas lamp, the sign reading "Fulton Street." She searched the faces now of the men strolling on the brick sidewalks, in Sunday coats and light pantaloons. One of them could be her cousin Brian!

There was no sign of the supercargo—"Maybe you should let me down here!" she called to Restored. " 'Tis the street of my cousin!"

But Restored rolled along, not wanting to stop. "Don't worry! Unless he's paralyzed, he'll be at the game anyway!"

Then above the grating of the cart, she heard a great dull roar. Restored stood up and excitedly gave the poor little horse a lash. They raced along, sparks flying from the cobbles. Po was afraid they'd upset. Ahead of them, on one side of the street, was an open grassy space. It was jammed with people, near as many as at Bantry Fair. They were all standing about, the women's and children's pink and green and magenta dresses gleaming out from the darker clothes of the men. The dull roar came again, louder. Larry and Grandpappy stood up now, shouting. From then on it was as if they were possessed.

Restored pulled the cart to a sudden stop, jumped out and ran off. Grandpappy clambered down, tied the horse to a hitching post and followed him. And then, that Larry ran off after them!

Po stood in the street, twisting a lock of black hair uneasily. She ought to go and find her cousin at Fulton and Pineapple Streets. But she was worried. He was only her mother's cousin, her own second cousin. True, she had heard, even in Ireland, he was a kind man. But what if not—what if he were like her cousin Frank? Or what if he didn't want to be bothered with her? "Wisha, it's maybe a little scared I am, though it's me has been traveling the thorny world this long while. What if he tells me to be off?"

And that Larry! And he running off, with never a backward glance! She kicked back a wave of self-pity that lapped the shore of her consciousness.

What if she never saw Larry again?

On second thought, she might just go and take a wee peep at this game that made them all into children. Besides, hadn't Restored said her cousin would be there surely?

Chapter Five

Po WAS so small she was able to work her way through the crowd until she was in the front row. But, there was nothing there, only a large open space of clay, beaten down hard by many feet, circled by this great crowd standing about.

Just then, the people on the side where she stood let out a great shout. A string of men had come trotting out, one by one, from a little tent she had not noticed before. They were dressed alike, in long gray trousers, white flannel shirts, and hats peaked like a rider at the Fair. Their middles were circled by wide belts of white, lettered "Putnams."

From the other side, a second file of men trotted from a tent, and a second shout went up. At the tag end of this group, hurrying, and still fastening on his belt, she saw Restored. She spelled out, on his belt, the word "Atlantics."

There was a little silence, like in a church when some ritual is to begin. Then, stooping way down to come out of the tent, appeared one of the biggest men she'd ever seen.

He was bigger than Larry. As he sauntered out with a little jocular roll, the crowd gave a joyful moan as if it were clasping him to its breast. He smiled a little and raised an enormous arm in greeting. They yelled "Bull! Bull Bender!" After that, things began happening too fast for Po. "Sure," she thought, "it's like moving day in hell!"

At first she could make nothing of it. She did not know the why of the mad surges of delight, the fierce rages, the screaming exultations, the joyful frenzies. But suddenly, on that Sunday in 1857, in Fulton Street, in Brooklyn, Po felt tears come to her eyes.

She wanted, deeply, urgently, for her father to be here. All her fears, in Fall River, on the ship, seemed washed away in a flood of sunlight.

On the field, the men flashed about, stretching their bodies in long beautiful arcs, or leaped into the air to catch the ball with easeful sureness in bare cupped hands. Yes, these were the tall men! And running with the full swinging strides he had told her of! And the men watching let out their entire lung content in complete anger, or threw an arm over the shoulder next them, in some feeling where no dregs of hate remained in their eyes.

And even if small squat row houses pressed close in around this open field, and it was no longer dewy morning, but afternoon, the feeling of joy, of exuberance, was here! Of a people, running, shouting, raging, anxious, but caught-up, possessed by the delight of their own activity. If they were gusty with anger, or screaming mad with joy, ready to fight or to embrace, they were also flashing, fleet, agile, boss of themselves. They seemed lost in a feeling of oneness.

She remembered the thin gray men like sheep sucked into and out of the thread mills in Fall River. In Ireland, such men had starved. In Fall River, they had food enough to keep alive, but it was as if they had been compressed into small flat molds. All the sap and color and change had gone from them. On a Sunday afternoon such as this, they sat in drab houses, too tired to move. Again she thought of her Da, and the cellar they'd lived in. But . . . no more of that! He hadn't made it. But, ah, wouldn't he be glad she had!

She understood about Larry and Restored now. She understood about this game of ball called base. Suddenly, at the next roar, she screamed too, in mad delight, not knowing what the play was, but happy to lose herself the way the crowd had. That big man they called Bull was standing out there, waving a club. She sensed they were all the mighty Bull, waving the club . . . or at least, his smaller brother.

She longed to know why the crowd was possessed with rage or delight. Next her stood a mild plump man in velveteen jacket, who smelled of beer and the long meerschaum he smoked. Suddenly, the crowd groaned, the mild man snatched off his peaked cap and jumped on it.

"Please! What happened?" she demanded of him.

He shrieked at her in German, as his eyes popped with rage. Po shrank back, half scared. But after a few moments, a player ran around the playing field, and the crowd seemed to be happy again. A thin dark man with beautiful mustachios kissed another mustachioed man next him. Po longed to share the general bliss. Timidly, she plucked mustachio's arm.

"What happened?" White teeth flashed, his hands made intricate gestures. She was inundated by a flood of Italian. She began to feel she'd gotten to heaven, but couldn't speak the language.

Then she saw a slender narrow-chested lad watching her with a smile. She remembered half-starved students around Trinity who looked like him. He had dark hair above a bulging white forehead, and dark eyes burned in an intense face. He leaned toward her so she could hear him above the crowd and gave her the glad tidings: "Twinkle-Toes made third base!"

Everything about this game must be learned as fast as possible. Maybe girls played it! Now it seemed all the players were walking, on or off the field. There was a lull in the shouting. Po asked the dark-eyed one, "Is it far to a street called Pineapple?"

"No. Close. Looking for someone?"

"My cousin. Brian Brady."

"That runs Brady's Gardens? He's around. Saw him a while ago. My name's David Posen."

"I'm his cousin, Po O'Reilly, come from Ireland."

"Just stand here! I'll keep watching for him!"

But after a while, Po found herself looking, not for Brian, but Larry. Where had he gone? Then she saw the blonde girl in the greenish-blue dress.

Most of the women had their eyes on some man's exploits on the field, but this girl was smiling with full red lips at someone sitting on the ground near by. She twirled her tiny blue ruffled parasol and wriggled about so the curve of her breasts showed above her low-cut dress. Then the man she was flirting with stood up. It was Larry.

He crossed to her. Po could see that look of bursting out laughing on his face, his bright hair above the enormous shoulders. She had a strange sensation. Po guessed she was hungry or something. She felt so empty. Then a kind of frozen rigidity settled in her, as if she had to keep her eyes unwaveringly on Larry. Dressed conspicuously, the girl still did not look like the street women in Cork. She was young, eighteen or nineteen, fresh, and yes . . . she was beautiful. Po could hear the girl's loud unself-conscious laugh, as she looked up into Larry's face invitingly.

"And who is that girl," Po asked Dave, "with that butter-y hair on her?"

"Who? Oh . . . there! That's Louise Denis!"

Intent as she was on what was happening between these two, Po suddenly felt a strangeness in the air around her, like a cloud going before the sun. The people near her fell silent, became motionless, only their eyes turning to look at someone.

A big man was coming through the crowd. He was not as big as the Bull, but he was as massive as Larry, and in a certain way, built like Larry. His heavy shoulders, like Larry's, gave you the same feeling of power. But if they were built alike as two stony fountains, from Larry sunny water seemed to leap high in the air, while this man made you think of just the inflexible stone.

"And who is that, then?" Po asked Dave.

Dave stared at the man, with no fear, but a blank look. "William Hymes."

About thirty-five, Hymes's features were heavy and immobile-looking, and under the new but dusty-looking beaver, his hair was dullish brown and sparse. Po wondered why everyone seemed to look at him with such blank wooden expressions. He was common-looking as anyone here, his snuff-colored double-breasted tail coat no better than the crowd's. He looked even a little ill-kempt and his white stock was dingy. His glance was certainly not threatening. Indeed he paid no attention to anyone. He walked straight across the field, though, as if, seeing him, the game would suspend. It did.

Then Po saw Hymes was headed toward Louise Denis. Louise saw him coming, too, and made the great thing of flirting with Larry, laughing with wide sensuous red mouth up into Larry's face.

Then the clod was thrown. Po could not understand it. For what was the poor man doing but chasing some light-of-love, a thing accepted long since by the human race. The clod had landed in front of Hymes. In this crowd of expert tossers of balls, it could not have been meant to hit him. It was an expression of an emotion.

Hymes turned heavily, his massive shoulders hunched awkwardly. She felt a kind of admiration for him, for he stood, one against many, looking at the crowd with stolid courage.

By the time he turned, Louise had disappeared.

Hymes kept coming, though, straight toward Larry.

And then, it was a strange thing, but Larry seemed to lower his head with almost the same gesture as Hymes. You could think they were two great bulls, lords of the herd.

Then Hymes turned and walked off in the direction in which Louise had disappeared.

The game began again, quickly, as if some dark shadow, some apparition had appeared to claim all this sparkling zest, and they wanted to play again quickly, to forget they had seen it. They seemed to blink their eyes in the sun, to push the shadow back into their consciousness; as if they sensed it hovered, waiting to claim them; as if they feared the heady exuberance they breathed this day might evaporate like dew.

Po felt angry. She had been so caught up with the feeling of the free, happy, screaming crowd. She didn't want anything to spoil that. "But—why—" she hardly knew how to ask Dave to explain. "You'd think he owned the place!"

"It's likely he does!" Dave's eyes looked over the heads of the crowd an instant, as if seeing the shadow. Then suddenly he gave a shout. "There's Brian! Brian Brady!"

Po felt herself trembling. The shadows that had dulled her at Fall River fell again. What if Brian did not want to be bothered with her? Or what if he did not like her?

Then she caught sight of the man Dave was bringing, and she knew it was all right. She wanted to laugh and cry, and guessed what she felt was homesickness. The thick brown hair, the deep-set

33

gray eyes, were as familiar as a thatched roof. The cliff of his chin jutting between cascades of sidewhiskers was as like home as a whiff of the green downs, or the mist off Ballybunian. Only he should not have been wearing a round bowler hat, a checkered vest and a blue coat with velvet lapels. Knee pants, gray wool stockings and a knit cap would have looked more natural.

A little boy of six clung to his coat tails, another lad about ten was at his side.

Then Brian grabbed her hands in great ham-like fists, and warmth ran all through her. "Hugh O'Reilly's girl!" Delight and surprise and love were all mixed up in his gray eyes. "Happy it is I am to lay eyes on you! Let me look at you now! Sure, darlint, your eyes are deep blue as the Lake of Sheelin! And look at the face on her, Dave, pretty as a blushy rose!"

The little boys were not his sons. They were just friends, and they ran back to watch the game now.

"But your father? Where is he?"

"He's dead, Brian!"

"Ah, surra, it's that blaggard New England. If he'd but come to Brooklyn now, he'd be alive and singing! And Cousin Frank?"

Po looked at Brian's good-natured face. She could not speak. Then she said in a rush, "I ran away from there, Brian." She could not look at him or go on.

"It's all right, darlint. I'll not question you. You had reasons. And how was it you got here?"

"It was on a ship, and I stowing away!"

"Stowing away, is it?" Brian's eyes sparkled. "A slip of a girl! Well, that's done now! You'll stay with me. Mamie'll be glad to see you!"

At that moment, the crowd gave a great angry shout, and Brian dropped her hands and ran to the edge of the crowd, asking what had happened. Then she heard him yell in a dreadful voice: "The dirty dog! He tripped him as he went past! Didn't I see him with me own eyes? He oughta be hung!" After a few minutes, when the excitement died, he came back.

"Ah, poor Hugh," he sighed, "that lovely singer! I can hear him yet, singing 'Fair Athlone.' And to think he is dead!"

But just then there was the crack of a ball, the crowd yelled, and Brian was gone, screaming, red-faced. He came back soon, pulling his mouth down into mournful lines again.

"So poor Hugh is gone! I remember hearing of the crazy name he gave you!" But his eyes kept darting out to the field. A strident voice called, "Str—i-ke!" Brian's eyes blazed, and he ran off, screeching, "You're the blackest robber ever walked on Myrtle Avenue! Your

34

mither was blind and your father an idjit!" Po thought it wonderful to hear him. When he returned again, he said, "Never mind me, darlint!" and he set his mouth in mournful lines again.

"Tis a game, this!" Po's eyes sparkled.

"You've seen nothing. Wait now till you see the Excelsiors play! That's the team Dave and I play on!"

Himself played! Ah, marvel! Somehow Po began to have the feeling these Excelsiors must be the wonder of the known world. The game had stopped while they hunted for a lost ball.

Some of the crowd, while they waited, clustered around a man, who was reading aloud to them from a newspaper. "There's Walt," said Brian. "Come on, let's hear what it is he's reading to them!"

This Walt was a big man, and though he seemed only in his late thirties, his beard was streaked with gray. The crowd was dressed in Sunday coats with high white collars and string ties, but Walt wore a red flannel shirt open at the neck, and a large round felt hat on the back of his head. He stopped reading a moment and looked up, and she saw his strange seer-like pale blue eyes. He began to read again in a deep resonant voice, and Po saw the print across the outspread newspaper, "New York Journal of Commerce." At first, she could make nothing of what he read, though in the crowd pressing in on him, she felt a gathering, outraged indignation. She listened, trying to understand why. Walt read on:

"Since Mr. Cartwright founded the first ball club,
the Knickerbockers of New York . . ."

Someone let forth a sneering catcall, but Walt went on, saying each word as if he wanted them to miss none:

". . . there have come into existence three other clubs, the
Eagles, Gothams and Empires of New York. These four clubs
represent baseball today in America."

There was a second of silence, then a low hissing sound. A moment later, when it let loose, Po realized this had been the crowd drawing breath to let out a roar of outrage. Po had heard cursing along the byways of Ireland. It had been rich, too, but not so pointed or venomous as this.

"The low-flung sneaking pot-bellied plush-assed bastards!" a player near her yelled, red in the face. "They never even mentioned our names!"

Walt glanced around, and then he went on blandly, as though he were reading something mild and non-explosive.

35

"Some of the most respected business men in New York play nowadays and the game threatens to supplant even the popular cricket. Our readers may remember Alexander Cartwright, who engaged in mercantile business on Fourth Street before he went to California in the gold rush several years ago. It was this New York business man who invented the game about ten years ago. . . ."

"Aaeeyow!" The crowd gave an outraged incredulous groan.

"Invented the game!" Dave Posen yelled, indignant. "Why Bull Bender played it upstate long ago as he can remember!"

Then Po caught her breath as she heard a familiar voice cry out from the back of the crowd: "We played it in New England from way back!" It was Larry.

Walt read on mercilessly:

"The Knickerbockers make the rules and run the game since they were the first club and are generally recognized as the best. . . ."

Po was almost frightened at the feeling let loose around her. A chunky player pounded one big fist into his open paw. "Champion of the world, huh?" he said bitterly. "Because they're scared to play anyone else."

Walt went on:

"The Knickerbockers are made up of some of the most solid and respectable business and professional men in New York. It is one of the tenets of this club, which has no doubt added to its strength, that no one can obtain admission to the club merely by being a good player. He must also have the reputation of a gentleman."

"So to play ball you gotta come on the *Mayflower!*" yelled the chunky player, as the rest groaned and called imprecations.

"I come on the Cauliflower," a tall rangy Atlantic called, "and I'll play 'em any day!"

Walt was folding the paper blandly. "You boys ought to put a piece in the paper yourselves! Maybe they don't know you're over here!"

Now Po saw, on the faces around her, the look she had seen on Restored, in the cart. Cold, earnest, solemn. Then the tall rangy man said, slow, heavy, grim, "They're gonna know soon!"

But now the game began again. Po kept demanding to know what it was that made the crowd roar, and Brian or Dave would start to

36

tell her . . . until something else happened on the field, and they would become too excited to finish.

After a time, there was a great roar, and the crowd chanted like a litany: "Bull, Bull Bender!"

"He's good, that one!" muttered Brian. "I gotta watch this, if the Excelsiors are to show they're best! Which we are!" A little man next to him took exception to this, and began to argue hotly.

But the whole crowd hung motionless as the Bull swung on his great club. Then there was a terrific crack as the ball struck. It glanced off to one side, wild, over the head of the crowd, with electric speed and force. So quickly, she could not be sure it happened, she saw Larry, standing there, reach up a big arm, and as easily as if he were plucking a flower, pull the ball down out of the air.

She saw Dave Posen look at Brian and Brian at him. "Who's he?" Brian asked. "Never saw him before!" Dave said. They exchanged a glance, then Dave disappeared in the crowd.

Suddenly, there were shrill piping whistles. The crowd called out, not in the big roar as before, but in individual angry screams. They began to rush in one direction.

"The police!" Brian yelled. "Trying to break up the game!"

The peelers? Trying to break up such a beautiful thing as the game! "But why?" Po demanded.

"Blue laws! It's Sunday!" The police were all over now, in tight uniforms, brandishing staves.

"When else can they have time to play?" Walt cried as a policeman rushed by.

"I'll bet William Hymes put them on us!" someone screamed. Some of the crowd began to fight back.

Baseball clubs were swinging now, and fists. Po saw Brian, flailing away with his fists at a policeman, and as she watched, mouth open to yell, she saw another policeman, fat, start toward Brian, stave upraised.

At this sudden rude violent break up of the happiest thing she had seen in America, Po had felt a swelling of outrage pound up into her ears. She didn't know where the impulse came from. Maybe from long generations of rebels. She found her fingers closing around a piece of earth. Her impulses were always too strong for her. When she heard the clunk as the clod hit the policeman's neck, just as he was about to strike Brian, she was scared, but she felt good, too.

The policeman reeled off to one side, with a startled hurt look.

Brian ran toward her. He grabbed her arm. "Come along now." He breathed hard. "We better git from here!" They ran.

Down Fulton Street that Sunday afternoon, Brian and Po went.

37

And so Po arrived at her new home. "Running from the constabulary!" Po thought. "And what better way to arrive? Sure, I love this place entirely!"

Chapter Six

"COME here now, Mamie!" Brian called. "See who's come to stay with us!" He disappeared down the hall.

Po sat on the edge of an unyielding horsehair settee, fingers of disquiet tightening around her throat.

Brady's Gardens was a three-story rectangle of red brick with the barroom on the street level, and they had reached Brian's flat by an outside stairway to the second floor. When Brian opened the shining plate glass door at the head of the stairs, Po had looked into the semi-gloom of a long narrow hall with four or five varnished doors opening off it, and the one at the end had been this parlor.

She could hear Brian's voice, a little excited, at the other end of the hall, giving, no doubt, the history of the sudden cousin from Ireland. It was asking a great deal, Po knew it, to come into someone's house, even in America, where potatoes need not be counted. And what if Mamie did not like her?

Perhaps it was only Po's feeling of hanging unsupported in midair that made the small square room seem so airless and gloomy. She felt even the gleam of a candle would have cheered her. But where were the candlesticks? A gas fixture of brass bowknots hung from a molded plaster ceiling, and ah, yes, there was a lamp! Carved ornately of alabaster, with its shade be-flowered and be-fringed, it stood on the ruffled cover of a round center table beside a book covered in purple velvet and stamped in gold "Fanny Fern's Thoughts on Flowers." But everything looked so untouchable, as if glued down, that Po gave up the daring notion of lighting the lamp.

And if Mamie did not like her? To stop this carking thought Po tried to admire the room. Staring at her from the maroon wallpaper with its pattern of sulphur-green wreaths, was a picture, in a heavy carved gilt frame. It had a view on it of a stag kicking out his dying gasp, and somehow the sight did not seem to ease Po at all.

Three chairs, matching the settee, ranged precisely against the opposite wall, their horsehair-covered seats looking as if never, no never, would they yield to any buttocks, queens' or hooligans'. Their stiff bosoms bore, like white temperance badges, square crocheted tidies.

Po could see the fireplace had been bricked off and papered over, but the varnished oak mantel remained. A clock ticked. Maybe Brian had been gone but a few minutes, but to Po it seemed a heavy weight of time. On the mantel, she discovered that the bronze statue of a lady holding aloft a bunch of grapes held the clock, set right in the middle of the poor woman's belly. Looking at it seemed only to add to Po's feeling of torment.

She'd look at their books then. But she could find only the purple velvet one, which she felt was not to be moved. In a corner, a cabinet with shelves held, not books, but china ornaments, and near it, on a molded terra cotta pedestal, was a large glass dome. Nailed down under the dome were wax flowers, but they looked so like a funeral wreath, Po shuddered from that too.

With a small miserable sigh, she sat down again, pulling her muddy brogans under her skirt, as the bright magenta roses in the mustard-green brussels carpet seemed to stare up at her with disdain.

The parlor of that Episcopal rector in the county Armagh, she remembered, had the same crowded rigid completeness—the whirling curlicues, the feeling that everything had been freshly varnished, and set to dry and must on no account be touched. The rector meant it to show how people of civilized gentility lived, an example to the poor ignorant peasantry, who had no advantages in their homes—except a warm fire and a feeling of tenderness.

When Brian and Mamie finally came in, Po got to her feet hastily, and remembered her manners in time to bob a curtsy and say, "God save all here!"

Mamie's dress of stone-colored taffeta stirred with a Sunday afternoon visiting frock's stiff rustle. It was fitted up close to her chin and down to her wrists, as if everything was under lock and key, valuable property, buy your ticket at the window. Even her fine brown hair was smoothed down in dew-laps over her ears and fastened under a flattening net, with no careless disposal of property.

"But what should I call her, Brian?" Mamie's tone was so sweet it seemed like cake icing which might crack at a touch. "I can hardly use that outlandish name! It's so queer! What will people think?"

"Call me Po, Cousin Mamie!"

"My name is Mae!" Po knew from her tone, she must never make that mistake again.

Mamie's face was oval, except for a small angular chin, and her features were undistinguishedly regular and pretty, except for the mouth. To match the pink and white enamel of her skin, her mouth should have fluted into tender curves. Instead it was sparse, as if

39

someone had dipped the tip of a knife blade in bluish pink paint and drawn a small straight line.

"Give the girl a bit to eat, Mamie!" Brian was clumping toward a front window, closed tight against the late afternoon sun. He burrowed through green plush lambrequins, arranged in tortured loops riveted to the wall with green glass rosettes, then through stiff lace curtains, and threw open the shutters. In the rays of the setting sun, the room seemed so rigid and neat it made Po sit up straight in spite of herself.

"Of course." Mamie closed the shutters Brian had opened and started toward the kitchen. "I'll make her a collation."

"What's this collation? Give her a plate of corn beef and cabbage!" Brian plopped down in a strange chair that rocked back and forth like a cradle.

When Mamie went to the kitchen, Po, hoping to make friends, followed her. In the kitchen, Po could see the fireplace had been bricked up, too. Perhaps with copper pans gleaming, iron pots standing sturdy on an open hearth, Po would not have felt so cheerless. Mamie moved a pan made of shiny tin on the stove, and turned and stared at Po's hands, when she offered to help.

"No, thank you." Mamie smiled her thin smile. She was of medium height and slender, and her figure was neat and compact under the tight stone-colored basque, with the tiny buttons down the front. As she moved about, all her movements seemed staccato.

By the time they came into the dining room, the last daylight was blanked out by the heavy lace curtains and maroon over-draperies and Brian lit the gas in a dome of green glass which hung just above the circular oak table.

As Po sipped cocoa from a floridly elegant cup, Mamie's gray-green eyes studied curiously Po's tangled hair and rumpled clothes. Po was hungry, and when food was good and this was, a great slice of meat between real white bread, it seemed indecent not to exclaim to God of the delight of it. "Ow! But it tastes good!" she ejaculated. Mamie looked startled, but glanced away, as if deciding to overlook a lapse.

Po felt pulled two ways. She wanted to be a credit to Brian, but—there was something about Mamie that made Po want to swear and be rowdy and tell one of Dermod the Tinker's strong stories. "And isn't it like her face had been starched now?" Po thought.

But Brian, reading at his newspaper, his face shiny and red from the sun, looked up. "You'll like it here in Brooklyn, darlint!" He folded his paper. "And Mamie'll help you make friends."

Mamie looked at him a moment, and for the first time Po noted an odd thing about Mamie's eyes. They were like unlighted windows of greenish-gray window glass. There was no shine behind them . . . not even when she looked at Brian.

"It's not so easy to break in." Mamie brushed an imaginary crumb from the cloth. "The best way is to join the St. Cecelia Singing Society. They'll take Irish, if you're refined. Then, if they see you're all right, you may be asked to join the Society for the Suppression of Vice in Brooklyn."

"Arrah, now, they'd be the good ones to be in with," Po said sociably, "in case you commit a vice, eh?"

Brian smiled and turned a sheet of his paper.

Mamie was around twenty-eight, but when she drew her mouth out thin, she looked older. "Oh, you don't understand. If they see you're really not like the other Irish, you may be asked to join the Tuesday Club!" She touched one of her dangling cameo earrings self-consciously. "I've been asked to join them!"

"It's yourself must have the easy time making friends," Po said agreeably, "with a saloon where you can treat all the ladies!"

Mamie drew back. Po saw the unlighted gray-green eyes looking at Brian. "The Gardens are a way to make money, now." Brian got up uneasily and moved toward the door, and then disappeared toward the parlor.

At once Mamie leaned forward, and Po had a premonition of what was coming.

"What I don't understand is"—with Brian gone, the cake-icing seemed to have tiny cracks in it—"why you left Fall River?"

Often in the deep underpart of the night, when nightmares begin, Po had turned over in her mind what might have happened to her in Fall River if it had not been her good luck to have been around and about a great deal, and not to have closed her eyes as she walked. Frank had been an overseer, and therefore could order you to remain after closing. But Po had resolved never to tell a human soul about Frank, who was a married man with children. With evil, what can one do but forget it? So that area of time became like one end of an ice pond with a fence around a cracked, dangerous place, and a sign warning "Keep Away!" How easily it could have happened that she would not have known to run, far off!

Po looked at Mamie's smooth pink and white enamel face, and faltered. "I thought I'd try my luck in Brooklyn!" She stopped. Then in a rush, went on. "There's Irish here, and I could maybe earn my bread"—she knew it had not been true in Fall River—"like my father and his father before, by singing!"

Mamie sat up straight, putting a square hand with rather rough coarse fingers on the table. She looked worried. "Things are different here! It is not a good element at all who earn their living by"—

41

it seemed as if she were saying stealing—"singing!" Abruptly, as if disturbed, she got up and removed the food and dishes to the kitchen. In a moment, however, she returned, and the thin sweetness of her manner had returned. "Maybe you can meet a young business man who is on the rise! A good thing for you!"

For no reason, Po saw Larry's hulking shoulders, his bright hair. "I'm never going to marry," she said angrily. "I'll manage! Don't worry about me!"

Loud steps pounded up the outside stairway. A knocker clacked. Mamie frowned slightly with a puzzled look. Then, with her staccato movements, she went to the door. From the dining room doorway, Po saw four young men crowded on the outside landing. A little boy about four clung to the hand of one.

"Is Brian in?" Po recognized David Posen, the thin intense young man who had found Brian for her.

Mamie held the door half open. She did not invite them in. "The Gardens are closed. It's Sunday."

The men looked abashed. "But this is ball business!"

"I'll see!" Po was startled at the coldness in Mamie's voice. As Mamie turned, leaving them standing outside, Po saw her face stiff and frozen.

"Who is it?" Brian came out of the parlor. "Well, for the love of God! Come in from the landing there! Ah, my little Hansy!" Without a word, the boy ran to Brian happily. Brian patted his shoulder and the boy looked up at him as if they were old friends.

"Come in! Come in!" The little boy's father came first. His blond hair was combed down in a flat curl in front and scooted out like a duck's tail in back, above the collar of his bright blue coat. His long light mustaches curved out in the same arc as his bandy legs, so that Po thought of two sets of parentheses, one small, one large. His pink face looked as if meant for jollity, but Po saw, even though he was but twenty-four or five, deep lines of tension on his forehead.

"This is Hans Schmidt, Mamie! First base for the Excelsiors." Then Brian said as if proclaiming power and honor, "And this is Tony Zambrini, Excelsior pitcher." Big Tony's muscles bulged under his striped jersey, his bright dark eyes and white teeth flashed in greeting.

The last man to come in was so broad and chunky Po was afraid he'd stick in the narrow passage like a wide-sterned boat. "Bushel Basket Jordan!" Brian hit his shoulder affectionately. "The best god-da—he's our catcher!"

Bushel Basket, about twenty-three or four, combed a large red hand embarrassedly through a bush of curly brown hair and shifted his quid. "Youse'll have to excuse us, Mrs. Brady," he said apologetically. "We wouldn't have come up, but it was important!"

"What are you saying, then?" Brian cried. "Come in with you now!" Po saw Brian cast an odd look at Mamie, but he motioned them toward the parlor. "This way, boys!" Po had the astonishing thought that these friends of Brian's had never been in his home before.

Well, if they were to have a fling of talk about that game, Po wasn't going to miss that! She joined herself to the group. "My cousin Po," said Brian. The men smiled and Po bobbed a curtsy.

In the parlor, the men looked the way Brian did—clumsy. As if they brought part of the field in with them. They smelled of grass. They seemed awkward, red-handed. Mamie followed and sat down, dress rustling, back straight. Hans took out his meerschaum pipe, glanced at Mamie, and put it back.

"Sorry I can't wet your whistles, boys. You know I don't drink!" Po wondered that he had no drop of essence by him. You'd think he never expected his friends to be here. Po looked at Mamie, hoping she would welcome these great, the Excelsiors, with coffee. But Mamie sat stiff, rigid, staring at the clod of dried mud beside Tony's foot. Tony saw her staring, too, and squirmed on the small stiff chair guiltily, as if he wished he could put the mud in his pocket.

But Dave's intense eager voice was spilling out with a rush. "Brian, it's that piece Walt read us! This afternoon! From the New York paper! That's why we came!"

"Like Walt told us"—Bushel Basket shifted his quid, excited—"we got to put a piece in too! He says if we make it up now he'll take it to Mr. Greeley when he gocs over tomorrow afternoon!"

Po could almost feel Bushel Basket's uncomfortable surprise as he paced about, looking, that Brian's house should be so poorly furnished. He shifted his quid, got redder in the face. Then he fumbled with the lace and plush draperies, clawed at the shutter, opened the window and leaned far out. When he straightened up, he looked acutely embarrassed, but relieved.

Hans Schmidt's little boy, Hansy, with his blond hair and blue coat cut like his father's, leaned against Brian's knee familiarly, listening to the men talk, and Brian absently stroked the boy's hair as he talked and as Mamie watched him, her lips thinned. Then, rather abruptly, she left the room.

Brian was saying, "Anyhow, I often thought how we ought to write the baseball rules down sometime. Sure, Dave knows them all, but what if he went away or something happened to him?"

"What are we waiting for?" Hans Schmidt asked, impatiently.

"Walt said he'd help us!" Dave said. "He ought to be here now!"

When Tony began telling them about his new baby, "A left hander," Dave slipped into the settee beside Po.

"Is everything fine?" he smiled at her.

"Strange and wonderful!" Po smiled back. "This Walt now, why is it you wait for him?"

"He knows how to make up a piece for a paper. He'll help us. He's helped me so much already. When I was printer's devil, he taught me to set type. Now he's on the *Brooklyn Times* he's going to teach me to be a newspaper man! He makes me read things! See—" He showed a thin shabby book in his jacket pocket. It was Shakespeare's *Sonnets*.

With Mamie gone, Brian seemed to loosen up, as did the others.

Hans Schmidt was saying, a deep worry line between his brows, "Four months now I got no job. Why? I served apprenticeship in a good yard in Hamburg, Germany. I'm a master workman!" He said this with assured pride. "I can carve ship's figureheads with the best. What happens? Van Leyn's stops making clippers, builds freight packets instead! No figureheads wanted! Oh, sure they offered me a job!" He looked around, almost bewildered. "Running a machine! It planes boards good as a man!" He had a sort of incredulous look on his face now. "I don't need my tools, they say! With my tools, I am a man, an asset! Without, what am I?"

"Aw, now Hansy, you'll get a job soon!" Bushel Basket said. "People'll always want figureheads!"

Now the knocker clacked and Brian went out and returned with Walt. They all hailed him happily. "Now we'll get a piece in!" Dave said.

Walt, casting about for a place to write, dragged a chair up to the center table, and Brian actually lit the lamp. Walt took off his big felt hat and put it on the floor beside him. Over his red flannel shirt, he wore a gray coat, its pockets sagging with papers and books. He fished out paper and pencil, put them on the table, then looked up, annoyed at the furbelowed lampshade blocking the light. Simply, he took the shade off and put it on the floor beside him. Then he picked up the purple velvet book, read the title, his nostrils flaring out, and put it on the floor. Po felt a twinge of surprise each time he moved something to discover it had not been glued down at all, it had just looked that way.

Po looked at Walt curiously, at the wide mouth with its serene benign curve in the graying beard. The look he cast about at them seemed almost tender.

"It's warm," he said, and not only opened the shutters and windows, but tucked back the muffle of lace and plush high up out of the way, so that great gusts of fresh spring evening air flooded into the room.

44

"Now, Dave," Walt said, at the table, "I'm only going to get you started. You write it! Merton's sick at the paper, and I can only stay a few minutes. Begin with how baseball first came to Brooklyn!"

"I'm the one to tell about that!" Bushel Basket spoke up. He took off his coat, revealing great damp sweat circles under the arms of his blue cotton shirt. Then he cleared his throat importantly. "Couple of years ago, me and Tony was walking over in Jersey one Sunday. We was outside this country place, Hoboken, at a spot called Elysian Fields, where these rich people go Sundays. The Knickerbockers was playing ball there. We watched them. We seen it was a good game, but they don't know how to play it." He hung his coat over the chair back and went on. "Well, we watched a couple of times till we had it down. Then we got measurements of the field, and we started a team. . . ."

"Fellows from the Shipyard, the Iron Works, anyone in the neighborhood that wanted to play!" Tony broke in, excited.

Bushel Basket glowered at Tony, and recaptured his story. "Well, after we got good, and we were—somethin' about Brooklyn, I guess, just nacherly makes a man a good ball player—why, we called a meetin', and we had by-laws, and all—"

"We actually thought we'd get official recognition," Dave broke in bitterly. "We knew we had the best team in America!"

"Yeah, but you better not put that in," Tony said doubtfully. "You know how them Atlantics is!"

A rush of clean air, perhaps all the way from the wide free sea, came hurtling itself into the room like a joyful puppy. It made Po feel fresh and cool, until she heard the shattering sound.

The pedestal with glass dome over the wax flowers had blown across the cabinet with the china ornaments. The floor was a litter of jagged glass shards, splintered china and wax flowers. It was as though the room had not been meant for the free rush of air or to have life flow in and out, and it had retaliated for the violation.

Mamie was in the doorway. She looked about the room. The curtains doubled back, exposing the room to the world, had a faintly bawdy look, like a lady with her skirts tucked too high. And the chair tidy, which had come off and which Dave had hung politely on the arm tip of the bronze statue, waved in the spring air, as if the bronze lady were waving to Mamie in drunken exhilaration.

The men stared around at Mamie through a haze of tobacco smoke, as if they had been caught in some misdemeanor. Mamie looked at the lamp shade on the floor, at the prized ornaments from the mantel pressed into use as ash trays. Then she turned and left.

The men looked uncomfortable. They went home soon afterward. After they had gone Mamie came in, picked up a piece of broken

45

glass, and stood staring at it. Brian patted her shoulder. "Ah, there now, Mamie, me girl, let's fergit it. No harm done. Come now, leave it be! I'll sweep out in the morning! And poor little Po," he said, "she must be dropping with sleep."

"I am that, Brian. It's been a rare full day!"

When Mamie lit the gas wall bracket in the third floor chamber, Po saw a dark ingrain carpet, a dark wood bureau, a washstand, and a bed of solid gold! But Po was glad she did not exclaim. She realized at once it was brass. She'd heard of such things. But she was going to sleep in a bed of brass!

Mamie was staring at Po's blouse, open at the throat. "How old are you?" She had a faintly disapproving tone.

"Sure, and what does she want me to do then, cut them off?" Po thought. "Sixteen," she said, taking off her skirt.

Then, as if she were demanding Po's baptismal certificate, she said, "Where are your petticoats?"

"Oh, Mae, I hate the draggy things!"

Mamie looked worried. "You will have to dress respectably here!"

The bedspread was so stiff with embroidery it looked like a writhing mass of serpents. Mamie explained it must be folded exactly so, the bolster put thus, the small ruffled pillow there. Po, tired and sleepy, sighed a little. With this one, now, you could never do such a thing as just jump into a bed!

But with Mamie gone, and the room dark, Po did not fall asleep at once. So much had happened. Perhaps Mamie would take the buckram out of her face tomorrow, and it would be better. And anyway, there had been the ball game. Drowsing off, Po seemed to hear the wonderful electrifying sound the baseball made as it cracked against the bat stick.

But suddenly she came awake, for she heard a door close, so plainly she thought it was her own.

Then she heard Brian's voice, hollow, as if coming through something. "Poor little Po. She's had the rocky time of it, I guess." Then she heard Mamie's "Has she?"

Po was wide awake now, feeling uneasy. Their bedroom must be under this room. Why were the voices so plain? Perhaps they came up a fireplace. Should she get up and try somehow to shut it off? But then there was silence, and Po drowsed off. But she woke again, startled. Brian's voice, hollow, but distinct, was saying, "Come to bed now, Mamie! You can't sit there by the window in the dark all night!"

Silence. Po hoped that was the end, but after a while she heard Mamie say, "Don't touch me!"

"Come on, now, Mamie!"

Po sat up, little prickles climbing her throat. What should she do?

46

Get up, walk around, make a noise? Let them know she could hear?

But then Mamie's voice, the words pouring out, came. "After I've struggled so! I'm going to be somebody! You're not going to drag me back, spoil everything. How am I ever going to be somebody when you . . . A dirty little Jew! A garlic-reeking dago! That low Bushel Basket! And that . . . that . . . Walt!"

"They're all good boys! Good ball players!"

"Ball players! Common! Low! Oh, I've tried so hard! If only you'd . . ."

"Come now, Mamie! You know I love you! You know I want you to be happy!"

"You want one thing, and you know it!"

Po was frozen with horror. What should she do? Now she did not dare move. It would be worse if they knew she had heard.

"It's natural to want them. Every man does!"

"I've told you and I've told you"—Mamie's voice had the low insistent sound of a water drip—"not till we get out of this place!"

"With children, if you love them, it doesn't matter!"

"That's the low Irish! Breeding children over a saloon!"

"The saloon's all right!" He was rough. Silence. "It's not like I had another trade!" There was a long silence then, and when Mamie spoke again her voice had changed.

"There's politics. Everyone likes you. Why can't you make use of that? Instead of wasting it on those fools, those ball players?"

Brian's tone was rough and thick. "They're all right!"

At last, there was silence. Po let out a long shuddering breath of relief.

After a while she heard the bed creak.

"Brian." Mamie sounded soft and sweet.

"Unh?"

"I met a woman whose husband is in politics. Selfridge is her name."

"Huh. Selfridge is one of Hymes's men!"

Silence. "They're building a new house on the Heights." Mamie's voice sounded dreamy now. "Some day, we'll be somebody. Respectable, important people will come and sit in our parlor. We'll have a house on the Heights. Big . . . big enough for children. Then—we'll have a son!'

When Po took her hands away from her ears long after, there was silence and she fell asleep.

47

Chapter Seven

P O WAS WAKENED at dawn by what sounded like hundreds of shuffling feet in the street below. But she knew she must be mistaken. It was in Fall River you woke in the bleak December daybreak to hear the rush of feet on pavements. Half asleep as she was, she remembered with joy, that she was in Brooklyn.

She turned over to go back to sleep. But it seemed to her she could still hear the hollow sound of many feet. The memory brought an uncomfortable feeling.

There was something she should be doing now in the grim December dawn. What was it? Something she dreaded above all things. Oh, yes. She must get up and dress, and lay out the two slices of bread for their breakfast . . . and waken her father. That was what she dreaded. He lay in the front room of their two, with her shawl and his old coat over him for extra warmth. He had always been slender, but now, in sleep, from the inside corners of his paper-thin lids, to his pale lips, deep lines were drawn, even in sleep. But in sleep, the coughing stopped, and the bitter aloof look that had lately come to his mouth was gone. Outside, she could hear the pouring feet and knew she must wake him. Sleep was the only luxury he had, and she must snatch it from him! Better let him sleep! But that would be bad for him, for the two dollars a week the mill paid her for working from six in the morning till seven-thirty in the evening could not feed them. She put out her hand to rouse him, but the hatefulness, her unwillingness, wakened her. She breathed a sigh. Ah! She had only been drowsing. She was in Brooklyn!

But half awake, it seemed to her she could still hear the slide of feet on pavement, and even when she drifted off, the sound persisted.

She was walking in the stream of operators in the half light of early morning, going in through the mill gates. But she was lost. She could not find herself. She could not tell herself from any of the others. Which was she? The mill regulations bade them all wear clean cotton dresses, and so they had all come to dress alike, in gray merrimac print dresses and coarse sacking aprons to take up the grease from the machines. They even came to look alike . . . the girls from hill farms in Maine, or from Ireland, or the mountains of Bohemia. Ah, how nice it had been when the girls from Bohemia first came. On their first days they wore their native dresses, beautiful in color and flow and embroidery. And they had carried little willow baskets, hand-woven, for their lunch. But soon, the rules caught up with them, too, and they had taken on the gray uniformity, and even carried their lunches like the rest in American tin pails.

Po turned over and slid back into a recurrent dream. She could smell the sickening inhuman smell of hot oil on the machines. The air was dead. What was it they hated so, she and her Da? It was the noise. The whir and grind and pound of the machines became at last a soundlessness in which you could hear nothing. All the operators became deaf and dumb people. They became less than human. You could not raise your voice in song as you worked, or even speak to your fellows, except by motions.

But the sound of feet was loud, she must rouse herself, dress . . . and oh, hateful, horrifying . . . snatch from her father his only solace, sleep.

She came wide awake in horror. The feet were plain on the cobbles. But they couldn't be! She was in Brooklyn, sleeping in a bed of brass in warm Brian's house, and he with a pretty American wife.

She sat up in bed. It was still dark, but she had been living at such a pitch of excitement the past days, it seemed as if she slept faster, too, and was ready to enter life again.

She opened the casement window of the dormer. She could hear the shuffling sound plainly now. A gas street lamp burned at the corner of Fulton and Pineapple. It flickered over what looked like a torrent of men and women.

She pulled back in, almost in fright. Were they here, too, then? The monsters that swallowed them all? She must know!

Mamie and Brian still slept. The flat was quiet. Then . . . she could not find her clothes. Mamie had taken them for some reason. But an urgency filled Po. She must see . . . she must know . . . if the enemy were here, too. Next to her third floor chamber was a storeroom. Hanging on a nail there she found an old shirt and pair of breeches, discarded by Brian. Well, it was dark, no one would see her. She got into the breeches and shirt and tiptoed silently downstairs and into the street.

Under the ghostly street lamp, Po saw she had not been mistaken. It was a current of men and women, and children. They moved down Fulton Street, bodies slanted forward, shoulders hunched, heads pulled down on chests.

Except for their feet, there was no sound. They didn't call to one another the way birds do in early morning when they begin to be about their birds' business. A kind of morose silence hung over them. And the sound on the pavement was not the smack, clean and hard, of fine new square boots. It was the off-center, slurred, blurred sound of thin-soled shoes, down at heel. Then Po saw them . . . the tin dinner pails. They were exactly like the ones they'd carried in Fall

49

River, and in the dark, the clothes they wore all looked the same, a dark grayish-brown. For a weird moment, Po felt as if it were the same current of people, flowing all the way down from Fall River and down this street in Brooklyn, eddying into mill gates here.

Po stepped out in the current. The smell of sweat and damp musty clothes smote her, as if the clothes perspired in the day before had gone on this morning, partly damp, for when would there have been time for the washing?

Next her in the crowd, she thought she recognized a man. He was one she had seen yesterday, flashing about the ball field, the one they called Twinkle-Toes. Now he looked sullen, gray, morose, an old cap pulled down on his head.

But then the current swirled and eddied, and men turned off and through a high wooden arch. Painted on it in large black letters, Po read "William Hymes, Iron Works." Hymes! That was the big man who had walked across the ball field yesterday and caused the play to stop.

Ahead, down the street, a strident bell clanged. Po had been pushed off to one side of the street, and the current she was in now seemed mostly women and little girls. In front of Po, an old woman wheezed along, helped by a small girl. A large black building, two stories high, loomed ahead. The crowd made a desperate lunge, as if to be inside the gate of this building before the bell clangor stopped. Po was caught in the terrible urgency. As if she had gotten too near the edge of a whirlpool, and was sucked down, she found herself inside the gate, and then inside a great cavernous room. The women and children hurried away, speeding to their places, but now, Po, as if hypnotized with horror, stood stock-still inside the room, unable to move.

The room was long and dim, lit by flickering gas jets on the walls. The windows, small, high up, were far above the work tables running around the blank wall. The women and children were scurrying to these, hurriedly pulling off their bonnets and shawls. Standing by the long tables, then, facing into the blank walls, they began, with an air of anxious tension, to work. What were those ghostly cages they worked on? Then, at the other end of the room Po saw a large sign: "Quimby Hoop Skirt Manufactory." The women were making hoop-skirt frames.

Under the big sign was another. It said, "The Lord watches thy every move." On a raised dais, Po saw a tall, flat-faced man in a black frock coat, hair plastered down, lower lip thrust out over his black beard, glaring at those last in their places. Then he tapped a ruler on his table, opened a book and read, glancing up often to be sure every operator worked. As tense fingers flew, manipulating whalebone and steel wires, he read, in a nasal sing-song voice: "The Lord is my shepherd, I shall not want."

A rough voice behind Po yelled, "Whatcha doin' here?" She ran as fast as if she were afraid she'd be captured and chained to work at a bench facing a blank wall. Soon she felt the free cobbles of Fulton Street under her feet.

The monsters were here, then, too, she thought, her heart still pounding hard. The yawning black buildings, waiting to swallow and chew you till you were gray and cowed and no good for anything but to serve them. Po tried to smile. She was going to be a singer. She hurried away from there as fast as she could go.

By now, the street was nearly empty, and the outline of the brick buildings began to stand out clear against a sky coloring and waking with luminous beginnings.

Po stood and watched the sky. It was that magic moment when the day might be going backward or forward, the few moments when the sky has the half radiance that could mean sunrise or sunset.

Coming up the street, as if from the river, Po saw a big man with a graying beard, a large hat on back of his head. She recognized him. It was Walt.

The street was deserted now. At a little distance, he raised his arm to her in a gesture of salute. Now he was near and she could see again his strange pale blue eyes. Somehow, Po knew he had been abroad in the land the whole night through. He had not been drinking . . . too many of that kind had passed under her eyes for her not to know . . . but there was something about the face, lined, grayish and sleepy, his rumpled coat. Well, many a one like that had she known, too, who walked the lone roads of the misty glens in Ireland, calling and crying and seeking for something. She returned his greeting gravely.

"So Brian Brady's cousin is up to see the day come in!"

" 'Tis a fine sight," Po said.

"I don't know your name." He smiled at her. "What is it?"

Po looked into his face. This one would understand.

"It's a long name and it's one my father gave me. He always said he was descended from kings, and I must have the name of a princess. But he knew some day we'd come surely to America. So, it must be an American princess. 'Twas from a book he got it. My name is"— Po looked up at the sky, opalescent, glowing, dark blue—"Pocahontas O'Reilly."

Walt repeated it, making each syllable ring like a little bell, the way her father had. It was as if he enjoyed the sound. In Fall River, they had laughed.

"A girl with such a beautiful name must be full of courage."

They looked up, silent for a moment, into the sky. So serene, radiant, untouched, pure, it would be a sacrilege not to be happy, to sing inwardly. How could everything not be richly full and joyous under it? She felt as she had at the ball game. She was glad she was here.

They were standing by the gate of the Iron Works. At that moment, the enormous tall smokestack began to pour forth thick, gummy belches of sulphurous black smoke. It drifted and spread and smeared and blotted out the opalescent sky.

Walt peered up at it, grimly. "Hot metal!" He sighed. "Down there"—he gestured toward the river—"are the Yards where they build the wooden ships. A man can hold a maul, or an axe, or a hammer, or plane, in his bare hand. But, you can't hold a ladle of hot metal in your hands. The whole thing is slipping, slipping away, out of their hands!" He seemed to have forgotten she was there, and walked on up the street.

Just then, Po glanced down, saw she was wearing Brian's breeches; Mae's face flashed into her mind. She turned and ran up Fulton Street as fast as she could go.

Chapter Eight

THROUGH the heavy lace curtains in the back parlor, Po could see the sky was blue outside, but small joy it was to her. All the morning she had been doing a fearful stint called "piecing a quilt."

Mamie was contending with a machine with a wheel and treadle that hummed and hawed and then spit forth her piece of dress material all seamed up! But Po was determined to look as though a device of the kind sat on every hearth from Kerry to Galway. Mamie seemed to feel Po was stupid enough as it was. She would not entrust her, even, with washing the elegantly flowered cups and saucers, but put her to this piecing. First, Mamie had cut up some fine strong material into little bits, then Po was to sew them together again, in a pattern.

Po's hands perspired, the thread knotted, some demon had blunted the needle. Any other girl could do this without a sigh, Po knew. It was this thing of patterns. She was no good at them. She remembered women, in front of sunny thatches in Limerick, making lace, their faces mindless, smug, as though they were sure that making an ancient pattern come out right was all life expected of them. They had an easy time of it after all. Po always felt she had to make up her pattern as she went along. "And 'tis that, maybe, that Mamie does not like in me."

The pieces were twisted, hopeless, now. "Sure, this is destroying me entirely." Po felt tears of frustrated strain near. Then she sensed Mamie had stopped work and was watching her.

" 'Tis the poor one I am around a house, Mae!" Then with deep guile, "A stupid Irish bog hopper like me! 'Twould serve me right if you put me below washing glasses in the Gardens!"

Mamie drew back sharply. "It's bad enough we have to live here! We don't have to mingle! If you must do something outside, better for you to go to Quimby's."

Quimby's! Po saw again the hoopskirt manufactory, with the dim rows of women and children facing a blank wall. The blood surged out of her face.

"Perhaps it would be better if you did go to Quimby's." Mamie looked worried. "It's quite a respectable class of girls, and they just sit all day. I've heard their overseer reads improving books to them. It keeps them out of mischief."

But for the time being Mamie apparently thought Po had better learn to make herself some clothes. "You look just like," she said accusingly, "an Irish greenhorn!" What does the woman expect me to look like then, a British grenadier? Po wondered. Mamie gave Po a paper-bound book with pictures of mincing ladies and told her to select a pattern, while she went to the kitchen.

Po tried to fix her mind on "yellow passementerie, draped over a festoon of sprigged challis, with gussets of apple-green silk." And right now, this minute of God's day, the Excelsiors might be down-stairs in the Gardens, and they arguing about ball plays, or having the fine jokes for themselves! She sighed. She could put the book down, slip through the door at the end of the hall she had seen Brian take this morning, and go down to the Gardens. But then she got thinking that Mamie wouldn't like it . . . and she read some more about "a violet cashmere cloak trimmed with gupere and white feather fringe. . . ." But the trouble with thinking was, you never got anything done, and that way, you never had any excitement.

But . . . Mamie might think of Quimby's again. Po picked up the book again and sighed. But, if a game were being played today? Po found herself putting the book down. She passed along the hall, opened the door and went down to the Gardens.

From the moment Po opened the door at the foot of the stairs and stepped onto the white sanded floor of the barroom, she loved Brady's Gardens. Strange how places made you feel. Mamie's flat above gave you a restless, uneasy creep, but the tack room in the great stables at Lough, where grooms and masters loafed . . . everyone wanted to be there. Or Kate Finn's cottage at Ballyhouna, where all gathered often to sing. It was a kind of magic some places had. Brady's Gardens, she sensed, was one of the places people liked to be.

You couldn't put a finger on it. Maybe it was himself behind the bar. In his shirt sleeves, with the black string tie and blue and brown checked waistcoat, he leaned one thick elbow on the scoured white wood, talking to a patron, receiving a confidence, giving advice, with a benign air, like a philosopher or priest. On the ball field Brian had seemed loud and gusty; in the flat, awkward, almost coarse. But now, as the cluster of gas lights in elegant brass curlicues gleamed across amber and red bottles, he turned, and his ham-like hands moved nimbly among the shining glasses. He had the look of a man who was doing what he most wanted and was best fitted for in all the world.

She searched the faces of the few people about, then impatiently realized she was looking for a pair of big hulking shoulders! That one! And he probably long gone to that California Ohio place! But the few men in the place had the easy look too. Two men in bowler hats played billiards at a shabby table, unhurried. A sailor sat absorbed in dominoes, an old Paddy with a fringe of white whiskers read the *Irish Mail,* his clay pipe making a cloud of blue smoke above him. He looked as if he were sure no woman would come and ask him, in a righteous voice, to move while she cleaned under him. Maybe that was what made the magic atmosphere . . . everyone was doing what he wanted.

For the room itself was but a low smoke-darkened thing, the white-washed walls nearly hidden by red and yellow circus advertisements, calendars, and framed lithographs. From where she stood, Po saw that the main entrance in the middle of the right wall on Pineapple Street was a short flight of steps above the street. Through the two windows facing on Fulton, and the four on Pineapple, one looked down, detached, on passersby. Maybe it was this gave the feeling of private snugness.

But those big double doors on the left wall? She stepped through one and into what seemed to her pure enchantment. Enclosed like a little world, in a high board fence, but open to a blue Brooklyn sky, was the grassy plot, dotted with small tables, known as the Gardens. Chinese lanterns criss-crossed over it, and at the far end . . . a little stage. Oh, what a place! Could one wish for anything more? She flew back to the barroom.

"Brian," she demanded, breathless, eyes dancing, "is it shows you have, too?"

"That we do! On Wednesday nights, we light the lanterns, and the young couples sit out there with their glass. On Saturday nights are the Free-and-Easy's. Anyone that's feeling good gits up and dances a jig or sings a song. All the boys are there, the Excelsiors and all."

Po drew a deep breath. She had something on her mind. Of course, girls would never play the game. That would be too good to be true. But, maybe, maybe, she could somehow belong. She must know. She had not seen the Excelsiors play, but in her mind she knew them to be the most courageous, the most nimble, the blinding marvel of the world.

"Brian," she began, tense, "if a girl, say like me, has a relative is an Excelsior, say like you—does that mean the girl belongs too? You know, like it is with politics or a church?"

"Well . . . no."

"But . . . I can *be* an Excelsior?" Po watched his face, intently.

Brian's fingers combed the whiskers which flowed back from his cliff-like chin and considered.

"Well, you can't belong like deciding captain, or anything. You can belong, sort of in spirit. Like most of the Excelsiors come from around this neighborhood, and I guess most people around Hewes and Marcy would say they were Atlantics."

There was no ritual or ceremony, then, like becoming a Mason or a Catholic. It was more inside you. If that was all, then she belonged. She could tell, already it was sort of like a religion, though, because you got a blind loyalty, a passionate identification. Po remembered a line from a book in school: "When I die," said Queen Mary, "the word Calais will be found imprinted on my heart!" Po guessed that when she died the word Excelsiors would be found on hers. Po had become an Excelsior.

But, as she stood tasting this glory, a sound stabbed through the neighborhood. Later she would identify it as one of the rhythms of life in this street in Brooklyn. It was the noon whistle at the Hymes Iron Works. A new device, the workman who blew it seemed to love to let it speak out its power.

A great flood came pouring up Fulton Street, up the steps, through the doors. Brian rushed wildly to the kitchen. In less than two minutes, there was not an inch of space at the bar. The long tables, already set with heavy crockery, were filling. The cook, who had been preparing for this all morning, rushed from the kitchen, holding aloft great platters of corn beef and cabbage, and dashed back. No orders were taken. There was but the one dish. You took that.

Like a chip, Po had been washed into the open kitchen door. The Negro cook thrust a platter of corn beef and cabbage at her. "Fo' the Excelsior table!" he shouted at her over the din of talk, dishes, and cutlery.

55

Po was to find each team had a table, hallowed by custom, for itself and supporters. Also, that, just as Dent's Chop House down the street was the center for men from the Clipper ships, Brady's was the center for baseball men. Its very floor boards and walls seemed soaked with baseball talk.

Po, staggering out under the two-foot platter, identified the Excelsiors' table because Hans and Dave Posen sat there. It seemed impossible for platters to be emptied so quickly. She hurried in and out.

The first onslaught over, she stood a moment by the Excelsior table, eyes dancing, mouth agape. Dave Posen looked at her, his dark eyes leaping up with warm feeling. His shirt sleeves and bare arms were stained with blue and black ink. His talk rushed at her, intense as the brook bursting down from Kileen.

"The Apprentice Library is back on Cranberry Street," he ran on. "I'll get you some books, if you like to read. What do you like best?"

Po liked everything best. Being alive. Put to it, she said, "I sing a bit."

Dave said eagerly that he and Walt would take her to the opera. In New York.

But Brian had hurried over to Dave and leaned down. "What happened to that big young feller? The one caught the ball yesterday! Did you find him?"

Po's heart jumped. They must mean Larry, who else?

"Not only did I find him," Dave shouted back over the noise, "I got him a room in Battle Row."

"Git him a job?"

"Took him to the shipyard this morning. Grogan asks, 'Does he play ball?' This big fellow—name's Larry—says, 'With the best!' So of course Grogan takes him on, thinking he'll play with the Excelsiors."

Larry would play with her team!

"We could use a fellow like that . . . shoulders near big as Bull's!" Brian said.

"But we haven't got him! Seems as he was coming into town, he met Restored Jones, and of course he told him the Atlantics were the team. Now this Larry's holding out. Says he'll play only with the best!"

A poor hopeless thing like the Atlantics best!

"I hear he is a pitcher! You should have got him!" Brian exclaimed.

"I'll work on him when he comes in. I can maybe find a way!"

Larry might be jouncing in that door at any minute then!

Po tried to listen, to miss nothing, yet keep her eyes peeled on the door. But, instead of Larry, through the door came—the supercargo from the *Red Tanager*.

She stood, fastened to the floor, parching to death with fear. He stopped inside the door, glanced about, went to the bar.

Po loosened her feet from their horrified paralysis, and sped to the kitchen. Through its half-open door, she could watch him. Wouldn't it be a thing now if he found her and made the cry against her, had her arrested! In front of the Excelsiors! And Larry might be flashing in that door any minute, and he not only a stowaway, but had knocked the man down with a great fist.

The supercargo was searching for someone, she could see that. He was served with brandy, but even as he lifted the curved glass, his toad eyes darted here and there.

Just then Po sensed that strange murmuring tension she had felt once before—in the crowd at the ball game. Coming up the outside steps, with an absent frown, like a busy man called out on some urgent errand, his beaver hat rubbed the wrong way in careless patches, his brown tail coat unbuttoned, was William Hymes. He glanced around then, seeking someone. Then Po saw something astonishing. A glance passed between the supercargo and Hymes. The supercargo hastily swallowed the brandy, paid, went out. Hymes followed.

Why, the supercargo had been waiting for Hymes! Strange! Well, thanks be to God he'd missed Larry, anyway!

Now she saw Walt come in, and a group of men gather around Walt and Dave Posen, while Dave read to them from the piece Walt had him finish for the newspaper.

Looking at Dave—frowning, excited, his high forehead already lined—she thought somehow of Bethel Court in Dublin, and the starving children there. How could Dave, she wondered, play with and against these brawny molders and hewers? But Brian said, "Dave's not a notorious player, but he has the elegant brain on him. He's our strateegist!"

A tall lanky man with a rectangular jaw, wearing butternut shirt and breeches, a long whip stuck in his boot top, was standing up, arguing angrily. Brian said it was Hank Collins, a teamster at Quimby's, and left fielder, called "Death-to-Flying-Things" because he could catch anything passing through the air.

"Death-to-Flying-Things" was pounding the butt end of his whip on the table to mark each grim word. "No piece is going to be any good that don't put in the real trut' about them Knickerbockers."

A pale fellow in soiled white shirt, dark serge coat and bowler hat, a clerk at the shipyard named Melvin, spoke up quickly, looking scared. "Oh, now! Be careful! We got to watch what we say! The Knickerbockers are smart educated men. They won't play us because we don't play by their rules!"

The men crowded in closer, flaring down at the clerk. Po could feel their intensity. "Then why don't they call a convention and let everyone in on them sacred rules?" a man at the Excelsior table shouted. And another cried out as he glared around, "Do they got to be first in everything?"

"In the shop, the yard, the foundry, so easy it is to be lost, to be nothing, nobody." Hans Schmidt's light blue eyes had a disturbed look. "We'd like to be first in something!"

"We're best"—Dave was firm—"and we want to be recognized officially!"

"They'll take the game from you"—Hans's voice was tense, and his face muscles strained, and Po saw the furrows between his eyes deepen—"just like they'll get your tools!"

The men fidgeted impatiently, looked away.

Hans was calm now, his voice quiet. "Because now I do only odd jobs I got more time to read, to think." He flared up again. "I tell you it is all the same thing! Just like this game. We got to hang on! Hang on to our tools! To our game!"

"Maybe we are only fooling ourselves, with all our play-offs." Dave frowned, and looked bitter. "What if they still don't pay any attention to us?"

Hans leaned forward. "Is baseball just for them then?"

"Death-to-Flying-Things" was standing up, with the look Po had seen on the face of Restored Jones in the cart. Cold, resolute, almost solemn. She saw it now on the others, too. It was like some smoldering thing, in them long and darkly brooded on, was now near the point of explosion.

"When we finish our play-offs, and know who's champion of Brooklyn"—he cracked his long whip expertly over the heads of the crowd till it snapped like the crack of a rifle—"we'll send one . . . more . . . challenge!"

Suddenly, a pathway opened from the door to the Atlantics' table. Surrounded by a crowd of smaller men, team mates, admiring hangers-on, who moved with him like a retinue, The Bull came in. As he crossed toward the table, the floor trembled under the pound of his heavy boots.

When Po had first seen Larry, he had reminded her of a giant in an old Irish tale. But the Bull, he was the thing itself. She had the same sense of his being an impossibility.

Nothing small could have hewn his face; only wind, fierce sun, great fights, and jobs of work that would have killed another man. His face and arms, bare to the elbow, were ruddy and rough-textured as one of Dermod the Tinker's copper ingots. Blue eyes, with startlingly clear whites, shone out of his coppery face like small lakes glistering from a brown prairie.

Once upon a time, when the Bull first came to Brooklyn, he'd worn a fox-skin cap with hanging tail. Now, his head was bare. His hair and beard, black as a crow's, bushed out from his face with such virility Po felt she'd get a magnetic shock if she touched them. His shirt of green flannel stretched tight over a rock-like chest. Over that, he wore a bright plaid vest, trimmed with yellow buckskin fringe, for the Bull had once been a shanty boy. A wide cowhide belt held up the brown tent of linsey-woolsey that made his breeches. Po thought, as she stared at his advancing high boots, "It's a whole animal it must have taken to make the man boots to be walking in!"

He used to carry a hunting knife, too, but now his only weapons were his fists, which to Po looked like two boulders from Croagh Mernan. His legs seemed thick as those of the stone giants in the cairn there. His voice, as he talked to his followers, sounded as if he were hailing them through a deep forest.

Now he was passing the Excelsiors' table, and Po could see his shoulders, so massive they made her think of the dam at Lough Carra, which held back the great waters.

Three men jumped up quickly from the long bench at the Atlantics' table to make room for the Bull. As he sat down, he pounded the table impatiently. One of his team mates ran to the kitchen to hurry the cook. A platter, not a plate, of corn beef and cabbage, was set before him. It disappeared. An admirer ran and fetched it full again.

Po sat staring, wide-eyed, fascinated. She saw that the mug the Bull drank from was twice as large as the other men's and that he seemed to drain it in one or two long swallows. When the mug was empty, he pounded, till it trembled, upon the bare table. Po thought of Jack-and-the-Beanstalk's Giant, yelling for blood. One of the Bull's followers hurried to the bar to fill the great mug. It was then Po saw the printing on it: "Sarse's Ginger Beer."

Po looked amazed at Dave Posen, who sat near her. "No Galway man would thin his blood with anything but the real essence!"

"His mother was a member of the Temperance Society," Dave explained.

Just then, Po heard the gurgle of an emptying bottle, and saw Brian pour a pint of Bushmill's whiskey into the mug.

"Now, would you think," Po marveled, "a buckeen that size would have such delicate feelings!" Her eyes were still wide. "How did he grow so big!"

"You want the truth"—Walt leaned toward her, his eyes laughing —"or what they say about him?"

"Oh, the lies! Arrah, they're more interesting!"

"Well, they're mostly wish lies! What do the men long to do? Work fourteen hours at hard labor and not be worn out? Speak up to the boss and make him tremble? Hug three girls at once? Likker up constantly, yet not die? The Bull can do it, and with flourishes. I happen to know the Bull's father was a no-count shanty boy up-state, but better not say a thing like that in Brooklyn. According to them, you'd think he was born out of a clap of thunder. The idea of the Bull does everybody good. They've got to have something to live by!" And Walt looked at the Bull fondly.

Po watched the Bull wolfing down great forkfuls of corn beef.

"Over at the shipyard where he works"—Dave's eyes gleamed— "they say they wanted to launch a packet one day. The Bull stood on the East River bank, and gave the packet a shove. But he shoved too hard. The ship went clear over to the New York side of the river, ricocheted off Staten Island, and went sailing off down the Narrows. They forgot to tell him just to give it a little push!"

"They know it's impossible, but they like to brag that he can step up the spar of a schooner by himself," Walt said, "and lay three decks in a single day! But the reason they worship him is, he can play ball like a natural-born fool!" Walt shoved back his empty plate and leaned back.

To Po it seemed the Bull must have materialized out of the mists off Lough Lene. "But how did he come here to Brooklyn?"

Without answering, Walt turned around in his place and called over the din, to the Bull. The Bull called back a warm loud greeting, hailing Walt with an upraised arm.

"Bull," Walt called, "this young lady we have here is Brian's cousin! Her name is Po O'Reilly!"

The Bull grinned, showing great yellow buck teeth in the black waves of his beard. He leaned toward her, across his table. Po found herself looking into child-like eyes.

"Howdy! You come from up-state?"

"It's from Ireland I am," Po called back. To herself she thought, "And if we had a few buckeens like you there, it's long ago we'd have stopped paying rates to England." Aloud she said rather wistfully, "Sure, it's not from Galway you come, is it?"

"Not me!" He waved an arm, thick as a wagon axle, toward the north. "I come from up yonder!"

"Tell Po about when you were a shanty boy up there, Bull!" Dave called to him. Around them, the din became quiet. The men near them hung on his words. Po saw an expression on their faces which seemed odd. It was sort of a dreamy longing. The Bull's story, Po would learn, was never the same. It was Variations on a Theme.

A long gurgle from the ginger beer mug, and the Bull smacked his lips politely, and daintily batted off a few drops of whiskey with a boulder-like hand. He leaned back on the bench.

"Well, now, I was dropped in the mountains at the top of the

Delyware River. Even before I was old enough to go girl-stalking, I was a shanty boy. But . . . I guv it up!"

"Why was that, Bull?" an adoring follower spoke on cue.

"I was usin' up the trees too fast. Warn't hardly any big pines left . . . only little old sixty-foot hemlocks. Why, one day, after I'd chopped down six eighty-foot pines, it come to me I was de-populatin' the forest. Besides, when I was choppin', there was always a jam on the river. I cut too fast for the river to float the logs away. So I guv up bein' a shanty boy. I walked forty miles into the crossroads one day, and become a rafter. I'd start out, at the top of the Delyware, with my raft, maybe a thousand foot of lumber. That raft'd be fifty feet wide, and I'd have a forty-foot oar to shove her agin rapids, around bends. I'd take her down to Philadelphy or Trenton. One day, I'd brang my logs to Trenton, drunk up all their whiskey, wore out all their wimmen, and I begun to feel life had foozled out on me. I says, Bull, what next? I decided to follow them logs to find out what happened to them. I got me on board a lumber schooner. It hove to in Brooklyn. . . ."

"In Van Leyn's shipyard!" spoke up an admirer.

"That's when I learned to build a ship. Course, it took me a couple days to git the hang of it. But after that, I was a ninety-proof shipwright!"

"Tell her about how you joined the Atlantics," put in a swelling team mate.

"I went out one day to let the inhabitants know a man has come to town. What do I find them doing? Trying to play ball! Why, I played the game since I was knee high to a oak tree!"

"You learned them how to play, didn't you, Bull?" Twinkle-Toes shouted, glaring over at the Excelsior table.

"Well," the Bull freshened himself up out of the ginger beer mug, wiped the back of his hand across his coffer-dam mouth and said, "Some men are demons at lumberjackin'. Some at countin' up figgers. Some at huggin' wimmen, or soaking up likker. Well, I ain't no slouch at them things. But when it comes to my real true demon-ing, why"— he looked around as if hoping someone would deny it—"it's baseball!"

Po had sat entranced. She'd been seeing the shadows of the forest, hearing the Bull's axe ring out on mountain peaks, watching him push a forty-foot oar against the river. Suddenly, she was brought up short. How could the Bull have gotten mixed up with those mis'rable little Atlantics?

Now her eyes were on the door constantly. And then . . . Larry came in. Her heart, like a swimmer poised above a deep lake, stood still a moment. Then it took a dizzy plunge to the bottom of the lake.

Finally, it came up, panting. "Bedad, it's the bright hair, and the heft of him, and the big mough laughing, that distracts me!" she told herself crossly. But she knew it was something else too. It was what she had noticed when she had first seen him in the hold of the *Red Tanager*. It was the shine like a fresh sunny meadow wet with dew.

It was clear to her as the sun on the River Lee, that to balance against this rock, this mountain, this Bull—the Excelsiors would have to have Larry!

He had been late coming, because, for a joke, he'd been told to hold a certain wooden pin in place until relieved. After a while, he realized he'd been given a green hand's welcome. Then he laughed and followed the others. The joke on him didn't bother him. "He always looks," Po thought "as if everything was the great joke."

"There's that Larry!" Brian had come to the table beside Dave Posen, and put his hand on Dave's shoulder, urgently. "Git him to our table quick, before Twinkle-Toes or someone sees him!"

Dave pushed through the crowd. Larry stood, glancing around the noisy crowded room. Po saw Dave take Larry's arm, and urge him toward the Excelsiors' table. But Larry stood, not inclined to hurry, looking around. Then his eyes lit on Po. He smiled at her, white teeth flashing. He started toward her, Dave trailing.

Now Larry was laughing down at her. "By Whittaker, Po, I'm glad you're all right!"

"The brass of the man," she thought, "and I could have been murdered by ruffians for all he'd have known, after he got watching that ball game!"

Then he said in a lower voice, "I saw you leave with your cousin! I knew you were all right!"

"Maybe it's the black lie," she thought as she flashed him a smile, "but it's got lace on it!"

She wondered if she ought to warn him that Rimshaw was in the neighborhood, but before she could speak, Dave put in, "Oh, you two know each other!"

Po thought, for a second, that Dave's burning dark eyes looked sad and hurt. She must have been wrong though, for already he had Larry sitting at the Excelsiors' table, and was talking to him like a brook in flood.

Brian, standing at Larry's shoulder, threw in a few pebbles as the brook raced by, but Tony, Hans, Bushel-Basket Jordan and the rest, just drank their ale and listened. They needed a big man, a good pitcher, to face up to the Bull. But—they were the Excelsiors. Did they have to coax?

"We practice evenings, whistle till dark. Smith and Degraw Streets.

Just come around," Dave was saying. "Anyone will tell you the Excelsiors are best!"

Larry heaped a heavy crockery plate full of corn beef and cabbage. "That's not the way I heard it!" He sounded positive.

"Why, the Excelsiors are first!" Dave was equally positive. "Just ask anyone!"

"I did! This morning. That fellow over at that table . . . that Twinkle-Toes!"

"But"—Dave's dark eyes spat fire—"he's an Atlantic!"

Now, Brian, standing in back, changed tactics. He became gentle, kindly. "Of course, Dave, maybe this boy belongs with one of the second-class teams, like them Atlantics. If he ain't such a good pitcher, you know!"

"Let me tell you"—Larry stopped with a fork of beef in mid-air, and looked stern—"I am the best pitcher in Massachusetts!"

Dave picked up the ball from Brian. His tone became sort of pitying. "They probably don't play so fast a game as we do here! You might be sort of handicapped with a team like the Excelsiors!"

"Hah!" Larry was scornful. "Why, we got some of the best teams going! And when I pitched, we won!"

"You're good, eh?" Dave said, goadingly.

"Listen, if you knew anyone up there, I wouldn't have to tell you!" Larry got his laughing look again. "Why, it got so, when the other team saw me playing, they'd just give up!"

Brian picked up Dave's ball. He goaded, "So . . . you think you are pretty good, eh?"

Dave turned and caught Brian's eye. They exchanged a wink, and Dave slipped out of his place. Po saw Dave go over to the Atlantics' table.

Larry looked jolly and laughing again. "I don't have to do a brag!" He began to eat. "The scores show if I can play!"

Po saw Dave talking to the Bull.

"I haven't got anything against the Excelsiors, you understand," Larry was telling Brian. "It's just that I heard of the Atlantics first, and they sound good to me!"

Po was in a tusset. The Atlantics! Those puny little things. She looked at Larry, exasperated. She thought that she'd seen this kind of a buck-o before. But he'd been hitched between the shafts of a jaunting car and his master would be beating him and cursing, and screaming to heaven, "What goes on in the mind of a mean-stubborn mule?"

Here he was making the mistake of a lifetime, throwing away all that heft on anyone but the Excelsiors! It was true, Po herself had never even seen them play. But it was something mystic, like joining a holy order. She *knew* they were best. For Larry's good she threw in,

"It's plain you were hiding behind the door when the sense was passed out! Can't you see the Excelsiors is the only team?"

Suddenly Larry leaned back. The laughing look was gone. He brought the flat of his hand down on the table. "Why does everyone think they can push me and nag me and make me do what they want? I know a striped kitten from a skunk! I won't be worried and pushed into things! I'm going to stand up free!"

Po had a sudden memory. It was so sharp, she wanted to reach up and put a hand over Brian's mouth to keep him from goading Larry any more. She remembered the grassy hillock where they'd hidden as they ran from Rimshaw. She could hear Larry saying, "I'm going to move around free!" Best leave him alone awhile. He wasn't in the mood!

Po glanced over at the Atlantics' table. Dave was still talking to the Bull. But now, the Bull's lower lip was thrust out above the black beard, and he glowered over at Larry. The Bull got up. In a moment, he was standing across the table from Larry, arms akimbo, looking down at him as if he were a comic insect.

"I hear tell," the Bull's voice boomed out, "there is some boy over here what claims he can play ball better than anyone!" The Bull had a sort of pleased anticipation in his voice. He hardly ever had a chance to knock any one down.

Everyone in the room seemed to pause and listen.

Brian spoke up, quick, cheerful. "Haven't you heard? Larry here, he's the best pitcher in New England!"

"Eeyah?" The Bull flashed a grim smile. Then he leaned down and stared into Larry's face. "Well, I am the best player in North America!"

Larry smiled, pleasantly enough.

The Bull's eyebrows, close above his blue eyes, drew together. "You don't believe it?"

All talk in the room had stopped. Everyone drew around them.

"North America's a big country!" Larry said cheerfully.

"It sure is!" The Bull glared.

"Almost as big as you think you are!" Larry calmly put in a fork of corned beef. There was a sort of awed rearing back from the crowd.

"You give me the lie!" The Bull stared, almost unbelieving such effrontery.

"Not at all. I just said North America's a lot of ground!"

"And I'm a lot of man!" the Bull said. "When it comes to that— I am the best ball player in the world!"

Larry looked up, as though he were mildly surprised. "You never played against me!"

The Bull's mouth dropped down at such insolence.

"I guess you just come to town and don't know nothing. Why, son, my middle name is Pulverize. Once, up in the mountains, a wild pant'er got into a argyment with me, which he is still regrettin'! I grabbed him by the tail and flung him so high I left him hanging on the point of a jaggedy star!"

"Well," Larry said, carefully loading up his fork with cabbage, "I haven't got the strength of a three day-old puppy, so you wouldn't want to do that with me. Only thing is"—Larry leaned back in his chair and looked at the Bull, mildly, pleasantly—"I—am—the—best ball player in Massachusetts."

Po saw the Bull's mouth pop open, his eyes start, at such daring. Then, she saw him control himself with a effort and speak pityingly: "Sonny, you just don't know who you are strutting in front of! Why, listen! Once when I was a lumberin', they needed ten seventy-foot logs at the bottom of the mountain, and the oxes had the cholery. I lashed 'em logs together, and with one hand, I carried 'em down the mountain, in the other hand carryin' a bucket of beer, and never spilt a drop!"

Larry looked at him. Then he smiled, pleasant-like.

The Bull stepped forward a little, menacingly, hopefully. "You call me a liar?"

"Oh, no!" Larry chewed a few moments calmly, and swallowed. Then he said, "I was just wondering if they weren't hollow logs!"

The Bull's boulder-like hands came forward and made fists. "Why, you. . . !"

Then he bellowed, in a rage, "You are aggravatin' me! Somebody better lull me down. I feel my blood bri'lin up! Last time I met up with a yankee like you, he was claimin' he could build ships faster than me! I had to take that nutmeg by the heels and dunk him like a paint brush in the tar barrel!"

Larry stared at the Bull now, with a bland look. "I am scared to shivers by the way you talk!"

The Bull leaned forward and pounded the table in rage. "Why, I can chaw you up! I'll give you such a whuppin' they'll take you for a dish of custard! And with a few trickles of kill-care in me, I could pin you up on the north pole for a flag!"

Larry glanced up, pleasantly. "Likely as not. I just drink sarsaparilla myself." Now he paused between each word. "But . . . I . . . *can* . . . play ball!"

Po looked at the copper-colored arms of the Bull and trembled. "Larry's got him in a flaming wax! Ooh! He'd best stop!"

But the Bull, as if he were sorry for Larry, gentled his tone again. "Listen, son. I will educate you as to who you are braggin' to! Once up in Cooperstown was a smart feller, jis' like you, thought he had

65

some kind of a trick ball he could throw around a curve, see! Well, I jis' took my favorite bat . . . Betsy, I called it . . . I took it, and bent it around with my bare hands into a curve. This fellow tosses me this trick ball, and I larrups it with Betsy. Would you believe it, that ball started chasin' that feller all over the field!"

"Is that a fact?" Larry stared at the Bull serenely, and went on eating.

"You don't believe it!" The Bull leaned over Larry, breathing hard. Po shivered.

"Certainly, I believe it. Do you think I'd call a gentleman a liar? Only thing . . . I was just thinking that bat must have been made out of green wood!"

"I'm glad you believe it, son, jis' for the sake of your ole mother. Because the last fellow got into a scrimmidge with me, they never bothered to scoop up the remains. Why, son . . . I kin not only fight better than you . . . I kin love more wimmin one after another, I kin dance better, I can sing better . . ." He stopped, as if hunting something to indicate his utter contempt of his foe, and then came out with, "I kin even *spit* further!" With that he stomped to the door, and spit across Fulton Street. He came back and glared down at Larry.

Larry calmly chewed his food and swallowed. "Now me," he said pleasantly, "I haven't got the strength of a fly's wing." He seemed to be taking them all into his confidence. "But"—he leaned back and looked blankly at the Bull—"I can play ball better than anyone I ever met!"

The Bull's coppery face turned a darker shade, the blue eyes under the close-hanging black brows darted lightning. "Do you talk ball . . . or do you play ball?" he yelled.

Larry jumped up, his jaw sticking out. "I play ball!"

"There ain't time for a game before the whistle blows, but I'll show you how we knock a ball in Brooklyn!"

"A ball-knockin' contest!" someone yelled. The bats and balls and baseball gear were kept at Brady's. They were stacked in a corner. A follower ran and fetched the Bull's war club. It was so big, Po felt powerful just looking at it. Someone handed Larry a bat. Suddenly, the whole crowd, sweeping Po with them, were in Fulton Street.

Larry and the Bull stood in the middle of the street swinging their bats. Tony ran down the street about fifty feet with a ball. The crowd yelled and screamed. The passersby in the street looked interested, and many stopped to watch. But none of them looked disturbed or even surprised at traffic being held up in the street for such a contest.

"This'll larn you, little boy," the Bull growled savagely. "I kin

66

beat any player out of New England with my legs bound, and one arm tied over my head!"

Brian gave the signal and Tony threw to Larry. Po heard the crack of the bat, sharp as a pistol. The white ball soared up toward the blue. The crowd turned their heads as it went up, up. The ball came down, far down near the ferry. Po wanted to cheer. But, at that moment, Tony threw to the Bull.

She heard the electric crack of the bat. The ball soared. Again the necks craned. Now, there was a little awed, ecstatic murmur, as the ball kept on going. It went over the ferry, out over the river mist. Maybe it went over the river. Or, maybe they only wanted it to. A glad yell broke out.

Po looked at Larry quickly. He stood, watching the place where the Bull's ball had disappeared.

One of the Bull's followers ran up and took the Bull's bat. The Bull dusted off his hands and let out a roar of laughter. "Like I said, son"—he put a hand on Larry's shoulder—"I am the best ball player in North America!"

Larry reddened a little. "I'd like to meet you on the ball field!"

The Bull roared again with Gargantuan laughter. "I seen you sittin' over at the table with them scrawny Excelsiors. Son, if you are playin' with them, you sure as hell are goin' to have the pleasure! Why, the Atlantics can fold 'em up and use 'em for a bar rag!"

The whistle from Hymes's pierced the neighborhood. The flood of men flowed off. In a few moments, the street was nearly empty. Po was watching Larry. She knew it was in the few minutes after a fight you really got to know someone, down to their gizzard.

Larry was looking after the Bull. His face was blank, expressionless. Then he said to Dave Posen, who was standing near, "Where'd you say the Excelsiors practiced?"

"Smith and Degraw."

"I'll be around tonight."

Chapter Nine

SOMETHING seemed to be tugging Po out into the street. Some magnetic thing beyond her. Stronger than the sensuous fingers of breeze that had reached in and touched her cheek in the gloomy parlor; more urgent than the spring sun on the brick sidewalk; strong enough, even, to make her put behind her, for this minute of God's time, the thought of Mamie's face, all starched up into displeasure.

Po had to come forth. "A person could famish to death from wanting anything so badly," Po decided.

In the street, the air was tonic as the flick of a whip. She sucked in a long breath. Only twice in the ten days since she'd come had she been out, and then under the steering eye of Mamie. A dreariness had seeped down into Po's marrow. Po O'Reilly, the Oul' Boul' one herself, had become anxious, anxious to please Mamie. But now, the bold sunny air made her spirits bubble up as they used to—long, long ago—ten days ago.

And here was Fulton Street, swirling and roaring and raging with life, and running itself down to the river. She wasn't sure how to get where she wanted to go. But vibrant hands seemed to draw her as if to urge, "Commince then, and you'll arrive!" She turned down Fulton Street.

Like plunging into the sea off Glengariff, it was. The sea there, rough and boisterous under its green sparkle, made you shout with laughter and almost not care where it bore you. And look now, that teamster, in his bright blue shirt, standing aloft on his great dray of barrels, flicking his long whip over his white horses, in sheer exuberance. When they plunged down the hill, he laughed as if to say, "What if we do get out of control!"

Boys screamed and darted, ignoring horse's hooves. Women's heels, clittering under their great skirts, hurried in or out of shops. Barrels of beer, with jolly thunder, rolled down on boards into basement grog shops, above which hung, at rakish angles, the shingles of doctors and lawyers.

"Po! Po O'Reilly!" Off Fulton Street, and a flight below the pavement, Dave Posen stood in an open door, with the legend over it, "Andrew H. Rome, Printer." Dave beckoned and smiled.

"I couldn't come up." Dave was running on eagerly, even as she came down the steps. "I'm supposed to mind shop. Where've you been?" The small shop was afloat with papers, printed bills, placards, pamphlets, loose sheets. "I've watched for you, I've waited!" He motioned with an inky arm for her to sit on a high stool. "Where've you been?"

Po wished she could tell him how it was with her. But what was the use of murmuring against the desolation that had come upon her? For, if, when she arrived, that first day or two, there had been the delight of the Gardens, the happy ball game, the feeling she belonged to the team and the knowing of Dave, and Walt, and the Bull, and . . . Larry . . . why, quickly, with a tight look of the mouth, and

68

words like knife flashes, Mamie had cut her off from all that. But . . . why complain? What could Po do? Where else go?

Dave's black eyes were merry as he looked at her. "What's the Irish word for darling?"

"So it's soothering some girl you are now!" Po flashed back. "Well, then, it's mavourneen. Mavourneen asthor!" Po had picked up one of the loose sheets, and looked at it, curious. "And what is this you are doing?"

"That's a book!"

"Yourself can print a book?" She looked at him, marveling.

"I'm a member in good standing of the International Typographers' Union!"

"To print a book! That's a wonderful thing, surely."

"Lots of famous men started as printers," Dave said, trying not to sound proud. "Ben Franklin, Horace Greeley!"

She picked up the sheet again, the ink still glistening damp. "And what is it, then?"

"It's Walt's book. We printed it for him last year. Now we're setting up a new edition for him. Poems, they are. Sort of crazy." Then, as if hastily defending his friend, "He writes good pieces for the newspaper, though."

Po looked at the damp sheet and read:

> "You are not thrown to the winds,
> You gather certainty and safety around yourself,
> Yourself, yourself, forever and ever.
> It is not that you should be undecided,
> But that you should be decided.
> Something long preparing and formless
> Is arrived and formed in you."

The words seemed to speak to her from the page. She frowned, excited. She wanted to read them again, to be sure she understood, but Dave was talking in an eager rush.

"And where were you yesterday? *That* was a ball game!"

Po dropped the sheet. "Is it the Excelsiors played, then," she said quickly, "and I missed them?"

"No, but they're going to! The Eckfords 've beat everyone in the play-offs. Now they got to face us. We'll kill them. Then, it'll be us against the Atlantics. That'll be the game! But, you'll be coming when we play the Eckfords?"

How could she bear it, then, the Excelsiors to play and she to miss it? She wanted to ask Dave if Larry had played . . . but somehow sensed the question would not make him happy.

Suddenly, the strong hands seemed to urge her forth again on her errand. She started to ask directions of Dave . . . then did not.

"Mavourneen," Dave called after her as she went up the steps. "Mavourneen asthor!" She turned, startled. "I'm just"—his eyes twinkled—"practicing my Irish!" With a flirt of her skirt, she ran up the steps into the street.

But talking to Dave made her feel good. Or was it only the errand she flew on that made everything seem so alive? As she passed the blacksmith shop, the sparks from the fire leaped in an air full of rhythmic pounding and the smell of burned hooves. The naked-arm smith in his long leather apron turned, and she saw he was one of the ball players who'd played the Sunday she arrived.

Now she passed an inn, the American Hotel, and even the men and women clambering into the orange-painted horse car marked Fulton Street, seemed brisk and doing. Ahead, she could see the river glinting. What she sought must be down there. She surged forward.

A wharf, its wooden arched entrance marked "Fulton Street Ferry, New York, Four Cents," jutted into the olive-green river. A ferry with rusty smokestack was coming in. A group, laden with shabby carpetbags and small rope-bound trunks, clinging to one another for support, stared about in the brilliant sun. Po's nose wrinkled from the remembered steerage smell. They stood, tremulous, half-smiles on their faces, but alert, ready to jump at a command. An old woman, with yellow parchment face under a bright red wig, clung to a young man in rabbinical clothing. A plump man in a blue coat smiled, but clung to his wife. Five children, each dragging some bundle, clung to her. The group moved up Fulton Street, staring. Po hoped they too would not be caught in some trap marked "Safety." "May the road rise with you!" she said softly after them.

Now a crowd pushed on the ferry, the bell rang, the boat shoved off, passengers calling back cheerful insults to the ferry master. Ah, Brooklyn! It was a dear child of a place!

A beautiful tangle of masts and furled sails lined the shore. Men in rigging shouted to men in drays, or those wheeling barrows along the cobbles. A long slender steamer with side paddle wheel pushed out toward the sea, its pennants straight out in the breeze. And all this wonder and throb and chant of people had been rolling and pounding forth close at hand, while she, fearful of making a mistake, had been shut up with Mamie, behind the green plush lambrequins over the tight and closed-down windows.

She felt someone watching her, and turned. It was Walt, his graying beard blowing in the breeze, his big felt hat on the back of his head. He smiled at her. Then with a sweep of his arm, including the river and lower Fulton Street, he asked, "Good?"

Po wanted to shout or break into a song, but she only nodded.

Walt pointed across the river, where the afternoon sun was turning the red brick into coral against the blue sky. "Manhattan!"

Po nodded. "That's where the Knickerbockers are!"

Walt laughed a great bellow which floated out over the river. She remembered the damp smeared sheet she had seen in the print shop. She thought Walt and her father would have liked each other, and she wished she could . . . if she knew how to explain it . . . ask Walt about the trap.

But he had been looking at her with his serene tender look. "What are you afraid of?"

In a sudden release she pointed back up the hill, where Quimby's and other black buildings reared. "Those . . . the . . . monsters!"

"Oh. The factories!"

"And is it in one of them I'll end then?"

Walt watched the white waves in the middle of the sunlit river. Then he said, "That's your no. What's your yes?"

"If I could maybe sing the songs that are in me!"

A strange look came over his face, sad but grim. But at that moment, a great sailing vessel came into view. Like a thing enchanted, it came sweeping up the river, every white sail taut. Its masts were so high, it seemed they might scrape tags of clouds off the sky.

"Yankee Clipper! The *Sea Witch!* A Brooklyn ship! Built right there"—he motioned north along the river—"by Brooklyn men!" Now the great ship was upon them. As she floated by, Po stood thranced. The ship seemed alive.

The men on her were singing a chanty. Walt waved his big hat. The men waved back. Po waved too. They pointed and laughed and waved. Now the Clipper was going on up the river.

"They've been to China"—Walt's voice was exultant—"or India! Just boys reared up on Joralemon Street, maybe, with nothing to go on but a few pieces of canvas. Over fathoms of water, and seas with no marked roads. They found their way and back!"

Suddenly he turned to Po and said abruptly, "How do you like that for a yes?"

But now the ferry was coming in. The deck hand threw a rope, Walt caught it, snubbed it down, yelling a greeting. Po saw the deck hand was Rooster O'Hanlon, one of the Excelsiors. Walt was aboard, a crowd pushed on, the ferry chugged out against the choppy waves.

She had meant to ask Walt for directions. Well, she'd find it herself! She started up Fulton Street, and about halfway up, heard, ahead of her in the crowd, a voice, a street merchant, chanting. For so long had she listened to Irish street ballads, noting words, comparing them with ones she knew, a voice singing in the street was picked up instantly.

> "Oysters from the bay, fresh as today!
> A pearl in each oyster, fresh from the bay!"

The oyster seller was ahead of her, a wooden yoke extended to arm's length across his shoulders, from each end of which hung a wooden pail marked "Dent's." Po could almost believe the voice was that of the African who had stowed away with her on the *Red Tanager!* But he had drowned trying to make shore! She hurried ahead.

Like when she saw a seed sprouted from two specks of clay on a rock, she felt a sudden elation. The cold enervating fog that was Mamie and the flat seemed to lift and float away. It was Juba! He had come through!

"Juba! Don't you know me?"

He walked faster. He turned into an alley. She followed.

"I seed you down the hill. I waits to see if you wants to speak to me."

Po had discovered it was no disgrace here to be caught talking friendly to an Englishman or a peeler, but an African was considered a slip of God's hand.

"Are you all right?" she asked.

"Got me a job so's I can eat and sleep!" White teeth flashed a smile. "Wash dishes, sweep out. When too many oysters at the bar, they send me out to cry them. You all right?" He peered intently at her.

Suddenly she was ashamed. "Yes!" she said positively. "I'll be all right!

"Juba, that supercargo from the ship, he's here!"

"I know. Dent's a place for seafaring men. I seed him from the kitchen. He ain't seed me. When I'm in the street, I watch all the time. That's how come I seed you."

"Juba, your wife and baby?"

"I'se lookin'! Up one street, down another. But they're here. I know!" His white teeth flashed, his glittering eyes lit. "I'll find 'em."

A passerby looked in the alley curiously at the white girl in conversation with the Negro. Without a word, Juba glided off. "Oysters! Oysters!"

Po took a long breath. Reading that strange poem of Walt's in the print shop; hearing Walt with his serene tender lips saying the words about the ships on unmarked roads; seeing Juba surviving, spite of all . . . it made her spring away from her creeping fears. Fears that if she did aught to displease or disturb Mamie, the safety of sure food and certain bed might be gone! "And isn't it the cruel old time I've been giving myself lately, though, shut up with herself within walls!" Suddenly she turned, full of roaring joy again, and went up the hill, singing:

> "I know where I'm going,
> I know who's going with me,
> I know who I'll love,
> But the dear knows who I'll marry. . . ."

Passersby smiled, amused.

> "Feather beds are soft,
> Painted rooms are bonny,
> But I'd leave them all,
> To go with my love Johnny. . . ."

Po smiled back now.

And wasn't it that big one with the bright hair on him she'd come forth to find? Wasn't it only the human thing to want to know what way it was with him at all? And not that alone. She wanted to give herself the joy of seeing him, and the way he reminded her of the fresh field bright with sun; to reassure herself that even if at Mamie's she had none of the joy, it was still in this place.

After a bit, she found what she had been seeking. On a lane off Fulton, a sign swung out from a high fence. "Nicholas Van Leyn and Son, Ship Builders." She saw the yard was el-shaped and extended to the river. Inside, great skeletons of ships reared on building ways, but among all the men pounding, carrying planks, guiding barrows, not a sight did she see of a big pair of shoulders with a bright head on them. She walked along the fence, peering, until she came to a part of the yard taken up by lumber stacks, with scarcely any men working. About to turn back, she saw him.

She wanted to cry out in pain. Humped slackly over some planks resting on a trestle, his great arm moving in small slow jerky movements, he was sandpapering a board. The heavy shoulders sagged, the head hung forward, even his hair looked dull and dusty. But his face stunned her. His mouth was not laughing, but hanging, as if his mind were away. His look was dead with distaste, without interest, and even, down to the bottom of his kidneys, boredom. A man in a tail coat walked briskly past, eyeing Larry disgustedly. "Laziest fellow ever I saw. Wonder we get anything done!"

Po remembered Larry and how he had looked as he plucked

the Bull's lightning ball from the air. She wanted to beat her fists on the fence and make them let him go.

Then he looked up and saw her, her face pressed between an opening in the fence.

Po's heart flittered like a caught butterfly, for she was sure he looked pleased. Light flowed over his face. "Where've you been?" he called out. "Eckfords beat the Continentals."

"And is it the best ball player in New England you still are?" She wanted to keep the dull look from his face.

"Hah! Don't you believe it? See that big knothole?" He pointed to the fence beside her. "Watch!"

Out of his back pocket had flashed a ball. He fingered it, glancing up and down, as if judging the whereabouts of the brisk man. He threw. The ball came through the hole. Po picked it up, and he came over to get it.

"Wait a little!" He was laughing down at her. "Grogan promised to let me leave early, so I could practice a new pitch! You can come with me, if you've nothing special to do!"

Divil a special thing had she!

Chapter Ten

THEY boarded a stage which rolled through the tollgates of a highway called the Flat Bush Plank Road. In a little time they came to a lonely green country place Larry said was Prospect Hill.

And here they were now in a little glen, not wild or misty like a glen in Wicklow, but with trees large and small and it spring and sunlight slanting through the trees. The sun loosened the fragrance of a wild crabapple tree, its bud tips still red among the snow of its bloom. "Ah!" Po exclaimed. "And isn't this a beauty of a place now!"

"It's a darb!" Larry looked around with satisfaction. "See that elm?" He pointed to where the fountain of branches curved down, covered now with a veil of moving delicate green lace. "From here, across that open grass, to the elm, it's exactly forty-five feet, same distance as from pitcher's box to home plate!"

74

He opened the brown paper picnic parcel bought in Dent's. Cold chicken and oyster pie it was!

Po looked up at the trees. A horse chestnut near them had its five-fingered leaves still clenched below its spiked buds, like candles not yet lit. It was still so early in spring, the maple leaves were tight curled coral feathers against the blue sky.

"And yourself was the clever one to have searched it out, and you only come!"

He winked, sitting beside her on the grass. Each blade seemed shiny, new minted, without a fleck on its silvery green. "Dave and Tony told me it'd be a good secret place to practice. They want to keep me under cover till we face the Atlantics in the final play-off. I got this new pitch, see, I'm working out. There's always Atlantic spies around when we practice back there in the lots!"

The pie had a flaky crust, and in it pieces of tender white chicken. Ah! how good it tasted!

Under the trees, the black earth was littered with cast-off bud tips, where blossom or leaf had burst forth, laboring in a new beginning. Po watched a land turtle creeping about, slowly, timidly.

"That's a hard life he's leading, that beast, and he so worried about himself he must have a house around him always to be peering out from." Po sighed. "And it's no better am I. And what way is that then for a natural-born woman to be living, that she can never lep or dance when she has a roaring joy in her?"

Larry, chicken pie in hand, looked at her. "Well! Last time I saw you, you were squaring off to take on the world single-handed!"

"I was scared then, on that ship, and before that, for a long time. But . . . a sure bed, a certain food, feeling safe . . . I tell you, it's not everything!"

He had picked up another pie, but he stopped—looked off, frowning a little. "I had a thing like that bothering me!" Then he said slowly, "But I fixed it!"

"How then?"

He put the pie down very carefully, and he looked off across the green, frowning. "By breaking my mother's heart!" he said bitterly. He was silent then, but it seemed to Po he wanted to talk. And after a bit, words began to come out of him, jerkily at first, then with a rush. "I guess, leaving up there, that was the hardest thing I've ever done! You'd think to hear me talk she was mean to me! All she ever did was watch over me like a baby. Every move I made. I knew it was just because she was fond of me. But I tell you I used to feel sometimes she was bad as those old Southern planters she would tongue lash when she was working to free a slave! But, I got away!"

Then he said, as if he were trying to make himself believe it, "I'm a free man!"

Po had meant to tell him her troubles, but he was telling his. "It's good to be free," Po said, troubled.

"Yes!" He looked uneasy. "Sometimes, even now I find myself waiting to be told come, go, stay, or don't! But last thing she said to me was I'd be back. That I'd never get anywhere without going to college, and without her and her relatives to help me!" He looked grim then, and picked up a twig and broke it into bits. "They sort of run things back there."

"Your father then, where is he at all?"

Larry was silent. After a bit, he reached into an inside pocket of his brown wool jacket and brought forth a small picture in a flat frame. He handed it to her. It was a daguerreotype of a man and woman, the man a giant with a blond beard, the woman, tiny, uncompromising, staring from under heavy black brows.

"She's . . . little, isn't she?" Po, for some reason, felt her heart failing her.

Larry dropped his eyes to the picture. After a while he said, "Almost as little as you!" Po felt depressed, she did not know why.

"Funny, how I remember you saying when we were on the *Red Tanager*, that I had the sense of a trained bear!"

"Ah, surely now, you'd pay no attention to anything the Irish might say and they in a temper!"

"Used to be a little peddler travel around with a bear up home. Always wondered how the bear got on that chain."

He reclaimed the daguerreotype and stared at it.

"I remember the day my father came home and told her he'd signed on as hand on a whaler. He was a lawyer. My mother's family, they were doctors, lawyers, ministers. My mother took on, and they backed her up. My father said he'd get to be a mate or a captain away from there and them."

"And did he then?"

Larry put the daguerreotype away carefully. He stood up. "He was lost second voyage out! Then"—and it seemed to Po he looked at her almost with hostility—"my mother just had me!"

Now he stretched his great arms, flexed his muscles. "You know" —he laughed, a little grim—"maybe that's why I liked baseball, and ducked school, and was always running to the field! That was one thing she couldn't tell me how to do!"

He threw off his jacket, took out the white ball, and called down to her, laughing, "See that slug with blue eyes and a drag in his off leg about to go in that knothole in the elm? He's about to get the surprise of his life!"

76

The ball, with lightning swiftness and a little hiss of air, hit directly above the knothole, then bounced back a bit and dropped to the ground.

"Ah, it's the brag of the world you are!" She laughed with delight.

"I guess maybe playing ball's the one thing I'm good at." He retrieved the ball and returned, curving his fingers over it. "When you're pitcher at a big game, and you feel all the people hanging on every muscle move, you stand there, sort of half-scared, but knowing you can deliver, too . . . why . . . it's . . . all right! And at that"—he threw the ball with rhythmic sureness—"I'm doing as much good, I guess, as being a lawyer!"

He ran and picked up the ball.

"Ah, I could catch it for you now," she called, "if I were another young fellow!"

He looked over, winked, and broke into his big laugh. "You're doing all right. I could have gotten Dave—usually do—but I thought this would be more fun!" And wasn't it true a man liked nothing so much as having a girl sit quietly and watch him doing what he did best?

Po leaned against a black tree, and looked up into pale leaf buds, still tight and hard. She, not knowing this tree, could not guess what the leaf would be like, or the blossom or fruit. Beyond, a white birch shivered in a light breeze, its tender small heart leaves and its seed tassels swaying, heavy freighted like a pendulum. Everything seemed starting, ready to become, nothing had been.

Larry, warming up as he ran repeatedly to reclaim the ball, threw off his shirt.

He would draw his arm far back, then give a strong under-arm throw, and the white ball arced through the bronze diagonals of late sun. And to think but a short space of time past, he had the gray dull look on him, like he could be dead or in jail. But now, as sun glinted across his hair and bare shoulders, he had the shine on him again, like the fresh field. He had an absorbed look on his face, as if he paid no attention to himself or anything else, except that one thing he was doing.

"And 'tis a wonderful thing to see a young man throwing a ball," Po thought, "and with muscles like the waves running under a swell of the summer sea. . . . And maybe everyone is handsome when they do a thing they love." Brian, nimble among the glasses of his bar; her Da, piping on a green, and young people lepping and thronging; maybe even herself when she sang a soft song. Otherwise you were an affront to nature, as if God leaned over His balustrade and said, "Be ugly then, and after all the great pick-over of things I am after

77

scattering about with a generous hand and what must you do but pick out something you look squint-eyed at!"

A bird, very fancy, as though he'd dressed up to go courting, with a cream-colored vest with speckles on it, lit, swaying, on a bush near by. He let forth a poignant liquid song. Far, far off in the woods, where dusk was beginning to brush the tree tops, his mate answered. The bush was covered with sharp bronze spiky buds, ready to spring open, take form, become. She felt like that. A languid but steady pulse seemed beating inside her. If she'd known gaiety in Ballyhouna, or sorrow in Fall River, she was glad they had not fallen on her now, at this instant, for so awake, wide open, ready to receive she was, she could not have borne them.

She had never been in love or known a man. There'd been kisses snatched at some larking, with like as not a slap to follow, and she and the boy laughing. Only once did she remember being stirred, and then it was ugly. She and her father had come in August dusk to a place where there was a Feis, a wedding. She'd danced, as often before, with Seumas, a handsome boy, a great dancer, for Po herself could jig and reel with the liveliest. But that night, he'd guided her to the crowd edge, off into an orchard, heavy with the odor of harvest apples, still dancing. Then, his mouth, hot hard, insistent, his body, hot and moist, against her. She hated him, was disgusted, repelled, jerked away. There'd been no face slapping, or laughing. Disturbed, she'd run off and would trust herself with no dancer all the night, but kept washing off her mouth.

Po walked to the blossoming crabapple and breathed in its scent. To look up into that glistening white, abuzz with a few late bees, was to feel life could hold little more—except to be loved.

From the bush, poignant, urgent, the he-bird called again. His mate answered shyly, coming forward through the wood.

Po looked at Larry and it came to her that she loved him. She loved him. She had said it in words. That's what had been the matter. She loved him, she wanted him, and she wanted him to want her. Now that she had said it, a lot of reason for strange dreams and sleepless nights evaporated.

Then, she remembered the grassy hillock, above the beach, how he had touched her hand—then said he wanted to walk free. She must not let him see how she felt, then. She must act as if nothing had happened.

Larry had stopped. He was putting on his shirt, and he came over toward her. The pulse inside was beating strongly now. She'd be all right, he'd never know—only he didn't touch her. She must keep him from touching her.

She could see his gray eyes looking down at her, and the look on him he had when she first saw him, as though he were ready to break into a great laugh.

"Off the grass now! Dew's falling!" He smiled down at her, and before she could spring away, he picked her up lightly and carried her to a granite boulder and set her upon it. But he did not let go of her. He caught hold of her two ankles, playfully, and held them. When his hands touched her bare ankles, thrust into her brogans, an electric shock seemed to go up her legs, seemed to settle somewhere above the pit of her stomach, and she felt warm and moist and yearning in a strange way she had never felt before. Her words, her mind, she could keep behind a decent curtain, but when he touched her, she could not keep her body from answering. "I'm destroyed! I'm destroyed!" she thought.

But he still held her ankles, playfully, looking down at her, laughing. "You know, back in Rockville, on a hill beyond town was a little pear tree, and the little pears on it . . . well! Sun'd put gold flecks on 'em, and little russet spots, and they were so curved and smooth, when you sunk your teeth into one, it was white and juicy and sweet, oh so sweet. Except right at the end, there was a sharp tang to the taste, a bitterness, a sharpness. That's what you're like, little Po!"

Ah, why didn't he let go of her ankles?

He did, but to put up a thick finger and rub it along the edge of her eyelash. "There, I been wanting to do that ever since I saw you! Your lashes are so long and black and jagged!" Then naturally, almost unconsciously, his hand cupped around her shoulder, then stroked her back from shoulder to hip.

She reached up to touch his face, but just then, she felt his caressing hand slacken, fall away from her hip. He let out a long hard breath, and on his face came a strange look, a guilty look. He left her. He, frowning, a worried look on him, picked up his jacket and began to put it on.

Like a small brown cloud, a hunched form swooped through the air and lighted in the shadowy boughs above them. All the birds near by set up a great fluttering, and crying, and flew off.

Larry had moved away from Po.

"What is it then?" Po cried.

He peered up at the hovering bird lurking in the gloom above. "An owl!" he said, as if she had meant to ask him what was the matter with the birds!

The dusk was heavy bronze now, the long diagonal shadows purple.

Po looked at Larry, puzzled, a little angry, yet wanting him. She had not tried to lure him. But she could. A shiver of breeze moved across the crabapple tree and the odor of the wide-open blossoms moved her face like a soft hand. And why not, then? She wanted him.

She knew songs, some very old, sung perhaps by a dark-haired woman on some hawthorn foamy white path beside a misty Irish sea, calling a lover; and she knew others, simple songs, and she knew when she sang them, with tenderness, out of a deep well of passionate warmth, why she would see the gnarled hand of Sean steal toward Kate; or Owen's eyes and Peg's eyes lep across the room to each other, as though they must burst out of there and be alone together. So, in the April dusk she sang. Her voice was not smooth like a ribbon of velvet, but had little cockleburs in it:

"Put your head, darling, darling, darling,
  Your darling black head, my heart above!
Oh, mouth of honey, with the thyme for fragrance,
  Who with heart in breast could deny you love?

Oh, many and many a young girl for me is pining,
  Letting her locks of gold to the cold wind free,
For me, the foremost of our gay young fellows,
  But I'd leave a hundred, pure love, for thee.

Then put your head, darling, darling, darling,
  Your darling black head my heart above,
Oh, mouth of honey, with the thyme for fragrance,
  Who with heart in breast could deny you love?"

The song stopped. Then he was beside her, his arms around her in the bronze dusk. And it seemed the only way the flame that leaped up in her would be beat out was with his arms, his body. He stroked her hair softly, the curve of her cheek, her throat. Then he gently curved his hand around the small round mound of her breast, and seemed to set vibrating a thousand notes from a tightly strung golden harp, whose strings could only be silenced by his hand laid on them.

Then he kissed her, and her whole body rose to him. His arms tightened around her, almost convulsively. Then she felt him stiffen and draw back again, breathing hard, and in a moment his voice came, low, strained and unnatural. "I shouldn't! I know you're a good girl!"

Po felt deep anger well up in her. And all the vibration of the thousand golden strings, instead of resolving in a chord, jangled painfully.

"A good girl, is it?" she thought. "And what now? Is a good girl not to be happy then?"

Larry was frowning, looking at his hands, uneasy. "I know it's wrong!"

How could anyone think of wrong on such a gold-bronze evening, and with blossoms and soft air? How could anyone get such a simple thing as love so mixed up?

"I get awful strong feelings. I know—well—I know you ought to respect a good girl—the same as your mother."

His mother, was it! Found some foggy morning under a cabbage, was he?

"With a fellow, it's . . . different. I haven't got words to tell you. Back in Rockville, the older men took me down to Red Row early, and the women there, why, well, it was different! I—got—feelings!"

And what did he suppose she was feeling then, and the strings vibrating in her like a whirlwind?

What was it? "Larry . . . is it a trained bear you fear I'll be making, and chaining you up?"

His breath came fast, and he spoke quick, loud, like a drowning man snatching at a straw. "Yes. That's it!" He repeated it to himself. "That's it!"

"But, I would never!"

Now he frowned, angry, as if she were trying to take the straw away from him. "I got to be sure no one coaching me from the side lines is going to get me off my throw!"

"It is maybe a bit of a habit I have, of ordering, from my father having the need of it! But . . . I can drop it away from me!"

Larry stepped away so quickly one might think he was in panic. "I'm going to be sure of myself first. I been on a chain so long. Maybe it's because you're little, like she is," he insisted. "I just want to be free. There's nothing the matter with me!"

It was dark now. Po felt as if she were battling some shadowy thing she could not see, lurking in the air around her.

"Come on," he said. "I'll take you home."

Po knew now that, somehow, the giant, the big one she had wanted to lean on, whose strength she had fallen in love with, was crippled; that she would have to help him by the muscles of her imagination. And somehow she must do this without letting him know, for if he felt she was running him, he was lost forever.

81

Chapter Eleven

M AMIE'S eyes narrowed a little as if she could hardly believe her ears. She stared silently. After a while she said one word. "No!"

"But, Mae, what's the harm in it?"

Mamie stared at her again, then emitted a short breath, as if she could hardly trust herself to speak. "It's not the kind of people I care to associate with!"

"But, Mae," Po said unhappily, "I'm not asking you to go! I'll go myself!"

Mamie arranged the teacups with the handles all pointing one way on the center table in the parlor. "No!" she said shortly, as if ending the discussion.

"But I can't see why it's wrong!"

"You are not going." Mamie spoke through closed teeth, as she savagely whisked imaginary dust from the table cover.

Po began to get angry. "Well, that day Brian and I stopped at the game, there were a lot of nice-looking women and girls there."

Mamie broke out, "No doubt! Like that blonde Louise Denis. Why, her mother was no more than—well—I wouldn't mention the word! Or that common Clarabel Jones!"

"But, Mae, if you'd only go once, you'd see! Why—"

"With all the people in this town ready to tear me down to their level, make small of me! What you do reflects on me!" She went out and closed the door with such a click, the lace curtain stirred a little.

The trouble was, Mamie was ignorant. She had never been to a game. How could she know? Po bit back baffled tears. A thought protruded into her bafflement. Mamie had no right to stop Po. But then, another thought jutted up. And what if Mamie made Brian send Po away? Po cursed inwardly. If only the game had been on another day. If only it had not been on this particular afternoon!

For Mrs. Archie Selfridge was coming, that afternoon, to call.

Mamie came back from the kitchen, with her staccato movements, carrying the silver cake basket, polished to a glitter.

"Don't use words like drunk! Or britches! Talk about the weather to her, or scenery!" Mamie's voice was like brittle sugar icing. Po could not decide if the dark cake it masked was hostility, worry, or fear. But the etiquette lesson went on. "Couldn't you talk about that castle where you stayed?"

Mrs. Selfridge was the wife of the chief clerk in the assessor's office in Court Street. While this did not make Mr. Selfridge the white-haired boy-o of Brooklyn, he, like an iceberg, carried nine-tenths of his power beneath the surface. "Mr. Hymes uses him to manage the most confidential affairs!" Mamie said, impressively.

For Mamie had heard of something she hoped would float Brian off the sand bar of the saloon, over to a glittering island shimmering somewhere ahead, of "respectability, a carriage, a house on the Heights!" Brooklyn was about to have running water. A reservoir was building. Soon water would run into the houses and wash basins of the rich and easy. A Water Commission, made up of solid estab-lished burghers, was already appointed. Mamie knew there had been no chance of getting Brian on that. But, underneath the city, would be built drains. There would be a Commission of Sewage. And it was for this Mamie had got herself into such a clenched fist. This afternoon's call seemed to be some kind of inspection she must meet and, long days ago, she had started preparing for the fearful occasion.

And so, all these days, while Mamie had been blathering the words "nice" and "pretty" and "refined" another word had been on her tongue constantly. That word was "sewage." Indeed, Po had once, infected with the general tension, referred to Mrs. Selfridge as "Mrs. Sewage—" It was that same evening she heard Mamie tell Brian, in her sugar-icing voice, that, "A young girl is too much of a respon-sibility!" And later, as if with deep kindliness, "that perhaps Po would be better off with that cousin back in Fall River."

But Po had helped Mamie polish the flat till it was nasty clean. Mamie had added a new lamp shade, and made herself a frock for the terrible occasion. She was a painstaking seamstress and the basque on the new sulphur-green poplin fitted like the peel of a potato, and the maltese lace collar, fastened with a cameo brooch, was the latest fashion. And all of it, including the exact words Mamie would use as she would take Mrs. Selfridge's parasol—all of it had come out of a holy catechism Mamie consulted, called Godey's Lady's Book.

For under Mamie's righteous assurance, Po sensed uneasiness. She was so easily disturbed. Everything must be perfect. "If you'd turn your toes out when you walk across a room," Mamie said nervously, trying to complete Po's presentability, "you'd look more refined."

" 'Tis a thing wants practicing," Po said apprehensively, hoping that in her anxiety she did not call the great one "Mrs. Sewage" and then trip herself from trying to walk like a duck. But she went upstairs to dress, worriedly, and exactly, as Mamie had set forth.

First she put on, over her chemise, a corset, a thing with great hooks down the front, but which, thanks be to God, came only to her hips. Over this went what Mamie called a corset cover, then long muslin drawers, ruffled with machine lace. Then Po got herself into, with only a little swearing, and that in a quiet lady-like way, a steel and whalebone hoop frame. Over this went a full muslin petticoat, its two flounces edged with straw braid to make them stick out more. The object was to make yourself look like you were perishing to death from hunger from the waist up, but blown up like a balloon from the waist down. On top of all this, she put on the new full skirt she had helped Mamie make of pale blue hit-or-miss calico, with its graduated rows of tucks.

Po liked the new basque well enough, though, for it was open at the top. She could breathe nearly natural. The sleeves were three-quarter length, and under the basque was worn a chemisette of white nainsook, tied up close to the throat and at the wrists with narrow black velvet ribbon.

Dutifully, Po had parted her hair in the center, drawn it back over her ears, sleek and straight. It was supposed to be flattened in the back into coils. But Po's black hair was stubbornly curly, and a sort of halo of fine hair hung like a nimbus over the sleekly drawn front, and wiry stray curl-ends popped out from the coils.

In Fall River, there had been little money for new American shoes, and the brogans Po arrived in made Mamie nervous. Once or twice, Mamie had given her little laugh when Po clumped into the room. It was curious about Mamie's laugh. She never used it because something was funny, but only to make a kind of comment—scorn, or disapproval, or rejection, or ridicule. Po felt the blood rush into her face once, as she came into a room, when Mamie remarked, with a small smile, that it sounded like a cow coming in.

The next evening at supper, Brian brought Po a present. It was a pair of American shoes. The lower parts were made of some lustrous thing, shiny as jet, called patent leather. The heels were so fine and dainty, but a quarter of an inch high, and the toes as pointed and slender as a columbine flower. And the uppers! Sure, they were black taffeta, quilted, and turned down around the ankles in a little cuff! The whole was bound round with fine black satin, and tied to the foot with three bows of the same. They were enchanting, and Po loved them.

Arrayed, she stood tiptoe to see herself in the greenish mirror over the bureau. Pocahontas O'Reilly from Ireland was gone.

Only the face was the same. The thin oval face, with pointed chin, and curved black brows with little points in the middle; the jaggedly black eyelashes, and the intensely dark blue eyes. In spite of all the tromping about, her skin was still milky white. She remembered one of the professors at Trinity saying to her father that she

84

looked a "tender imp." But only the face looked the same. The rest was someone she must still become.

Her old clothes hung, disheveled and mute, across the bed. Po knew that Mamie wanted anything that bespoke the Irish greenhorn out of sight. Coolly, Po began to fold them, to lay them away forever in the bottom drawer of the bureau. She picked up the worn white underbodice, its linen cool to the touch. She could see the old woman of Innismallock reach up into the rafters of her cottage and pull down the hank of flax out of which it was woven. But Po folded it up now.

She picked up her shawl. From long wear, it had taken on the curve of her head and shoulders. She stroked the soft wine dark wool, with flecks of color like motes of light, amethyst, scarlet, gold, cunningly woven into it. Then she folded it quickly. The skirt, still deep blue after all it had been through, she started to fold.

Her hand touched a little hole burned in the skirt, and she remembered the very fire, the spark! Something seemed to loosen from the woolen fabric. It was a fragrance, an essence, haunting as neglected tenderness. It was turf smoke. She remembered when her father had bought the dress.

They had been lacking for money for long, that time, walking roads, singing in village greens. They came to Dublin. The Society for the Preservation of Ancient Music had arranged a concert. He sang and played. The blue wool dress came of that. Her hands clenched around the little pile of old clothing. It was not only that all had been woven or spun by human hands, all had been made in love and paid for by a song.

She tried to put the dress and shawl in the drawer quickly. But the turf smoke seemed to loosen. It came up and strangled her. She seemed to hear the low wild ringing sound of an Irish harp, and her father's voice singing Deirdre's lament:

> "Dig the grave both deep and wide,
> Sick I am and fain would sleep,
> Dig the grave and make it ready,
> Lay me on my true love's body."

Suddenly Po buried her face in her clenched hands and sobbed wildly, wildly. The sobs came so uncontrollably it was as if some other person, not herself, inside her, were sobbing.

When she had gotten over it, she smoothed the things and put them away. It seemed like a last source of strength and love. She took the cruiskeen of water they kept on the washstand, and washed her face in cold water.

85

Then she ran down the stairs to try to fit herself into the ways of Mrs. Selfridge and the catechism according to Godey.

Listening, Po began to understand that Mrs. Selfridge—a meaty-looking woman in stiff brown merino with matter-of-fact eyes—was, in truth, making inspection. Herself planning to assail the Heights, Mrs. Selfridge was checking on possible cohorts, making certain Mamie would be a credit to her. It was astonishing how thorough she was. Little questions flicked out, were answered, Mamie's opinions checked.

"Po lived for over a year with a member of the nobility," Mamie said, pouring tea from the china pot. Po remembered Lady Dudevan, who went about in shabby riding pants, with a gangly Irish setter crowding her out of her chair. Then Po looked at Mamie, fingers curved in a set way, her eyes darting uneasily; and at Mrs. Selfridge, whose eyes seemed to keep adding up little totals of credits for stylishness, or subtracting sums for non-conformity.

Watching them Po suddenly realized that just as Walt and Brian and Bushel Basket had outraged the room, Mrs. Selfridge and Mamie, with their rigid movements, uneasy eyes and hidden motives, seemed to belong in it. Po could see Mrs. Selfridge admiring the lamp shade. Of green bobbinet it was, with artificial flowers and vines sewn thickly all over it, the vines trailing below the shade. It was as though in this room it was fitting not only to shade, but disguise, anything as simple and necessary as light.

"And were you educated in Europe?" Mrs. Selfridge took a precise sip of tea.

"Ah, and wasn't it the nuns in Dublin themselves that gave me the great working-over."

"Oh!" Mrs. Selfridge asked at once. "Is she Catholic?"

"Oh, no," Mamie said hastily, "Protestant!" And, as Mrs. Selfridge accepted the statement, Po felt she had been admitted to this noble, sparkling company by the edge of her teeth.

Mamie rose from the settee, and handed the silver basket with the almond cakes. "I go to hear Henry Beecher myself."

"Really!" Mrs. Selfridge seemed to add up the silver basket, the cakes, and manner of handing them, to a quick total. "He's so low church!"

It was the first mistake Mamie had made. Po saw the pink and white enamel of her face strain into a tight smile.

Po got a sudden sense everything said and done was like the artificial flowers and vines masking the light. It was like the things in Godey's catechism. "Be something you weren't, what someone told you was better." Po could still recall tales about America she and her father had read before they came, of women—fighting Indians, starving, crossing deserts, but hanging on. Was it for this, then?

Po had lost track of the talk for a moment. Now she heard Mrs. Selfridge say, ". . . and Mr. Hymes was just walking across this field. They threw a clod at him. He's a fine man!" The injustice of it filled Mrs. Selfridge. "He has problems! That's what they never think of! Every week he pays them their money! Where would they be without him? Common roughs!"

"Oh, that element!" Mamie set her teacup down.

"It would never have happened if they hadn't been playing on Sunday! If I had my way, there'd be none of these rowdy ball games at all!"

No ball games! What was the woman thinking of?

"Oh, excuse me!" Mrs. Selfridge went on deliberately. "Your husband belongs to a ball club, doesn't he?"

"For business reasons," Mamie said hastily, "while he has the Gardens!"

"They're getting like the fire companies. Some of the best people *used* to belong."

Oh, if only Po could make them understand about the men on the sunlit field. It seemed she could see Mamie and Mrs. Selfridge turning off on a narrow little path that led into a thicket of dry sticks, instead of keeping to the boisterous bright highway.

"But 'tis a lovely game!" Po heard herself say, a flush on her face. "A sight to see!"

Mrs. Selfridge's meaty face turned, surprised. "Oh, the game itself! Perhaps there's no harm in it. But what I object to here in Brooklyn is the people who play it. I for one think there should be an ordinance against those great mobs of people carrying on that way!"

The doorknocker clacked. Po, through the window curtain, saw Dave Posen standing on the landing. Dave! He was the very one she needed! She wondered at his being there the afternoon of a game; but Dave with his sensitive face, his quick talk, he could explain to them all about the ball game.

Po sped down the hall. "Come in!" She held the door open.

Now she was urging him down the hall, introducing him to Mrs. Selfridge.

Mamie had a pinched frozen look, but then, anything unplanned bothered her. Mrs. Selfridge was staring at Dave's ink-stained hands, his shirt sleeves.

"I have to take the referee out in a hack. I thought maybe Po could come to the game!" Dave was smiling, shyly but happily.

Mamie seemed to quiver back from him. She took a long breath.

"Miss O'Reilly"—her voice had a thin quality—"does not care to associate with that element."

"Oh, Mamie!" Po broke out. "You don't understand! Why, this game of base—isn't it one of the happy things in America?"

"That's right!" Dave smiled.

"Oh!" Mrs. Selfridge had a half smile on her face, her eyes were half drooped as she looked at him. "Are you American born?"

At her tone, Po for some reason felt a flush rise to her cheeks. She turned quickly to Dave. He seemed to adjust a mask, blank, so that nothing could be read on his face.

He didn't bother to look at Mrs. Selfridge. "Yes." His voice was flat.

Mrs. Selfridge's eyes seemed to narrow a little. "And what do you *do?*" her voice bored in.

For some reason, Po felt on the defensive. She didn't know exactly why. Dave was her friend. She was proud of him.

"Dave's a printer!" she announced grandly.

"Oh!" Mrs. Selfridge smiled the half smile.

Po felt something unpleasant in the air. She made her voice sound like a fanfare of trumpets. "He's an International Journeyman!"

"Printer! Hmm . . . That's an odd occupation." Mrs. Selfridge glanced at Mamie with the half smile.

Mamie, copying Mrs. Selfridge's half smile and tone, said, "Isn't it unusual!"

"Odd, is it?" Po felt obscurely angry. "And he able to make a book with his fingers being that nimble!"

"Odd, I meant"—Mrs. Selfridge and Mamie were looking at each other now, as if enjoying some private nuance—"for one of his race!"

"Sticks of type aren't particular, Mrs. Selfridge." Dave was looking at the door, as if weary and wanting to go. "Well, I'll be going." He moved to the door. "Sorry you can't come, Po!" He was gone.

Po sat still. Big waves seemed to pound her one way, then another. She was angry. She was hurt. She was horrified for Dave. But, another wave said, "Be quiet! Be careful! Safety! Safety is silence!"

But she felt her face flush again. She heard her words come spilling out. "That . . . that was not a good thing to do, Mrs. Sewage!" Ah, now, there, she had done it. It had happened.

"I must go after him!" She stood up and looked firmly at Mamie. It was the first time she had openly defied her. "I am going to that game of base, Mamie!"

Chapter Twelve

"DAVE!"

By running, Po caught up with him before he reached the corner. But how could you ask pardon for hate and slyness? Dave turned then, and she sensed his strength. His face was calm, with a sort of ironical look.

"And would you take a girl, now, to that game of base, and she coaxing you, mister dear?"

She was beside him. He reached out and touched gently the black velvet ribbon at her wrist. Then she saw his eyes. She shrank back a little. It was too much like looking into a room with shades up, in a darkened house, and that room lit with a hundred candles. "And never let me catch you teasing this boy, Po O'Reilly," she told herself.

But a rusty open hack had clattered up to them and stopped. In the back seat sat Louise Denis, the blonde girl who'd had the great flirt with Larry that first Sunday at the game. Beside her sat Larry!

"Climb in!" Larry called.

"Come on!" Louise's voice was good-natured. "I'll sit in Larry's lap!"

"Out to Wheat Hill!" Larry called to the driver. "Corner Hewes and Marcy!"

"Stop at Portland Street first!" Dave cried. "Next door to Walt's! We got to pick up the referee!"

Rolling along Fulton Street, Po tried to be merry with Dave. But she kept looking, in spite of herself, at Louise and Larry. Louise didn't have to sit in Larry's lap! There was room enough! And look at her now, letting that smooth heavy coil of yellow hair brush against him! Leaning forward so her bosom swelled above her low-cut bodice! Po felt again the dull misery she'd gone through that first Sunday, watching them together, wanting to do something, but being frozen.

They careened around a corner. Louise, in mock terror, laughing, tightened an arm around Larry's neck. And he held her firmly around the waist, letting his hand remain snugly curved over her hip! No holding back with her, or torturing her, or worrying about her being too good!

Desperately, Po began a great bantering and joking with Dave. She made eyes at him. She felt a black satisfaction, too, when she saw that great stack of a Larry watching her. Suddenly, she was ashamed. She remembered Dave's eyes. She stopped using him.

"There's Clarabel! Restored Jones's sister! Stop the hack!" Louise cried. "I told her we'd pick her up!" Waving at them was a black-haired woman about thirty, with bright red cheeks and a red skirt.

The hack stopped. Clarabel climbed aboard, announcing with a rollicking laugh, "I'll hold all the men on *my* lap!"

But when Po was introduced as Brian's cousin, Clarabel turned, all hilarity vanishing, and looked at her, seriously, intently. "You know he's one of the best, don't you?" From her intensity, you'd almost think the woman was in love with him! Po smiled at the idea. No two women could be less alike than Mamie and this Clarabel, with her jovial voice, lively black eyes, ample bosom.

"Here!" Clarabel was hearty again. She tossed a small flat package into Louise's lap. "Present for you!"

"For me?" Louise laughed, opening it.

"Guess who from!"

Louise looked contemptuous. "Not from him again!"

"He can't understand anyone telling him no!"

"He's got to learn then!"

"He meets me accidentally on purpose on the street," Clarabel said. "Says he knows I'm a friend of yours! Will I give it to you? So I took it. I think, even if you don't like him, you could keep it!"

Louise had the package opened. It contained a silver arm bangle. She held it up, making a face.

"Watch this!" Louise stood up, teetering, in the hack. "I don't like nothing about you, William Hymes! Not your presents, nor the way you smell of the butt end of a dead cigar!" She hurled the bangle into the mud of the street.

"I forgot!" Clarabel said. "He sent you a message, too!"

"Sure, I know! He wants me to come to supper at his house. Tomorrow night!"

"He's walked wide and bullying through South Brooklyn so long, he thinks he's got the pick-over of any girl with straight legs that grows up there!"

"I'm not scared of him!"

"Hey, Louise!" Clarabel shouted. "You know something? He can't touch you, you working in New York and all! Maybe you're the one to really trip him up!"

"How?"

"There's more ways than one of beating someone to a frazzle! Tell him you'll meet him next Saturday in Brady's! Christy the Minstrel's coming, there'll be a crowd. Then, you be there with some good strong fellow, one that don't scare easy!"

"Larry!" Louise was laughing.

"And will we make a fool of Hymes!"

Po had a feeling of premonition. She wanted to clutch Larry by the arm and say, "Don't do this! Not to that man who stumped across the ball field! Don't make him ridiculous! Never about this particular thing, and in public!"

"Sure, I'll do it!" Larry squeezed Louise's waist, and laughed, carefree.

Po wanted to cry out. Then she remembered him telling her she wanted "to run things." She was silent. And she stayed silent when the hack stopped in front of a small frame house on Portland Street, and Dave darted in to get the referee.

The hack arrived at the field, and Dave and Larry hurried off with Mr. Sellers, the referee. Po, with Louise and Clarabel, walked toward the playing place.

Po was fascinated by these two, and curious, too. "The divil a care do they seem to have of what anyone might say of them! They seem so free!"

"Is it in New York you work?" Po asked Louise, as they sauntered toward the field.

Louise smiled good-naturedly. "At Barnum's. On Broadway."

"And what is it you do at all?"

"I'm a mermaid. A Fiji mermaid."

Think of that! There was an occupation!

"A good job, but you never know when some smart slick will make a fuss in the papers and claim there weren't any mermaids in Fiji!"

"I wish I had a job!"

"Barnum needs a Greek slave. For a tableau. You're kind of skinny, though." Louise was as unmalicious as a girl who can have any man she wants can afford to be. She looked Po over with a good-natured, professional eye. "Not enough breast meat. Fat up a little! Men like to think of a feather bed when they look at you!"

"And was it a minstrel you said would be at the Gardens on the Saturday of the week, then?"

"Sure. Christy. He's over at Niblo's. Comes over to Brooklyn to try stuff."

"It was a minstrel, my father was!"

"Hear that, Clarabel! And I never even knew they had blackface in Ireland!"

As they approached the field, the crowd, mostly men, became denser. Walking along with Louise and Clarabel, Po felt like a pale small cornflower between a big scarlet poppy and a full-blown pink rose.

Louise had a sensuous way of walking. It was as if she sloughed off little wisps of female essence, which hung in the air where she had passed, so that men instinctively turned after her, looking, like pointers on a scent. And Louise, smiling her wide knowing smile, touched the arms of men who spoke to her, or let the young boys brush against her great rose-colored skirt and tight-fitting white velour bodice, as if taking them into her cult. You could see the men liked her being there, looking at them, and dressed like that. She lent a relish to the game. And she liked the maleness, and their enjoying her. Watching her, Po had a sudden insight. She guessed Louise was not a "good girl." And she remembered Larry, his hand so familiarly on Louise's hip.

But now they were up at the edge of the playing place, and Dave and Larry came running back.

They were in uniform, but, as Dave explained, they were not going to play.

"They only use me when they're at the bottom of the barrel," Dave grinned. "Larry, we want to keep under wraps. This place"—he looked around—"is full of Atlantic spies!"

But something was going on around Mr. Sellers' chair. A paddle had been brought, someone spat on it, one man yelled, "Wet," another "Dry," and the paddle went spinning into the air. "Excelsiors win the toss!" Dave cried.

Po heard the roar of the happy excited crowd, and the first crack of a ball on an Excelsior bat! Oh, happy moment! It was beautiful! It was exciting! It was as good as she had thought. The free-running exhilaration, the happy loss of one's self!

Dave, over his shoulder, threw hasty explanations, when he wasn't too excited. But Po understood quickly, because she loved it.

"Git to second!" Dave screamed, as Tony knocked a high one. The Excelsiors, proud, confident, working with well-oiled cooperation, began to win a ball game.

Then with excited elation, Po saw Brian was the next striker. The sun gleamed on his wide white belt with the proud "Excelsiors" on it. He wore his blue peaked cap straight on his head, his whiskers flowing back in the spring breeze as he waved his bat stick. The big blue E on the white flannel, long-sleeved shirt, stretched over his chest, and the white cord on the side of his long blue trousers stood out smartly. His large feet were firmly planted in white-laced shoes with black toe caps. His great ham-like hands grasped at a thick stumpy bat. Po would notice later how the bats reflected their owners; a little man would surely provide himself with a big club, a regular post. But there stood her own cousin, ready to cover Limerick and the clan Brady with heaped-up honor.

She saw the Eckford pitcher make the underhand toss to the plate, and Brian let it go by, again and again.

"Striker can pass as many balls as he wants," Dave said. "That's the way to tire out the pitcher!" Finally, Brian's bat gave a crack which sent a thrill through Po. She yelled with excitement.

Brian had pounded past the little peg in the ground that marked first base, and was near the second, when the ball hit the ground, gave a long bounce, and an Eckford man caught it.

"Ha!" groaned Dave. "Out! That's one of those lace-pants Knickerbocker rules for you!" he said, disgusted. "Striker out on the bound!"

Bushel Basket was up next. He was captain, Dave told her. You had to be brave to be a catcher, everyone knew it. Po, hearing the stinging balls hit in their bare cupped hands, thought they were all brave. "A catcher hardly ever has any front teeth, after he's played awhile," Dave said. Po had noticed this peculiarity of Bushel Basket. "Yow!" They jumped in joy, and screamed as Bushel Basket sent a long one that hit the limb of a tree back of left field, and he came in for the first home run.

Bushel Basket had to leave, afterward, to go on night shift, but Thomsy Devlin took his place, and the game went on, the Excelsiors scoring again and again, so that by the fifth innings, the score was fifteen to nine.

Then, just as Tony stood poised, bat stick waving, suddenly the air was filled with the clangor of a fire tocsin.

"Fire! Fire!" came a great cry. The game stopped, as the fire bell came now in regular strokes. All listened, counting. Was it his house? Or his fire company called?

"It's the Miss Myrtle Company! Hey, Tony! Hank! Ansel! That's your company!"

Tony and Ansel and Hank stopped a moment, but, naturally, decided the game was more important than the fire. The game went on, the Excelsiors confident, and everything falling before them.

But, after they had played awhile, a burly man, red-faced, excited, burst on the field, screaming, "Tony! Hank! Ansel Dop! It's Battle Row! Your places are on fire! Tony! Your kids are in it!"

Tony and Ansel and Hank dropped bat sticks. They raced off.

"Want us to help?" their team mates yelled.

"Hell no! We'll take care of the fire! You win the game!" And they raced off.

Now Po saw Dave motion in all the Excelsiors, and Brian and Hans and Larry and the others stood close together, heads bent, talking.

"Play the game," an Eckford player taunted, "or forfeit!"

Brian ran out, then, and took Ansel's place at third base; Dave went to left field. Po saw that even now they wanted to keep Larry under cover as a pitcher. They put him in Hank's place in center field. Big Billy Beiderstein went in to pitch for the Excelsiors.

The Excelsiors were now short four of their best players. Even Po could feel the change. The beautiful teamwork was slowed. Before they could get going, the Eckfords scored three quick runs.

Then the best Eckford striker, Johnnie Hutchens, knocked a long one to left field over Dave's head for a home run. The Eckfords were moving up. The score stood fifteen to thirteen.

The Eckfords began to feel cocky. One of their strikers now struck a high one back of center field. Larry, by hard sprinting, made a beautiful running one-hand catch.

It was the first time Po had seen this, the first time she experienced the absolute personal satisfaction, when everything depended on someone, by speed, precision, eye and hand, catching a ball—and the wonderful sense of accomplishment and completion, when, surely and precisely, it was caught. Mr. Sellers called the Eckford striker out.

An angry uproar rose from the Eckford crowd. Larry, running, had held his cap in his hand. It was that hand that caught the ball. The Eckfords now screamed that the ball, hitting his cap, could not be counted an out.

Now it was that Po understood what Dave had meant when he told her the referee had to be a man of great strength of character and much respect in the community. Mr. Sellers, sitting in his straight chair, a little distance back from home plate, his high stovepipe hat reflecting the afternoon light, and his long dark beard stirring in the spring breeze, looked dignified and unruffled as the raging Eckford crowd swarmed around his chair. He sat, arms folded calmly in his black frock coat, his long legs crossed in wrinkled white linen trousers, unmoved. He said one word. "Out!"

But at the next innings, the substitute Excelsior pitcher, Big Billy Beiderstein, met the full force of the Eckford catcalls and jeers, and went to pieces. The Eckfords scored three more runs.

The Excelsior crowd groaned as Mr. Sellers picked up his knife and made three notches in the long stick, on the Eckford side. Unbelievable! The Eckfords were now ahead; the score, sixteen to fifteen.

Worried, Dave motioned the Excelsiors in for conclave. At the next innings, Larry went in to pitch.

By the time Larry had made three tosses, bullet-like, burning over the plate, precise, controlled, he had somehow rallied the Excelsiors again. He was so sure of himself. They became a team once more. After all, substitutes or not, they were the mighty Excelsiors, weren't they? While Larry kept the lightning balls burning across the plate, the Excelsiors, coming to bat, surged ahead. Po had the feeling that Larry was not even using the new throw.

The Excelsiors were in stride again. Po, with delight, watched the notches mount. At last, they were the first to score twenty-one runs! The Excelsiors had won! The crowd let out a great roar.

Now the captain of the Eckfords advanced to the middle of the field, holding the ball. Hans, as substitute captain for the Excelsiors, advanced to the center to meet him. The crowd was still, silent, watching this ceremony. The losing captain handed over the ball to the winning captain, and the Excelsiors gave another great shout.

The crowd was dispersing when three raging, red-faced men ran onto the field. Tony, Ansel and Hank! They motioned their team mates around them. Po watched, wondering.

Hank was so angry he could hardly speak. "There wasn't no fire!"

"It was nothing but a low-down Atlantic trick!" Ansel broke out.

"They just wanted the Eckfords to win," Tony growled, "so they'd face them in the play-offs, instead of us!"

"They was tryin' to make sure it was them got at the Knicker-bockers, and not us!" said Hank.

There was a moment of grim silence. They looked at each other.

"It ain't the kind of thing," Hank spat, "that the Excelsiors can let go by! It comes to me," he added, grim, "something has got to be done!"

"Not on the ball field. Oh, no. That's too easy! We know we can beat them there!" said Ansel.

"A lot of the Atlantics belong to the Miss Atlantic Fire Company," said Dave, looking deliberately from one face to the other.

"This thing has got to be studied," said Brian.

"Just one thing I know," said Ansel. "They are going to regret the day!"

"A lesson," Hank spat, "is going to be taught!"

Chapter Thirteen

IT WAS high noon when Po heard the alarm. Upstairs in the flat, she had been listening, waiting. She charged down the stairs and ran across Fulton Street with a running throng. Ahead, voluminous black smoke rolled.

It came from the windows of a sprawling building two stories high, covering a large part of a block. Built fifty years ago by the

Van Leyns for naval stores, and finally abandoned, its roof was partly down, its windows out.

But Po knew the fire was in the warehouse for one reason. It was in the heart of the territory covered and staked out as their own by the Miss Atlantic Fire Company. And on the Miss Atlantic Company were five of the Atlantic baseball team. And she knew it was at noon, because then many people would be abroad, to see and understand the black disgrace which was about to besmear the Miss Atlantic. The lesson was about to be taught.

Po had picked it all up avidly from Brian, and she, being a complete Excelsior, besides having a natural affinity for excitement and a good fight, panted down the street to miss nothing. She knew from Brian that your true Brooklyn man, right after his baseball club and his favorite son, felt his honor to be involved with the fire company he "ran with." And she knew that the Excelsiors, through the fire company they were identified with, the Miss Myrtle, were about to deal out justice, avenge insult, and forever put in their lowly place the Atlantics and their fire company, the Miss Atlantic.

It was the custom of the country, well understood and accepted by the inhabitants, that to get "first water" on a fire was the mark of honor, speed and *esprit de corps*. But to have a fire in your own territory taken over—with persons and property saved, bravery displayed, plaudits won by a rival company—was a bitter, black thing, which no company who ever expected to hold nozzles erect again could let happen.

So Po stood now, in the great gathering crowd, out of breath, excited, hoping every detail would work out as those brave and brawny darlings of the world, the Excelsiors, had planned. She noted with satisfaction how thick and black was the smoke pouring from the windows of the old warehouse.

And yes, there was chunky, bulky Ansel Dop, sitting, with the apparent innocence of a babe, on the nearest hydrant, connected with the cistern blocks away. And down the street Po could see Tony sitting on the second nearest hydrant. And thick clustered about Ansel and Tony were partisans and friends.

And here now, almost before the bell clangor ceased, brisk and nimble, came the Miss Myrtle Company, with Brian and Jim Tash and Hank, to take over the Miss Atlantic's fire. Naturally, knowing the hour, the very minute, standing by ready to flash forth before an astonished world, they came trotting swiftly along, in shiny helmets and red shirts, pulling behind them their sweet pride, the Miss Myrtle engine. It would be long minutes before the Miss Atlantic, taken by surprise, would get to its own fire.

Ansel leaped off the hydrant, the Miss Myrtle hose was attached, and an admiring shout went up from the crowd as the first point was scored. The Miss Myrtle had first water on the fire, and the Miss Atlantic was shown up to be a slow-witted, crippled, lame, stupid, paralyzed crowd of dull slobs! Po cheered with the crowd. Besides being a soul-and-body Excelsior, she was always for all cheaters, tricksters and smart-alecks having their faces ground in the dust.

The second disgrace which could befall a company was to be "washed." At a big fire, all the hand-pumped fire engines were hooked up, one after the other, as far as their hose would stretch, to the source of water. When the Miss Atlantic Company arrived at last with their engine, to meet the jeers of the crowd for a laggard appearance at their own fire, a battle broke out around the second nearest hydrant, held by Tony and the partisans and friends of the Miss Myrtle.

Driven off, Twinkle-Toes, captain of the Miss Atlantic Fire Company, decided to get water from the river. The Excelsiors, those intelligent, resourceful men, had foreseen what would happen. This fire, seemingly big, would attract other companies. Sure enough, here came the Shadrach J. Muldoon Company from Marcy Street. They made a hitch with the Miss Atlantic, and so stretched the hoses to the river.

This was what the Miss Myrtle had hoped for. If the company pumping in back of you pumped faster and harder than your company, thus causing the water to overflow your engine, you were said to be "washed." Great companies of men took solemn pride in maintaining their loves, their darlings, their beautiful engines—maiden and unwashed over many years. The Miss Atlantic engine, unsullied for five years, was about to be "washed."

After the hitch was made, husky partisans of the Excelsiors and Miss Myrtle immediately jumped to the aid of the Muldoon Company, and such terrible whooshing and pumping, and springing in to replace a winded pumper took place as made the Muldoons stand bewildered.

Twinkle-Toes, captain of the Miss Atlantic, looked back down the hill, dismayed. Hastily, he sent partisans back to try to cut the hose, stand on it, anything, to keep their engine unsullied and "unwashed." Stopping the water from going on the fire was as nothing compared to this catastrophe. But his cohorts were driven away from the hose. Slowly the water rose, and Twinkle-Toes stood and wept as water overflowed the unsullied Miss Atlantic. They were "washed."

Somehow, the crowd began to sense now that this was more than a warehouse fire. It was a field of honor.

And just then, something unplanned happened. Clarabel had not been in on any of the plans for the disgrace of the Miss Atlantic Company. After all, she was the sister of Restored Jones, the oysterman from Long Island who had brought Larry and Po to Brooklyn. And Restored was an Atlantic. Now Clarabel was trusted and liked in most things. But, in such a delicate matter as the honor of one's baseball team or fire company, how far could trust go?

Clarabel was an unplanned event. She (currently working at Quimby's) had long used the warehouse as a convenient and private spot for a noontime rendezvous. Baffled by the thick smoke, driven back to the second floor, she now appeared at a second-story window, screaming for aid and succor. A sheepish male, trapped with her, peered over her shoulder.

Clarabel was a hefty woman. Larry, though not a fire company member, was an Excelsior, and he, as having the required brawn, was elected to the honor of rescuing the lady.

"Hold on there, sonny!" It was the Bull. He had not responded to the fire call at first, thinking it not worth bothering about. But partisan couriers had sped with news that his brother Atlantics and the Miss Atlantic Company were being besmirched. Like an avenging giant, he came, to sweep down and forever disjoint anyone attempting to dishonor his friends. He thrust Larry away. "I will attend to this little job!"

As Clarabel screamed for succor, Larry clenched his fist and swung at the Bull. The Bull let out a roar, and with his open hand, gave Larry a great shove that sent him sprawling. Larry was up, red-faced, eyes blazing, and rushed back at him, as Clarabel screamed despairingly.

Now the Bull grabbed Larry by the shirt, hit him a great cuff, then gave him another harder shove, which sent him spinning and reeling far back into the crowd. Before Larry could come back at him, the Bull dusted off his hands contemptuously and, amid cheers, walked into the smoke.

It seemed a long time to the buzzing, milling crowd before he reappeared. Finally, there he was at last, in the doorway. The crowd gave a yell of acclaim, and the Bull, to give them their moment, stopped in the door to let them take in just how a real fire-fighter worked.

Over his shoulder was slung the squawking Clarabel. He held her by the knees. Over the other shoulder was a heavy sack of some stores, and under his other arm, a small keg. He dragged along—a hand through his belt—Clarabel's companion. The stores were probably of no value. But it was the spirit of the thing.

"That ain't no real fire." He glowered at the Miss Myrtle Company. "Lot of rags, making smoke—"

But just then a sense-stunning explosion blasted from the warehouse in back of him.

For a few moments, no one knew what was happening. The crowd scattered up the street. The Bull, with Clarabel on his shoulder, fell flat on his face, stunned.

His mates ran forward, helped him to his feet. Clarabel, stunned, almost hysterical, could think of but one thing: to get away, far and fast. She ran. The Bull, looking like a surprised baby, was helped down the street toward the obvious remedy—a dollop of revival-water, whiskey.

It was lucky it all happened as it did. The first, smaller explosion had warned the crowd back. For now a second, heavier explosion vibrated and rocked through the area. Afterward, they would know some saltpeter had been left inside. Now, all they knew was that the old warehouse had gone toward the sky in pieces.

But the Excelsiors and the Miss Myrtle Company were not to be swerved from the path of avenging their honor. A third and horrible disgrace waited the cringing Miss Atlantic. Their pet, the cherished pride of men who spent their Sunday mornings polishing her, over long years, their beautiful engine was to be ravished.

There she stood, her polished mahogany sides, with the inlays of sandal-wood, outlined with mother-of-pearl. Each oval inlay was decorated with a bunch of pale blue forget-me-nots, or a basket of pink roses. Her pumping arms were silver-plated, polished to gleam; her wheels were gilded. On her front panel, the painted picture of a curvish lady, draped in gauze, bore aloft a banner "Miss Atlantic."

But the men of the Miss Myrtle Company seized the "Miss Atlantic" in all her delicate grace. She was not without defenders, but with the Bull removed from the battlefield, the Excelsior-Miss Myrtle partisans were not to be denied.

She was pelted with mud. Then, with no shred of honor left, she was taken away and placed on the rooftree of the Miss Myrtle Company, a terrible warning, telling the world, "Don't meddle with the Miss Myrtle Company, nor the mighty Excelsiors!" The lesson had been taught.

The warehouse was gone. The black and gaping empty place stretched desolate and ugly. Ugly and desolate, that is, to most gazers. But not to one.

That one was Larry. He stood, gazing at the littered stretch of ground, covered with brick and blackened timbers. His face got a rapt look. His eyes sparked up with a sudden exhilarating dream. He cried out in rapture: "What a site for a ball field!"

Chapter Fourteen

Po had stolen, like a thief in the night, or in the twilight, rather, down to the Gardens. She sat, now, as people began to come in for the Saturday night Free-and-Easy, waiting, in a far corner, and watching the door from Pineapple Street for Mr. Christy to come in.

Po hated being sly. Open battle was more her style. But, if Mamie, knew, she'd have beaten her buttoned-up breast, and called upon an aghast heaven to witness Po's wanton doings—besides stopping her.

For Mamie had not allowed Po's going off to the Eckford game, and with Dave, to pass without decrees. Brian, too, was included in the accusing disapproval, when in tears, Mamie said, "After all my work, my planning!" True, Brian patted Po's shoulder, and looked relieved, for not a word, not a feeler, had come from the Sewage Commission. But then Mamie handed down the tablets of stone. Po must run to no more low ball games, consort not in the barroom, run not with undesirable elements. If she did, Mamie "could not take the responsibility." And had even talked of Cousin Frank in Fall River.

Piling higher and higher inside Po had come the feeling that dependent pudding, even eaten under protection, had not much taste. "Wasn't it . . . or was it? . . . better then, to go waltzing out into the free and freezing world again?" And wasn't Christy a one who might know of some way she could earn her bread by the songs she knew? Louise had said he was part of a whole company of minstrels that sang on the Broadway in New York. "If I could but get you, Christy, mister honey, to hear me sing, now!"

Po watched Tony. A sailmaker in Naples, and now at the Yard, and—Tony flashed a gleaming smile at her—"member Journeyman Sailmakers Protective Union!"—as his needle-scarred fingers expertly wound yarn over the raw rubber, making a baseball. He stitched on the sheepskin and balanced the ball expertly in a brown hand. "Now I take it to a grocer scale! Gotta weigh six and a half ounces. Then . . . it'll play like hell!"

Walt sat at the same table, writing on a scrap of paper, a news story. "Another slaver slipped through the harbor patrol. A gruesome business." Walt wrote words, crossed them out.

Watching Tony, Po had not noticed the young man at first. About twenty-three, slender, with crisp blond hair, expensively dressed in a putty-colored cutaway with velvet lapels, and a blue stock with white speckles embroidered on it, he stood, looking about, smiling. He stared at Po, then smiled charmingly. Po, thinking he somehow knew her, smiled back. He bowed elegantly. Then Po reddened, realizing he had been flirting.

When Brian came back to the bar, the young man ordered Madeira, and when he was served, he leaned forward, and in a pleasant, casual, well-modulated voice asked Brian, "Could you tell me where I might find a man named Hans Schmidt?"

Brian called Hans.

"I hear you make excellent bat sticks! Mr. Grogan told me!"

"Yah?" said Hans, surprised.

"I'd like to order a dozen. The best ash. I like mine fairly long, rather thick in the handle. I'll need them soon!"

"Yah?" Still surprised, but glad of odd jobs, Hans said, "All right!"

"Here is something in advance." He laid down a bill. "I'll come back for the sticks next week!"

The men around the bar, open-mouthed, stood staring.

Po had retreated to a table by herself at one side, and now, the young man, glass in hand, moved away from the bar and toward Po.

Po saw him coming. "And 'tis maybe time I displayed myself as a woman of the world," she thought, "who can catch an elegant buck-o like this!"

"Ah! Lady Violet-Blue-Eyes, I believe!" He smiled charmingly down at her. "Only fancy meeting your ladyship here!"

"And isn't it the Duke of Kilmally himself, and your grace going in disguise!" Po flashed back.

But Po could see the men at the bar had drawn together, heads bent in low excited talk. They kept looking over at the young man in a kind of wild surmise. She saw Hank come over to the table.

"Howdy!" Hank's eyes were wide and fascinated. His voice was quiet. "You play on some ball club around here?"

The young man smiled pleasantly. "Over in New York."

You could hear the beer tap drip, it was suddenly so quiet.

"Is that a fact?" said Hank softly, as if not to startle the quarry. "What team?"

There was not a sound in the barroom. The young man took a casual sip of Madeira. "The Knickerbockers."

There was a sudden indrawn breath around the room. Then the men at the bar advanced gently, treading softly, toward the table. They made a wide circle.

"Sure like to meet your team on the field." Hank seemed just to breathe the words, softly, innocently. The others held their breath.

"Oh," said the elegant young man, with a pleasant smile, "do you have a baseball team over here, too?"

Hank's tight leash broke. "We have the best goddam team——" But

Brian stepped forward quickly, while one of the other men caught Hank's arm, pulling him back.

"We have a pretty fair team over here." Brian's tone was controlled. "Like to meet your team sometime!"

"Why," the young man was pleasant, casual, "don't you challenge us then?"

For a moment, Brian lost control, his eyes darted fire, he clawed his whiskers. The others drew in a closer circle, glaring down at the young man. Then Brian said, "We sent so many challenges, we lost count!"

"Really?" The young man sipped his wine slowly. "I've just been taken in as a junior member. Been away, at Groton and Harvard. Perhaps the challenges weren't couched in proper terms."

"Sich as?"

"Oh, something like—'To the honorable secretary, Knickerbocker Club. We invite you to a friendly match, to be played at your convenience.' "

"Write it down, Dave!" someone yelled. Dave seized a beer tab and wrote.

"Best use white vellum, if you have it!"

"We're fresh out," said Dave. But he got a scrap of paper from Walt, and wrote.

"Now maybe they'll answer us!" said Brian as Dave wrote. "All we ever got before was they wouldn't play because we didn't know the rules!"

"Why don't they call a meeting so we can all get together on them rules, then?" Hank exploded.

"Oh, it isn't done that way at all!" The young man was pleasant. "The Knickerbockers, being the oldest team, hand down the rules."

Rooster, who had been taking aboard a skinful of Bushmill's, suddenly cried out, "It's givernment without representation!"

The young man had finished his wine. He rose.

"Will you take this challenge over for us?" asked Dave, handing him the slip of paper.

"And see that it gets to the right place?" asked Brian.

"And gets an answer!" growled Hank.

"Why, yes, certainly. Glad to!"

The young man tossed a coin down. Then to Po he said softly, "I'll see you next week when I call for the sticks, Lady Violet-Blue-Eyes." He went to the door.

"The bat sticks," Hans called after him. "Who'll I hold them for?"

"Coventry Van Leyn!" He was casual, unhurried, as he strolled out.

As soon as he was gone, an irrepressible yell broke out. Suddenly, the Knickerbocker game seemed so near, so possible, everyone fell to

Christy, in square spectacles, stood before the gas lamps in front of the stage, and introduced himself as Professor Hornswoggle, demonstrating his miraculous invention.

"Lad-eez! Have you ever been in a . . . er . . . a"—he rolled his eyes suggestively—"a situation where you wished you were not wearing a hoop? My invention is what you need!"

He motioned, and out came Louise, walking with downcast eyes, coy, with mincing steps.

"With my patent skirt adjustor, ladeez, you are always in control of any . . . er . . . a . . ."—he pretended embarrassment—"situation. I demonstrate!" He grasped the green tassel hanging outside Louise's skirt, but now he managed it so, instead of the hoop frame collapsing, it slowly rose over Louise's head, revealing her ruffled drawers. Louise pretended acute horror.

"Oh, a slight mistake, ladeez! It will never happen to you . . . unless you wish it to!" The crowd loved Louise, and she loved doing this. She ran off now amid calls and laughter.

Christy judged his comicality a success.

Now a female band, made up of some of the more daring girls from Quimby's, with Clarabel beating the bass drum, played a tune called "A Violet from Mother's Grave."

As the music beat out against the darkness, Po became aware of dark eyes gleaming near her. "Juba!" Po cried happily.

"First time I hears music! Nothin' but stones and bricks and closed-up streets! I got me a little ole banjo I make from a cheese box, and I plays to myself, but this the first time I hears anyone sittin' and playin' music!"

Some sailors from the Navy Yard were dancing a hornpipe, but Po wanted them to get through. She was impatient to hear a real American minstrel.

At last the little curtains parted. At first, she didn't recognize Christy. His face had been made black, except for a hideous white streak around his mouth, he wore strange and ridiculous clothes, and sang a song called "Gittin' up Stairs!" Po was confused. She was not sure she liked it. She couldn't say why, exactly. Then, suddenly, something struck her. Why! Christy was imitating a singer like Juba!

When the curtains closed on Christy, with the crowd clapping and cheering, Po tried to coax Juba to the stage, urging him to sing. But he was too abashed to go up on the stage. Standing in the half dark, swaying, weaving about rhythmically, his banjo reverberating, he sang the "Eel Catchers' Glee." The crowd clapped. They didn't care what it was. The more beer they drank, the more they loved everything and everybody.

But here was Christy! Excited, he grabbed Juba's arm, urged him around backstage. After a while, when they did not return, Po, a little worried about Juba, slipped back.

Christy, wearing Juba's old hat, using Juba's cheese box banjo, was trying to pick up Juba's weaving rhythm of steps and Juba's song.

"I can't quite get that bit in there!" Christy was saying impatiently.

"He wants my ole hat, wants my song!" Juba looked at Po, ready to laugh, as at the crazily inexplicable.

Po couldn't quite understand either. Why didn't Christy just let Juba *do* it? But Christy, excited and impatient, kept trying the song over. Po gave it up and went back to her table.

Now the crowd was calling for performers. They called for the Excelsior Quartet, and Ansel, Hans, Jim and Rooster sang a song called "Jeannie with the Light Brown Hair." They called for the Bull, and he, in a tremendous belly-buster of a bass voice sang "Stone Blind Jonny, Fill up the Bowl." Next they demanded Brian, and he recited "The Night Before Larry Was Stretched."

But just then something happened which made Po forget all about Brian. Larry had come in. But that was not what gave Po a sense of foreboding. He went and sat with Louise. They talked and laughed, yes. But it was not that which gave Po a sense of chill worry. It was hearing Clarabel boom out to Larry, "Nine o'clock. He's coming!"

They were going on with the joke on Hymes! Po saw Louise go backstage. Larry sat alone. It must be nearly nine o'clock now!

In a few moments, Hymes came in. His heavy frame moved awkwardly through the small tables. People glanced at him with blank faces. He sat down at an empty table, not looking around, eyes on the heavy gold watch which he put down in front of him. She had heard how he usually had his underlings do his pursuing for him. He seemed such a rigid man, she could guess Louise's forcing him to come himself was a strain. In his clothes he had made some awkward concession to the pursuit of love; his coat was unwrinkled, his stock fresh. But he had not an air of lusty joy about him, rather a secret look as if there was shame in his errand.

To be a butt was not a role this heavy, inflexible man could accept. In some reluctant way, Po felt on his side—for what could be bitterer than to be apart, and be laughed at? It was all wrong—every way.

She found herself half out of her seat, wanting to rush to Larry's table, scold him, coax him, order him, not to go on. But—she could hear him saying that she was "trying to run him again!" But, in spite of all, she had to warn him. She went quickly to Larry's table. Words poured out of her. "Isn't it the foolish thing, now, and you but lately come, to make a fearful enemy of that man?"

"Ah," Larry scoffed, "I can lick him in a minute!"

Oh, how could she find quick words to make him see this was not going to be just a flailing of someone with your fists?

This was useless! Minutes were slipping away. She'd go backstage, try to persuade Louise not to go on with the joke, or if she must, not to use Larry!

In front of the curtain the Shadrach Muldoon Fire Company Sextette was harmonizing a song called "The Awful Fate of Lucy Baker." In back of it, Louise was transforming herself into a mermaid.

Barnum's had been closed for a few days because of a small fire, and Louise was putting on the costume she used there. It delighted her, and seemed a great joke to her friends and neighbors, that what New Yorkers had to pay for, she gave to Brooklyn for love and fun.

Louise called to Po with careless good nature. "Help me get into this tail! That Clarabel was supposed to!" Louise smiled at Po with her wide red smile.

Louise had loosed her heavy yellow hair. In fact, it was a part of her costume. She was arranging it to make herself decent, for she was bare as a flower from the waist up. Then, as Louise got herself into the green-sequined stuffed tail, Po suddenly saw that Louise had no hips! She was flat, straight. "And isn't it, now, like God fitted her up with that round beautiful face, and those round blue eyes, and that heavy weight of gold hair, and put a lovely throat on her, a big red mouth, and exquisite breasts, and then said, 'There, that's enough for ye!' " And Louise was doing all right. The tail was heavily padded into swelling hips. "Arrah," thought Po with a quink of malice, "I'm not so rich in the front, maybe, but leastway, I don't hang me hips in the cupboard at night."

Louise was a few years older than Po, perhaps eighteen or nineteen, and she had a certain calm good-natured assurance. It was like she was saying, "I got nothing to lose!" How could Po make Louise see quickly that this joke on Hymes might unleash something on all of them better kept prisoned up?

"Would you listen to me," Po broke out, worried, "if I was telling you that to make a black mock of Hymes, and in front of all, is a heavy dangerous thing?"

Louise combed out her yellow hair. "Sure, it could be for some girl who might lose her job, or whose family might get evicted."

But Po was thinking of Larry. Louise arranged her hair one

way, then another. "If anyone's ever going to show South Brooklyn someone can stand up to Hymes, I'm the one. All I hope is, Hymes tries to hit Larry! That's all! Just once!"

Did she think it would be over then? Po remembered how Hymes's face had looked that Sunday at the ball game when the clod had been thrown.

But Louise was fastening the lacings at the side of her fish tail. "Best thing's happened for a long time. Hymes isn't married, you know. And he won't go to a regular house. No, it's got to be fresh, young, and on the wing! Well, the next time he tries to scare some girl, don't tell me she won't remember that Louise told him off, and lived to tell the tale!"

"But what's going to happen to Larry after?" Po was thinking. Aloud she said, " 'Tis to me a strange joke!"

"You don't get the full beauty of it, that's all!" Louise was spreading her hair carefully over her bosom. "You just came! Hymes knows I'm not scared of losing my innocence. That was taken care of before I got out of Public School 38, and good riddance I say! You got to strip for action sometime, anyway! No sir, he's going to know there's only one reason. I can't stand him!"

"But . . ." Po did not know what to say.

"I work for my living, and I've earned one luxury, I guess, and that's to pick who I'll lay with, and it sure as God's not going to be him!"

"But don't humiliate him in front of all!"

Louise changed. She looked angry. Po saw that if Larry had no hate, Louise had!

"Look! My dad, a big Slav he was, drove the stage out to Montauk, got carried off sudden when the cholera came to South Seventh. Ma wouldn't send us out to beg. We got evicted."

"But Hymes couldn't help it, and . . ."

"The hell he couldn't! He owned the house! Oh, sure, maybe he knew nothing about it, but why didn't he? Why didn't he know what his agent did? It's time he was made to feel people are human, got feelings!"

The firemen were finishing their song with a long drawn-out chord. Louise began arranging herself seductively on what appeared to be a big sea shell, and Po realized that she could not stop the joke.

The mermaid act was over. Louise, in a bright green satin dress, with her hair in great smooth yellow coils again, came rippling across the Gardens.

No one looked at Hymes, no one seemed to pay attention to what was about to happen, but there was a hushed sort of shiver.

Only Larry, that great baby, sat there, half smiling, as if he were just getting ready to take part in a saloon brawl.

Louise was coming toward Hymes's table. She had to pass it to reach Larry's. Hymes did not get up. He pushed back a chair for her. Something passed over his face that was undoubtedly meant to be a smile of greeting.

Louise paused at his table. She did not sit down in the proffered chair. She stood looking down at him.

"Did you really think I was going to your house for supper?" she said, not bothering to speak low, so her friends could enjoy the joke, too. "Why, no woman who could help herself would let you touch her with a ten-foot pole! I don't like you, or anything about you, not the way you look, or smell, or talk, or act! I'm going out with a man I can look at without wanting to puke! And oh, those presents you sent me! I threw them in the gutter! The man I'm going with don't have to give me presents, nor coax me. I'm going because I like him. And it's for free!"

Louise passed on. There was still the same quiet, the pretense of not seeing, by the crowd. Louise sat down at Larry's table, and began to laugh and talk to him.

But Po had eyes for one thing only. She watched Hymes's face. She was scared. His face was still as stone, and quiet. Then he got up, with a still slowness. He walked deliberately toward the table where Louise and Larry sat. She saw Larry clench his fists, get ready. Now the crowd turned heads, watching the table, silent.

Then what Po feared happened. Hymes said nothing to Louise. He ignored her. He said nothing to Larry either. But he stood, carefully, unmercifully studying Larry, as if etching his face on some sinister granite tablet. Then he turned and walked away. He had nearly reached the wicket gate leading to Fulton Street when someone laughed. Then another and another. But Po was frightened.

Chapter Fifteen

AS SOON after supper as she could, Po would run down the hill to the site of the razed warehouse. She might catch a glimpse of Larry working, sometimes with others, sometimes alone.

"I'm going to make us a ball field!"

Larry had said it, and reservoirs of energy seemed to pour forth. Obstacles seemed as nothing. He drove himself, and the others. He became a combination general and draft horse.

"It's so close to work, we can practice at noon! Evenings, we won't lose time getting some place! If we hurry, we can use it to get ready for the Atlantic game! Practicing every minute like that, we'll ruin 'em!"

Already, Larry and the Excelsiors had cleared the fallen bricks and timbers. Luckily, there had been no basement under the great ramshackle warehouse. They were leveling the ground now, pocked by holes and ridged with hummocks after the explosion.

It was late that evening, nearly dusk, when Po got there. Only three men were working, Larry and two others. Soon the two others left. Larry worked on. Po had heard Brian tell how Larry worked on the field, by lantern light, far into the night.

Po lingered, watching Larry's spade, with clean easy sweeps, eat into a ridge. The clods fell with a rattle into a wheelbarrow. He straightened up a moment, his face streaked with perspiration and dust. As she watched his spade slice into the hard hummock, quickly, purposefully, she remembered how he had looked, gray, slack, when she had seen him sandpapering a plank in the shipyard. She could hear the foreman saying, "Laziest fellow ever I seen!" The spade made a little ringing sound as it chopped again and again into the earth. The early morning shine was gone from Larry now, but he didn't look dull and apathetic as he had in the shipyard, either. He had a kind of absorbed look.

The next evening when Po came, more men were at work. Around her on the brick walk, the Excelsior Muffins and other neighborhood children darted and screamed or leaped over piled timbers. One boy stopped suddenly, looking in at the men working on the field.

"That's my pa, spadin'," he said, as if proud and surprised. The other boys stopped, too, and stared. It was as if they were trying to take in the strange sight of their fathers, using the wheelbarrows and shovels which they used all day every day, but now, making something for their own use.

Po watched, too. Dave was all over, trying to do things too heavy for him, positive, angry, shouting orders. Larry worked steadily, taking an order, giving one. They were trying to make a ball field, weren't they?

That evening, Hans Schmidt had brought his delicate carpenter's tools to measure and make all straight. Now Hans peered down the base lines, sharp, finicky. When the others shrugged off the difference of a few inches one way or the other, and seemed to feel life would go on about the same if a line weren't straight, Hans got red-faced, sarcastic.

"Shoemakers!" he snarled, as if hurling the lowest epithet.

Over near third base, Tony, his arms raised to heaven, was screaming curses at a placid munching goat. Having heard that some teams were now using bags to mark bases, Tony had stitched the canvas Jim Tash had brought up from his ship chandler's shop into base bags stuffed with hay. The goat had eaten the bases overnight. "Better stick to pegs!" Bushel Basket growled, sinking his mattock in hard earth.

Now Po saw two Excelsior Muffins stagger up with a great bucket of beer. Brian had to stay at the Gardens in the evening, so he had sent this down. It sloshed over as the boys put it on the ground, and the first man to drink had to bend down and lap it up. The last one raised the bucket and tilted it back to drink. But daylight was slipping off.

"If we had more light!'

"At the Navy Yard, they on'y work ten hours!"

Ten hours! They stopped a moment, looking off over the Brooklyn roofs, trying to assimilate this. Why, if you started, say at six in the morning, you'd be through at four! In the afternoon! You could— why, what couldn't you do! They looked off with a half-bemused look.

Larry had been measuring the daylight left. "We can't put it off any longer," he called out. "We got to figure how to get those stones out!"

Hearing this, the men, who were scattered about the field, each solving his own little problem, drew in.

The outer foundations of the warehouse had either fallen from the explosion, or were far enough from the playing lines not to obstruct. But part of the support of the center of the building still stood—six or eight heavy stones, jutting a couple of feet above the earth. They angled stubbornly between the pitcher's box and first base.

The men walked around the stones now, frowning, or, lips protruding, studying the problem.

Then Larry squatted down, chewing a thumb, eyes narrowed, looking at the stones. Bushel Basket came over and stood, legs crossed, leaning on his shovel. Tony came and stood, and Ansel, resting an arm on his mattock. Dave and Rooster squatted down near Larry. Hank stood, one booted foot up on a stone, stroking his long lean face. They had become a group now, a sort of engineering council.

Po liked the look on their faces. It was as if they were saying, "We'll figure it! Among us, we know enough!"

Bushel Basket, the iron molder, spat a long meditative arc of tobacco juice and spoke. The others listened.

"If we got us a long heavy iron ramrod, and all butted her—we could ram 'em out of there!"

They pondered, considering this, respecting it.

Then Ansel, balancing on the mattock head, spoke, and they listened. Ansel was a shipwright, and it seemed to him it was with ropes they could do it. "Git a good hemp over 'em. Jerk 'em out!"

Rooster, the deck hand, spoke, quick, excited. "Yeah, with ropes. Git a rope over 'em!"

They studied this a moment.

"If we had the Bull now," Dave said, "bet he could jerk 'em out like a row of rotten teeth!" The others looked at him dourly, as if he'd said something childish. This was an Excelsior project. What the hell? Did they have to go getting the Atlantics in on it?

Larry squatted down, chewed his thumb silently, frowning.

Big Tony spoke. "Seems like we could git in there and dig 'em out!"

"Digging'd take too long! We want the field in time for Atlantic practice!" Larry said quickly.

Then Death-to-Flying-Things, the teamster at Quimby's, one boot up on a stone, his long lantern jaw moving rhythmically, spat a long careful arc, and spoke. They listened, thoughtful. "We could pull them out—but what we want's a horse! Looks like I got to borrow Ethel. She's the gray, best of my team!"

"Ole man Quimby let you?"

"He don't need to be bothered about it. I'll jis' give him the benefit of the doubt of being neighborly. The night watchman's a bastard, but hell, how can he say no? It's for a *ball field!*"

The next evening, when Po got there, the men were waiting for Hank to come with the gray horse, Ethel. Daylight was sifting away, when, instead of the teamster with his horse, came a messenger of disaster.

The watchman at Quimby's had tried to stop the teamster from borrowing Ethel. Naturally, Hank had given him an opinion with his fists. The watchman wanted to have Hank put in the cell-house for trying to steal a horse.

The men looked at each other.

"We better git to Hughie McLaughlain quick!"

Po had heard of this Hughie before. He had been a boss at the Navy Yard, and was still called "Boss." But now, he hung out in the fire house in the basement of City Hall. When any such flagrant miscarriage of justice as this threatened, Hughie could unsnarl it. And, as nearly as Po could understand, all they needed to do to keep this ready refuge, this means of making the unreasonable reasonable— all they needed to do was vote as Hughie suggested.

"Don't need all to go!" Larry yelled after them as they dropped shovels. "We'll never get done in time! We got to have a practice field before the Atlantic game!" But they surged up the hill.

Larry walked about, kicking clods of earth, impatient, angry. He stared up into the sky, as if guessing the moment of daylight. He walked around the stones, frowning. He kicked over the great coils of strong hemp Jim Tash had brought up from his shop, ready to use if Hank brought the horse.

As if with the sudden release of energy of a plan, Larry began to dig with a mattock the ground around the first and smallest stone.

Then Po saw him fling out the great coil of rope and, squatting on his hams, study out some problem. She saw him fooling with the rope, knotting it, trying it. Then he slipped the rope over his shoulders, made into a kind of harness. She saw him study again how to fasten the rope to the stone. That done, she saw him walk off, and begin to pull.

She felt her own body strain, and sweat start from her, as she watched his muscles bulge out around the rope as he heaved. She wanted to cry out to him, "Leave off now, before you destroy yourself." Then, she saw the stone quiver. It moved. He strained forward. With a sudden "fwoosh" the dirt around it caved, it fell forward. Po heard herself let out a little cry of triumph.

He looked over at her then, in the dusk, as if surprised to see her. He waved and shouted, with a laugh, "One down!"

But the men did not come back to work on the field the next evening, for a sudden unseasonable blast of heat, sticky, furry with humidity, fell on Brooklyn.

People moved as if drugged. Horses lingered pathetically at watering troughs. The tender spring leaves and grass quivered back from this too-early assault of the sun. And the Excelsiors stayed at home, after working twelve or fourteen hours, and tried to keep cool in their narrow frame houses on Portland Street, or in their boarding houses on Sand, or in the great gray tenement known as Battle Row.

All except Larry.

Po had gasped as she stepped on the hot brick walk to slip down the hill for her usual few minutes after supper. Larry was working when she came. Then she saw Dave and Bushel Basket come up the hill from the other direction, slowly, as if pushing against damp flapping blankets of humidity.

"The Atlantic game's only ten days off!" Larry was ranging about impatiently. "Let's get these stones out!"

Po saw the three fasten on the ropes and pull, with groans and teeth clenching, two more stones. Then Bushel Basket threw down his end of the rope.

"I'm going to get me a beer! Too hot!" And Dave agreed.

But Larry, looking impatient and grim, stayed. Two big stones remained. He fastened on the ropes.

It seemed to Po she pulled and strained and let go her breath when he did. She found herself wiping off sweat. When he strained forward again, she wanted to call to him, "Give it up, Larry! It's too much!" But Larry was heaving again, red-faced. The stone stood grim, rigid.

But he leaned in again, and after a time, Po saw the stone loosen, waver, then slowly, slowly fall forward.

Caught up in Larry's struggle with the stone, she did not know when Hymes had come. She sensed the silent rock-like gray shadow behind her, by the little start of terror that shivered over her. Even in the heat, her sweating hands turned cold. She remembered it was the way she had felt that night at the Gardens when Larry had made a mock of Hymes. But Hymes soon returned to his buggy, and drove off.

She wondered if Larry had noticed Hymes. Should she warn Larry? About what? She didn't quite know.

Swiftly she crossed the field in the deepening twilight to where Larry worked.

"Larry! Hymes was here. Did you know!"

Larry laughed. "A man can look at a field!"

"But"—Po faltered, not knowing exactly what she feared—"what if—"

"I can lick him any day!" Larry coiled the rope out of the way.

"With fists, maybe!"

"What can he do?" Larry straightened up and ran a grimy hand through his bright hair. "You don't suppose we put in all this work without getting in the clear?" Larry sat down a moment on a fallen stone. "We got Grogan, he's foreman at the Yard, and a baseball crank if there ever was one, to ask Van Leyn if we could use the field. Only condition was, we had to pile all the usable brick and timbers down at the Yard. We did that!"

"But—"

"Aah!" Larry laughed, unconcerned. "They say Hymes used to play ball! When he first came here! He wasn't any good, though, and he gave it up. He's got to be the star! So now maybe the poor bastard's just looking at the field, wishing he could play!" Larry wiped sweat from his face with his shirt tail, and started back to work. "'Bout one more evening, and she's done!"

The next evening, Mamie carped about Po always running out on "these short walks after supper," but Po had to come. She wanted to see Larry when he finished.

The unseasonable heat blanket still slumped, damp and sloggy, over the town. No one came to work on the field but Larry. By the time Po got there, he was already tugging at the last stone.

Dusk had fallen before it was out. Then he had to dump wheelbarrow loads of dirt from the pile near third base to fill the hole where the stones had been. The moon had risen before the hole was filled. Po knew she should run home quickly, but she wanted to be there, to know he had finished it. He was pounding the dirt down now, his shovel going up and flailing down, hitting it hard and flat.

Then, across the street, Po saw a big man walking along slowly, glancing over. She could not be sure, but it looked like Hymes. Or did she just imagine it?

The shovel, beating against the earth, made a hollow ring, ramming the dirt down hard. The moon was up higher, now, over Quimby's, flooding the field with silver. Finally, Larry straightened up and looked over the field.

He came over to where she stood now, dragging his shovel. He stood panting. It was done, but he was too winded to speak.

After a while he caught his breath. Larry looked at the field, coated silver by the moon. Then he began to feel good. "We got a ball field!"

Po knew the others had worked hard, too, but they had come and gone. Larry had worked every free moment, far into the night. He had hunched, pushed, strained, and shoved, not even thinking of who was doing the most, having one idea. "Yessir!" he exulted, "we got us a field!"

The damp blanket of too-early humidity hung over Brooklyn that night. Po was restless, sleeping in snatches. It seemed to her she could hear the jingle of harness from somewhere; the sound of stones rattling on shovels; the strike of a pick in the earth. Toward morning it cooled off, but she could not sleep. She slipped out into the silent street.

Dawn had not yet come. Far down the hill, she could see lantern gleams moving on the ball field! Maybe some of the men, thinking to work in the cool of the night, had come back. Then she remembered Larry had finished it. The work was done.

She had a strange tight feeling of disquiet as she sped down the hill to find out who swung the lanterns.

Men were working. Strangers. Eight, nine, ten of them. They must have been digging all night.

All the carefully and laboriously pounded and tamped-down earth had been dug up. The base pegs were gone. A hole gaped in front of home plate. There was a big hole near center, one near first. Dirt and rocks had not been piled, but scattered about. Po wondered if the humidity was making her have a nightmare. She blinked her eyes, shrinking back from the bitter sight. Then she thought of Larry, who would be coming along here in a few minutes.

Dawn was coming now. People were stirring. Soon they began to come down the street toward their work.

After a while some of the Excelsiors arrived. They stood beside her, silent, stunned.

Then she saw Larry coming down the street. Whistling, he was, and pounding along, no doubt ready to brag to the others that the field was finished.

He came up to the open space and stopped. He looked stupefied. She saw him wipe his hand across his face, as if thinking he must be dreaming and wanted to wake himself up. But—the monstrous sight was not to be wiped away.

The men in the field began throwing their tools in a wagon.

"Hey, you!" Tony yelled, fierce. "What'd you do this for?"

Most of the men paid no attention. One answered, as if surprised, "We wuz hired, mister!"

"By who?" glowered Ansel, fists ready to swing.

"Why, by the South Street Construction Company."

"Ain't no company like that here!"

"Over in New York—South Street."

"But—why—what for?"

"We just dig when and where we're told. Guess someone's putting up a building!"

The Excelsiors held back their fists. What was the use of a fight? These were just slobs doing a job of work. But the Excelsiors looked at each other with a sort of gray, sick look. Then they hurried off to work.

All but Larry. He stood, very still. Po had never taken her eyes from him.

She wanted to touch his hand, now, speak to him, comfort him, but she could only stand, looking at his face.

He stood rock-still, frozen. The other men had protested. Larry had said not a single word.

Po felt a little sick. At first she didn't know why, and then she did. It was the way Larry looked. It reminded her of something. And when she knew what it was she wanted to scream out, as if to ward off some hovering blight.

Suddenly she didn't mind about the holes in the field. It was only a field, a piece of dirt. But Larry! Maybe it was because his face was so fresh and unused that the look on it stood out so stark and ugly. He stood silent, rock-like, sullen. Po realized with horror that she had never heard Hymes speak a word. Never. He had only stood and looked. And the way he looked was the way Larry was looking now.

Hadn't she heard it many a time, around a fire, or at a wake, the fearful tale of how a man became like the person or thing he hated! The look on his face now was cold hate.

"Larry!" she cried out in terror, running toward him.

But he swung away, and went down the hill to the shipyard, cold and silent.

Chapter Sixteen

NONE of the baseball men of Brooklyn liked the field being dug up. But it was one of those things that could happen, like losing a job, or having a little one die of fever. It was bad. But you went on. You found another place to practice. And it was going to be a great contest, wasn't it?

But Larry didn't go on. "Hardly comes to practice!" Brian complained. "And then picks fights! You'd think nothing bad ever happened to anyone before!"

Walking out at sunset, Po saw, in the bar, and at tables near by, the men gathered in animated talk. Apart, at a table by himself, Larry brooded. Even sitting down he looked big, his massive shoulders bulging under his brown jacket, his throat rising from his open white shirt, his bright hair tumbled. He looked just as he had the first day she'd seen him in the ship's hold—except for his face. Looking at that, Po felt a little sick tremble in her stomach. Then he had looked as if the world were a great joke and he about to burst into a laugh. But all the early morning shine was gone now, as if a harsh dry wind had blown over the great meadow and dried up the dew.

Maybe the shine had been there because everything seemed possible. If he came to Brooklyn, why, he'd get on the big team all right! If he'd gone to California, he'd have conquered there, wouldn't he? But—what if he were blocked by some detached thing having nothing to do with muscles, separate from courage, having only to do with what was owned? What if, now, everything were not possible?

Maybe that's why Po felt a shiver, looking at Larry's face. It was as if, striding across the great meadow, glisteny with dew, he'd fallen into a hole dug to trip him. Instead of shrugging and going on, he stood

117

transfixed, hands clenched, brow frowning with malevolence, trying to find his enemy. And as he stood there, the dew was evaporating, oh so quickly, from the meadow. On impulse, though the Gardens had been interdicted—Po went in. But Larry did not want to talk.

Just then a shout of derisive laughter rose at the bar. Brian had been delivered by hand, an impressive invitation. It was for a testimonial dinner, arranged by friends and well-wishers of—William Hymes.

Po saw Larry straighten up.

"There's a catch in it, I bet me second-best britches!" Brian slapped the invitation on the bar. "Sometimes these b'hoys, after they make a pile, get a yen for a political office, or a title!"

Larry came to the bar and snatched up the invitation. "Mansion House!" he sneered. "Thursday evening! Speeches by friends! Ha! I'll make a speech for them!" It was as if all this time he had been brooding because he could not grapple with his enemy. Now his eyes blazed.

"Ah now, Larry boy, git over it! How about practice tomorra—" Brian began. But Larry threw the invitation down and flung out of the bar.

Upstairs, the invitation met with satisfaction, for Mamie still had high hopes in the affair of the Sewage, and it was through Mrs. Selfridge the invitation had come. It had not even occurred to Brian that he would go—but he was going.

Mamie and Po were to go too. It was the custom for ladies to be admitted later for the speechmaking. They were to sit in their best toilettes, in a gallery, and admire the flow of wit and lend spice to the gentlemen's enjoyment by their polite handclapping.

Mamie had become galvanized with one of her terrible clenched-up strivings. For, after she had persuaded Brian he was going, she had seen this could be an occasion when Po might catch the eye of some "rising young man." She was so sure that was the best thing that could happen to Po. And Po did not argue because, one morning, a sudden flare of light seemed to illumine Mamie. Po felt as though she'd never seen her before, and even then, only darkly.

Mamie had decided Po must have a party dress. That particular morning Mamie was kneeling, pinning up the yards of its hem, a worried frown between her brows, her tense fingers flying. Mamie was not stupid about ways to catch the eye of a "rising young man," either, for the dress was cloud-white organdy with a pale blue sash, and with her black curls pinned high and falling in a cascade down the back of her neck, Po was astonished at herself. But, looking down at Mamie's tight back, Po realized: "She must always be making people do things they've no wish for, like making Brian go to the dinner. What could be crueler hard than that? It's not that the poor woman expects to have any hilarious time herself at this dinner! And isn't it like all times, she must be struggling up some cliff, trying to get to some safe place where she can relax? You'd think there was some lurking thing about she feared, and that only by raising herself far up could she avoid it! What was it she feared?" Po didn't know—but somehow, after that, she couldn't add to Mamie's strain by arguing about the "Rising Young Man."

Besides, Po herself had begun to be eager and excited about the dinner. The reason was the huge colored engraving that had hung in the library of the castle at Lough. The engraving was called "The Founding Fathers of the U.S. of A., in Council over the Future of the Infant Republic." The name of each figure was designated in flowing script, and in the long afternoons in the library, she had studied their faces. Noble, stern men, they had looked serene in a purpose apart from and bigger than themselves.

And now, according to Mamie, at this dinner would be the pillars —the Governor, the Senator, the head of the hospital, prominent lawyers, editors, all would be there—the heirs of the men in the engraving. They were a part of her new land she had not seen. And at the dinner, she would not only see but hear them!

The evening came for the dinner, and Brian went off scowling in his Sunday coat. Mamie, her black taffeta rustling importantly, stood with a little frown, regarding Po's toilette. But Po sensed a real interest, like an aunt's or a sister's, in Mamie's critical eye. Then, grand in a hired hack, Mamie and Po drove to the Mansion House and were shown to the gallery with its rows of gilt chairs. To some of the ladies already present, Mamie nodded perfunctorily, as if affronted at the sight of them. Others, like Mrs. Selfridge, she greeted with obvious respect. Now Po leaned over the railing and looked down on the large banquet hall.

The hall was shaped like the one in the colored engraving, with high square windows, but here, crystal chandeliers gleamed down on white damask.

Twenty-five or thirty guests were seated along a head table facing into the room, and more guests, well over a hundred, were seated at smaller tables.

Po found herself glancing at these nervously. She realized now that she had been afraid, all the time, that Larry might come here. She searched the smaller tables. Why, there was Brian, looking glum, at a small table near the door. And there, at a table at an angle to the head table, with four or five other men, all writing busily, and wearing white badges marked Press, sat Walt, writing and chatting quietly with the others. But, as she breathed a sigh of relief—Larry was not here!

Relaxed now, and ready to take it all in, her eye swept the head table, where sat the men who carried on for the Founders. At first they all looked alike, in smooth broadcloth, high stocks and slicked-down hair—only the array of beards ranged behind the white damask was fascinating in variety. Now she began to study each face. Was there a one here who looked like Washington, noble and stern? Yes, there was one! Maybe he would actually speak!

Was there a one like Franklin? That little man on his feet, talking, who seemed the Master of Ceremonies—certainly not he. For, as he looked around the room from behind his high white stock, his face had an expression which seemed to say, "I've caught many people cheating, and I am watching you!" Well, he could have gotten in by mistake.

"That's Mr. Jenkins!" Mamie whispered. "A lawyer from New York. Handles Mr. Hymes's affairs!"

They were drinking toasts, though, just as one might have imagined they would be—to "The Constitution" and "Liberty" and "The Flag." Then Mr. Jenkins was reading messages and letters of regret from the Governor and the Senator and others.

There was the guest of honor himself, William Hymes, behind the red roses. His black broadcloth coat was so bunched up around his heavy shoulders, it somehow failed to make him look elegant. Po thought of the stony fountain again, from which no watery music played, for he sat, massive, silent, only showing his pleasure by a slightly heightened color. She could remember no face like his on the engraving, but then, he was an enigma to her. She had never heard him utter a word. Perhaps he would speak tonight.

But suddenly she began to pay attention to what Mr. Jenkins, in his precise fussy voice, was saying. "—will now tell you something of the early life of our honored guest, and how he came into the city with nothing but a Bible, his mother's blessing, and one silver dollar, and rose to his present substance."

Po sat forward, excited. For wasn't it in every shebeen in Ireland you heard tales of these miracles—how a fellow with nothing but his bare hands, and a shilling wrapped up in a pocket handkerchief and it dirty, went into a wilderness, and built a town, or a railroad, or a great works. But never were the stories clear just how the miracle was done. Now she'd get the whole way of it.

"—born on a small cattle farm in Washington county," Jenkins' precise voice was mincing on, "he earned his first money driving cattle into the city for sale." Po could see Hymes, in the dust of the road, with a whip, driving the tired dumb cattle into the city.

"Now, we have a surprise for our honored guest!" Two waiters came in bearing aloft a great piece of white confectionery and placed it on the center of the table.

"This, my friends," Jenkins announced, "is an exact replica of the humble log home in which our illustrious guest was born!" Po sat back, a little impatient at the applause. Was there anyone, even back in Ireland, who didn't know that anybody who was anyone in America was born in a log hut? She wished they'd get on to the interesting part.

"In the city," Jenkins went on, "William saw the wealth of the great merchants and shipping men of South Street. It fired him with ambition to accumulate substance, too. He secured a job sweeping out at three dollars the week for Mr. Phelps, the well-known iron merchant. Williams patterned himself after Mr. Phelps in every way. No one could ever accuse William of wasting time in reading idle books, but at this time he acquired two volumes which influenced his whole career. A Spence's Advanced Arithmetic, and a book on single entry bookkeeping. Soon he rose to clerk at twelve dollars the week. But now, to carry on the story, let me introduce Mr. Elias Winkler, Manager of the Long Island Steam Rail Road, and a business associate."

Now Po did sit forward on the little gilt chair. For the man he introduced was the one who reminded her of General Washington in the engraving! And wasn't it the honorable good thing he was doing, too, making the steam cars shuttle back and forth, carrying people to farms or cities, bringing in cattle, and taking back plows! Mr. Winkler had a high noble brow, and a sonorous voice, and she loved him.

But after compliments all around to the guests, he went on to how he first knew Mr. Hymes at the time Hymes took over the old Phoenix Works, which sold bolts to his company. Then he went on to a lot of gnish-gnash which Po found hard going. She'd pick up a word like "investments" or "earnings" and then be lost again. But Mr. Winkler ended up with an air of triumph. "And so when I say to you, that when Mr. Hymes took over the Phoenix it was losing fifteen thousand dollars annually, and now it is second largest in money earned on this side of the river—what more need I say? To my mind that tells the whole story of the man we honor tonight!" He was sitting down and Po still hadn't learned how Hymes jumped from clerk to the owning of an Iron Works. She found herself for some reason vaguely disappointed, too, in the man who looked like General Washington.

But now Jenkins was introducing a thin nervous-looking man and Po felt hopeful and eager again, for this was a Mr. Ridgeway, and who was he? None other than the man responsible for turning on the magic lights in the town! And wouldn't that be a wonderful thing to do? Every evening to send forth your gnomes, the lamplighters, and make the entire place to spring into light! Mr. Ridgeway didn't look, though, like a man who lit lamps. He looked as if he had a gnawing pain in his belly.

Mr. Ridgeway gave greetings and compliments to all concerned. Then he went on, too, at length, with a lot of talk of "net profit" and "fiscal years" and "good yields" and finally ended up by saying how much respect he had for Hymes in the way he'd increased business. "Every such gain helps everyone, certainly helped his company, to make more money."

What a strange thing! He didn't seem to feel that he deserved any honor or acclaim about lighting the lamps, and never even mentioned that!

Po began to fidget, and feel the white organdy bodice fitted too tightly, and glanced down at Brian. What she saw caused her to sit bolt upright in alarm. Larry was coming in.

He slipped in quietly, and as, from time to time, other men had come in to hear the speeches, no one paid any attention to him—no one but Brian. Larry sat at an empty seat near him, and Brian put a hand on his arm, and spoke to Larry as if pleading with him. But Larry shook off his hand, and stared ahead, looking stonily at Hymes.

And now more men spoke, including a wide, sanctimonious-looking man in a high white stock who Po thought might be Henry Ward Beecher, but who turned out to be Simon Quimby, who owned the hoopskirt factory. Mr. Quimby said piously that God was smiling on America this year, for the volume of business was up. Mr. Van Leyn, who owned the Brooklyn shipyard had sent regrets, but another man who made ships spoke, going on much the same way. Even the doctor who was head of the hospital gave the news that he had been able to close the books evenly this year, thanks to a thousand-dollar donation from Mr. Hymes. But Po could not pay any attention. Her eyes were unable to pull away from Larry.

Larry looked strange. For one thing, he wore a respectable blue coat she had never seen before. His hair was slicked down flat to his head, like all the other guests. He wore a stock, carefully tied. If she had ever seen him wearing one before, it had looked as if he had finished tieing it by grinning in the mirror and saying, "to hell with it!" Maybe this careful manner was the way he would have looked if he had stayed in New Bedford with his uncles and his mother. But it was his face that disturbed Po. She didn't want to look at it. If she had seen him for the first time as he was now, she would not have loved him.

Now a man with sandy mutton-chop whiskers Mamie said was Mr.

Archie Selfridge got up and spoke. But Po, worried about Larry, only half heard him as he went on: "I feel we should do more than drink toasts," and his voice had an accusing, righteous tone, "to the man who inspires this spontaneous demonstration of appreciation. Able men, men who have demonstrated their fitness are needed to run our great state. No doubt, Mr. Hymes, burdened as he is, would be reluctant to assume more responsibility, but I feel we should make an attempt to recruit him. Why do we not urge him to accept a place on the Democratic ticket for the office of senator in the legislature of New York State?"

Hands beat together, some even tapped with spoons on glasses. Many turned their heads to look at a man Po knew was Hughie McLaughlain. But Hughie McLaughlain sat as expressionless as Hymes himself.

When several people, including a tenant who told how Hymes loaned him money when he was in trouble, rose from their seats to second the idea of the nomination, Po, apprehensive, was watching Larry. He started to get to his feet as if to speak, but Brian spoke urgently to him, and pulled him back with a strong hand.

Then Jenkins was on his feet again, speaking. "And so, my friends, you may ask, how did Mr. Hymes accomplish what he did? Early in life, he heard of Mr. Astor's motto of thrift, honesty, industry. He resolved to follow it! And today we see the result."

In spite of her worry about Larry, Po had a sense of being cheated. She hadn't learned the way it was the miracle had been accomplished. Why, she knew lots of fellows, in Ireland and here, who had industry and thrift and honesty go leor, and they didn't come prancing out with an Iron Works in their pocket.

But Jenkins was going on. "Here is a man who has never forgotten the moral teachings of his mother. Inflexible in judgment, utilitarian in character, I give you a four-square, all-around American, William Hymes!"

Hymes was going to speak!

Hymes stood up, his heavy bull-like shoulders straining under his broadcloth coat. He was silent, as polite clapping circled the room. Then he began to speak. He was saying nothing remarkable, just thanking them all for kindness, but Po sat bolt upright in her chair, frightened at the sound of his voice.

It was a harsh voice, grating and curiously flat, without timbre, and she had the strange sensation she had heard it before, at some dreadful moment of her life. It brought back a sensation of desperation, without bringing the memory of where or when. But, she must be wrong. She listened now, straining to remember, to place it.

"—When I came to the city, I landed at the foot of Liberty

123

Street. I hadn't a friend. Didn't know a soul. I can tell you, walking around then, I never thought I'd ever be attending a dinner like this!"

Po still felt the fright the voice aroused in her. Had she heard it in Fall River? Suddenly it seemed to her it had something to do with Larry. But when she had seen Hymes in the Gardens, or watching the field, she was sure she had not heard him speak. She tried to pick up some word that would be a clue.

"—but I guess the thing I'm proudest of is—I saw we could make more money by changing over from charcoal, as fuel in the Works, to coal. Yessir, even though we had to bring it all the way over the mountains from Pennsylvania! And I think by pushing that I can take some credit for making money for all of us!" Hymes went on, but Po didn't hear.

She was watching Larry, with a sort of sick feeling. For after a while when Hymes sat down, amid clapping, she saw Larry, in spite of Brian, jerk to his feet and, in a loud, harsh voice, begin to speak rapidly, before he could be broken in on.

"Up where I come from, anyone can speak his piece in meeting! And since this is a spontaneous demonstration of affection, let me put in my word!"

Po knew now why she hadn't wanted to look at his face. He looked the way he had when he discovered the wreck of the field. The same look Hymes had when they played the trick on him. Cold, still, planning hate. Not lined there yet, not etched—but the same look.

She guessed it took courage in a way to do what Larry was doing, to stand up here. But she didn't admire him. He wasn't fighting for his ball field, only downing his personal enemy.

"I hear you think this Hymes is quite a man!" Larry rushed on. "Well, let me tell you—" But Jenkins had jumped to his feet, an indignant red mantling his face. Hymes leaned out and stared at Larry, then spoke quietly to Jenkins. Larry went on quickly, shouting now. "There are a lot of men in this town, everyone that plays the game called baseball, that wouldn't vote for him for outhouse cleaner!"

Jenkins broke in, his voice sharp as a needle. "I must ask you, sir—" But Larry rushed on. "A lot of us worked hard, nigh killed ourselves, making a ball field, and this fine Mr. Hymes"—Larry glared at him—"had it dug up!"

Jenkins had beckoned to three burly waiters, who were rushing toward Larry. The guests were buzzing, some demanding Larry be thrown out, others wanting to hear him. But the waiters had seized Larry, and were rushing him toward the door.

Jenkins was talking, with shocked righteousness. "Mr. Hymes informs me this was land he had legally acquired, and on which he was starting to erect a building—"

"Why'nt he tell us that?" Larry shouted back over his shoulder. "Why'd he let us finish, and then—" The waiters had him out of the door.

Jenkins looked shocked. "Is an honest property owner, who will be paying taxes on improved land, to be attacked by an irresponsible young vagrant?" But Po didn't wait to hear.

In the street, as she ran, Po was in time to see Larry swing at the men ejecting him. They turned then and ran back in. They'd done all they were told to do.

Larry was brushing off his sleeve under the gaslight when she ran up.

"Larry!"

"Po!" His face had a drained white look. "Oh, were you in there?" His voice was flat and tired. "You're dressed up! You look pretty."

Po felt she had something of fearful importance she must make him see, and she didn't know exactly how to say it.

"Larry! That Hymes! I was watching his face! That's why I ran after you—"

Larry looked snarling again. "If he fights dirty, I can too!"

Oh, how could she make him see? "And is it happy you feel now?"

"He had it coming!" He sounded sullen.

"And you, is it better you are feeling?" she insisted.

"What kind of fighting was that he did? Like hitting me with a stone when I'm bent over tieing my shoe!"

Oh, if she could but find the right words. "Larry, if a fellow gets you eating yourself up with hate—why who wins?"

The gaslight flickered down on his face. He had a sort of bafflement. She loved him, she wanted to smooth the bafflement away from his face with her hands, but she could only reach up and brush dust from his coat.

One or two people came out from the dinner into the street. One was Walt, and he sauntered up to them on the sidewalk, stopped, listening to Po.

"Larry, quit off this now," she pleaded. "He'll mark you in the end!"

Larry's fist clenched. "How do you figure?"

Walt put his hand on Larry's shoulder soothingly. Po could see she had not made Larry understand at all, at all. Oh, how could she? "Larry, back in Ballyhouna were two families, the Dermods and the Breens. Over a stony patch it was a quarrel grew between them the like of which for bitterness would blight the praties in the field. 'Tis a devouring thing when breathing men lie down in the night and rise up in the day with hate using up their inside strength, and they spending all their time of light figuring how to hurt the other. And it's God's truth, Larry, and you must listen to me, what with the dwelling on their enmity, and the terrible concentrating on each other of their hate, why after a lengthy time, they began to look alike!"

"Aw, more of your big stories!" He frowned.

"Stories is it," her words came tumbling, "and you changed already! Do you know who you looked like standing in there, with the greeching hate glistening from your face like poison? Like nobody else but that great ugly Hymes himself!"

"She's right, Larry." Walt was gentle.

"What did you want me to do?" Larry glowered. "Stand and take his digging up the field? Sure, I had it in my craw for him! But we're even now! I'm over it, I tell you! It's done. I'm going back to ball playing! And I don't need anyone to tell me what to do!" And he flung off into the darkness.

Po started after him. "Larry!"

But Walt spoke then. "Let him go now. The soreness is still there. Later, you'll talk to him. You'll know what to say!"

She looked after Larry, troubled. "I wish I did!"

"Why, who could know better? You love him and it will all spring from that. He's a strong fellow, and he can think, and he can feel. But you can see!"

It was a flattery thing to have Walt speak to her the like she was a woman grown—still and all, she wished he didn't expect her to have answers. She didn't see. She didn't know.

More of the people were beginning to come from the dinner. "Come along." Walt with his open white collar, his big simple clean look, seemed so sure, so serene. "We'll walk along home together." And Po taking four or five brisk steps to his one long rolling one, they went up the street, while bugs circled around the pools of lamp light in the spring night.

"You know"—Walt looked down at her—"I've been watching that lad since he came here. He has a lot of that mighty man, Bull Bender, in him. So has Hymes, you know. They're the conquerors, the dominators. And the three of them, coming here from the outer lands, to the gathering place of the forces, where island, rivers, ocean meet! What will the conquerers conquer, I ask? The Bull, he still wants to swing a wild pant'er over his head—only soon, the wild pant'ers will be gone. But Hymes and Larry, what will they conquer? For you know, both of them—Hymes from the hardscrabble farm, Larry from the tight New England town—have the same background. It rests on the same two dark pillars—worship of money, and denial of man's and woman's sex—of sex, the clef on the symphony of life! So, when Hymes comes, what does he conquer?"

"He made somehow a great fancy Iron Works for himself!"

"He didn't make—he got. He's not an Iron Master. He bought a bankrupt works, hired men cunning in the art to run it. He's not a maker, only a getter. But, is that evil? When he arrived at South Street, did he find songs to be sung, armies to be defeated? No! Only things to be piled in great sterile piles with oneself on top, the tallest pile under the greatest conqueror. And didn't he draw from the very air there that the worth of a man was not what he was, or made, but what he got?"

Walt had a resonant voice, but Po, trotting along beside him, had hard going understanding his meaning. But now he began on Larry, and somehow that seemed easier to understand.

"But when Larry came, what did he conquer? He's still using his strength, I guess, to fight free of the two dark pillars he sprang from—but he's moving on. But where? That's the question mark. He can become anything. Now, he's trying to build a baseball team to conquer the world. For a young fellow, is that bad? See how it is connected somehow with everyone else, it's not sterile. And then what? What will become of him? Who can say?"

He turned suddenly and looked down at Po. "That's why you're going to watch out, and use your eyes for far-seeing, because in the end—it all springs from women!"

From women, was it? And didn't he know she'd hardly be seventeen come Michaelmas? People always, she thought crossly, expected too much of her.

"And now—" He stopped walking in his earnestness and gazed down at her a moment, under the gas lamp on Fulton Street. "What did you think of all you saw tonight? How did it strike you?"

Now didn't the man know she was nothing but an unbeknownst little Irish girl? "It's hardly for the likes of me to say anything of the like of them, and they the great ones in every way!"

"Indeed?" He seemed genuinely surprised. "Why not?"

She would have liked to have told him about her vague feeling of disappointment—how she had actually hoped to find the inheritors of the noble stern faces with the serene purpose in the engravings—only now that she thought of it in cold blood, it seemed childish. But he was waiting patiently.

Po was inherently polite, and she had been a guest. She was searching for the words. "Well, now," she began, "all the time they were talking, my heart was scalded for them. For wasn't it like they'd all been tricked by some blaggard American leprechaun, who'd thranced away from them all the lovely ships, and the magic lights, and the whistling steam cars, and the strong iron, and turned them into—money!"

"A new evil spirit?" Walt said bemused, and they walked on again, he seeming lost in thought. "And yet," he said finally, as if talking to the spring night, "is acquisitiveness new? The danger is, at this moment, great wells of human intuition, of invention, have been tapped. The greedy, piping this into private reservoirs, can rise to power unheard of before. But, was it evil, then, for Ericson to invent a screw propeller? Or greedy for Cooper to have built the little engine?"

He sounded so deeply sad, Po tried to think of something to cheer him up. "Ah, now, if only the iron and the lovely ships and all, could come un-thranced again!"

Walt turned and looked at her, and she was surprised to see that he wasn't sad at all, but really serene and sure. "Oh, you must not regret, you must not look back. If the mold is awry, you must mold anew!"

She was taken aback. She had nothing to do with it! Didn't he know she'd but lately come? "Why," she faltered, "I only spoke of the un-thrancing to cheer you up!"

Now they had come to the steps leading up to Brian's flat, and he looked down at her, large, simple, his manner confident and serene. "Oh, I don't need to be cheered up! Who would confine, even with a dream, the beautiful possibilities of growth? For there is you!"

"Me, is it?" she said, taken aback. Why, she hardly knew what the man was talking about! She didn't want to *try* to know! He with his remolding and his growing! It was all very flattery to be talked to like a woman grown, but when he began making her responsible for things! It was bad enough when he said she must watch over Larry, and now what must he do but be throwing the whole shebang into her lap!

But he was turning away, calm, serene. "Good night." And he went on up Fulton Street.

She stood there in the Brooklyn night, as the poplars stirred, not feeling serene or sure. She had a mixed-up indignant feeling, like he was imposing on her, expecting too much. Why, didn't he know she was only— But, ah, now, she thought crossly, he was daft, surely.

Chapter Seventeen

P̶O DID not see Larry again for some time, but Walt's words, and his expecting her to be a woman grown, stayed with her and made her uncomfortable. It was maybe because of that she quarreled with Mamie.

On that particular evening, Mamie, getting ready to go to a meeting in Mr. Beecher's church, called out to her, like a general issuing a terse order for attack, "Put on the rose-colored dimity and come with me! Joseph Cooper's to be there!"

All Po's inner forces marshaled instantly in alarm. Mamie had seized on this idea of a "rising young man" for Po and kept worrying it like a dog with a bone. Did she dare openly defy? It was so much easier to do as you were bid. But some obscure struggle seethed in Po explosively.

She stood tense. "I'd as leave not go!" She faced Mamie finally, her cheeks burning.

A quick frown appeared between Mamie's brows. She stared at Po in baffled disappointment. "Why not? I tell you I've considered everything, and he's the best one! A young man from a respectable family! And a clerk in Mr. Selfridge's office, too!"

"He'd maybe"—Po's defiance faltered—"not care for me!"

"Don't think that way, or you'll never get married! You're pretty enough! You can manage if you just let me teach you how to do!"

A defiant stubbornness rose in Po. "I'm not going!"

"Oh!" Mamie tapped her foot, exasperated. "After all my work. Making you new clothes! Trying to get the Irish out of your speech!"

"And that's a foolish thing," Po flared up, "for you could as easy rinse the aroma off a brandy cork!"

"You could do it if you tried!" Mamie said firmly. "Can't you see if you could marry someone like that, you'd have a respectable, secure position?"

"Maybe," Po said darkly, "I don't want to be respectable and secure!"

Mamie stared at her in baffled anger. "What are you talking about?"

Po looked at her a long moment, then broke out, "I'm saying that I'll be making my own pattern!"

"Oh, you just want to oppose me!" Mamie stared at her, as if she were too exasperated to go on. Then, she whisked out of the room, closing the door with an angry little click.

Po felt a little scared at what she had done. It was all very well to be a woman grown, and stand up and say what you would do and would not do—but then you had to take the consequences. Mamie would go to Brian—Mamie would think of Fall River. Though slanting sun fingers still held back the twilight, Po ran upstairs to her third floor room, and with trembling hands closed the door, as if she could shut out the consequences.

She threw herself on the bed and closed her eyes. She'd call up the memory of a time she thought of as the Pale Gold Day. She only called it up in bad times, for it was like a valuable medicine, and she did not want to indulge in it too often, for fear it would fail to soothe her when she needed it.

Part of the radiant buoyancy of that far-off day bathed in pale gold light sprang from the fact that she wasn't sure how old she was when it happened and so it was easier to feel as if it might be now.

It had been a Sunday morning, though, and she and her father were going walking. Po stood waiting, knowing all would be happily arranged, with no effort from her. A pair of hands, perhaps her mother's, placed Po's caubeen on her head, buttoned gloves on her hands. Po didn't even have to make any decision about where to walk. Her father would do that. They were going along the wall back from the sea. Po longed to go there herself, to explore all the silver tracks that went darting off below—but the way was beset with dangers, bad boys, a black dog. Now her father put down a bony warm hand and clasped hers firmly. She could see his thin legs, the mend on his brown tweed breeches, the scuffs on his brogans.

When the wall got higher, she did not have to worry or take care, for he always picked her up and carried her. Her father wasn't strong; she a big girl to be carried. It was as if they both knew this, but he enjoyed, maybe, being to her, at least, all powerful, and she even now remembered the wonderful warm safe feeling of being carried, effortless, sheltered against the wind by his cape. Then the pale gold light faded.

Po rose then, and walked around the room restlessly. After a while, she went unhappily downstairs to the Gardens. When she came in, Brian was not to be seen, but Larry was there. His back was toward her, but she saw his bright hair, his powerful shoulders hunched forward as he leaned on a table.

Then her heart squeezed down, became small and hard. Louise's dress of pale green looked sulphurous to Po under the gaslight. Louise leaned back, laughing, her body moving up under the tight green silk. She jumped up, tugged at Larry teasingly, pulling him toward the door.

But Bushel Basket, at the bar, stopped Larry, and spoke to him in a low voice. Larry shrugged off Bushel Basket's hand angrily.

"Have I ever missed practice yet? No one tells me when to come!" Larry said defiantly. "I'm my own boss!" He walked cockily to the door. Louise and Larry went down Pineapple Street together.

And as Po stood looking after them with a forlorn lost feeling, Brian came into the bar from the stairs leading down from the flat. From his face, Po saw Mamie had been talking to him. Perhaps she had sent down for him while Po was on the third floor.

Brian came over to Po, nervously. "Well, darlint!" He seemed to be making an effort to sound cheerful, as if he wished everything could be pleasant. Brian and Po sat down at a little table, then, near the wall, and Brian took out his pipe. As if postponing something, he began to fill it carefully.

"Mamie is, maybe, a little—prickly," he said finally. "You see—" He stopped.

"Sometimes"—the words came out of Po, tortured, wanting him to deny it—"I feel I shouldn't stay here with you!"

Brian was instantly contrite, his eyes warm. "What's this you are saying? Why and what would I do now for someone to laugh at a joke?"

Po grasped this desperately. It was true; poor Mamie had no humorous feelings. She could not understand Irish jokes. Sometimes Po and Brian would shriek with laughter while Mamie looked at them as if they were daft.

"Whisht now, aren't you like a breath from my family in Ireland? And the way you love the Gardens, isn't that a comfort now?" Po seized this hungrily too. Mamie didn't appreciate the Gardens. "And the game now—isn't it a marvel the way you took to it?" Real concern was in his warm gray eyes.

Po clutched at the idea of his need for her. It was not, she thought, that she was scared of starting off alone again, or having to decide, take consequences, always be wary, alert. It was not that she was afraid to struggle and make her own pattern. No. She had to accept Brian's shelter, because he needed her.

But Brian's face looked teased, and he seemed to have a lot of trouble getting his pipe lit. He didn't look at Po then, but said, uneasily, "A man has to have peace in his own house!"

Po felt her stomach quiver uneasily.

"You're a girl of sense. You'll take no hurt at anything I say!"

Po felt a cold chill mount.

Brian nervously turned his tobacco pouch over and over, then he looked around as if he were hunting the path out of a thorn patch.

"I was thinking how maybe"—he glanced up at Po, harassed—"it'd be best if we try to go along with Mamie's ways!" Then he burst out in a rush, "It's just that I want Mamie to be contented!

We get along fine as long as nothing stirs her up. And I been thinking I might tell you how things have been with her. You'd understand her better. Mamie's had a hard time!"

"Don't tell me," Po said quickly, "if Mamie wouldn't like it."

Brian's face got stubborn. "Still and all, if you're to live here, it will help keep all calm and easy. I can talk to you. You've knocked about a bit. I can expect you to act like you was older!"

At this Po felt a bad familiar feeling.

"You see"—Brian hesitated—"Mamie was left an orphan at fifteen. She went then to live with her aunt by marriage, who kept a boarding house in Manhattan. First class it was, over on Ann Street, the like where travelers would put up. I stayed there myself when first I came, for I'd the price of the Limerick farm in me pocket and could afford it."

Brian's pipe was out again, and he stopped to light it, frowning. "At first, I didn't even know I was in love with Mamie. It was on'y long after when I had the Gardens and all, that I persuaded her to marry the clumsy like of me. She was a pretty delicate thing, but terrible strict and shy all times. But I always felt that was on account of the way that blaggard aunt treated her. She took great care of her own fine daughters, and did well by them, but Mamie she disregarded. Off the aunt and her daughters would go, leaving Mamie to work, the like she was no better than a slavey! Being treated so was extra hard for Mamie, for she'd been reared delicate. Not that her Da had it—he was but a customs clerk over in Jersey—but he had treated her like a little queen. Mamie was an on'y child, and to speak God's truth, I guess they'd spoiled her! And then to be so careless treated after, like she was nothing!"

Po thought of how Mamie was always trying to prove she was somebody.

Brian sighed. "It made her turrible straight-laced and cold for a long time—I guess she'll change afterwhile, as soon as she gets over having to feel like she must be perfect!"

Suddenly Po understood why Brian loved the ball game, why he lived his real life in the Gardens.

"But Brian—" Po's voice rose a little, pleading.

But Brian looked irritated, as if he hoped Po had understood. He spoke slow and heavily. "I want Mamie to feel right and good. That's why I don't cross her. Once we have children, she'll be all right; everything'll be fine. Once she settles down and feels easier, we'll have them. I know it!"

Dave Posen came in just then, and his face lit up, seeing Po. He crossed quickly to their table.

"Brian! I promised I'd take Po over to Manhattan for a lark

one of these times. It's been kind of hard to, on account of practice for the Atlantic game, but how about this evening?"

Brian looked relieved somehow, as if he were worried to have made Po unhappy, and glad now if she could have some fun.

"Mamie won't like it," Po said.

Brian looked a little harassed, but he spoke warmly. "You go on now, and enjoy yourself!"

Chapter Eighteen

THEY STOOD at the rail, Po and Dave. The ferry boat passed over the gently chopping waves toward the roof tops Po had looked at so often—Manhattan.

It was a fair warm evening, the white-branched clouds turning coral in the sunset. A hay boat, crossing near them, loosened the fragrance of Long Island farms over the water. Po felt sparkles of excitement running all through her.

Sea breeze from the upper bay whipped Po's ruffled skirt against Dave's legs. Only slightly taller than she, he looked at her, smiling. "I'm glad you're little!" She saw his hands on the rail, thin, sensitive and calloused, with dark ink stains on the fingernails.

"I haven't been progressing with the Irish language"—he leaned toward her, eyes smiling—"the way I should have. What did you tell me was the Irish word for kiss?"

"When the Irish say it, they're all ready, for the word is"—and she formed her lips, mischief in her eye—"pogue!"

He leaned closer, but stopped, hesitant, shy.

Ah, isn't he the nice lad, she thought, and looking handsome, too, in his short blue jacket with the gleam-y brass buttons, the checked pantaloons on him, and his blue cap set so jaunty in his dark curly hair! Yes, he was a right lad, with deep places in him the like of a well of cool water, but he could joke and be tender, too.

Wouldn't it be the wonderful thing now, if a certain large buckeen had some of this tenderness about him? If only Larry and Dave had been mixed up and rolled out into one! Wouldn't that be a fine fiery man!

"First, we'll try to get in the opera!" Dave smiled at her. "Walt and I go lots of times, but I never took a girl before!" He delicately touched the white nainsook frill at her wrist. "I never wanted to!"

Up from the ferry on Fulton Street, they turned into the Broadway.

It was that moment after sunset, when the sky, greenish-blue, still glistened with opal light. Lamplighters were moving along with their tapers, as if they were lighting up the city to greet the boy and girl from Brooklyn. The lozenge-shaped gas lamps began to glow lemon-colored against the red brick buildings.

Always attuned to sounds, Po was bewildered by the rattle of the iron and wood wheels rolling over the paving. Purse-proud black carriages, canvas-covered freight wagons, and common yellow stages, all moved noisily—to somewhere. The moving crowd on the pavement, gay, old, beautiful, sneering, laughing, jabbering, seemed to strain to make themselves heard above the wheel noise as they moved along, going—someplace. In the air above, all was glitter and light. In the gutters, greenish ooze and filth stagnated, sending up foul sewage odors.

But Dave seized her arm and hurried her along. When they got to the Opera House—disappointment. It was a gala night for some returned Italian singer. Not a seat to be had! Dave looked chagrined, but Po, excited by the flurry and gush of life about her, was almost glad to turn and walk up the Broadway again.

"There'll be singing at Niblo's Gardens," Dave said. Of course, it wasn't opera, but Po could hear what the music was like at a concert saloon. "Come on." And he guided her along the Broadway toward Prince Street.

The street lights shone bright now, because it was darker. The crowd was changing subtly, too. Toward the brilliant lights, pale, ragged women crept from the unlit streets in back of the Broadway. Thin-legged, dirty—crossing-sweepers, flower-sellers, beggars, drunks. And from the murky alleys, creeping toward the glare, street women appeared with soiled shawls and bonnets with broken plumes.

And now, spilling out of doorways which has been silent earlier in the evening, came raucous laughter, yellow light and brazen music. "They're concert saloons, too," Dave said, hurrying her along, "but don't worry, Niblo's is respectable."

Girls, young, gaudily dressed, were going in and out of these doors, some alone, some leading men. In front of one, a girl, not more than fourteen was importuning a middle-aged man. "Come on, this place is fine. I work here!"

Po looked back, appalled, as Dave hurried her along. "She's never a singer, is she?" she asked anxiously.

"No, just what they call a Waiter Girl. I knew one once from—"

Suddenly a man reached out from the curb and seized Dave's arm familiarly and held it as Dave tried to pull away. The man's furtive chin seemed buried so deep in his tightly buttoned-up brown coat you could wonder where his words came from. "Dave! Stop! You're my boy! Got a fine job for you! Money! Say—" Dave had jerked away savagely, and walked on hastily. "Now is that a way," the furtive man called after him, "to pass up a friend?"

Dave looked straight ahead, ashamed, grim. "Don't look back at him! He's no friend. A bad one! Always trying to recruit boys from Battle Row to help him in his games! He used to live there. He works the railroad stations, the packet line wharves; picks up young girls! Promises them jobs. I'd hate to think how many of those Waiter Girls he got started in the life! He's a—pimp!"

But here was Niblo's. It was fancy. The entrance was marble, sort of Moorish, and the open gardens beyond, where Po and Dave sat at a small table and had an ice cream, were filled with shrubberies clipped to look like a dog or a man. There were plaster statues of trolls and small fountains with artificial lights. A man with face made black like Christy sang American minstrel songs. Po applauded, for she would never want Dave to feel she wasn't enjoying herself. She clapped too, for the singing of a red-haired woman in an elaborate pink ball dress who sang "Found Dead in the Snow," though to speak truth when Po tried, as always when she heard a new song, to learn the melody and words, it all clogged in the wheels of her mind like stale syrup.

Po was not sorry to come out again in the street, with its voices strident above the horsecar bells and the clatter of wheels. Po listened, trying to catch the sound of the city, its hum. In Limerick, the air seemed to vibrate with pipers, fiddlers and songs. In Dublin, the sound had seemed like an old woman humming a tender lullaby. In Boston, where she and her father had landed, the sound had seemed like an angular teacher, humming through his nose—a hymn. Fall River—that place, it never did resolve itself into a chord, but was always jangle, jar, screech and grind. This Broadway now—Po listened—it was like, maybe, a beautiful woman, singing very loud, a sentimental song.

Dave thought it would be fun to go to Bleecker Street to a beer cellar called Pfaff's, where they might meet Walt, and ride home with him on the ferry. It was too early, though. Walt wouldn't be there yet. They might, in the meantime, to pass a little time, drop in to Tammany Hall, where Walt and he often went to the Sunday lectures. They could just hear if there were any interesting speakers.

When they got there, the hall was echoing and half empty, but the audience—men in respectable black coats, workers in checked shirt sleeves and vests, students with books, women of all ages, sat at the front in an intense cluster, their eyes on a woman lecturer. She was a slender woman about forty, in a handsome white dress, with smooth dark hair and grave eyes. On the platform with her were six women. Their sheer white bonnets and fichus over their gray dresses indicated they were Quakers. They sat close to the speaker, three on each side, unmoving. Po smiled to herself, they looked so like a bodyguard.

The lecturer raised a delicate white hand, and her limpid diction made every low syllable penetrate. "It must not be true in America that sex, class or color limits freedom! The equal rights of human beings are here proclaimed! I speak to mechanics, uniting for the discovery of their rights! I speak to all saddened, and enslaved! I speak to women!"

Po felt as if the speaker's eyes suddenly lit on her, and stayed there. "Women must not be helpless children, but free agents!"

Now the lecturer looked around at her audience with large grave eyes. "I speak for the foundations of a society where kind feelings and kind actions are the only religion! Respect for the feelings and liberties of others, the only restraint. I speak for a society where affection shall form the only marriage. . . ."

Yells of protest broke from some of the men. Others jumped to their feet, shook their fists threateningly at the lecturer.

And now Po saw that the Quaker women were really a bodyguard. As if to protect their charge, and at the same time assure her saying whatever she willed, they moved in closer, forming a square. Then they stared calmly, with serene blandness, at the noisy objectors, as if to shake a gently admonishing finger at unruly children. After a time, as the unruffled calm stares of the bodyguard persisted, the cries subsided, the lecturer continued.

The slender speaker looked around. Then, Po felt there could be no mistake, this time the dark eyes looked directly into hers. Po felt as if she probed, saw clearly, then spoke out what she saw.

"You women make some of your own fetters! You look for the ancient road, so beaten into the earth it is nothing more than a rut! You haven't the courage to strike out across an open field, to make a new path! You'd rather walk knee-deep in the old dust!"

Po squirmed uneasily, trying to escape the grave eyes of the speaker.

"Self-support is the first outward requirement of any human being, man or woman! Life is a becoming—"

The personal duel she seemed in with the lecturer was so real to Po, she jumped, startled, when Dave plucked her sleeve.

"Come on! We better go or we might miss Walt!"

Reluctantly, looking backward, Po left. She felt stirred up, as if she needed to defend herself against some accuser.

And even as they went down the street, and Dave kept chattering on about this beer cellar where they were going being a place where sporting-men and actresses came, and newspapermen, and writers and artists, Po hardly heard him. The splintering words uttered so delicately by the woman lecturer kept jibing at her, magnified now like ringing taunts.

"Wasn't that the queer old thing she was saying!" Po finally broke out, troubled. "Do you think self-support is the first requirement of every human being?"

"Why, sure." Dave's tone was so quick and positive, Po was a little taken aback.

Po frowned miserably. "I wonder my brains out if maybe I shouldn't leave Brian's."

"Oh"—Dave's eyes glowed in denial—"that's different!" His eyes touched her hair, her cheek; then he said shyly, "He's lucky to have you."

But Po felt upset and guilty. Why did she have to keep tormenting herself this way? Suddenly she realized all this moiling and roiling had begun because of Walt's words! And he acting like she was a woman grown, responsible for things! Now, would you think a few words that you let slip in, innocent as babes, could go roistering on and disturbing the peace, like a pair of glen men come to the inn of a Saturday night?

She hadn't been able to argue back with the lecturer. Well, she'd pick an argument with Walt now, and have it out! Then maybe all this goading and scorning of herself would quit off! As they went down the cellar entry to find Walt, Dave was smiling, but Po had jousting in her eyes.

They came into a large low room, smoky, with an outdoor garden beyond. Pfaff himself, enormously fat, pointed beyond to where Walt sat at a table, alone, his big felt hat on the floor against his chair, his old gray coat sagging with papers and books. He was delighted to see them. He had been writing on a large sheet of white paper, but now, he listened with complete happy absorption as Dave's words came tumbling out, recounting their lark. "And so, finally, we had to go to Niblo's!" Dave ended.

"And after, we heard a lady, lecturing with the delicate sweet voice on her," Po said, a little grimly, "with her small hands tumbling, down around our heads all the great pillars, and jaunting jibes at everyone to make them walk free!"

Walt turned all his attention to Po, studying her face. He spoke finally, in a gentle tone. "And what did you think of that?"

But this time Po was ready for him—ready to show him how unfair anyone, including herself, was, to expect her to stand alone. "All I could think was that it's little the likes of her would know of being shivery or empty of food or having to fight against the Eaters do be creeping at all times about the world to devour others!" Po was angry at everybody now. "She like as not has a neat round yearly sum from her granddad"—Po was sarcastic—"with her talking so brawny. And like as not a mighty husband, and four roaring brothers to protect her at all times, and be standing up to take the heavy fists in the face for her. Easy enough to be brave then!"

Walt's eyes dwelt on Po, but he was silent. Finally, almost angrily, she glanced up at him, feeling his look.

But his eyes were looking at her with sober tenderness. Po began to feel uneasy again, seeing how he looked through and far beyond her, the like he expected her to be a great deal more than a smallish Irish girl with nothing much to her but some songs.

Then he pulled out of his coat pocket a mass of notebooks, loose sheets, folded papers. He searched through them until he found a single sheet he looked for. Then his large hand with the blond hair on its back gently shoved the paper toward her, until it was under her eyes.

He began to chat with Dave then, about the doings in Rome's print shop, and whether the Atlantics or Excelsiors had a better team.

The handwriting was simple, neither massive nor too fine, and even though it had been interlined and scratched out many a time, it was plain enough to read, the like she couldn't pretend she couldn't.

"Not I, any one else, can travel the road for you,
You must travel it for yourself,
It is not far, it is within reach,
Perhaps you have been on it since you were born and did
   not know.
Perhaps it is everywhere on water and on land."

She came to some scribbled-out lines, then went on.

"Shoulder your duds, dear child, and I will mine, and let us
   hasten forth,
Wonderful cities and free nations we will fetch as we go.
Long have you timidly waded, holding a plank by the shore,
Now I will you to be a bold swimmer,
To jump off in the midst of the sea, rise again, and nod to
   me, shout, and laughingly dash your hair!"

Even on the ferry going home, Po felt stirred up, vaguely angry at herself, at everyone. She wished she hadn't brought the argument up. She felt worse than ever! Instead of expelling the first roisterers, all she had done was to let more of Walt's words slip in to disturb the snug safety of the inn.

Chapter Nineteen

P O STOOD surprised, for this was the first time that Larry had come up to the door of the flat, the first time he had ever sought her out like this. She glanced at his face eagerly. But his eyes looked troubled as he said, "Po, could I talk to you?"

She snatched up a fichu for her shoulders, and closed the door after her. Going down the stairs with him, she seemed to float buoyantly.

But in Fulton Street, they could not talk over the loud grind of the horsecars, the rush of foot traffic. "Come on," he said impatiently, "we'll walk out toward the Heights. Quieter there!"

She cast a speculative look at him. Maybe he had heard about her trip with Dave and was jealous. She sighed a little. There was something disturbed and urgent in his manner, but she was afraid it was not about her. Hymes? She remembered her fear as she saw the cold planning look on Hymes's face after Larry spoke out against him at the dinner. She'd heard that Selfridge, Hymes's man, had gone to Grogan, foreman at Van Leyn's, to demand Larry be fired. But the story went that Grogan, a baseball crank, retorted that if anyone thought he, Grogan, was going to fire the best pitcher in Brooklyn right before the Atlantic game, they were crazy.

Whatever it was, she could see that to Larry, it was some kind of a crisis.

"Is it Hymes done something to hurt you?" she ventured as they hurried along.

"Huh!" Larry said scornfully, not slacking his pace. "About the only way he could hurt me is to break my pitching arm. I'd like to see him try." And he made a big fist.

"What trouble has struck you, then!"

"I had a letter from my mother!" the words leaped out with bitterness. "A crewman on the New Bedford packet saw me here. She sent my uncle Adams down to talk to me! I told him I was staying! Yesterday, this came!" He thrust the letter at Po, as if getting rid of a burden he should never have been expected to carry.

As Po read, the black curlicues on the white paper seemed to curl upward with small grasping fingers. "Dear Son: Your uncle, Dr. Bradford Wainwright, informs me I am ill of a heart ailment, and need you by me at all times. I know your duty to your mother will not be forgotten. Your uncle Adams tells me with pain and shame, of your being a vagrant workman in a shipyard, squandering your life on that game of base. But, your mother does not blame you, dear little son. I foresaw you would need our help. For, my son, you could be the best ball player in the world, and it would amount to nothing. I believe and pray you will yet make a success of yourself in some business or profession that your uncles and I and everyone here can respect. But we can talk of this when you return. I enclose money for packet fare, which should bring you at once, as my condition is serious."

Why should he be so deeply upset, he with his shouting he was his own boss? But he was looking at Po, expecting something of her, as if he had shown her his hurt place and she was slow at doing anything about it. "'Tis only a letter," she faltered, handing it to him.

"But, I don't know what to do!" he burst out, almost petulantly, taking the letter unwillingly as if he did not want to pick up its burden again.

Engrossed in the letter, Po had hardly noticed as they passed the narrow-shouldered brownstone houses—Mamie's dream of elegance—nor paid much attention as the houses thinned, and finally there were no more houses. The brick street had turned into a stone walk through low shrubs and trees, the stone walk had widened into a terrace or platform of flat stones, along a stone wall set into the bluff.

Larry walked toward the wall and plumped down, half sitting on the guard rail that ran along its top. The wall had evidently been built to keep the bluff from crumbling into the marsh below. He sat, legs spread apart, as if waiting for her to help him.

But, seeing the muddy marsh below, with its dank weeds and glints of water showing through, Po was suddenly reminded of the Bog at Necroe, in the north country where they had lived when she was very small. And remembering the Bog at Necroe, and what had happened to her there when she was a little girl, she suddenly wanted Larry to comfort her.

She stepped close into him between his spread knees. His troubled gray eyes were on a level with hers. But he, intent on his own problems, glanced quickly at her, with a little surprised frown, as if to say, "This is no time for fooling!" Then he reddened. "Better not lean against me!" He held her away from him. "I don't know how strong this support is!" Then he glanced at her as if not understanding why she didn't help him at once with his problem.

He got up, impatiently, and walked back to where the trees began, and Po followed him. He flung himself down on a fallen tree, the heavy man-sinews of shoulders bulging, hands, strong enough to pick up a hogshead, slack between his knees. But his eyes implored Po, "Do something! Get me out of this!"

"Is it sick she is, truly?"

"I don't know!" he burst out. "One thing I know"—he kicked some clay viciously—"if I'm going good, look out! She seems to be able to pick, like a witch, the moment to trip me! To spoil whatever I'm trying to do, make it seem nothing!"

He seized hold of a good-sized branch on the dead tree, jerked it off, with one splintering pull. "I don't care if she doesn't like it—it means more to me to pitch against the Atlantics and win, to get to play the Knickerbockers, than to rub together some money got by smart tricks as a lawyer or ship broker back in New Bedford!" He lashed the near-by shrubs with the branch. "Why does she think I have to earn the prizes she sets up? I'll set up my own prizes!"

And Po saw that, because this was the first prize he had set up himself, the first weight he tried to lift alone, it was all important for him that it come about. And now, added to all her other feelings about playing the Knickerbockers, was this: To someone else it would only be a game. To Larry, at this moment, it was a matter of heavier weight.

"Why don't you just forget the letter," she began, but he broke in impatiently, frowning.

"But, you read it! She says she's sick! And doesn't she know just how to get me off my stride! To make me feel guilty!"

Po remembered having thought of Gulliver, a giant, pinned down to a strand by a thousand slender cords, when Larry had first talked of his mother. The giant had risen, walked off, but the cords must have been woven by a sorceress, for they dangled, tripping him. And even as he tried to fight free of them, he looked imploringly at Po, as if to cry out to her, "I can't walk without help!"

Po felt a surprising surge of something almost like triumph. He'd gone off with Louise for the night, all right, shouting his strength, but when he needed help, tenderness, he'd come to Po. She crossed to him, put her hand on his shoulders. There were, maybe, compensations in being a "good girl." And, maybe, too—more ways than one of being carried.

Suddenly, he put his arms around her waist, leaned forward and

141

buried his face in her small warm breast. Po felt a strange heady feeling go through her. A feeling of sure, absolute power. How easy it was to pick up the trailing cords, to fasten them down.

She stroked his bright hair. Then she heard her voice, calm, sure, as if knowing, without doubt, exactly what he should do. "Now then, you must go at once to the people you know on the packet line. You must get them to find out is she sick, or what way she is at all!"

He sighed as though his tensions were loosening. Then he looked up at her and nodded. Po felt a strange sense of guilt. He nodded again, obediently, unquestioningly. She had the feeling if she had told him to go home to New Bedford, he might have gone with the same relieved nod.

He took her hand to start back then, for he was overdue at some practice. But it was surprising what small comfort it was to feel his big warm clasp. Po drew her hand away. You could think she was punishing herself for something, depriving herself of the joy of walking back, hand in hand, with him.

"I guess I'll be staying here the while," she said miserably, "to watch the ships go in and out."

And as she watched his big form hurrying away, she had again the strange feeling of guilt.

Po turned away impatiently. The divil take it all! Wasn't she destroyed enough these days with her quivers and qualms about leaving Brian's, and now what must she do but add to it this strange feeling about Larry!

She went out to the railing and looked below. But the view of the marsh was small comfort, for it reminded her again of the Bog at Necroe, and the lesson she had learned there. And now that it had started, the memory of Necroe rose in her like marsh water. For even though she had been but a paistin, she still remembered the sensations of that time when she had to struggle across the dark bog alone. And she could never forget it had happened because she wanted to explore with feet and hands as well as eyes, all by herself, the silver tracks in the bog.

She had gone with her father along the sea wall, and as usual, at the high place, he had carried her. But that day, the longing to explore by herself overcame her. She had jumped from his arms, sped back along the wall to the lower end, sprung off and tried to run down a silver track. Cold sludge rose over her ankles, her knees. When she looked back, her father had been lying beside the wall. He had jumped after her, or had fallen, startled.

He did not answer her wail. After bleak ages, men came and carried him away. They paid no attention to her. They thought she was able to take care of herself. And so, fearful, wary, alert every second, having, terrified, to decide when the earth before her was quicksand or not, she found, finally, the few inches of firm earth, and, with the desperate necessity not to slip, to keep on it, she struggled out alone.

Po sighed deeply. Her father had been sick a long time after that, she remembered, and it was about that time her mother died. But she knew it was not only the actual memory of that day at Necroe that stayed with her. It was the deep inner knowing it had taught her. You could start out brawny and roaring across the bog, but if you lost your footing, there was no one to carry you. And she often thought of the dark world out there as a bog. It was dangerous! One could hear often the despairing cry, see the hands disappear as someone slipped.

And it seemed to her some people moved over the bog, bent over with the weight of those who insisted on being carried. Others went alone, with fearful eyes on the ground. Others—and these she loved to think of—went surefooted, nimble, looking at clouds or marsh birds, seeming never to worry about the path!

"Arrah, now," she told herself scornfully, "is it for a safe warm shelter I'd be willing to give Brian the hard trouble; or if I don't, but let Mamie rule my life, never be free or independent, or self-willed?

"Whist!" she thought ruefully. "And who is this sneering at food and a warm bed and safety?" It had not been so long but she could remember how it felt to go the day with but a piece of bread. And how it felt to come in after twelve hours in the mill, fingers mumbling with cold, to a fireless room. And how it felt to have the vicious supercargo of the *Tanager* advancing toward her. "And isn't it only that I've been living here fat and easy this while, I can think so scornful of bread and fire and safety?"

For she faced now what she had always sensed, even before Brian talked to her. She was a cause of tension in the flat. Telling herself she was a help and comfort to Brian was only a way of excusing herself for letting him carry her. Wanting to use people—that's what got everything mixed up. Maybe that's what made Brian so unsure of his own footing. He loved Mamie, yes, but he wanted to use her, too. He wanted her to give him children.

Lights began to come on over in Manhattan, so that it glowed like an enchanted island. Walt's words, written on the scrap of paper she had seen at Pfaff's, came gently tapping at her mind, not roistering now, but sober and serene.

"I nor anyone else can travel the road for you,
    You must travel it for yourself—"

The wind had swept the evening sky clear of all the ragged clouds now. Po felt curiously empty and spent, too. Things came to her sad, but rubbed clean and clear. She sighed. For all the time, waiting in there had been the final window shade inside herself she had not wanted to lift.

It was the guilty feeling she had about Larry.

For soon, he'd know if his mother were sick or not. Soon he'd come back crying for help. Not to Louise! Louise wasn't a "good girl" like his mother. He'd come crying to Po! And all Po would have to do was tell him what to do. It was easy as sin. Why, she could weave those cords fine and strong as the woman in New Bedford, fastening the giant to the ground again!

And when Larry came back crying to Po, would she be able to, maybe, ridicule him, sting him, push his head out of her lap?

Evening chill began to soak into her and she shivered.

Po wondered at herself. For she had quit off Fall River alone, without all this twisting and turning. She had stowed on the ship, jumped into the water; and in Ireland, too, she had fronted dangers, yes, even the time long ago, she had struggled out of the bog. Why should she be destroying herself now with her "will I or won't I?"

This was a more delicate, troublous thing, she saw. "For those times what was I doing but saving my own skin! It had been 'live!' or 'die!' This is for someone else, for Brian, for Larry."

This was her first free decision, she guessed, removed away from bread and fire or safety. Larry would soon be making his first free decision too, to tell his mother no, or not. But he wouldn't have to make it. Po would make it for him. Or would she?

With the wind down, the world seemed quiet, listening for her answer. A ripple of light glimmered over the water from a mooring lantern, she could hear the jangle of some boat watchman's keys. Inside, she felt as flat and gray as the sky. All the excitement was gone. You knew just how everything was. No one was going to carry you, and you had to be responsible, too, for not hobbling anyone else. Being a woman grown, she guessed, was not going to be much fun. There was a price attached to the joy of standing on your own two feet.

For she knew she must start out alone again, not only to help Brian, but to get away from Larry, not be at hand for him. Otherwise she would not be able to keep her hands off the trailing cords.

Chapter Twenty

To BE ALIVE in that place in that little space of time before the Atlantic-Excelsior play-off was to feel that game was the most important thing in the world. Oh, perhaps the inhabitants of the streets running along the Heights were above it all. The others seemed as if possessed.

And the town was not divided in any comfortable geographical way in two camps. It was honeycombed. The teams already eliminated in the play-offs lined up fiercely on one side or the other. And with them, their families, friends, and team partisans. You were an Atlantic or an Excelsior. You were regarded with suspicion until it was known clearly which. Partisanship made jagged cracks across families, dulled or fanned romances. Life in the town took on somewhat the excitement of wartime. It was complicated. One must walk warily. And on all sides there was discrimination. There were the minor discriminations, like Mr. Schultz, the butcher, an Atlantic, giving all the good cuts of meat to the wives of the Atlantics. It was some time before Mamie, who loathed the very word baseball, realized why her cuts of meat were now always skimped, stringy, and gristly. In Mr. Schultz's mind, Brian's wife was "one of them Excelsiors."

Or if you glanced down Middagh Street at nightfall, when the lamplighter was lighting the lamps, and saw that he lit some lamps and left others dark, you had no doubt the lamplighter was an Excelsior and the areas left unlighted were inhabited by clusters of Atlantics.

There were major discriminations, too. For instance, law enforcement was a chancy thing. When the boys of the Excelsior Muffins engaged the boys of the Atlantic Bantams with stones in a pitched battle on York Street, householders kept indoors and only ran for the police when too many windows were broken. Since the two policemen who came were Atlantics, naturally, they assumed only the Excelsior Muffins should be taken in. But at the cell-house, Mr. Waters, the Chief, was an Excelsior. Naturally, he let them go.

Reverend Ginty, of the Reformed Church, seemed to be discriminating, too, and most unfairly, when he prayed for an Atlantic victory. What was he trying to do, get an advance word in at Headquarters? But when Reverend Bell, of the United Church, who was as good a man as Ginty, prayed for an Excelsior triumph, why one plea cancelled the other.

The *Eagle* and *Journal* and *Times* at first printed what they thought to be non-discriminatory accounts of the two teams. But when editions were torn up and buildings mud-smeared, they learned it was impossible to be neutral enough.

But it was in the matter of transportation that life became really difficult, especially if you had to ride a horsecar or a ferry boat to work.

If the horsecar driver was an Atlantic, and you, a flagrant, known Excelsior, were waiting on a corner, do you think the driver would sully his car with you? Certainly not. You could stand there till you rotted.

Once, a pitched battle broke out in a horsecar, between Atlantic and Excelsior partisans, and at its height the horses bolted. As they plunged down Fulton Street, the horsecar careening from side to side, pedestrians scattering before it, the battle inside never stopped until the horses ran themselves out and the car stopped and then both sides carried their injured away.

But it was on the ferries that war was waged to the hilt.

It had begun with Rooster O'Hanlon, who played second base on the Excelsiors and who was a deck hand on the Fulton Ferry.

It had always been the custom, if a passenger could be seen running down the hill to the ferry, to wait for him, and like as not when he came aboard, there was a cheer. But, one morning, Rooster, seeing the person racing for the ferry was one of the blackest of the Atlantics, gave the three taps on the bell and the ferry started.

However, there were Atlantics aboard. The Atlantics knocked out the wheelman, and ran the boat back and picked up the stranded Atlantic, amid wild cheers from their partisans.

Next morning, the Excelsiors were ready for them. They gathered in a compact knot at the wooden arch. When Rooster's boat came in, they rushed aboard, the gate was clanged shut, three bells sounded and the boat took off, leaving all the waiting Atlantics, many of whom worked in the shipyards on Corlears Hook, on shore. Naturally, the Excelsiors called back unkind words, and naturally, the Atlantics tried to pull up cobbles to throw, but the ferry was too far out by that time.

Then some Atlantic, brooding on the glory of his side, figured out a way to let the world know the Excelsiors were nothing but low-flung ruffians. With some others, he managed to substitute, in the night, the ferry used to carry horse manure from the city stables to Long Island, for the ferry used in the early morning. The Atlantics, warned, used the Hamilton Avenue Ferry that day, and the Excelsiors were shunned by sniffing people all day.

Mr. Grogan, the foreman at the shipyard, was a baseball crank. But he was also an astute man. He took advantage, one day, of all this free floating energy. By carrying back and forth belittling remarks, he managed to pit the shipwrights who were on the Excelsior side against those who were on the Atlantic side. In a single day, he got half the curved frames fitted to the heavy keel pieces of a packet just put down. Nicholas Van Leyn, visiting his yard that afternoon from his office in Wall Street in New York, was surprised and pleased to see the packet for some reason so far advanced.

But feeling among the men got pretty tense, and it was carried over, that evening, to Brady's.

Long before this, it had seemed to Brian wise, if anyone were to have their ale in peace, to draw a chalk line down the middle of the floor. On one side Atlantics, on the other, Excelsiors. On this particular evening, Clarabel came in, and crossed over on the Excelsior side of the chalk line, chatting with Brian.

Now it was rumored that Clarabel had offered to sleep with the first man to make a home run, regardless of team. This was probably a libel, but hysteria had mounted to such a pitch, that now, as Clarabel stood on the Excelsior side, chatting and listening to the talk, some of the Excelsiors gave her black looks. After all, her brother, Restored, was an Atlantic. Others muttered and moved away from her. Suddenly someone yelled, "She's a spy! Put her back over on the other side!"

But the Bull intervened. He gave the man, who would have pushed Clarabel over the chalk line, a great shove, not bothering to hit him with a closed fist. Then he gallantly seized Clarabel around the waist.

"Come on over with a good ball team!" he growled.

The teams had to move around to secret practice places, too. The Excelsiors often went out to Prospect Hill. The tollgate keeper on the Flat Bush Road was an Excelsior, and with a few handy boys by his side, it was very difficult for any Atlantic to get past the tollgate if the Excelsiors were at practice beyond.

Once, Po, walking in the street, met Dave Posen. With a conspiratorial air, he motioned her to one side.

"We found out where the Atlantics are practicing this evening. We want someone they don't know to go see if they're working out a strange pitcher, besides the Bull."

Po's eyes lit, color flamed into her cheeks with excitement. "I'll go!" She felt like a new recruit suddenly entrusted with a secret mission for a general. Larry would be pleased with her, too. Dave whispered directions, and like true conspirators, they parted quickly, with no more words.

Po walked rapidly, repeating directions. "Up DeKalb to Cumberland. Down Cumberland to Lafayette." She kept walking rapidly. After a while she came to the lane with the high board fence at the end. This was it. The fence ran around two sides of an open place. Men and a few women stood about, watching the play intently. No one seemed to pay any special attention to her as she slipped in quietly.

Yes, there was the Bull pitching. Twinkle-Toes was catcher.

She remembered this Twinkle-Toes. She remembered seeing him, the day after she arrived, in that early dawn work-bound stream of men and women. Sodden and gray, an old cap pulled down on his head, he had gone hunching along toward the Iron Works.

She'd been with Dave in Twinkle-Toes' house since then. He lived, like many of the others, in a three-story wooden building, a family to a floor. Knowing now that most of the men earned one dollar and fifty cents a day, Po had not been too surprised to find Twinkle-Toes' wife, shoulders hunched over and eyes squinted under an oil lamp, making artificial flowers.

If at first Po might have wondered how these men could work twelve or fourteen hours, then throw themselves into this game as if possessed, she felt closer to them now, and dimly understood.

As she watched him, Twinkle-Toes cupped two hands to his mouth, and let out his full lung power, yelling at a fielder, who threw him the ball. She watched Twinkle-Toes catch it with sure hands. Yes, she thought she understood why they were so possessed.

With a sure flick of the wrist, you could catch the ball. A problem was solved. Out there, on the field, you were expert, equal to all occasions. Sometimes your foot slipped, or your hand or eye was not quite quick enough, and you didn't catch the bullet of lightning that was the ball. Sometimes someone else was faster than you. But usually you were out there battling with ease and speed and great skill. You were a great fellow. You could win! Sometimes you lost, but that simply put an edge of excitement on the battle. The big thing was—you *could* win. You often did. And it was a glorious feeling.

And when you turned away and talked it all over in Brady's or Dent's, that was wonderful, too, and prolonged the wonderful feeling that if you were just skillful enough, and fast enough, and tough enough, everything could be solved. You *could* win.

Suddenly, in her soul, Po committed a black disloyalty. She didn't care which team won! It didn't matter! What mattered was they have the recognition, the dignity, the acceptance, of getting to play with the Knickerbockers, the big team, the champions! She could hear Hans Schmidt saying fiercely, "We wanta be first in something!"

But this disloyalty was only for a moment. Then she remembered she was a spy on a secret mission, and she became an Excelsior again. She watched the play, memorizing who was playing where.

It was then Po experienced what it was like to be a discovered spy in enemy territory. At first, she just felt two of the men looking at her. Then a woman whispered to a man, staring at her. Three turned and stared. Then four or five moved toward her, surrounded her, blocking her view. They stared, stonily. One of them must have recognized her as Brian's cousin, an Excelsior in girl's clothing! Po felt terror. She turned and ran. One of the men started after her, but as she sped away, he turned and went back. Po's heart was pounding. Her first assignment as an Excelsior—and scared off! She hoped Dave didn't tell Larry.

Next day, something happened that caused all the intensity about the game to spurt up with an even more zestful flame.

Coventry Van Leyn dropped in at Brady's again, to order bat sticks for a friend. Young Van Leyn told them the Knickerbockers were holding a general club meeting on Thursday. At that meeting, he would officially present the Brooklyn challenge!

The test with the Knickerbockers, so long deferred it had begun almost to seem like some legendary tournament, would actually soon be scheduled! The flame spurted up so high perhaps it was just as well the Atlantic-Excelsior play-off was at hand. Emotions were getting too explosive.

Chapter Twenty-one

IT WAS KNOWN from the first the game could never be played on the home grounds of either the Atlantics or the Excelsiors. The field on Wheat Hill, at the summit of Hewes and Marcy, had been picked as large enough and—it was hoped—sufficiently neutral.

The streets took on a deserted look that day, as the clock on City Hall neared one—game time. A woman from an isolated farm on Long Island, teaming down Fulton Street to the barber to have a tooth drawn, discovered his shop closed. When she found the Emporium, then the Hay and Feed Store, and the Tax Office locked, she suddenly whipped up her team for home. Maybe cholera had come again.

Afterward Po heard how, in the courthouse, about that time, a lawyer addressed the court: "Judge, my client, Harv Gilbert, wasn't even around when the money was stolen. He has witnesses! Four of them!"

"Four!" The judge glared indignantly. "Why, that'll take us all afternoon!" He stuck out his lower lip. "This hearing's postponed till tomorrow! Sheriff, put the prisoner back in the cell-house!"

Everyone moved quickly toward the door. They were late now. But the prisoner let out a scream of outrage that could be heard on Court Street. "A stinking, low-down trick! All you runnin' to that game, and puttin' me back in jail! It's inhuman and cruel!"

The judge sat down again, pursed his lips, and pulled his ear. "Tell you what, sheriff! Put the cuffs on Harv, and take him along with you to the game! That way, nobody can complain!"

It worked out fine, except the sheriff was an Excelsior and Harv an Atlantic.

The factories, the foundries, the yards were emptied, too.

At Van Leyn's, the foreman Grogan, who would as soon have missed the game as lose his right eye, had arranged for a shortage of materials that day, and the yard closed at noon.

But at Hymes's, it was not so simple. William Hymes, who spent most of his time in his office on Washington Street, where he handled his other business affairs as well, employed a superintendent to run the Iron Works. The superintendent did not dare to close the plant. Everyone, of course, took the afternoon off, but with loss of pay.

Some of the more spirited girls at the hoopskirt factory petitioned for the afternoon. When the request reached the office in New York, straight-laced Simon Quimby said he thought it unwise for the girls to go, and said no.

Po had no trouble in finding Wheat Hill. She'd gone there to the Eckford game. Now, as she came up to the immense crowd standing about the field, she could feel the almost unbearable tension. This game had been argued and weighed in every cranny of Brooklyn. Who could guess the winner? Even the weather seemed uncertain and chancy, with masses of stormy torn clouds passing over a gray sky.

Po worked her way through the crowd. She wanted to get close enough to the bench along the third base line where the Excelsiors sat to feel she was one with them.

The crowd bubbled and seethed. Why didn't the game begin? A rumor went about they were waiting on Death-to-Flying-Things, left fielder for the Excelsiors, the teamster at Quimby's. Perhaps he couldn't get away!

Then Po heard a sound like the twittering of many birds. Triumphantly cracking his great whip in the air, came Death-to-Flying-Things, driving his big-wheeled dray right across the open grass toward the playing space. Packed in the dray were the girls from the hoopskirt factory. Death-to-Flying-Things had told them, "If everybody takes the afternoon off, can he fire all of you?"

Now the referee bugled through his heavy brown beard the magic words. "Pla-ay Ba-a-wl!" They came just in time. One more moment of compression, and all the corked-up hope and uncertainty might have exploded of its own power.

Tony Zambrini's bat stick connected with the Bull's pitch with an electrifying crack. The crowd let out a deep roar. The Atlantic-Excelsior game had begun.

But the Atlantic third baseman, chunky Gus Bering, who owned the Hay and Feed Store on Washington Street, caught Tony's ball on the bound. Tony was out. Then Bushel Basket and Hans Schmidt, a little edgy, struck out. But the Excelsior crowd wasn't worried. The boys were trying too hard, that was all!

Po stood on tiptoe, now, to see who would come in to pitch for the Excelsiors. This had been a touchy and debated thing. It was felt Tony, long the Excelsior pitcher, should have a chance at the Atlantics. Tony came in. Po guessed that Larry, who was a good fielder, too, would be fitted in when needed.

Now the Bull stood, massy shoulders and arms bulging under the gray Atlantic uniform, enormous hands waving the bat stick. Tony pitched. Cr-l-mp! The Bull knocked a crusher far out in right field. By the time Big Billy Beiderstein got the ball in, the Bull stood triumphantly on second base. The Atlantic crowd screamed their ecstasy. This was it! He was their boy! The Bull would win for them.

Restored Jones came up to strike. Across the field, Po could see Restored's granddaddy, the light shining on his faded Revolutionary soldier's coat and his white beard, as he danced up and down, screaming, "Kill 'em, Restored!" But Restored struck out.

Then Twinkle-Toes topped the ball and beat Tony's throw to first. Now with the Bull on third and Twinkle-Toes on first, Johnny Kosansky, Atlantic second baseman, came up to strike. Johnny—Po knew from Dave—worked nights in a tailor shop on Gold Street and studied law in Columbia College days. Johnny struck to right field. The Bull and Twinkle-Toes came in. The score stood two for the Atlantics, nothing for the Excelsiors.

"And wouldn't you think no one ever made a score before, the way those wind-baggy Atlantics are screaming?" Po muttered. And the Excelsior crowd yelled, "Just wait till we get started!"

But somehow, all the luck seemed to fall in those braggy Atlantics' lap. The Atlantics, discovering Big Billy in the right field was a weak spot, kept trying to hit there. Every time they got through, the Atlantics carried on and bellowed their triumph. It was all right to yell, Po thought, but those Atlantics had the nasty gloating way with them. Wasn't there any justice in heaven? Were they to have all the luck?

The Excelsior crowd were still cheerful, though, yelling encouragement to their favorite players. But in the next innings, bad luck dogged them again. At the end of the third innings, the unbelievable score stood eight to nothing in favor of the Atlantics! The Excelsior crowd looked at one another out of the corners of their eyes. Was it possible they could *lose?*

Now Larry came in to pitch for the Excelsiors. Tony replaced Big Billy at right field. The Excelsiors drew a deep breath. Weren't they the great and mighty Excelsiors? They'd show 'em!

Watching, Po understood why the Excelsiors had kept Larry hidden.

Even she could see he had the Atlantic strikers confused. He had a peculiar wrist throw, and you'd almost think, if such a thing were possible, the ball made a curved path instead of a straight one. But he only sneaked this in now and again. Sometimes he'd throw a slow ball. Sometimes a hard straight fast one. The strikers were not used to this. Larry struck three men out.

The Excelsior crowd, now feeling the righteous had at last been given the nod by heaven, let loose their pent-up feelings! The great satisfied shout that rose to the Brooklyn sky seemed to bounce back from the bank of gray clouds overhead.

In the fifth innings, Larry held the Atlantics hitless. Then Bushel Basket, that brave and brawny darling of the world, made a home run for the Excelsiors. Rooster and Death-to-Flying-Things both scored in front of him.

The Atlantics began to get that dogged look now. Their partisans were yelling, loud, but sharper, and excited.

By the end of the sixth innings, the game was flowing in a different direction. The score stood eight for the Atlantics and seven for the Excelsiors.

Both crowds were beside themselves now. They yelled excitedly at every move. Dull roars of pain rose when a man struck out, high ecstatic screams at a run, full-throated yells of triumph as the score mounted.

And now, too, the Atlantic crowd began to shout sarcastic words at Larry. He was somehow taking advantage of their side, with his sneaky throws. But Larry kept steadily on, pitching brilliantly, as if he were enjoying himself, mixing the balls up, bewildering the strikers.

Perhaps emotions that day had been too wrought upon. Perhaps if the game had gone more steadily, without such sharp teetering, nothing would have happened. But, at that moment, the Bull came up to strike.

He combed two enormous hands through his great black beard, picked up his mighty bat stick like it was a war club, and strode to the plate. Larry stood eyeing him a moment. Then he made the mistake of smiling.

The Bull glowered at him. The crowd began to heckle. Larry threw. The Bull gave a mighty swing, and drove the ball on a low line directly at Larry. Before Larry could put his hand out, it hit him smartly on the shin. It knocked his feet out from under him. He fell prone.

Instantly, the Excelsiors screamed murder, and swarmed on the field.

"So! They can't beat us at ball! They got to kill our pitcher!"

The Atlantic crowd rushed onto the field, too, to protect their players. The playing space was a mass of angry men, demanding fair play, and offering to kill anyone who touched any of their players.

Po caught a moment's glimpse of Larry, hands cupped to his mouth, red-faced, screaming that he was all right. He had not been hurt. Just knocked off his feet. But it was no use. Taut emotions had exploded. The immense crowd swirled and shoved over the field, screaming for fair play.

Now Po saw the referee standing on his chair, screaming, "This here game's called!" But no one paid any attention to him.

In all the angry voices and confusion, something came to Po more important than screaming for the Excelsiors. They had to have a champion to put up against the Knickerbockers! It was needful for their souls. And now this! A spluttering off of all their fine zest.

She saw Larry, a ring of players around him, haranguing them, red-faced, excited. More players and some of the crowd gathered around this knot, listening. Then she saw Larry, and this knot of people, move off the field, and heard a shout, "Goin' to Brady's!"

When Po came into the Gardens, Brian was behind the bar, but leaning far over, listening to someone talking. The Atlantic and Excelsior players, and their flame-hot followers who had left the brawling field and come here, were gathered in an intent, frowning knot, listening to someone. Po recognized Larry's voice. But, even as she watched, the group broke. Some walked away, disgusted, muttering. But Larry's voice became more positive, more insistent.

"—because what is it we been trying to do?" he was demanding.

"Git a champion!" said Twinkle-Toes.

"Sure—but why?" Larry's voice was quick and loud.

"Settle it, that's why!"

"No! We want to beat the Knickerbockers. That Knickerbocker—that young Van Leyn—the one that was here for the bat sticks—he told us he'd deliver our challenge sure this week, didn't he? And where are we? We haven't even got a champion team to meet them!"

The Bull slapped a big open hand down on the bar. "We'll have us another play-off tomorrow!"

"And feeling so worked up now, everyone ready to murder? How would it end? In a lot of bloody heads this time!"

"There ain't no Atlantics that's scared of bloody heads!"

"The Excelsiors aren't scared of anything either. But how's that going to beat the Knickerbockers?"

"Yeah—and that's what we need to do!" Twinkle-Toes put in, frowning. "We need that! You know what them Knicks remind me of? A big fat man sittin' on a box, keepin' out all the air and light! And who's in that box? We are! I hear they's a lot of baseball clubs around the country. I bet we're good enough to beat any of 'em. But we ain't never goin' to be anythin' but a bunch of neighborhood clubs fightin' among ourselves until we blast them Knicks off that box!"

"Who's arguin'?" said the Bull.

"And if we play off again, and another fight, nothing's going to be changed!"

"We got to get us the best team there is!" Larry said, hot, excited, his eyes darting around, his color high. "So good no one can stand before it!"

"That's what we been tryin' to do!"

"We know ourselves it was a pretty fine balance between the Atlantics and Excelsiors! But what if we had all the good players on one team!"

"All the good players on the Atlantics and Excelsiors?" Twinkle-Toes frowned, surprised.

"No! All the good players in Brooklyn!" Larry ran his fingers through his bright hair excitedly, frowning, excited, intent. "Let every club put forward their best men!"

"You ain't been in Brooklyn long, son! They'd kill each other decidin'!" Bushel Basket snorted.

"I don't think so!" Larry was quick and positive.

Twinkle-Toes spoke now. He was still frowning thoughtfully, and his words came slower. "If it means beatin' the Knicks—If it means bein' champion of the world—" He looked around at the others now as though some vision were rising in him. "For that—maybe we could forget that stuff—! For that, we could all be blood brothers!"

Dave spoke in a rush of words now, excited. "Larry! You mean, have the Bull and Johnny Kosansky, and you and Bushel Basket and Tony all on one team!"

"And there's more!" Larry was excited. "Who do you think could beat a team like that?"

"No one!" Dave's eyes glowed.

There was silence. But the men were looking into space, with a

154

kind of dawning brightness on their face, or a half-smile, thinking of all the wealth of skill, of nimbleness they had to draw on! Of the sheer undefeatability of such a team!

"Bushel Basket could be catcher," said Twinkle-Toes softly, almost dreamily. Bushel Basket was an Excelsior, and Twinkle-Toes was the Atlantic catcher.

"And Curly Vos of the Putnams, at center," someone breathed, half-smiling, dreamily.

"Naw! Johnnie Hutchens, that Eckford fellow!"

"To pick a team like that, golly," Larry said, "that can't be done here, in a minute! We got to think about it, stew about it—"

"Brother!" Twinkle-Toes broke in. "A team like that! We gotta *pray* about it!"

"If we can pick 'em without favor," Larry said, "we got enough good players in Brooklyn, to make a—team of champions!"

Now they began to look at the Bull out of the corner of their eyes. He had not said a word. If he didn't go along, it was no use. The crowd would go with him.

"I been studyin'," he said finally. He scratched his shock of wiry black hair. "Now, *I'm* good. I'm *real* good—and the Atlantics is *pretty* good! But a whole team like that—why, they'd be *real* good, too! It'd be like Larry says—so good no one could stand before it!" It was all right! The Bull agreed! Now everyone began enjoying the idea, rolling it over and adding to it.

"The players oughtn't to be selected by the club!" Dave's words came out with a rush and excitement. "There's bound to be human feelings enter into this! Now, we all know who's the best individual players in Brooklyn. Everyone ought to pick 'em!"

Brian spoke. "That's a wise thing you speak there. Davey boy! Let's drink to it!"

Brian set up a long row of glasses along the bar. He brought out the Bushmill's. The fact that Brian, who rarely drank, poured a glass for himself, added to the solemnity of the occasion.

Each man raised his glass. Po felt a little cold chill run down her spine and her breath came fast. It was a kind of dedication, she felt. She was still an Excelsior, yes, but she was part of a broader, deeper thing now.

In spirit, she raised a glass, too. Sleante! Abu! Up the Brooklyn team!

Chapter Twenty-two

EXCITED TALK about the new team still ran high in the barroom, but Po, though she wanted to hear it, slipped out. The moment had come. Even though she'd planned it for several days, she began to feel an empty sensation in her stomach like hunger, though she wasn't hungry—only maybe a little scared.

In the kitchen in back of the barroom, the African cook glanced up from his stove inquiringly. "Will you give this to Brian Brady?" She handed the cook the note she had written earlier. "That time he is through this evening!"

The cook nodded, mouth agape, and Po moved quickly to the outdoor gardens. From back of piled chairs, where she had placed it that morning, she picked up the box with her belongings. Out through the garden gate, down Fulton, she walked swiftly, not allowing herself a glance back.

But when she reached the arched ferry gate, the incoming ferry was still far out in the river. She looked back up the hill then, to where, warm together, Dave and Brian and Larry talked in the barroom. She wanted the boat to come in quickly. Waiting, you got thinking, and then—feeling. But, when she glanced out on the river again, and the ferry loomed large and close in, her hands turned cold as they gripped the cords around her box. Well, she was not going to turn back now.

Her own particular demon told her the time had come to go. Not only because of Larry, and her seeing it would be better for that lad if she were away from him for a while. Not only because of Brian and her knowing she was a cause of tension in the flat. These things, yes, and then, something more.

It was a stark flash she had of what was ahead. The Excelsior game had pointed it all up for her. Long ago, Mamie had announced that Po was to go to no more rowdy ball games. Yet it was unthinkable to Po, an Excelsior herself, that she not go. And Po saw she would always be involving Brian in trouble, or bowing down coward-like, or doing things underhandedly, the like in a year's time maybe she would hardly be knowing herself if she passed herself on the street, but would be asking, "Who is that miserable creature with no sap in her at all?"

So, knowing if she went to the Excelsior game, she could not go back to Brian's, she had gone.

She had not dared talk it over with Brian. He would be unhappy, feel he had failed her. It might cause him to quarrel with Mamie. Best go quietly, quickly, and let him know as soon as possible when she was safe and settled.

The incoming ferry sounded six strokes. Po picked up her box, paid her four pennies, and firmly went on board. The bell sounded three strokes, the ferry moved out into the water.

She walked up to the bow and sat down, not afraid of anyone seeing her, for everyone she knew had been at the Excelsior game. She was wearing the pale blue calico with the white nainsook chemisette, fastened at throat and wrists with narrow black velvet, and a white rice straw bonnet, with a cluster of forget-me-nots under the brim, and now, as the breeze from the river struck her, she tied the bonnet ribbons tightly under her chin. In her reticule was nearly ten dollars— the two she had when she came, and pocket money Brian had given her from time to time and she had not spent.

She had planned to go at once to some small, respectable hotel for the night, but, because the game had not been played to a finish, she had gotten away earlier than she expected. It was only about three o'clock. That was good. She could begin at once, this afternoon, to try to find a job. She would leave her box at the baggage office near the ferry. She had seen people leaving parcels and boxes there when she had crossed with Dave. Then, she would have several hours of daylight to try to get herself established, so she could begin at once to earn money.

Her plans were simple. She wanted to get a place singing. Christy had told her Irish songs were not wanted. She needed a chance to learn American songs like those the singer in Niblo's had sung. But that would take time. She must at once find some kind of a situation, anything, so she could live. This was the worst part of her plan, the beginning part, this was the uncertain, shaky part—trying to get herself that place.

The ferry pulled into the New York wharf and she felt its bump with a little tremor of scared excitement. She had crossed the river.

She deposited her box in the baggage office, and walked briskly up crowded Fulton Street in New York.

Her first try, she decided, would be at some of the women's clothing shops she had seen along Broadway. She came to one—Brodie's. Not a large shop, but behind its gleaming show window, was displayed a lady's green velvet mantilla, richly bordered with sable fur.

Inside, a woman clerk met her with an expression showing she considered Po a most unimpressive customer, and when Po explained her business, the woman languidly waved to the rear, where a man sat behind a high desk.

He regarded Po over his white stock with a look of distaste.

"Could you use my services as a clerk, sir? I've a pair of willing feet, and a cheerful disposition."

The man looked at her, slight pain being added to his distaste. "Experienced?"

Po licked her lips and dropped her eyes, as if confessing a fault. "No, sir."

The man shook his head, slowly but positively, No, and began to write again in the ledger in front of him.

But in the sunny street, in the rushing throngs, Po cheered herself up. She'd made a mistake going into such a rich shop. She'd heard of a store called Stewart's, with a general trade.

She had no trouble in finding Stewart's, a large place, and she boldly asked for Mr. Stewart. The clerk smiled, and said if it was about a situation to talk to Mr. Zimmers. Mr. Zimmers, a man with mutton chop whiskers and a formal black coat, looked at her kindly, but as if he had talked to a dozen girls just like her that day.

"References, I presume?"

"No, none, sir."

"No experience, and no references? I'm afraid we could not use you. Why don't you try an Intelligence Office? They know of situations." And he raised a pencil to beckon the next person waiting for him.

In the street, she decided trying an Intelligence Office might be a good idea. She went up the Broadway quickly, looking, and finally, saw a sign, "Intelligence Office," on a side street.

Po went down a few steps in the large clean light basement room which had been partitioned off into several compartments. On the door of one of the smaller compartments Po read "Employers." Outside this door, a man, his hands crossed on his walking stick, sat on a long wooden settle.

On the door of a large compartment, it said "Servants," and next this, behind a desk, sat the manager, a thin woman with a red nose and frosty blue eyes. She wore a shawl, as if against the drafts from the frequently opening door.

"Fee's fifty cents," she told Po at once in a clipped voice. "Payable in advance!"

Po paid. If she could get a place quickly, it was worth it.

"Situations open now," the woman droned from a list, "maid-of-all-work, four dollars a month, seamstress, two-fifty a week, nurse maid, five dollars a month— What kind of experience you had?"

"Why—well—" Po flushed a little. "I'm a . . . singer."

"No calls," the woman said and read again. "Embroiderer, governess—"

"I could try that!"

"Go in that door, and wait."

Po went in the large compartment. Twenty or thirty girls and women, some shabby, some well dressed, cheerful and morose, sat silently, without chat, on wooden benches around the wall. Po sat on the edge of a bench timidly. "With all this pick, they'll never take me!" she thought.

After what seemed to Po a long time, during which girls kept going out and coming in, the manager opened the door and beckoned to Po. In the room marked Employers, Po was confronted by an elegantly dressed woman about forty, who stared at her coldly.

"Well, if you don't know enough to curtsy to me when you come into a room," the woman broke out peevishly, "you've certainly never served for anyone of consequence. You won't do!" And Po retired in disgrace.

But as she was passing the man sitting on the wooden settle, he spoke to her. He had a large fleshy face, coarse, but merry-looking. "Did I hear you say you was a singer?"

"I can sing," Po said, surprised.

"Well, now, just sit down here a minute!" He picked up his pipe hat from the settle to make room for her. "A pretty little thing like you don't want to go being a slavey somewhere. I know a fellow, a good friend of mine, has a restaurant, and he uses singers there sometimes. Think he might use you! I'll introduce you!"

Po looked surprised and excited. "Isn't that a kindly thing now?"

"Come on"—he rose good-naturedly—"it's up the street." And he guided Po out into the street.

In the Broadway, she could see his coat was shabby, the white tabs of his neck cloth not fresh, his fleshy nose was inflamed red, but he smiled down at her pleasantly. He raised his stick, then, and hailed a yellow Broadway stage.

"It's six-eight blocks from here," he said as the stage stopped in front of them. "We may as well ride!" He helped Po aboard.

The stage was crowded, and they could not get seats together. The stage rumbled along, the driver cracking his whip over the clumping horses.

Then, sitting there, in the rumbling, crowded stage, a frightening recollection flashed on Po. She remembered the furtive-faced man in the tight brown coat who had stopped Dave on the Broadway that evening. She could hear Dave saying grimly, "A pimp. Recruits girls. Promises jobs— They end up as Waiter Girls at those concert saloons—" Then she remembered the young girl, gaudily dressed, she had seen luring the middle-aged man into one of the places.

Oh, she flushed in shamed rage, how stupid she had been! What a dolt! She must get out of the stage, quickly. The man looked over at her, and nodded and smiled. Thank heaven it was a public place. All she would have to do was get up, when the stage stopped, and run. If he followed her, she would— The stage ground to a stop while a passenger got on, but Po, her heart racing, had jumped off. She heard the man cry out protestingly after her, but the stage rumbled on up the street. Po turned and ran.

She guessed she had better go back to the Intelligence Office. She should have asked the manager about the man before she left. At any rate, she considered, it would be as safe a place as any.

She hurried back, angry, scared, railing inwardly at herself for not having more sense.

But back in the Intelligence Office, the manager looked at her, surprised. "Oh, it's you. Thought I saw you go out with Mr. Fripps! He's the well-known wine merchant. A very kind man!"

Now Po's confidence in her own judgment was shaken. "Until I know my way about," she told herself, "I'd best try only for some safe place as nurse maid or seamstress. Time enough later, when I can better tell what's what, to think of singing."

After her scare, the idea of a dull domestic place seemed happy, secure and completely desirable. She went back in the large room with the other applicants, and sat down to wait.

From time to time, employers would come to the door. They would look over all the girls and women, then beckon to one.

No one beckoned to Po.

Then one employer came to the door whose look went past Po at first—but returned. He looked so respectable and safe and dull, in his long-tailed black coat, his gray vest with the heavy gold chain across it, she hoped he would beckon to her. He looked rather dour, but Po guessed it was because of his clothes, and his pasty pallor, rather than his expression, for he seemed to have none. He looked at Po unenthusiastically, just impassive, but—he beckoned.

The manager introduced them. He was Mr. Thompson and he needed a nursery governess.

He did not bother to take Po in the interviewing room, but stood by the manager's desk. "Have you any experience in that line?"

"No," Po admitted, afraid that was the end.

"Do you have relatives living here?"

"Not in this city." After all, Brian lived in Brooklyn. Now, she thought, he'll ask for references, and that will end it. But he said, "The salary is ten dollars a month and board." His voice was expressionless.

Po had the impression he was perhaps doing this errand for his wife, was rather bored by it.

But Po nodded, and began to wonder uneasily if she could remember enough mathematics to teach children.

"And how old are they, sir?"

"They?" He shot her a cold glance.

"The children?"

"Oh, six and eight!"

That would not be so bad, Po thought. "Boys or girls?"

"Uh . . . a boy and a girl." He looked preoccupied, and as if he had other affairs on his mind. "Are you ready to start at once?"

"Yes, sir, at once."

"My house is up in Yorkville. That's a way out the Third Avenue. I'll be driving out there as soon as I finish my other business in town. We may as well start."

With a nod to the manager, and her nod and smile back, Po and Mr. Thompson left.

A rusty-looking gig waited outside, which Mr. Thompson drove himself. He had to see a man yet in the leather district, and he might be a little late. She could wait at his sister's house until he was ready to go. They could pick up her box when they started to Yorkville.

He drove along the Broadway until they came to Canal Street. He turned off and then made a few more turns, before he stopped in front of a brownstone house, one of many on a quiet, tree-shaded street.

It was nearly six o'clock now, and the setting sun lit up the blank windows with their shades drawn tight, and the gleaming brass plate on the door, as they went up the high steps.

Mr. Thompson gave a short ring. At once the door was opened by a Negro serving woman. She disappeared, leaving them standing in the hall.

Po saw the house was richly furnished. Heavy folding doors into rooms off the long hall were closed tightly. Then Mr. Thompson's sister appeared from the back of the house, her black brocade dress rustling as she came.

"This is my sister, Mrs. Modilani. Her name is O'Reilly. We're going to drive on tonight!"

Mrs. Modilani was a heavy square woman, not fat, strictly corseted, with small diamond earrings trembling in her ears. Her eyelids hooded her eyes in a peculiar manner, so that Po thought of a turtle. Being unenthusiastic must run in the family, Po thought, for she was as impassive as Mr. Thompson.

At first, Po had feared the women of Mr. Thompson's family would not be as easily satisfied—that they would begin to ask for her references, about her experience. But Mrs. Modilani did not seem interested one way or the other.

"She can use the small back room," she said to the serving woman. The serving woman took Po up the heavily carpeted stairs. Po glanced back. She could see Mr. Thompson and Mrs. Modilani standing there, looking after her, impassively.

The room was plainly furnished, a single bed and bureau, and a worn carpet, but there was an armchair, and Po sank down in it gratefully, suddenly exhausted.

"Will you have some supper?" the serving woman asked at the door.

"Why, yes, and thank you!" Now that was very kindly of them, not only letting her wait here in comfort, but feeding her as well!

In about ten minutes, the serving woman returned with a tray which she placed on the little table, and removed the covering napkin.

"Thank you kindly. It's hungry I am, and I not having eaten this while!" Po smiled at her as the woman left.

Po had an odd sensation just then. She thought she heard a click, almost like a door latch. But she shrugged, and fell upon the food. It was a sandwich, delicious. There was a pot of tea, too, with cream and sugar.

By the time she had finished, she felt revived.

"And wasn't I the lucky one to find a place so quickly. A nursery governess!" It would take a little scratching of her brains to remember how to spell and do sums—but she could sing to them and tell them the fine stories, anyhow.

She ought to take the tray back down stairs. The serving woman had been so kindly, bringing it up. The kitchen would not be hard to find. Po would save the woman an extra trip. She picked up the tray and went to the door. But the door was locked.

Chapter Twenty-three

PO KNEW she must be wrong. The door was probably jammed. She laid the tray on the table carefully. With both hands she tried the door again. It was locked. A sudden wave of panic made her rattle it wildly.

Maybe the serving woman had turned the latch, without thinking, not meaning to.

Suddenly Po darted around the room, touching the walls as if she expected to find another door. Two sides of the room were papered with bumpy brown wallpaper, the other two paneled in scabrous, varnished wood. Her knees were trembling as she reached the single window.

The red draperies were faded to the color of dried blood. When she touched them, stale dust gritted down on her, as if all manner of evil smells and sounds had settled for years in the folds. She jerked aside the lace curtains, soiled to unwholesome gray, and a dead moth fell down on her arm. The dusty glass pane seemed to open on a blank brick wall. Outside it was nearly dark.

Po unfastened the window latch, and opened the window. In the advancing darkness, she thought at first she was looking through another curtain of wide black meshes. When she put her hand out, she felt only scaly metal. Close-meshed, heavy iron wire bolted to the outside of the building covered the window tightly.

"And couldn't it be that Mrs. Modilani is frightened all times of thieves?" Po turned into the room, trying to shrug airily. Why, all Po had to do—she tried smiling—was to attract attention, let Mrs. Modilani know the door had been mistakenly locked.

Po rattled the door. Silence. Then she pounded on it with a fist. No answering footsteps came running to her aid.

She called out, "Mrs. Modilani!" Alarm made her voice shrill. "The door is locked!"

She had heard no footsteps approaching, but suddenly she heard Mrs. Modilani's voice, malevolent, as if detached in the air, outside the door. Po remembered the heavy carpet and how footfalls had died in it. "Stop that noise!"

"Open this door!" Po screamed. "Let me out of here!"

"Be quiet, d'y hear me?" Her voice was harsh with threat. "Or I'll come in there and quiet you!" Po heard her muttering angrily as if she were going down the hall. "Disturbing the whole house like that!"

Po's knees suddenly seemed to buckle under her. She found herself sitting on the floor. In the deepening gloom, even the sagging bed, the cheap bureau, seemed like crouching forms, ready to spring. From the dusty carpet, the reek of creosote, around a splotch of some horrible stain, assailed her.

She was, and no use to fool herself, locked in. She had better face what that meant.

A sudden rage at herself brought angry tears. How could she have been such a stupid, slow-witted, green fool? How could she? Dave had warned her! She'd known these things could happen! And then, like a witless, silly fool, to be trapped! Why hadn't she seen? In contempt of herself, she pounded the floor with her fists.

Was it that Intelligence Office? But she recalled the waiting girls.

the employers coming and going, the manager. No, that was a legitimate place. Mr. Thompson? But who could have guessed he was not a respectable householder? This house? On a respectable street, and she coming into it in broad daylight? What could have warned her about it? Nothing.

She stood up now, facing the door, fists clenched. There was nothing to have warned her. She pounded her fist into a small open hand, not in rage at herself now, but at the world. It was the Eaters again, creeping and devouring. How could human beings be like that? She ground her foot into the floor as though to crush all such. Let that Mrs. Modilani come in! Just let her! Po kicked the door in violent anger. Standing there, facing the door, words poured out of her mouth, a curse she had heard in her childhood. "May the black murdered hands of Seumas O'Reilly choke you till your blood turns black and your heart falls soft and rotten from your breast!"

But there was no sound. The house was silent. Only an odor of sour stale cheap perfume, musk, assailed her.

Po sat on the edge of the bed, from which the odor of dead perspiration rose. It was no good cursing, or clenching her fist. She'd better clench her brain. Get herself out of this before—her stomach seemed to cringe and crawl away from her body—something happened.

She must try to think. It was no use pleading with Mrs. Modilani. The serving woman? When she came back for the tray? Maybe, if Po pleaded, she might help her get out of the house.

Like a child who knows no one hears, but gives one last sob— Po rattled the door again; then she sat on the bed, in the musty room, in the silent house, and waited.

To Po it seemed a miserable long time before the latch was finally thrown, and the heavy-moving serving woman came in. A candle lit her immobile bronze face. She picked up the tray, put the candle holder on the tray and turned to the door.

But Po's words came in a pleading rush. "Won't you help me? Oh, please!" The woman was already at the door. "Maybe it's daughters you have yourself!" At this the woman turned and Po saw her eyes, glinting white in the candlelight with some savage hurt. "Help me!" Po's voice rose childishly.

The door was open. With a wild bound Po lunged toward it. A heavy bronze arm shot out and hurled Po back toward the bed. Without a word, the woman went out, and to Po the latch bumping against the wood felt like a thump against her own flesh.

Po sat for a long time then, until thought and hopeless motions for getting out began to chase themselves in mad circles in her brain.

Then, in the silent shut-off room, the whisper of a movement warned her someone—something—was near her. She sat rigid, listening with her whole body. Then, she heard somewhere, she could not tell where, but close, oh, too close, a slow rustling, a sly, steady, sliding noise.

The room was dark. Frantically, she sprang up and groped for the candle on the bureau. Fear turned her fingers to stiff, wildly flailing sticks. Then, she found it, the match grated on the candle holder. She lit the candle.

She saw her face in the streaked mirror, her eyes starting in terror —for, in the silent, airless room, closed up, sealed off—the candle flame moved—as if in a draft. Her shadow writhed against the wall as the flame bent.

She stood stark still now, mind and body listening. For a long time there was no sound. She relaxed a little then, and went and sat down weakly on the bed.

She waited. After a time, she heard a woman's mad drunken laugh, then a man's growling rumble. She remembered the heavy carpet, which killed footsteps, made voices seem to materialize out of nothing. The man and woman must have come up the stairs, and were passing down the hall. Po heard the door in the next room open and close. The woman laughed again, unmistakably drunk. The man answered with a loose curse.

Po stood, shrinking against the wall. She heard creakings of a bed, the man's guttural tones, then silence. After a while, Po went over and sat on the bed. A long time passed. She began to get over her first fear and to wonder if she should call out, plead to them for aid, but just then the man's voice rose in a horrible curse. She heard the door thrown open in the next room, heard their voices in a drunken quarrel, fading as they went down stairs.

The house was tomb-like and still again, with only the odors seemingly alive. Then, somewhere close at hand, she heard the whisper of a footfall. She drew back her head to scream but no sound came forth.

She stood in silent fear. She heard then, a creaking, as though something, someone, rested weight on ancient flooring. Perhaps it was a bat lost and dying somewhere in the partitions of the house.

Po went unsteadily to the mirror, the candle shining up in her face—then she jerked forward in fear.

In the mirror she saw a dark rectangle moving along the wall. So near hysteria was she that she wanted to weep at the mad unreasonableness of this. Then, she saw a small, dirty, claw-like hand on the edge of the dark rectangle.

The wood paneling on the wall was set in large rectangles, outlined in molding. One of these rectangles, about three feet above the ground, was sliding back. A figure came through the small opening, then stood silently, blinking at her in the candlelight with malevolent impudence.

"Huh!" He seemed to spit in contempt. "Dey got one of youse in here! I t'ought it was Minnie!" He was about twelve years old. His face was dusty, with dirt or pallor; his brown hair grew so far down, Po thought of mouse's hair. Even his eyes, like black glass buttons, were mouse-like.

"If you'll help me get out of here, Mr. Boy, honey," Po burst out pleadingly, "I'll give you"—she remembered the ten dollars in her reticule—"a vast large sum of money!"

He smiled, a sneering, cynical smile, and took a wallet from a pocket, like a mouse taking something from his fur.

"Pah! I got money!" His tone was jeering. "Got any candy?"

"Oh, I'll get you the great wagon load of it, if you'll help me now. They told me I was going to Yorkville—"

"Yorkville? Nah, he takes 'em to Albany!"

"No, Yorkville!"

"Nah—dey run a big house in Albany."

Suddenly Po remembered Mr. Thompson's light gig. Well, if he tried taking her any place in that, she thought savagely, she'd get away.

"Dey got a big closed carriage. Dey waits till dey gits three or four. I t'ink dey's fixin' to go tonight late."

Po realized her hope was to make this mouse boy stay and talk, to find out all she could.

"What makes you so dirty?" She tried to pick a fight with him.

"Anh, you'd be dirty, too, if youse worked dem panels!"

"What do you mean—work the panels?"

"Why—I'm a panel boy!"

Whatever it was, he was proud of it. She'd make him talk. "And what is that, for the love of hivven?"

"Why, see, de fella comes in. He leaves his pants dere—on dat chair, see? I can git in the panel, git de cash outa his pocket book, stuff it with somethin' else, git back out and close de panel, and he never knows no one's been here! Madame, she says I'm one of de best panel boys in de business!" The black eyes sent out sparks of pride.

"But"—Po thought if she could just get him talking, get him friendly—"don't the fella call out for the peeler when he finds his cash gone?"

"Nah . . . she on'y works de panel game in dese rooms up here. Let's 'em out to tramps, see? De tramps has the feller out in the street again by dat time. Downstairs is her reg'lar girls. Aggie, dat's me mudder, she gotta room down dere!"

"So I'm to go to Albany?"

"Yah, and if youse try duckin', youse just git slugged!"

But Po was thinking that if she could once get outside, she could—

"And the policeman on this beat, he's a friend of Madame's, and he don't like no trouble!"

Voices sounded suddenly from the hall, passing Po's door. A woman, laughing, talking in a high shrill voice, a man's guttural. They did not go in the next room, but went on down the hall, evidently on the other side. The panel boy was standing, intent, a sly leer on his face, listening to the door opening, closing. Then, swiftly, silently, he climbed through the panel, slid it closed and was gone.

Albany was it! Anger rose in her now. Well, they'd have to drag her screaming the whole way. She'd get away! She'd show them!

But she must figure. Her brow knit in a furrow of terrible concentration. Then her heart failed her. What if they did get her as far as this Albany? She was lost there for sure. She'd never find her way back.

Her eye fell on the panel. He'd gotten through. She was not as small as the panel boy, but she was slender and little. If only the door in the next room was open!

She ran to the panel. Shaking it, scratching at it, frantically rubbing it, she struggled in vain. Then, something she did must have opened it, for now she could slide it back with her hands. She felt it move wider. It was open.

She peered in. A narrow low passage, perhaps only a wide space between the partitions, smelling of dust and active mice. She climbed through, feet first.

A thin stripe of light showed where the panel into the other room opened. If only the door were unlocked! What if the boy were still in the other room? She stopped and listened. There was no sound.

Po opened the panel into the other room and squeezed through. A gas lamp burned there, perhaps left by the departing couple.

She knew she would have to move quickly. Someone might come and discover she had gone. She remembered she'd left the other panel open. She flew to the door. It was not locked. She opened the door a careful crack. The hall was empty. Just then she heard voices rise in loud talk down the hall, and she heard a door click, as though someone stood with it in hand. She moved back, and waited, breathless.

When all was silent, she moved into the hall, her feet lost in the deadening carpet.

She tiptoed down the carpeted stairs. Her heart pounded in wild thuds, her mouth was dry, but every nerve and muscle seemed alert. It was in the downstairs hall she felt the danger lay. From its gloomy depths, Mrs. Modilani might appear. Or Mr. Thompson, or the serving woman. What if they were watching her now, as she went down the steps so quietly, laughing at her, ready to pounce?

She passed the bronze statue holding the colored lamp. Now she could see the front door. But—what if it were locked.

It was. She stood, blank despair assailing her. She was afraid to move for fear a sound would make the large folding door into the front room go grating back, and Mrs. Modilani would appear.

In the corner of the hall stood a dusty blue china umbrella stand. In it a woman's broken parasol, a man's heavy feruled umbrella, stood upright. She seized the heavy umbrella, raised the handle over her head, and with all her strength and ten times more supplied by fear, she swung down with all her might, through the long plate glass panel of the front door.

The splintering of glass reverberated through the house. For a few seconds there was no movement or sound. Then—the door to the front room began to rumble back. But Po was climbing through the shattered glass, tearing her skirt, cutting her arm.

She saw the great folding doors open now, and Mrs. Modilani's malevolent face, her mouth opened as she shouted something. But terror had pulsed through Po, and she leaped down the steps, and ran up the street, trying to keep in the shadow of the trees.

Chapter Twenty-four

HER FEET, as she ran, scuffed along the brick streets with the frightened scurry of dry leaves. Loathing of the people she'd escaped gave extra breath to her fear. She turned a corner, ran into an unlit street and slackened, for this dark way could lead anywhere.

A gaslit street intersected. She sped along it. Closed carriages, their passengers riding safely over sinking mud, rolled along in regular decent rhythms.

A breathless pain in her side made Po pause, panting. She didn't know where she was. But even a hurrying, homeward-bound man, loaf under arm, she did not dare accost. Mr. Thompsons were abroad in the land. Fear blew breath into her lungs again. She sped on until her leg muscles refused any longer to tense themselves.

Ahead, a few gaunt trees lurked near a stony statue and some benches. She sank on a bench, drooping forward, exhausted.

What if she went into one of the tall houses, close-packed along this street, and asked help? Behind snug windows, lamps lit sheltered people moving in small safe patterns. But which door might open onto a deadening carpet, leading to a musty locked room?

Everyone was safe on firm ground. Only she was cut off, with no place to stand.

She thought of Brian's face, and even his whiskers seemed to glow with warmth. There was the safe brass bed under the sloping eaves. No one could trick her there—they couldn't even see her, for she would be colorless.

A man approached the little park. Po started up. She hated the man walking the street—and everyone who could not let her rest a moment in peace. Trees had always been her friends, but these were hostile. They threw leering shadows. Her loitering here could be mis-construed. She walked fiercely and rapidly away.

It was a black night, moonless, only an occasional lamp starring the gloom.

Then—she smelled the river. The ferry! If she could get to the ferry, she would go back to Brooklyn. It was a fine thing to talk big! To want to make your own way! But freedom was a chancy thing.

What time it was she had no idea, but perhaps the ferry ran all night. With the river on her left, if she walked south far enough, she must come to the ferry. Swiftly, filled with contempt and hatred of everything, she moved down long blocks of looming warehouses. After a long time, she saw lights gleaming on the painted white wood of the ferry wharf, but she was too weary to feel anything but a longing to sit down in a safe light place.

A few people were waiting. A ferry had just left. Then she saw the clock inside the lighted ticket office. It was only half past ten.

More people came in, filling the place with easy chatter about unexciting everyday pleasures. Po sat down on a bench, feeling a stranger, bitterly apart. More people kept arriving. Some lined up to retrieve parcels or umbrellas or bags left in the baggage office on the wharf.

She remembered her own box. She thought of how she had felt, so sure of herself, when she left it there, and swallowed hard. Although she had lost her bonnet in that house, she still clutched her reticule with her baggage check. Po rose and walked over to the waiting line.

Suddenly—she didn't know why—maybe it was the docile blank faces of the people getting into line, like ciphers in a row—but she felt herself stiffen into a resistance.

She didn't want to go back.

She sat down again on the bench to wrestle with this. A ferry came in, the crowd rushed on. Po did not get on. She'd catch the next one, maybe.

After a time, more people began to collect on the wharf for the next ferry. They waited, some with sleepy half-smiles, some reading newspapers. It was about this time she and Dave and Walt had come here on their way home that night. She wondered if Walt would be in that café, writing at that table.

She remembered his serene, patient look, like he regarded her as important. If she could talk to him, maybe.

It was about eleven. Suddenly, she got up, went out of the ferry wharf, up Fulton to the Broadway. Stages rolled along. She boarded one, paid her fare, and asked to be let down at Bleecker Street.

But when she was at the entry leading down to the beer cellar, she hesitated. Still, what harm could come from going in to see, and if he were there, if he would talk to her, maybe— She went down the steps and pushed upon the heavy door.

In the el-shaped room, several parties, men and women, sat at large, round tables, eating, drinking, absorbed in laughing talk. The talk died as she passed one table, and one of the men turned to stare after her. She tried to look haughty and hurried past. She turned the corner of the el into the back of the room, toward the place where they had found Walt.

Walt's table was empty.

Po stood swaying a little, a bitter taste in back of her throat. She had so wanted him to be there, a kindly, known face. Everything that had happened that day seemed to gather into a heavy stone pendulum that swung against the back of her skull. She needed to sit down a minute.

Spicy steam rose from the plate of a fat man who ate noisily at a near-by table. She was hungry. She felt her money in her reticule. She'd order some food. Then she could better decide what to do. She sank down at the empty table.

A dumpy German waiter thrust a long menu at her. Exhausted, she stared at its meaningless jumble of words.

Then—a young man was standing across the table from her,

smiling charmingly, bowing deferentially. Light glanced across his crisp fair hair, over his beautiful gray broadcloth coat.

"Lady Violet-Blue-Eyes!"

It was Coventry Van Leyn, the young man who had come to Brady's to order the bat sticks!

As if she had been lost at sea for days, and his the first friendly hail from dry land, he looked to her incredibly wonderful, pleasant, kindly. She even summoned a little rag-tag of raillery.

"Why, your grace!"

"Eating alone?" His amazement was delicately complimentary. "May I sit down?" He slipped into the opposite chair. "I pierced your disguise, my lady. Are you displeased? I learned your name!" And he smiled as if he were amused even at saying it: "Pocahontas O'Reilly!"

Gently, he took the heavy menu card from her hand. "If you haven't eaten here before, allow me!" He spoke with quick, low assurance, and the waiter sped off.

Wearily, Po hoped Coventry's seeing her alone, in a café at this hour was not going to lead to any misunderstandings. "I was looking for a friend, a man who usually sits at this table—"

"Walt!" He smiled disarmingly at her. "He was in and gone—just left a few minutes ago!" She wondered if she had better not go at once. But she was so hungry, she so needed to sit a minute.

"Do I detect an air—oh, very slight—of trouble?"

She knew it was unwise. But she so longed to speak into a sympathetic ear.

"I've left my cousin's house!" Coventry raised his eyebrows, smiling as though some astonishing plum had fallen into his lap.

"And it's trying to get myself settled is causing me a little difficulty."

"But"—sympathetically, he stroked the tablecloth near where her hand rested, as though he would not presume to stroke her hand—"that should not be hard!" She guessed he was about twenty-three, but with his pleasant brown eyes and smiling sensual lips, crisp, fair hair, and clean tubbed skin, he looked as if he never yet had had to raise his voice, or strain, or hurry, or frown. He leaned forward and smiled as though he were amused and charmed by her. "On the contrary!"

"I can't stay here long," she said uneasily, "because I must find, yet tonight, a small respectable hotel!"

Now, but with the delicacy one might reassure a friend, he did touch her hand. "Say no more! It's already done! My family has a house out on the tundra, away up on the Fifth Avenue. But I have rooms at the Astor!"

"I need to find my own place—" Po spoke quickly.

"Now simply don't worry any more about it!" Two waiters, no doubt made quick and obsequious by Coventry, appeared. One bore a covered silver dish with a flame under it. He lifted the lid, loosing an agonizingly delicious odor, and announced solemnly, "Lobster Newburg." The other waiter, deft under Coventry's knowing eye, gently loosened the cork on a pale wine, German-labeled. "Now eat your supper," Coventry commanded, taking a critical sip of the wine.

Po did not drink the wine, but she fell greedily upon the food. She guessed she should not have spoken to him. Things were getting complicated.

"You're an extraordinarily charming child, do you know?" Coventry leaned forward, smiling, kindly, interested.

She looked at him a moment. She'd eat quickly, leave.

The flame under the silver dish flared up, and the wine in the rich sauce sent out a heady fragrance. "See how blue that flame is? That's what your eyes are like—fiery, intense, blue, like jewels alive. And then, put them behind those black silk lashes—and it's quite delightful, really!"

If he had only been looking at her eyelashes, Po might have enjoyed this more. But his eye ran over the roundness of her shoulders, down her arms, down her throat into the opening of her bodice, over her small round breasts—like a tailor measuring someone for clothes. She saw he was a little puzzled by her, but he was enjoying the uncertainty. He hoped for something, and he might bring it about, and he was enjoying the game, the hope of victory. But she was too worn out to fence.

And in a way, she could see, too, that he really meant to be kind.

A burst of laughter bellowed out from the large round table around the el. "My friends make wassail!" He smiled.

"Cov!" A woman's throaty voice called, "Where's Coventry?"

"They'll get on without me," he smiled at Po. "I like this better!" And the way he rested his arms on the table and leaned toward her, smiling, Po saw he had decided she was fair game.

Po looked at him steadily, with no coquetry. She wished she could say right out, "The answer is no."

"Cov!" The woman's voice was more insistent. "Where are you?"

"Perhaps you'd best go back to your friends!" Po said.

"Why, I wouldn't think of leaving you alone! All sorts of things could happen!" Po had to smile at his cheek.

But his friends came now to him. One of them, anyway. A fascinating-looking woman about twenty-six or eight came around the corner from the large table. She was not tipsy, but she had been drinking, and she looked at Po in amused astonishment.

Richly dressed in cinnamon-brown velvet, great emerald ear drops, the exact color of her green eyes, trembled against her creamy high-boned cheeks. Her red hair, under a topaz velvet bonnet brim, was not done in the conventional sleek fashion, but in seemingly careless ringlets. The figure-revealing plainness of her dress, the good-natured smile on her large mouth, the possessive camaraderie of her hand on Coventry's shoulder, all had the artful simplicity of sophistication.

"Carlotta, love! Sit down and help me!" And he looked up at her with as innocent a little-boy smile as if he had really been earnestly engaged only in helping his neighbor. "You must give this child some advice! And wait till you hear her name! It's Pocahontas O'Reilly!" He brought this out as if he deserved credit for discovering it.

Carlotta burst into good-natured laughter and sat down. "What are we drinking? Get me some brandy, Cov!" The hovering waiter sped away.

"This," Coventry managed to put a delicate fanfare in his voice, "is Mrs. Bradford! She's playing in the *Lady of Lyons* at the National Theater. The best actress in New York!"

"No one but Coventry and I know it, though. That's why I play second ingenues and maids!" Carlotta's large mouth smiled with deprecating charm, and the emerald ear drops glinted.

Po looked admiringly at Carlotta's beautiful red ringlets. "So it's in the theater you are! 'Tis partly that I've come for. I'm a singer, and it's that kind of work I am looking for!"

The waiter brought a dark bottle of London Dock brandy. Po declined, and Coventry poured Carlotta a large drink, and poured one for himself.

And then Po heard herself spilling out to these strangers, as they sipped their brandy, all her hopes and vague plans. She was a little embarrassed at herself, bragging about how many old ballads and street songs and antique lays she knew. "But never an American song! So it's a job I must get—any kind of a job—while I try to find the knack of American singing!"

Mrs. Bradford was a little bored, her attention had wandered. Coventry poured her another brandy.

"Coventry," Carlotta's voice was brooding, "do y'know why I was looking for you? Marion Fielding just told me that rotten Augusta has been working against me again! But I suppose I shouldn't talk about Augusta to you! After all, she's your mother!"

Coventry instantly and indignantly rejected this. "She's my step-mother! And if you heard that Augusta had Mrs. Rhinelander take you off the cotillion list—she did!"

"Why?" Carlotta's green eyes glinted with angry passion. "Why? I suppose she told her that because I was in the theater, I was no longer in society!"

"That's what she said! But she did really on account of you and the Count Ossi, and the week-end at Saratoga!"

"Jealous!" Carlotta broke out passionately. "Jealous!"

Po felt as if she were eavesdropping. She couldn't stay here any longer. She rose. She had to find a hotel.

Coventry was instantly contrite. "Now you're not to worry. I told you I'd take care of it!" He pulled her back down to the table, and addressed Carlotta. "We have to find her a safe place to stay! Now let me see! There'd be—no, that wouldn't do!" He sat a moment, drumming on the table cloth. Then his whole face lit up with prankish merriment.

"Carlotta!" he laughed. "I have just gotten such an idea as will stun you with its sheer devilish cleverness!"

Then Po heard another one of those American practical jokes they were so fond of, that they would go to such trouble to arrange.

The joke was on Augusta, of course, but, at the same time, it would solve Po's problem of a comfortable safe place to stay.

The idea was to give Po some hilariously important references, that anyone who wasn't a rank snob like Augusta would see through in a minute, and send Po there for a situation in the household. Then, at some future moment, they would contrive to make Augusta's being taken in a source of public humiliation for darling Augusta.

With great laughter, more brandy, and enjoying Augusta's anticipated embarrassment, they planned the details. "I wish we could send her as a cook. She could put some ground glass in Augusta's pate de fois gras!" They were both enthusiastic about the idea now.

"Ha!" Po thought. "It's mad they both are!" Aloud she said, "Belike it's the great joke you could nearly die laughing at, and I'd like to oblige you, and thank you kindly—but to make the story short—I won't do it!"

But by this time they were both so enamored of the practical joke, they sprang to defend it, to try to make it attractive to Po.

"You could go as a parlor maid!" Carlotta said coaxingly. "It'll be easy! And it's ideal for you. Coventry, we can trick her out in that English nurse maid's bonnet I wore last year in *Money*. Remember what a fuddy-duddy it was!"

"It can't fail," Coventry broke in, laughing. "Pretend you were in service abroad. I'll write the reference, and if I make it from some titled person, Augusta'll fall in a swoon."

"Is it a convict you'd have me, then, and wearing prison stripes and chains, belike, if I'm found out?" Po set her chin stubbornly. "I won't do it!"

Carlotta tapped her thumb on her white teeth and looked at Po reflectively. Finally, she said, as if pulling out a trump, "You go, and if you get the place and stay awhile, why, I'll introduce you to the manager of Niblo's Gardens!"

Po wavered. Of course, she'd seen a certain charm in the notion from the first—if it would work. And she remembered, too, how it was with the below-stairs staff back in the castle at Lough, and knew the servants in a great house had an easy time of it. But still—going with a lying reference. On the other hand—if Carlotta would do as she said! "I'll do it then—if you get me from the prison if I'm thrown there!"

But they sprang in at once, scoffing at this, reassuring her of their immense cleverness, and planning all the details.

"The title'll have to be a real one," Carlotta said, "for she sleeps with a Burke's Peerage in the room!"

Coventry picked up a newspaper from the leather seat along the wall, and leafed through it. After a while, he read out, "Lord Cecil Bathurst presided at the spring meeting of the Marylebone Cricket Club, at Lord's—

"We'll address the letter to Augusta personally, as if she were such a famous hostess, he'd heard of her over there." He sent the waiter flying for writing materials, and when they came, with glee and zest began to compose. "A servant from the staff of my country house, O'Reilly is a faithful second maid. I would appreciate it if you would assist her to a suitable place in your own establishment, or in that of one of your distinguished friends."

"This will fetch her." Coventry laughed, and wrote: "I plan to visit America soon, and trust I may have the pleasure of calling on you to thank you!"

Carlotta laughed and clapped her hands at this. Then Coventry took the letter to the other table, to have one of his friends recopy it, so Augusta would not recognize the hand.

They decided Po must go home with Carlotta for tonight. They'd go through Carlotta's theatrical wardrobe, and do Po up handsomely.

A hansom cab took them to Carlotta's second floor rooms on Houston Street near the theater. The rooms were beautifully decorated with delicate green draperies, and bowls of white lilac stood about on the floor and the piano. A Negro maid took Carlotta's bonnet.

Coventry seemed to know where everything was. He left his coat in Carlotta's room, brought out a fresh bottle of brandy and glasses from a cabinet. Po had the feeling this was not the first night he had spent there.

The exactly right maid's bonnet and shawl were found. All was arranged. Po was put to bed in a small room then, off the one where Coventry and Carlotta sat. Until nearly four, Po kept waking and hearing snatches of conversation. Then all was quiet.

Chapter Twenty-five

NOON SUN came in through the delicate green draperies of Carlotta's rooms, but Carlotta and Coventry still slept. Carlotta's Negro maid had given Po some breakfast, and now Po stood in front of the long gilt mirror in the front room.

She took up the English nurse maid's bonnet, with the white ruching across the front and the streamers down the back, and settled it firmly on her head. The brown merino shawl was fastened primly over her shoulders. Then, as the authentic touch Carlotta had insisted on, she drew on the gray cotton gloves.

To give herself confidence, Po felt the stiff square of the letter of recommendation in her reticule, addressed to "Mrs. Nicholas Van Leyn, Thirty-seventh Street at the Fifth Avenue," and went out to have another try at the wide world.

The day sparkled. Po forgot yesterday. She began to feel that life was a lark and she the girl to lark it—in other words, to feel her usual self.

Briskly, she moved along the street, through charcoal sellers, wood sellers, water sellers, all crying their wares, until she came to a broad avenue. Hansom cabs waited there in a patient line.

Po walked boldly over. The first man was asleep in his cab. She went to the second. He sprang down, and held the door open. A tall man, high-shouldered, with a shock of straight black hair falling over his forehead under his high rusty beaver.

Po stopped cannily. "First and all, you must tell me—what is the price now for driving me to Thirty-seventh Street at the Fifth Avenue?"

The cabby's gray eyes sparkled into life, and he stared at her, a slow smile breaking, without answering her.

"It's from the glens you are, so that there must still be a little of the turf smoke about you—with that soft, velvety tongue on you!"

"The County of Wicklow, is it maybe?" Po cried in delight at his voice. The long lantern jaw and Roman nose, it was a familiar type face to her. "Or Tipperary, maybe?" Brian's speech had begun to sharpen into American angles, but this man's still had the soft green mistiness of the glens.

"Killeney Bay!" he cried. "The parish of Bruy! And yourself now, if you'll speak some more—"

"It's in Ballyhouna I was born, in Limerick, but I've traveled all vales and glens in Innis Fail!"

They stood there, gazing at one another, tears crinkling behind their eyes. They each wanted the same thing—to hear the other speak some more, because of all the warm, wistful smells, and breezes and voices it recalled. If they could have sat down and had a dish of talk by the roadside now—but there was only a curb on the Fifth Avenue.

"But tell me now, is that the high-costing ride to where I'm going?"

"Git in, git in, talk no more to me of money!" he said impatiently, as if she were being uncivil. "Sure, you're going up there on Murray Hill but for one reason—a situation, I know!"

She climbed in, the door banged shut, off they trotted, the horses' hooves ringing clear in the fresh sparkling air.

The further up this broad dignified avenue they drove, the larger the houses became and the further apart, so that by the time they got to Thirtieth Street many were set almost in parks.

They passed a granite mansion with Doric columns and the cabby pointed a whip and called down, "That fellah got his making a swill they drink here called sarsaparilla!" Then, as they passed a frowning marble palace at Thirty-fourth Street, "And that one"—he pointed— "belongs to a b'hoy named Billy Astor. He made his by gittin' here first!"

Now they were near Thirty-seventh. "Is it to the Van Leyns' you are going?"

"It is that! Is it aught you know of them?"

"Why, the fellah himself, this Van Leyn, had an old brick mansion down on Washington Square, but it's said this new wife made him build this place up here. A gothic villa, they calls it!"

The cab stopped, and Po got down. "Go in that side door," he pointed, and Po was grateful he had saved her from her first error. "I'll wait a bit, so in case you've no luck, I can take you back!"

Po smiled up at him on the box, bolstered by the thought of a man from Killeney Bay standing by. Then she crossed the avenue.

Towers and turrets rose from the large house. It reminded you, sort of, of a castle, but it was made of stucco instead of stone and in the grounds, covering nearly a block, with tight-clipped hedges in front and kitchen gardens in the rear, the trees seemed to have been but lately planted. She clutched the letter in her hand, took a deep breath, and lifted the knocker on the gothic arched side door.

A beautiful butler, with handsome calves and plum-colored livery, appeared, regarding her with the warmth of a stony statue. On the strength of the letter, which Coventry had marked "From Cecil, Lord Bathurst," Po was suffered to sit upon a velvet chair in the marble hall. The beautiful curved calves disappeared with the letter on a silver salver. He went into a room off the hall from which animated voices flew out like twittering birds.

Through the window, Po saw a barouche draw up smartly before the front of the house and stand waiting. She guessed Mrs. Van Leyn was about to drive out. At this moment, chatting with a handsome man with curving, black mustaches, and a woman fashionably dressed for driving, Augusta Van Leyn, holding the unopened letter in her hand, came into the hall.

Looking at this great lady with the diamond cross on her bare bosom, Po blinked. This beauty, about thirty-five, tall, with strong jet brows against a white skin, with her white silk bonnet trimmed with purplish-red grapes setting off her abundant black hair, and the rich folds of her dark crimson taffeta gown topped by a bertha of exquisite lace of the kind the nuns in Dublin spent patient years making—this was "darling Augusta." And, looking at her, Po tried to reconcile the snatches of brutally candid conversation she had heard from her step-son and Carlotta during the long hours of the night.

From the rear of the hall, a man in the striped apron of a gardener now appeared carrying a flat wide wicker basket heaped with plump pink strawberries. Augusta examined these carelessly.

"Put my card on these, Scoreby." She addressed the butler. "And have them delivered by hand to the Commander of the English naval ship that's just in at the battery!"

Her friends broke in with gay banter at this. "Trust Augusta to find a distinguished visitor before anyone else!"

Augusta was opening the letter now, and bantering back. "Those British naval uniforms will look most handsome at my Saturday morning reception!" Now she glanced through the letter rapidly, and laughed again, this time with triumph. "Just listen to this—and it's from—" Here she glanced up to be sure they were impressed, and to enjoy their being—"Lord Bathurst!" She read phrases. "He's heard of me as a hostess! Recommends one of his household staff—" Augusta sent a cursory cold glance at Po. Then she ended on a note of triumph, "And—he may come here!"

Augusta came toward Po then. Po, remembering the woman in the Intelligence Office, sprang to her feet, and ducked a curtsy.

"You are O'Reilly?"

"Yes, m'lady!" It had bobbed out without Po planning it, but it was evidently not a fatal error.

"Scoreby"—Augusta was already moving off—"take care of her. I'll fit her in as a second maid—or to help you in the pantry. I'll talk about it when I return!"

A maid handed Augusta a carriage mantle of heavily embroidered white silk and a scarlet taffeta parasol with a long carved handle of wrought ivory. Augusta, with a rich rustle, swept out of the hall toward her barouche, her friends following.

Scoreby turned and looked at Po like she could be the queerest old bit of straw blown up on a door step.

"Come"—his nostrils quivered faintly with distaste—"with me!"

Chapter Twenty-six

THE WAGES, it turned out, were ten dollars a month, with livery furnished. Best of all, Po would have, once a week, a whole day and a night out. She hoped she could go, then, from Thirty-seventh Street into the lower city, to the concert saloons, to absorb the American songs.

Borrowing a stamp from Scoreby, she had written Brian at once, telling him she was safe, and would come back to see him as soon as she could. She decided for the present to give him no address, for she still felt shaky there, not only because of the joke of Carlotta and Coventry, but because she had to bluff a great deal in other ways.

However, knowing the servants in a great house were apt to be rank snobs, she would get out of a tight fix, when scolded by the head chamber for some ignorance, by haughtily declaring that Lady Dudevan's chamber put the bolster over the coroneted monogram, or whatever the matter in dispute might be. She never admitted she had only been a guest at Lough, and knew nothing whatever about the linen room.

Scoreby, she soon learned, was what in Bethel Court would have been called a posy, with a young footman in a near-by great house as special friend. And she soon saw that Scoreby managed by gossip, intrigue, and eavesdropping, to make himself valuable to Augusta, for he was clever in all kinds of message carrying and secret arrangements, taking special relish in flouting Mr. Van Leyn, the husband.

At first, Scoreby looked on Po with delicate disdain, but when he saw her reject decisively the advances of the lusty gardener, he contemplated her speculatively. Later, he moved her downstairs to the butler's pantry, where she washed glasses and polished silver. She guessed he meant to train her, as being small and unnoticeable, to relay all kinds of morsels of information to him.

And it was amazing, how scandalously quick, from a servant's eye view, you got down to the bare bones of a family life. Po soon came to know which of the men who flocked in and out to receptions and teas was Augusta's present favorite—and it was not Nicholas Van Leyn.

One day, Count Ossi, he of the black mustaches, who was helping Augusta arrange a bal masque before she left for Newport, had been announced and was being shown upstairs. On the second floor, next Augusta's bed chamber—with its canopied bed enthroned on an Aubusson rug, with a bathing room next where water gushed into a marble tub if you so much as turned a brass handle—was her sumptuous private sitting room, crowded with gilt mirrors and red damask furniture.

As Count Ossi was going toward Augusta's sitting room, he passed, in the upper hall, Coventry. Po saw the Count, with a little flourish, bow mockingly.

Then Scoreby sent Po, with a sharp command, to dust the day room.

Po was glad of this chore, though. For it was what Po had discovered in Mr. Van Leyn's day room on the first floor, that kept her obedient under the stings and sneerings of Scoreby's orders. Because of what she had seen, she felt she must on no account, and certainly not at this moment, lose this situation.

It was a large room, and, from the long heavy table with green leather chairs about it, Po guessed Nicholas might occasionally transact business there. The room was severe but impressive, with solid black walnut furniture. Po wondered if perhaps this one room had been transferred from the brick mansion on Washington Square.

From behind heavy gold frames, grim faces, one surrounded by a frilled neck ruff, gloomed down. One portrait, with a brass plate reading, "Pieter Van Leyn, 1670," stared across glumly at another marked "Willem Van Leyn, 1724." There was a portrait of Nicholas' first wife, too, a Dutch-looking lady, with a long aristocratic nose and prominent blue eyes, and beautiful color sketches of full rigged ships, bearing the legend, "Van Leyn, Builders."

But it was none of these that had excited Po and determined her to stay there, ears open and eyes wide, as long as she could. It was, in fact, a large picture, neatly framed on the wall, gray-toned, the kind they called a photo-graph. It was of nine gentlemen with elegant beards, in baseball costumes. Underneath the legend read, "Knickerbocker Baseball Club, Nicholas Van Leyn, President."

Po dusted without hurrying, for she knew Nicholas would not return for some time. He led a clock-like existence. He rose not too early, breakfasted alone—for Augusta never appeared and Coventry came and went in the house—was driven down to his office on the Wall Street, or to the shipyard in Brooklyn, and in the later afternoon returned, sometimes to find the house overflowing with one of Augusta's receptions.

But it was what happened on Tuesday afternoons that had Po watching the poor man's every move. Then, Nicholas came home early. Several of his friends might call for him. One of these friends looked familiar to Po, and she finally placed him as Mr. Jenkins, the lawyer who had been toastmaster at the testimonial dinner for Hymes in Brooklyn. This Jenkins and a few others appeared in baseball uniforms with "Knickerbockers" written bold as brass across the belts.

After a little leisurely drinking, and accompanied by some of the servants to carry the gear, they were driven some blocks south to an open grassy place at Twenty-fifth street called Madison Square. There, Po was told, they practiced.

And oh, wasn't Po going down there as soon as she could manage to get away to watch them! And when she went to Brooklyn to visit Brian and see Larry, wouldn't she have the great bits to tell them! Why, she could be the spy of all spies! So she gloated over her situation and jumped quickly to please Scoreby when he spoke. Not only was she in the family of a Knickerbocker—she had stumbled into a whole nest of Knickerbockers!

She had just pulled a stool over to the fireplace, to dust the glass-encased wooden models of Van Leyn-built ships, when Coventry came into the room.

He came in with a thoughtful frown, but seeing Po, smiled at her. "Ah! It's you!" Then he asked kindly, "Are you getting on all right?"

Po got down from the stool. "Oh, yes! Except the joke worries me!"

"The joke!" He looked absent-minded, as if he were worried about other things. "Oh," he said as if remembering, "that! Well, you're safe here, and you're happy, aren't you?"

"Oh, it's the fine place, for it'll be giving me the time to learn the way of American singing!"

His eyes kept wandering toward the door, but he said still kindly enough, "Well, then, why don't you stay?"

"I'd like it fine! 'Twas only the joke was—"

Suddenly he glanced out into the hall toward the stairs. "I've more to worry about than playing jokes on her!"

Then, as Po began to dust the gold frame of the oil of the plumpish man in a commodore's cap, holding a silver cup marked "Blackwell's Island Yacht Regatta, 1841," Coventry came up beside her, and stared absently at the picture.

" 'Tis that of your father, isn't it?" Po turned to him.

He replied grimly, "That's how he was before. That's when he was happy!" He turned away then, and looked around the room uneasily.

But Po had to scurry just then, and gather up her brass polish and cleaning cloths and duster, for Nicholas Van Leyn had come in. He was not on schedule. Except for days when the Knickerbockers practiced, he rarely came home this early.

Nicholas was older than Augusta by some ten years, he being around forty-five. With his plump patrician face, his sandy side whiskers, his fair hair, he looked a duller, older, puffed-out version of Coventry, and the father and son, Po had discovered, were very fond of one another.

Usually Nicholas was pleasant to the servants, in the manner of a lord. He paid no attention, or hardly saw them, just reached out a hand, and whatever he wanted was placed in it. It was only when some detail of his well-cushioned existence went wrong that he looked at the servants or spoke, and then in a calm and kindly way, being sure that seeing the error of their ways, they would immediately be more alert in his service.

But today, his calm pleasantness had been ruffled by some wind off-shore. He still carried his stick crooked over his arm, and he stared at a handful of letters and papers he held in one hand. Before Po could get into the hall, she heard him say, not in his usual calm tone, to Coventry, "Will you ask your step-mother to come here?" And he did not add, "If she is not engaged."

Po suspected the letters and papers Nicholas stared at, so disturbed, might have something to do with overdue bills. It was current below-stairs that money was not as plentiful as formerly, and that Nicholas was not as sharp a businessman as his father and grandfather had been. And the house was run with senseless extravagance—rich food purchased and allowed to spoil. Suddenly, there would come an area of retrenchment, like a woman who has allowed bills to accumulate, being confronted with creditors or lack of funds, making a hasty resolution to economize. Expensive peacocks, lately purchased as ornaments for the rear garden, were suddenly killed and roasted for fowl, because they were costly to feed. The servants, while carelessly piling up waste, sneered at the master for allowing it.

Then, as Po was putting away the cleaning things in the pantry, Scoreby appeared. He was in an annoyed swivet.

Two conversations, both of which he felt he must hear, were going on at the same time. But one was upstairs, the other down. Coventry had remained in Augusta's sitting room, with Count Ossi! Unquestionably, something beautifully unpleasant would occur! Po knew very well that a certain spot in the linen cupboard upstairs commanded most of what was said in Augusta's sitting room. Indeed, it was this which kept the feud going between Scoreby and the Head Chamber. Both knew knowledge was power, and the Head Chamber felt that vantage spot was her vested right, and she was not going to be ousted by Scoreby.

But here came Augusta now, trailing her white embroidered muslin frock down the stairs, her heels making an angry click, as she moved toward the day room. Without question, there would be another horrible scene over extravagance. It seemed to Scoreby that fate was purposely irritating that day! Why did both conversations have to occur at once? He elected to cover the upstairs sitting room conversation, as being more unusual.

It was then he showed Po what she had suspected, that there was a certain spot in the butler's pantry, where, innocently polishing silver, one could hear the conversation in Nicholas' day room—especially if the talkers had the grace to keep at that end of the room. The butler's pantry, between the dining hall and the day room, jutted out on one of the house's many angles, and if the oriel window facing the pantry were open slightly—and Scoreby saw, in warm weather, that it was—the talk in the day room could be distinctly heard.

Po did not like her commission—but she did not want to lose her situation either. She resolved she would stand there, but not listen, and would make up some wish-wash when Scoreby asked her to report.

It was easy at first not to hear, for the voices in the day room, both Augusta's and Van Leyn's were low—but suddenly she heard Augusta's voice raised, sharp: "Get it like you did before!"

Po was ashamed of hearing, and started to move out of the pantry, but the voices died. Perhaps they had moved to the other end of the room.

Then she could hear papers crackling, and occasionally an angry phrase from Van Leyn, as if he were pacing up and down, and what she heard came when he was at her end of the room. "If you could stay at a hotel in Newport—but to take a cottage, transport all the servants—I tell you I can't afford—"

The conversation was fragmentary now and Po tried to shut it out. Then she heard Augusta's voice, louder and taunting: "Look at those ancestors of yours! You can't tell me that they didn't do a lot worse to get what they did!"

Po slipped out into the hall so as not to hear. But when she was there, she was in an agony for fear Scoreby would come down and discover she had left her post. She stood fidgeting in the hall, until she heard a door open in the upstairs hall, and thinking Scoreby was coming, she sped back to the pantry. She heard Augusta in a towering rage now.

"I know he's coming here this afternoon! All you have to do is to tell him yes!"

"No! I won't do it!"

Scoreby appeared then, on silent footsteps, and, with finger on his lips for her silence, motioned her to leave, that he would take over.

The rest of the afternoon, Po could not help wondering who it was they had mentioned as coming, and what it was that Van Leyn was going to say no to.

But she was sick of the atmosphere of conniving in the house. It was no planning of hers that put her in the pantry on a ladder, reaching down the extra sherbet cups for Augusta's musicale that evening, at the moment when whoever it was Van Leyn expected arrived.

But, being there, she heard a voice and, hearing it, she, for the first time in that house, dropped and broke a piece of glass. Scoreby was in the conservatory, superintending the cutting of flowers, and did not come running at the sound. Po got down off the ladder, but stood, a piece of crystal in her hand, her mouth open in surprise.

It was the voice she heard in the day room that astonished her. It was the voice, flat, grating, without timbre, she had heard at the testimonial dinner! The voice that had brought the sensation of some anxious, desperate moment in her life, without bringing the memory of when or where. She must be mistaken! She listened, straining. No, it was the same voice, the voice of William Hymes.

She went wildly through her memory, ransacking all the drawers and closets. When? At what black moment? She listened tense now, as the voice went on.

"—can lay hands on a hundred ton iron-screw steamer. It's priced at sixty thousand, dirt cheap, and the boilers are good enough to last ninety days anyhow!"

Was it in Fall River, in the mill, she had first heard him? No, it was something about ships.

"I am sure"—she heard Van Leyn then, coldly polite—"I wish you the best of luck!"

"Hah! You know I don't waste time visiting! Here are the facts! With the ship at sixty; stores, crew and coal at two hundred thousand; and a cargo at seventy-five thousand—the whole venture'll take three hundred thousand!"

Po strained, her whole body leaning forward, listening, trying to remember. Was it in New Bedford?

"A great deal of money." Van Leyn's voice was cool and calm.

"Put in three hundred thousand, take out five hundred thousand. Where else could you turn that much profit in ninety days?"

"Of course"—Van Leyn was suave—"the risk is great, as you cannot insure!"

"This is venture capital!"

Desperately, Po searched for the place she had heard that strange flat voice. It was something about the sea.

"And besides, the risk is reduced, for I got someone to keep tab on things for me at sea—a reliable supercargo!"

It was that word, that like a crash of cymbals, sent echoes reverberating through Po. That night on the *Red Tanager!* The supercargo discovering them in the hold! She remembered the supercargo mentioning a "Big One," who was to get off in a small boat. She remembered then, how someone called down an order to the supercargo in the hold, someone she had not seen, but who had a harsh, grating voice, strangely flat, without timbre. The voice she heard now in the Van Leyns' day room, under the Van Leyn portraits, was the one she had heard on the *Red Tanager.*

But surely she must be mistaken. She wasn't bothered about eavesdropping now. She listened with all her might, only worried for fear Scoreby would come and send her packing.

"—every venture's turned out well. One of them, unless I miss my guess, built this house for you! Must be pretty expensive to run, eh? I had a feeling you'd want to take another subscription, and I'm willing!"

"Well, thank you, but—" Poor Mr. Van Leyn sounded unhappy and driven, Po thought. She wished she could help him. "I wanted to tell you. The risk—"

"No more risk than before. All sound, trustworthy people. The Spanish bank will take one-half as before, Jenkins and me each a sixth, and you can pick up the last sixth."

"Thank you for thinking of me, but—I must decline."

"Well, now—I don't see how you can!"

"What do you mean?"

"Well, I don't like to mention it—but the shipyard owes me a great deal for materials."

"Are you questioning my credit?"

"Of course not. But—just let me explain how things are with me. I have just been able to pick up a franchise for a new ferry to

Brooklyn. That took cash! I got two ventures at sea already, with cash capital in this, so, while I don't pretend I'm a poor man, I need ready cash!"

"Let me tell you before you go further," Van Leyn broke in, "that even if I wished to, I couldn't subscribe. I haven't the cash."

"Well, now, what I was thinking. You got a packet well along! You can raise fifty thousand on that!"

"No!" Van Leyn's voice sounded harassed now, but sharp. "I am counting on that to pay—"

"Of course, you remember I have your note for the materials I furnished the Yard. I could have that packet attached. But why do we have to do that? Why don't you raise the fifty thousand on the packet yourself, put it in the venture, and in ninety days all your worries are over!"

There was a long silence, and when Van Leyn broke out, his voice was sharp, anguished. "This is the last time I can take such risks!"

"What are you doing?" Po jumped at Scoreby's sharp voice. He stood, his hands full of roses to be arranged, frowning at her. "Didn't you hear me call? Why, you've broken something! Go at once to the scullery and bring me several containers—"

But Po hardly heard the peevish words buzzing around her head like angry bees as she moved off. She kept hearing Nicholas Van Leyn's voice as he said, "—the last time!" and wondering at the anguish in it.

Chapter Twenty-seven

THE MORE Po thought of it, the surer she was that William Hymes was the man on the *Red Tanager*. She remembered the day she had seen the supercargo Rimshaw meet Hymes, in Brady's Gardens in Brooklyn.

She remembered, too, how she had wondered at Hymes owning the Iron Works, and wondered if it were by these Ventures they talked of. Whatever they were, they could hardly be anything wrong, or a man like Nicholas Van Leyn would hardly be in them. Yet—there was something strange about it, too.

In a way, it was none of her business, and yet, ever since Larry had cried out at Hymes at the testimonial dinner—and whether for that reason or not, it was a fact that Hymes was not nominated for the political office—Po had feared that somehow, sometime, Hymes would do something to injure Larry. And since there was evidently something queer going on, maybe it would be a good thing if she knew what.

So the next Tuesday afternoon, when Mr. Jenkins, the lawyer, dropped in for a drink before he and Nicholas left for baseball practice in the Madison Square, and Po heard the word "Hymes," she managed to take a very long time serving the Madeira. They were inclined to fall silent, though, when she was in the day room.

Po had made a resolution never to listen in the pantry again, or take part in any gossip about the family's private affairs, but when it came to the Knickerbockers, that was different. If you were a spy, like in war, you did all kinds of things. So—she would eavesdrop about baseball. It was a code she had made up. Maybe, she reflected, that's how laws were made. You made up rules that fitted in with what you wanted to do anyway, then you felt all right, because you were following a code.

Now she flew to the post in the pantry, and only hoped Scoreby would remain in and about the front parlor where Augusta had visitors. He usually did, ignoring Mr. Van Leyn's dull friends, who were, in his opinion, extremely uninteresting.

Po could hear Jenkins talking now, in his precise, fussy voice. "You're not finding it easy to move from Clippers to steam, and I'll tell you why, Nicholas. Because, with iron steamers, you just can't keep in your little closed circle like you do on wooden hulls and get orders. You have to get out with all kinds of people and hustle."

"But, Jenkins"—Van Leyn's voice had its usual casual pleasant sound now—"I'm convinced that people will tire of all this hustle, as you call it. Then this country will come back, for leadership, to men of station. It has to!"

"Now, I'm different. I try to move with the times!"

"Things have never been right in this country since Andrew Jackson was in the White House!"

"There's something in what you say." Jenkins sighed. "I hear you're in with us on the new venture."

"For the last time. This house is expensive."

"I've been telling Hymes that, but—he asked me to look out for a place for him."

"Over here!" She could hear the amazement in Van Leyn's voice.

"On the Fifth Avenue, as a matter of fact. You know I think you have him all wrong, Nicholas. He doesn't like the ventures any more than we do. But he has a great scheme afoot, and he needs cash for it. It'll benefit thousands. He's acquired a franchise for a new ferry."

"So he told me."

"There's competition, other ferries, but he's a good fighter, an able chap. He'll pull it off. I have great faith in him. Of course—he'll need some others in with him when the company is organized. Do y'know that last year the Union Ferry Company earned twelve per cent profit? It's not much, but a public utility is sure. People have to go back and forth. And I'm sure Hymes will remember his friends when it comes to letting out the stock, and setting up a Board of Directors."

"I admit the chap has many good sound qualities."

"I'm glad you feel that way, Nicholas, because I told him I'd mention something to you. He knows you're President of the Knicker-bockers. He wanted to know if you wouldn't put him up for membership."

"In the Knickerbockers!" She could hear Van Leyn's astonishment. "You're not serious!"

"Oh, yes, I am. He's really touching about it. In some ways he's just a child. Has romantic notions that belonging to a certain club will put the right mark on him socially. It's all part of his buying a house here on this street, and establishing himself here. I think he means to look out for a suitable wife, too. In a way, I admire the chap tremendously. He's trying to make something of himself—socially, too."

"But that's hopeless."

"Well, I don't know, Nicholas. I think you're a little cut off from things. Anyone who can do the things he has done deserves the best."

"But the Knickerbockers! He wouldn't be happy! He doesn't belong there!

"I've wondered about that myself."

"And it's not only my putting him up. No one would vote for him!"

"Well, I don't know. I think you may not find as much opposition as you might expect. Quimby knows about the ferry franchise, Brinton of the *Journal of Commerce* knows about it. And, remember, the Manhattan Gas Light buys iron from him!"

"But the Knickerbockers! That's the one group where we are all on equal footing, can relax, talk about business freely if we want to! I'm not going to put him up!"

"I think that's unwise, Nicholas."

But they went out and got in the carriage then, Jenkins' man carrying their gear, and were driven off to practice. For all her listening, Po felt she had learned mighty little.

But she did discover one thing that day that got her excited again. In the kitchen entry there was kept a large leather-bound book with blank pages. Every day Scoreby carried this to Augusta. In it she noted down menus, guests expected, parties scheduled. And, right after the entry: "Wednesday, tea, for Commander Bunshire of the British warship, and three of his officers—" (the strawberries must have been effective, Po guessed)—"pate de fois gras, curacao rum for the gentlemen," another entry read: "Thursday, lunch meeting, Board of Directors of Mr. Van Leyn's club, the Knickerbockers. Terrapin, with Mr. Van Leyn's own sauce."

Why, maybe at that meeting Coventry would present the Brooklyn challenge! And Po might be able to report back to Brooklyn not only that she was in a strategic spot to spy—but she could bring back news that the Knickerbocker game was scheduled at last! She had planned to go back to Brooklyn on her first day out, but now she decided to wait until after the Knickerbocker meeting.

Instead, on her first day out, she would be about her purpose of learning American songs.

Po had considered trying to find Louise in her mermaid act at Barnum's on the Broadway, to ask if she would tell Po where she might go to hear songs. But Po felt a reluctance to ask Louise. She liked her good nature, her free ways, but, in another way, she didn't like her. She was, and Po grimaced wryly, jealous of Louise with Larry and that was the ugly truth.

But, in the Van Leyn house, there were many newspapers about. There was the *Herald*, where she could read such items as, "On Tuesday, as General Tom Thumb's mother was in the 27th Street railroad station, some adroit rascal filched her carpetbag." And there was the *Clipper*, where she could read that, "Mrs. Bradford had a small supper in her rooms for Charlotte Cushman, after the opening of *School for Scandal*," or that, "August Belmont's mare Lady Owen is touted to win at Newport."

It was in the *Clipper* that she found advertisements for Bryant's Minstrels—"Comicalities, musicians, and vocalists, at 482 Broadway, at thirty past seven every night, admission twenty-five cents." And there she read that at Wood's Minstrels, 444 Broadway, Miss Gibbs was giving tableaux and musical entertainment. These places must be like theaters, where she could safely go alone.

Her first day out, Po took the horse-drawn omnibus that passed every hour to the lower city. She went, in the afternoon, to Burtis' Varieties, which advertised "all the musical talent in the country of any account, admission ten cents." For supper, she went to an oyster parlor that had singing waiters, and in the evening to Woods'. And then—just as she was going home, she had some unbelievable luck.

On a side street, in a dusty small window marked Firth and Pond, Music Publishers, she saw printed copies of some of the songs she had heard that day. She purchased them. This meant she could really learn the words, for with the exaggerated way the singers sang them, these had been hard to understand. And then, just as she was turning away, she saw, next to Firth and Pond, a store selling second-hand musical instruments, guns, knives. It was a pawn shop. But what held her transfixed was a small Irish harp.

Some of the keys were missing. It had been painted over, none too skillfully, to hide its antiquity—but, there it stood. Ten dollars, the sign said. Po stood, lost in musing, looking at it. What immigrant, what sad soul, a harper, come brave to the new world, had lost his tongue, his voice, discouraged, given up, maybe dead. Oh, if she but had that little harp, she would love it so, coax it back into singing! It would be a comfort to her, and she could play it privately betimes in her own room. For to speak truth, she did not like the songs she had tried so hard to learn that afternoon.

When she got off the stage that night, with her little roll of music sheets under her arm, it was late, nearly eleven o'clock. The Van Leyn house was dark in front. Po knew Augusta had gone to a charity ball being conducted by a Mrs. Astor, and half the servants were having their day off. Only a light glowed in the oriel windows jutting out slightly from the house, in the day room, and a dim light on the third floor, in some servant's room. A sleepy scullery maid let Po in at the kitchen entrance. As she went into the kitchen entry, the signal showing the bell had been pulled in the day room clicked in the box on the wall. Scoreby was out. Po whipped off her bonnet and shawl. She was not in livery. Augusta or Scoreby might have flayed her alive, but Van Leyn would not notice.

When Po opened the day room door, yellow light streamed from under the green glass lamp shade, across the heavy walnut table, and made amber ridges of the folds of Nicholas Van Leyn's brown velvet smoking jacket. He sat in a high-backed armchair, erect, but at ease, belonging there.

Sitting on the edge of a straight chair across from him, his shoulders humped forward so that the seams of his black coat strained awkwardly, one large square hand stiffly on his knee, the other holding an incongruously fragile wine glass, sat William Hymes.

It was strange, Po thought, but when she had overheard these two talking before, she had felt vaguely sorry for Van Leyn. Now, seeing Van Leyn, his smooth fair hair, his cool brown eyes in the calm plump face regarding Hymes from behind a wall of courtesy, she felt vaguely sorry for Hymes.

For once, Hymes's expressionless face had a spark in it—and to Po it suggested suffering.

As usual, Van Leyn did not look at the answerer to his ring.

"Crackers and cheese, please!" Po had a little tremor of terror wondering if Hymes had seen her in Brooklyn, might recognize her. But his eyes never left Van Leyn's face.

Po turned to go. Beside the dark gleaming bottle of Malmsley Madeira she saw one glass almost full. Nicholas had drunk just enough to fulfill his duties as a host.

Po returned quickly with the thin English sea biscuits and aromatic cheese she had seen Scoreby serve.

As she started up to her room, she paused. What if they were talking about the Knickerbockers? Jenkins had mentioned Hymes and the Knickerbockers. Well, she'd listen for a moment, with half an ear, just to see.

Through the oriel window, in the quiet of the night, with only crickets in the back garden chirping, the voices from the day room sounded clearly.

Hymes's voice had a note she had never heard before, a sort of incredulous outrage, the way a decent man would feel at black injustice. Ah, they *were* talking about the Knickerbockers!

"The Knickerbockers to you means just another club, but to me, at this moment, it's the background I need, so I can do the things I want to do for this city. I helped Brooklyn! Now I want to cross the river!"

"But"—Nicholas' voice had a kindliness to it which made it seem cruel—"I do not feel you yourself would be happy in the club!"

"I'm no different than anyone else! The same things make me happy! I worked hard, built up everything I have from nothing. I'm not ashamed of my struggles! I'm proud of them! But now I want what everyone wants! A fine comfortable home to found a family in that'll take care of what I've done, and make it grow. How you can block a man that never hurt you, I don't understand! Who else would have helped you, when you needed it most, to a hundred fifty per cent profit? I gave a great deal of time and energy in fitting up the vessels, in worrying about every detail. I did all the dirty work. You have the benefit of my judgment of men in picking out crew and captains and supercargoes. All you did was put in money. Yet now, when I ask a small return of this friendship, you go out of your way to hurt me!"

"It seems to me this is all quite uncalled for!" Van Leyn's voice was not so cool and courteous now. "After all, it's in devilish bad taste for you to come here and question your exclusion from a club!"

"Excluding people!" Hymes's voice was stronger now with righteous indignation. "That's not the way we do things in this country! If a man's able to get anything—no one can keep him out. It's a terrible thing when men that have been associated in business as we have—I've always been honest with you—have to come to a thing like this! What if I got mad? What if for instance, I put certain ship's manifests in the hands of the Federal Court here? Or, what if I turned them over to that fool Greeley, to make a holiday with in the *Tribune?*"

"You see what I mean, sir, about your not belonging to the Knickerbockers! Not that I am concerned with your threats! You're involved as much as I am!"

"Except in that second venture. D'you remember? We sent out three, the bark *Red Tanager,* the bark *Wanderer,* and the schooner *Gertrude.* Each took a ship, for convenience. Each had the papers in our individual names. You elected to underwrite the bark *Wanderer.*"

"The papers were destroyed, as usual!"

"The supercargo didn't destroy the papers for the bark *Wanderer,* showing a list of cargo in detail and where landed. They're in my safe in Brooklyn, showing you, and you alone, carried through that venture!

"I never hurt anyone who doesn't hurt me. But—if a man does hurt me, or balk me or get in my way, I know how to handle that. I'll tell you how. I find out what it is that man sets store by, what he wants most, what he's struggling for. When I find out, then I hit him, just there, hard, on that one spot. Now, for instance, if it got out about my sending out the ventures, I wouldn't like it. It'd hurt my business. I'd do a great deal to keep it from happening. But—it wouldn't kill me. A man that's come up the way I have's gotta know the men around him. And I know the spot to hit you on. You like belonging to what I call—the Righteous Rulers. You're where you are not for anything much you done, but because you're supposed to stand for something. So with you . . . it's your name. And like I said—if it came out about me, I wouldn't like it. But—it'd kill you!"

"Sir, I bid you good evening!" And Mr. Van Leyn's voice had the goaded anguished sound again.

Chapter Twenty-eight

SCOREBY was in one of his moods. The Board of Directors of the Knickerbocker Baseball Club was to be served with a buffet lunch in the day room, and he considered the whole middle-class affair distinctly beneath his talents.

"Merchants!" he said superciliously. "High-class clerks!" Scoreby prided himself on knowing all about the guests in the house, his specialties being Debt, Drink, and Depravity—but as to Dullness, he couldn't be bothered. "Blair! Superintendent of a Carriage Works on Barclay Street!" He sniffed. "And Granger! Owns a plant on Water Street, making horseshoes!" And as for Shelton, Manager of Arnold Constable, what was he but a glorified ribbon clerk? True, Fielding was connected with the Bank of New York, but, Scoreby was sure, in no very distinguished capacity. Haviland was the only one in Society, and that only by virtue of an old family, for he still lived in his ancient house on unfashionable Broome Street.

Augusta, too, who, Po had come to learn, was not quite secure herself in Society, had gone off to some affair, not deeming the lunch of sufficient importance to see that all went smoothly. Nobody was excited about the meeting—except Po.

When Po went in, she nearly dropped the platter of hot cheese trifles being offered with the terrapin, what with staring at this cluster of breathing Knickerbockers, so much like legendary dragons had they come to seem. She wondered if Coventry had already given the challenge to Nicholas, and thought excitedly how it was going to be taking the town-shaking news back to Brooklyn that the challenge had been received and the date for a game set.

She tried to hurry them as much as possible, snatching plates when she dared, but they went dawdling on, never mentioning baseball. Then Haviland, from behind his dignified brown beard, said, "Lord Guernsey's visiting in this country. He's a power in the Marylebone Cricket Club. It'd be a decent thing to have him to one of our games, don't you agree!" They all did, and Nicholas said he'd see that a carriage was sent, to conduct him to the next game with the Gothams at Elysian Fields.

Scoreby sent Po to the kitchen for something, and as she returned she could see all the men listening to Nicholas Van Leyn in a kind of reverent silence. Every once in a while, as he said a certain word, they seemed to bow their heads for a few seconds. It reminded her of monks saying their beads, and making a genuflection at a sacred word. She wondered what the sacred word was Van Leyn was saying, and drew in close to listen. The word was fran-chise.

But then they went dribbling on about the annual meeting that was to be held on Saturday, and finally, after the cloth had been removed, and walnuts, brandy and cigars left, Scoreby, glad to be through with the stupid affair, departed.

Po flew to the listening place in the pantry in time to hear Nicholas say: "It's always been our custom, as you know, for this Board to look into the suitability of new members, and, if we pass them, they're taken in with no more formality. I'd like to present for membership, my son Coventry, who's been, as most of your sons are, a junior member. Coventry's through with Harvard, or, at any rate"—he chuckled—"they're through with him! He'll be here now coming in with me at the Yard, and I'm proposing him as senior member." There was no discussion. Coventry was voted in with suitable pleasantries.

In a low voice, Van Leyn proposed the name of William Hymes. Immediately, Fielding said he wanted to second it. He thought it'd be a good thing. Haviland said he didn't know the chap, but if Nicholas backed him, that was sufficient for him. They voted. Hymes was elected. William Hymes was a Knickerbocker! Arrah, now, wouldn't Po have the pocketful of rare gossip to take back to Brooklyn!

Coventry must have come in then, for Po heard his pleasant cheerful voice, and the board members chaffing him about being dropped from college, and congratulating him on being a senior member.

At last, she heard what she'd been waiting for!

"By the way, gentlemen," Coventry said, "I have a challenge for the club."

"From one of the New York clubs?" Nicholas asked, surprised. "They usually write us formally."

"This is from a team over on Long Island. In Brooklyn."

"Oh." Fielding was flat. "You're new in the club, Coventry."

Haviland broke out testily, "They're always badgering us! I tell you, the New York Yacht Club isn't annoyed that way. But then, there you have it! In baseball, all you need is a ball and a bat stick!"

"But about the challenge—" Coventry put in.

"We've always stayed right with the three other New York clubs. They play by our rules, and that way, we know where we are!" Blair said pleasantly.

"But—if we claim to be champions, how can we—" Coventry seemed a little taken aback.

"You see"—Haviland was kindly informative for the sake of young Coventry—"we pattern ourselves on the Marylebone Cricket Club of Lord's. Now they've handed down the rules for cricket, and say who's eligible, generation after generation, and it's worked out very well. And what's good enough for the Marylebone is good enough for us!"

"But"—Coventry seemed a little bewildered—"what do we do about the challenge?"

"Oh, just ignore it!"

Po felt very lonely in her room that night. The other girls in the house had sweethearts, and on time off would go out walking with them, up around Forty-second Street, where there was a big reservoir. It was a sort of Lovers' Lane. She had never minded being alone before, but now, she kept seeing Brooklyn faces—Tony, and Bushel Basket, and the Bull, and Brian, and Dave and Twinkle-Toes, when they learned they were as far away from beating the Knickerbockers as ever.

If only Larry could talk up to those old jackeens! Po thought about the annual meeting they'd mentioned. And it wasn't at all that a sight of Larry would do her a power of good that gave her an idea and set her to writing a letter! But once the idea came, she grappled with it.

It took her quite a while to figure it out, but finally she finished:

> Dear Larry:
> The challenge wasn't paid any attention to. The Knicker-bocker Baseball Club holds their annual meeting on Saturday here at Van Leyn's, 37th Street and the Fifth Avenue, at three.
> P. O'Reilly

Finished, she read it over. Then she thought, "Now, isn't that the queerest old love letter ever was written!"

"Erie Railroad closed up a point." Thomas Fielding, of the Bank of New York, and second baseman of the Knickerbocker Baseball Club, put one smooth hand under the tails of his handsome olive-green coat, and helped himself to the pâté de fois gras canapes Po was offering from an antique silver plate.

Nicholas Van Leyn, impressive in a beautifully fitted plum-colored tail coat, rich brocade waistcoat with pearl buttons, and elegant buff nankeen trousers falling in faultless drape to his polished boots, nodded, and helped Fielding to some of his best London Dock brandy. The Knickerbocker Baseball Club Annual Meeting was in sedate motion.

When twenty-five or thirty gentlemen, complete with whiskers, tail coats, cigars and glasses of liquid, stood or sat about in the day room, even that ample chamber seemed crowded. Scoreby, with eyelids drooping, as if in faint pain, offered Polish ham, cold woodcock, salmon and turkey at a side table, with port, champagne, brandy and—as something suitable for a group of brawny athletes—London brown stout.

They were a handsome lot of gentlemen, well stuffed into their nice green or blue or brown coats, with the pearly drab tight trousers on them, and pretty flowery waistcoats. They looked a little on the solid side for running bases or leaping for a fly ball, and Po wondered which one pitched. She looked, too, for missing front teeth, trying to guess which one might be their catcher.

Darting in and out with canapes, she remembered the time she had spied for the Excelsiors at the Atlantic game. This was certainly not the same. For one thing, she kept straining to hear something about baseball. But all she could pick up were scraps like Haviland, glass of port in hand, angrily telling Blair, "These damn Southerners, running up a bill of two or three hundred million with us up here for finished goods, then talking of seceding! We're going to have to fight them yet!" She darted to another group, only to hear Jenkins fussily declaring, "We Whigs are going to have to put up a strong candidate, that's plain!" And Granger nodded glumly as he said, "It's got to be someone to stop this advocating free land in the west! Drains off all the labor supply!" Po moved on to another group, but there was no baseball there either, for Mr. Shelton was wrothily declaring, "This new third party—these Republicans—aren't helping any! And Greeley and that bunch of radicals going ahead with it!"

Then there was a Dr. Allen, a man with a big crookedy nose, a curly black beard and a booming laugh, who talked and joked beamingly with everyone, and stared about as if with amazed amusement. He even tweaked Po's cheek and winked at her, but Po could see he just wanted her to feel that she was one of the party. He tossed off a brandy himself, and then demanded to see Quimby's tongue. Po hoped if ever she had a baby, he'd be around to deliver it—it would be so nice for the baby to meet, first of all, his look of amazed amusement.

And then Po stopped in her tracks. William Hymes came in. His movements were rigid, he stood awkwardly, holding an unlit cigar. His black coat and waistcoat and stock weren't pretty like the others. But in spite of that, he was not embarrassed. He even looked around a little contemptuously, as though he knew his own worth. And he was not let alone long either. Jenkins brought Haviland over to introduce him, and soon a little group of seven or eight were gathered, listening with rapt absorption to Jenkins and Hymes. Po hadn't heard a single word about baseball yet, and she slithered through the crowd to see if this were it. And then, she saw the same thing she'd watched at the board meeting. As Hymes talked, his listeners, every once in a while, bowed their heads for a few seconds, as if some sacred word had been said. Po drew near. Yes, it was the same word— the word fran-chise.

The serving over, and the meeting about to begin, Scoreby disappeared upstairs, for Augusta had friends in her sitting room. Po was in command of the pantry.

By the time she got there, and, busily polishing silver, could hear what was going on, the meeting had started, and Hymes, as a new member, was being introduced.

She didn't hear a word about baseball. Ah, at last! Here it came! They began to talk of the game at Elysian Fields in Hoboken the following week, with the New York Gothams.

But instead of arguing strategy, and who was to pitch, they began to talk about the menu for the banquet they were to give the Gothams afterward at the St. Denis! All went peacefully as they voted on green turtle soup à la reine, fresh salmon with lobster sauce, pâté de fois gras and truffles, but when they got to broiled grouse or compote de pigeon, a real tangle ensued. Mr. Quimby was a staunch advocate of the pigeon, as he'd gotten a recipe from the chef at the Greenbriar at White Sulphur, and he felt it important they hold their own with the Gothams in being able to select decent food. They settled the problem by referring it to a committee. Then Nicholas Van Leyn said they couldn't be disgraced in the matter of wines either, and he'd take care of that.

In the middle of an acrimonious debate about changing the style of the Knickerbocker hat, Po heard the front door bell chime. It was Scoreby's duty to answer it, and she guessed he'd taken care of it, for after a while she heard the front door open, and voices in the hall.

In the meantime, in the meeting, some radical was advocating the abandonment of the straw boater with the blue ribbon with Knickerbockers on it, for some kind of a cap, and this was meeting with conservative opposition.

Then, suddenly, Po, in the pantry, was electrified. She heard Larry's voice! He seemed to be at the other end of the room, but his voice sounded full and round and pleasant. He was saying something about being sorry to break in on the meeting, and that he brought greetings from the baseball clubs of Brooklyn.

Could it really be he? Like a flash she was in the hall. The day room door stood ajar. How had he gotten Scoreby to usher him in? Then, she saw.

They were right inside the door, and their backs were toward her, but there they stood on their brawny legs, those darlings of the world, those sons of light and laughter—Larry, Tony, and the Bull!

Seeing the Bull there, Po guessed why Scoreby had come to see eye to eye with them on showing them into the meeting! Ah, now they'd come to grips with it! Now, the Knickerbockers could never refuse to play them!

Then, Po saw inside the room, something that squeezed down

her excitement, and replaced it with disquietude. Sitting directly opposite the door, so that Po could see his face plainly, sat William Hymes. His feet planted solidly on the floor, he leaned forward a little, looking at Larry. On his face was an expression Po had seen before—in the Gardens, after they had made Hymes the butt—and again, when Larry had burst out against him at the testimonial dinner.

But Larry was talking on, courteous, unabashed.

"We have the best team on Long Island, the Brooklyn All Stars. We feel we're even strong enough to challenge for the championship such an illustrious team as the Knickerbockers. We propose a series, best of three, winner to be declared champion of the world!"

She saw some of the Knickerbockers eyeing the Bull, starting at his feet and traveling upward, in dismay.

"I may say, gentlemen, that baseball means a great deal to us over there. We know that you gentlemen, as the oldest team in New York, must feel as deeply as we do about the game. We've been working toward this moment a long time. It means everything to us!"

Then Po saw Hymes's face. A look was dawning there—a look of satisfaction. Burning into Po's mind came Hymes's words, overheard as he talked to Nicholas Van Leyn. "I find out what a man's struggling for, what means most to him! Then—" She wished Larry had not been quite so talkative.

Now Nicholas Van Leyn, courteous, calm, was taking charge of the situation.

"Thank you so much for coming, gentlemen." He bowed with impeccable courtesy. "We'll take the matter under consideration."

Po saw Larry's hands go out, as if in protest, but Van Leyn went on suavely. "Now, if you'll excuse us? We are pressed a little for time, and we *are* in the middle of a meeting!"

Po fled before Larry and the Bull and Tony could turn, and perhaps see her. By the time she got back to her listening post in the pantry, the outer door had closed on the men from Brooklyn and the Knickerbocker meeting was going on again.

Po recognized the loud jovial voice of Dr. Allen. "—guess Haviland and I are the only members left of the original club. It'd stir us up a little, be good for our livers, to play those young men! Don't you agree, Haviland?"

Haviland's voice was guarded, "Well, I don't know. We've always kept to the four New York clubs. Once you let down the bars, the whole thing gets out of control! After all, we've had these challenges before!"

Someone, she guessed Mr. Shelton, the Manager of Arnold Constable, said worriedly, "Did you see the size of that one with the beard? After all, we've always played our own style game."

Then Po heard Nicholas Van Leyn say in his calm mild voice: "They're worthy, upstanding chaps, I'm sure! But, would you say, people one might invite to lunch?"

"Besides"—Po recognized the precise, fussy voice of Jenkins— "the club and the games have been a place where we could talk affairs rather freely. It's useful to all of us in that respect!"

"Come, gentlemen," Dr. Allen's hearty voice rallied them. "Where's your sporting spirit? Let's play them! I demand it be put to a vote!"

A vote was taken. But there was not much feeling about it. The result seemed foreknown, for even as the vote counting was going on, Po heard someone who must have been near the open window say, "Look here, Granger, if you want to expand over there at the horseshoe plant, drop in at the bank. I can easily arrange a loan. Money's a plentiful. All that gold from California, you know!"

"May do that, Fielding. Got my warehouse bulging, holding for even higher prices."

Then the vote was announced. Five had voted to play a series with the challengers, the rest voted solidly against.

"The old jackeens," Po raged to herself. There they were, keeping Brooklyn from the joy of being champion, yet they themselves weren't getting any joy out of it! They didn't deserve the game! They were—using it! Using it in their merchant-ing! And soon as you used something, people or things, and didn't accept it joyously for what it was in itself, it got all spoiled!

Now Po knew she'd be no roaring heroine, taking home fine news to Brooklyn, and she thought of the faces in Brooklyn, and the bowed-down hearts, when all found out their mission to Manhattan had failed.

Yet somehow, somehow, Po thought grimly, they'd manage to blast those Knickerbockers, planted so solidly on the lid, sky high. And then, the men of the game in Brooklyn, who didn't try to use the game but loved it for its own sake, would come into their own.

But, even as she thought that, a disquieting picture flashed into her mind. It was Hymes's look of satisfaction as Larry said, "It means everything to us!" You'd think a man like Hymes would not bother, but hate did strange things to people.

All day she carried the letter inside her dress, where its edges cut happily. She didn't take it out to read. She didn't need to. It was the best letter ever she'd received, and good as a lengthy book of passionate love verses. She stopped now under the raspberry bushes in the kitchen garden on Murray Hill, and opened it again, just for the pleasure of seeing the large, square boyish hand. She read:

Something is missing over here. I think it is you. When are you coming back?

Larry

Chapter Twenty-nine

PO RAN down the steps of Rome's print shop in Brooklyn. It was her first afternoon back in Brooklyn and she wanted Dave to know she'd tried to see him.

"He's not working here any more!" Mr. Rome looked over his glasses. "Baseball! Baseball!" His voice rose like a man tried beyond reason. "I got sick and I got tired! So let him play his baseball, I said!"

But when she inquired at Dave's boarding house, she found he'd gone back to live in Battle Row. Battle Row, she knew, though she'd never been there, was a place one sank back to only in times of stress. Now, she *must* find him.

At the end of a narrow alley, close lined with falling-down wooden dwellings, pigsties and livery stables, three wooden tenement buildings huddled together, packed with nearly a hundred families.

Gray-looking children, thin legs protruding shoeless from under their one ragged garment, played in the offal-plastered alley, down which a wide gutter flowed with greenish ooze. The children shrieked and swarmed about, the same as if they had been playing in some sunlit field.

Smaller ones played a ring game, hands circled, in the widest space available, the dark passageway between the tenements. But the space was so narrow, the ring was squeezed out of shape. Instead of a joyous round O, it was a thin oval. Even skipping, hand in hand, inside the ring, they could not fling themselves in abandon, but must watch and turn abruptly at the corner. Po wondered if they'd ever played the game, which she remembered from her own childhood, in a full round circle. Had they always had to play it squeezed out in this narrow ellipse?

Inside the sagging building, the narrow dark hall was littered with decaying garbage, and the stench of unwashed humans and too-close privies struck her like a blow. Through doors half open in the heat, she could see into small dank rooms. Amid a chaos of bedding, clothes, and cooking utensils, six or eight people crowded, two or three of them, in the light from a single narrow window, feverishly stitching on piles of men's garments.

In none of the rooms did she see Dave. About to knock on a closed door, a man's voice suddenly warned: "Don't go in there, gal! They's cholera!"

The banister going up the treacherously steep narrow littered stairs was loose, and in the half dark she discovered only in time where steps were missing. Above, she almost fell over a huddled man, sick, sleeping or drunk, and she saw another stretched beyond him. They looked up and stared at her, thin human faces huddled together in haggard wretchedness. Inside the flats, pale-looking women and children worked frowningly on piles of bright cloth flowers and feathers. The stench of too many people, working, living, dying, too crowded, hit her.

Behind a door at the end of the hall, wrangling voices rose, the door flung open, a man sped past her and out of the building. She recognized him as one of the ball players on the Putnams team. A frowning, harassed woman peered after him a moment before she shut the door.

Suddenly Po was glad there was a baseball field for the Putnams player. For all the men. She thought, then, of the face of the frowning, harassed woman behind the door. Where was her baseball field?

Maybe it was the dark close air, the stench, made her feel so, but she stood there, eyes down, crying inside herself, ashamed, ashamed for someone, for something! Why did she feel so? Why, Bethel Court in Dublin was as bad or worse than this!

Yes, but Dublin was an ancient city, the sins and sorrows of centuries of mistakes crying from the paving. The ancient stones of Bethel Court had been once a great lord's castle and stables, long abandoned. But this—she looked around where cholera seemed to peer from doors, fever grin from dank walls—this was new shiny America! How could it ever have happened? These buildings had actually been built, not as a castle, but for these people to live in! How could this galled sore, this accreted filth have come so soon? America seemed not old enough to have accumulated such a place.

Po stood there, terribly angry and ashamed of the world.

Then she heard music, sweetly played, floating with light notes through the noisome hallway. Doors began to open. Unwashed, dull-looking men and women moved out toward the music. It flowed, sweet and bright, through the air. Po went with the others toward it.

The musicians, an old bass fiddler, a thin violinist, a flute player in a ragged cap, stood there, playing. They lived in the house, a woman next to Po explained. They were street musicians and played at weddings or parties. "But often, they play like this for us, for nothing. How we enjoy it!" The windows were full now, listening.

The children crept close. The music was like rain falling, soft, clean, washing all fresh. They played an old song tune, soft and beautiful, and some of the older men and women sang snatches softly. They played a dance tune then, and, in the confined space, children and some of the older people, too, danced. Even in Battle Row, life had wondrous moments.

Then she heard a happy shout, "Po!" Dave had found her. "How glad I am to see you!" His eyes glowed, he seized her and danced her around. "I'll bet you've never been danced with for joy!"

And Dave was not in the least bit downhearted or concerned about Mr. Rome's getting tired of too much baseball. As they walked down Fulton Street, he was talking excitedly: "Why, I can get a job any place in this country! I'm a jour printer! Franklin even got a job in England!"

And his words came rushing like the waterfall at Kilkallen, pouring out all that had happened, was happening.

"And so, Walt, he often does pieces for Mr. Greeley, and he was in Greeley's office, and Greeley, he was very cranky about all these people dropping in there, wanting to know about when baseball matches were to be played! Instead of worrying about the inflated currency, or getting the Homestead Law passed! 'Worrying about where to get bat sticks!' he said. 'I'm thinking of putting a reporter on it, so I won't be bothered!'"

Of course Walt thought of Dave, out of a job. And now Dave was writing down all about matches played and to be played, and Walt was taking them to Mr. Greeley, who was actually going to give Dave money for them! Dave laughed ecstatically. "Money for writing down about baseball matches!" And Dave hoped to do some for the *Clipper,* too, and the *Spirit of the Times.*

The black news of the turned-down challenge had spread quick as the potato blight over the town, and Po had begun to tell Dave about the game at Elysian Fields, and he was trying to tell her about a plan he had, when Po stopped listening to him. Ahead of her, coming down Fulton Street, was Larry.

They both saw each other at the same moment. Then, nearly bowling over passersby, they ran toward each other.

"Po!" he called.

By the time she thought of Dave, and looked back, he had disappeared.

They went back to the lonely spot on Prospect Hill where Larry had practiced ball. Then, an April dusk had trembled expectantly; now, the elm trees' virginal buds were mature leaves, fighting a day to day battle with insects. A brilliant June midday sun beat down hard and forcefully. Every plant, as if its time of growing were short and must be accomplished, seemed deeply busy about its affairs.

They came under the crabapple tree. Po, remembering its scent, looked up. A lightning-splintered branch trailed partly on the grass. But like some ugly little miracle, even though but a slender connection with the main trunk remained—there on the branch hard green crabapples, fighting off insects, pushing themselves out of shape to squeeze past a dead limb that partly smothered them, were growing. And seeing them, Po suddenly had the same surge of hope she had in finding Juba in the street, and when she and Larry saw each other alive on the beach.

Larry took her hand and smiled down at her, that way her heart began to make up a great poem. She dropped her eyelids then, afraid the poem would go speaking itself out through her eyes. Suddenly she had a great need to tell him of a fine thing had happened to her that day.

"Larry," she began, "you must listen how it was with me today when I came back to Brian's. Poor Mamie, she must be perfect herself, and everyone around her must be perfect, for she is always trying to get back to that time when all bowed down to her. I knew she'd not like my being in service, thinking if people knew 'twould belittle her. I tell you this so you may know 'twas not easy to face her!"

Po had seized his other hand in her excitement, and he looked at her, intent and serious, as if he sensed Po was trying to tell him something that had to do with their happiness, and he was striving to understand.

"Always before, I acted like a child to her, scared to let out my anger. But today, could I believe my own ears, when I heard myself talking to her, telling her what I was hoping to do—and me that free and easy and gentle. It was like I humored her. You could think she was the little girl and I the woman grown. I wasn't scared of her! And it came to me, Larry, 'tis so you must do about whatever is eating at you back in New Bedford!"

"Mamie is a lot different from my mother!" He dropped Po's hands, frowning, and turned away. "She has ways! One fellow on the packet says she's fine; another said he heard in the town she was very sick! Maybe she just wants to torment me, make me come back."

But Po pressed on. "It's easy and gentle you must be with her, but firm. See what way it is with her—if she be sick or not—and if she needs it, see she has help!"

"If it were only that!" He kicked at the grass, threw himself down almost angrily. The grass was no longer shiny green, but dusty, struggling to get itself seeded, and he sat frowning, silent, for a long time. When he spoke, the words came slow, almost tortured. "It's funny, your being a little like her! You sort of expected things of me that I didn't—that I couldn't—" He stopped, and then, when he went on, each word seemed to be wrenched out of him. "I can get along with everybody but your kind of a girl!"

Something told Po to stand very still.

When he spoke next, his words came still slower and heavier. "I never talked like this to anyone before!" Suddenly he burst out, "I can whup anything with my fists—but how can you beat your own mother! Why"—he looked aghast—"you'd think I hated her! How can you hate your own mother?" he cried out. "Haven't I heard it every Sunday, with brimstone and sulphur, 'honor thy father and mother'?"

Po hardly moved, thinking of the Bible, and the man casting forth a devil. "Yes, I hate her!" he cried. "When my father left, I had to be everything! She used me!"

Po sat down on the grass beside him then, and took his head into her lap. She remembered she had run away from this very thing, afraid he would bury his head in her lap like a small boy. Now she knew it had been herself she'd been running from, afraid she would shackle him. She felt strong enough not to now.

Her hand explored his face tenderly. The bump on his nose bridge, where he'd been assailed by a baseball, the pale freckles at the top of his forehead, the square strong white teeth, and the mouth, fresh and clean, now that the look of hate he'd had a moment since had gone. Ah, he was a right lad! Po's small hands were square and useful-looking, but nimble and never awkward. If she plucked gently at the strings, might not the tautness go, so that the wind of the morning could vibrate in him and music go loosening around the world?

And then, just as Walt had said it would, it came to Po what she must pass on to Larry! And striving so hard to pass it on to Larry, she suddenly began to understand her own experience with Mamie!

"Larry!" Po said, excited all over again. "I see now why I was so scared of Mamie! 'Twas maybe something in me knew I didn't like her, but was using her house as a snug safe ledge. And I didn't care much for myself in consequence. Now, you see, I'm not using her, so I don't despise myself!"

Suddenly she saw that liking herself inside now, she felt she deserved to be loved, and she wanted Larry to begin liking himself, too. "For then," she thought with a warm glow, "maybe he can love me too!"

In her amazement at this discovery, she stood up, almost ready to shout.

"It's you thinking, Larry, all the while you are mean bad for hating her! You're away from her, and she can't punish you, so what must you do but punish yourself, that way you would not even enjoy a girl like me, and she kissing you, and loving you!"

Larry sat, frowning. His face was troubled. Po came up beside him, and started to put an arm around his neck, but he reached up and took her hand and held it, and suddenly she saw he had taken her hand exactly as if she were his mother, and she looking down at him as if he were a small boy.

She jerked her hand away. "Larry, stand up!"

Puzzled, he got to his feet.

"You can shout out your declaration of independence and ring bells and shoot off guns—but you don't believe it yourself! You must go back there. Have it out with her, talk to her kindly and walk away!"

"If I only could."

"It's what you must do."

He sat frowning for a long time, and she could see he was fighting some battle inside himself. At last he said, slowly, "Maybe you're right. Yes, maybe you are! I'll go!"

Other people could smile and say, "That little thing!" but Po knew that with some it could be slaying their thousands, with some crossing the river alone to find a job, with others, a baseball game or—going home to face their mother.

Then Po laughed. She saw that, though Larry was big, she little, though they came from different soil, from childhoods strange to each other—inside them the same thing was going on—they were both trying to quit off being green and hard and misshapen. Maybe it would be as grim a struggle as the blighted crabapples were having. Po didn't even see the shape he and she were to grow into— but something insisted.

She felt very happy. Ah, but now, surely, there'd come a time when they would shout across the mist to each other the way they had that morning on the beach! Not about their flesh and bone, but about this part that made them push and struggle and painfully insist. Then they could cry out, "Look, we have come through!"

205

Chapter Thirty

EVEN BEFORE Po left Brooklyn that night, the Brooklyn baseball men knew they would not take no for an answer. Ideas were tossed about. Strategy formulated.

Dave's plan seemed most promising. The Knickerbockers' position rested on reputation, didn't it? Reputation was what people thought. What if articles appeared in the *Clipper,* the *Spirit of the Times,* the *Tribune?* Between Dave and Walt, with his newspaper friends, wasn't this possible? A little jeering laughter, in Walt's opinion, might be a deadly weapon. A few public taunts at the withered state of the Knickerbocker laurel crown would soften things up—and then—at the next public appearance of the Knickerbockers at Elysian Fields—

Lord Guernsey had indicated his gracious willingness to observe the native Americans at a game they had probably copied from the British, and Augusta Van Leyn had heard of his acceptance. She was not, naturally, going to let slip the chance of playing hostess to nobility.

It was to be a simple rustic affair in the country air of Hoboken, with Scoreby, Po, and the gardener in footman's livery following in the victoria with the rugs and tents and cushions and the eight hampers of food and wine.

Everyone seemed pleased that day. Augusta, dressed for the country in a Marie Antoinette shepherdess dress of primrose yellow, its overskirt fastened up with knots of rosebuds, carried, like any simple maid, her flat milan straw hat over one arm by its blue velvet streamers. But, as she stepped into the first barouche with Lord Guernsey and opened her primrose silk parasol, its gilt handle fashioned like a shepherdess crook, she had a rather triumphant air. Nicholas, always at his best in the role of host, got in and they drove off.

Even Scoreby was in spirits, for he considered the picnic a challenge. Though heavens fell, he meant to see Lord Guernsey had his oysters cold and his squab *au vin* hot, even though he, Scoreby, had to nurse the silver tureen over the charcoal brazier on his lap all the way across the Hudson River.

They crossed on the Barclay Street Ferry, and rode through the pleasant green of Hoboken to the resort called Elysian Fields. Greensward swept away under beautiful spreading trees. The Hudson River sparkled between the elms. Ships, white sails gleaming, drifted by.

Only the smoke from an occasional side wheel steam vessel reminded one of the city across the river.

But even as she helped serve the collation, Po could observe that many things were going on besides the eating of sweetbreads ballotine with cognac jelly. For one thing, a wan girl, who turned out to be Agatha, Quimby's daughter, was trying to attract Coventry Van Leyn, to his boredom. Mrs. Blair and Mrs Shelton were trying to attract Mrs. Haviland, to her boredom. Mrs. Haviland was trying to attract Lord Guernsey and being regarded fishily. And then, to top all these goings on—Po's eyes widened—Hymes was staring at Augusta! And that lady, with the fine flaunting figure on her, was regarding Hymes with an arrogant smile. "Two of a kind are those beauties!" Po thought. "And let me not be by if ever the fur flew between them!"

The athletes of the Knickerbocker team did not spare the sweetbreads or the green-gage ice cream, and Po, who was waiting eagerly to see the Knickerbockers at play, was afraid they were all going to have to go off somewhere and take a nap before they could begin. But, after much merchant chat, and cigars, and wine, the Gothams, another lot of pleasant and well-cushioned gentlemen, arrived in their carriages.

Victorias, gigs, landaulets, came now in great numbers, and lined the edge of the playing field. Ladies in elegant toilettes, tiny parasols shading their pretty faces, sat with their escorts in the vehicles to view the game, with chatter and gay calls from carriage to carriage.

The Knickerbockers disappeared into their striped dressing tent. Hymes and Jenkins and some of the other Knickerbockers, who were evidently not going to play in this game, congregated about this Knickerbocker stronghold. And then, after a lengthy time, out came the athletes!

The Knickerbockers, elegant in nicely pressed uniforms of blue wool pantaloons, white flannel shirts with dark blue bands, wide patent leather belts with "Knickerbockers" on them, trotted out, their chip straw hats at a jaunty angle. Only two of the Excelsiors wore beards, the Bull and Brian, but the Knickerbockers had lovely fine curly ones, cut in fancy shapes. And now, from their side, came the Gothams.

No roar of welcome greeted the teams, only a splatter of polite handclapping. The referee, his straight chair safely off at one side, called out politely, "Gentlemen, begin the play!"

The Knickerbockers were at bat.

Mr. Fielding of the Bank of New York held the bat stick at ready. He passed two or three balls, then pipped one out to center field. Before the Gotham fielder, a rather heavy-set man, reached the ball and tossed it in, Mr. Fielding had gently cantered around to second base. Glad handpatting greeted this feat.

Now Mr. Shelton, Manager of Arnold Constable, was up. Holding the bat stick straight-armed, he hit. The ball bounded pleasantly toward third base. But the Gotham base tender muffed it, and Mr. Shelton trotted along to first base, smiling pleasantly at the ladies as he came. Above the polite handclapping some one, no doubt made rowdy with wine, called, "Well played, Shelton!"

The Knickerbockers' score was mounting, amid pleased murmurs from their contingent. The sides changed, and Po discovered Coventry pitched, and quite well, and Mr. Quimby was catcher. But he seemed to have a different style of play from Bushel Basket Jordan, for he stood cautiously far back from home plate, thus giving the ball a chance to bound before he caught it. Mr. Quimby had all his front teeth.

The Knickerbockers were well ahead when Coventry sent a long skimmer through the trees at left field. But the Gotham fielder was chatting with one of the ladies in a near-by carriage, and Coventry had plenty of time to make a home run. No roar of delight assaulted the heavens though, no tragic groans, no desperate frenzies. Po thought of how it was in Brooklyn, with maybe the Bull making a home run. The Knickerbockers and their ladies didn't seem to fling themselves into the game the way they did in Brooklyn.

But by the fifth innings, the Knickerbockers ahead, the game stopped while the athletes got their wind. Men servants brought out cold drinks and towels to mop pink faces.

Then, what Po had been hoping and waiting for all the time, happened.

A hansom cab drove up and stopped at the edge of the field. And who should come sashaying out, daring and jaunty as King Davie out to assault Goliath, but Dave Posen in a new dark suit, a white press ticket in his hat, followed by two men Po didn't know, wearing press tickets in their bowlers! After them came Death-to-Flying-Things Collins, the man who could catch anything flying through the air. All Po could think, seeing him, was that he'd sacrificed a day's pay to come. And then—out stepped Larry. Po was a little surprised, seeing him, but maybe he had had time to go to New Bedford and return.

Under Scoreby's direction, all the silver and linen had been re-packed in the hampers. What if Scoreby picked this moment to decide to return to Manhattan! Fate could not be so cruel! Po squirmed away in the crowd, deciding to get lost quickly. She worked her way in and around carriages, to the striped tent with the gay Knickerbocker pennant.

Po got close enough to hear Dave's voice ring out, unnecessarily loud, as if he hoped he'd attract as much attention as possible: "May we speak to the secretary of the Knickerbockers?"

Lord Guernsey and Jenkins had been chatting, amid a group of non-playing Knickerbockers—Hymes, Blair and others. Jenkins turned, lips pursed fussily, frowning. But Po saw him take in the press badges. Dave's read impressively, *Tribune*; one of the others was *Clipper*, and the other *Spirit of the Times*.

"I'm the secretary," Jenkins said.

The men of the press ostentatiously got out pencils and pads and stared at him. Then Dave spoke, loudly. "The Knickerbockers claim to be champion baseball club of America, but we hear you won't accept any challenges!" A crowd began to gather, listening.

"Would you care to make a statement?" the man from the *Clipper* asked Jenkins, pencil poised. "Glad to print your side!"

Jenkins looked from one to the other, his face turning an angry red. He finally spoke through tight lips. "We accept all challenges!"

"Oh," Larry's words sailed out like a lance, "no you don't!"

At Larry's voice, Hymes turned around squarely, and looked at him. His face got the cold, blank stare Po had seen before, and it always frightened her.

"Naturally, we can play only with teams that play by the correct rules!" Jenkins snapped out.

By this time the listening crowd had grown.

"Are them rules anywhere, anywhere, I ask you," Death-to-Flying-Things broke out, "so's the teams from Jersey or Brooklyn can get at them?"

Jenkins' face turned a kind of purplish red. Lord Guernsey stared, open-mouthed. "Extraordinary!" he exclaimed.

Jenkins looked around furiously at his club mates. But not one of them made any attempt to rescue him from the awkward situation. Hymes kept staring at Larry. The other Knickerbockers looked at the press badges, licked their lips, and seemed to have nothing special to say. Finally, Jenkins came out contemptuously, "All the teams that are eligible already know our rules!"

"Who says who's eligible?" Death-to-Flying-Things roared, starting toward Jenkins, but Larry held him back.

Larry stepped forward then, and Po saw Hymes take a little step forward and the cold set look freeze on his face.

Larry's voice rang out clear. Po was always proud to see the way Larry handled himself with men. He was firm, but not rattled or angry. "You ought to call a convention, and let everyone in on the rules!"

Hymes's face changed. He got the look of slow deep satisfaction she had seen when Larry had shown before what mattered to him.

Hymes touched Jenkins on the arm, and when he turned, Hymes motioned him aside with his head. Blair and some of the others standing about joined this little group.

Nicholas Van Leyn stepped forward. "We have no objection to anyone playing the game who wishes." Nicholas was unruffled and polite.

"So long as they don't challenge you bein' champion!" Death-to-Flying-Things broke out. "Well, we do! And what's more, if you don't call a convention, we will!"

Lord Guernsey dropped his eyeglass in astonishment.

Dave, writing busily, said, "We'll print that!" And the *Clipper* man smiled and wrote, and the *Spirit* man, seemingly enjoying himself hugely, wrote.

But now Jenkins stepped forward. He was not red-faced now, but as if taking charge and wanting to settle the whole uncalled-for and awkward situation as quickly as possible. He cleared his throat, then announced with cold dignity: "As a matter of fact, we are already planning a convention of the baseball clubs."

"Can we quote that?" Dave snapped, pencil poised.

Mr. Jenkins glared. "Are you questioning my word?"

"Where will it be?" Larry broke in.

"When's what I'm askin'," Death-to-Flying-Things growled.

Jenkins drew his short frame up with cold dignity. "Notice of the time and place will be given to the press—uh—tomorrow."

"We'll be around!" the *Clipper* man said.

Po could see by the light in Larry's eyes, by the faces of the other Brooklyn men, they felt they had won the inning. Po cried out for them a silent, "Up, Brooklyn!" but in her heart, she was not so gay. She had been watching Hymes's face. She could still remember Hymes's words: "I find out just what it is a man's struggling for."

Then Po heard Scoreby's peevish "O'Reilly!" and ducked beneath an empty victoria and came up on the other side in time to gasp "Here, sir," before he called again. He and the gardener were packed, ready to go home, and as Po drove off with them, she could see Dave and Larry, standing, with incredulous smiles, watching the Knickerbockers at play. But Death-to-Flying-Things, he stood roaring like he'd catch his death from laughing.

Next day, Po found it in the *Clipper,* right next to the news of the races at Saratoga. She hated the Knickerbockers when she took in what they had done, but, somehow, remembering Hymes's look of satisfaction, she was not really surprised. She read:

"The Knickerbocker Baseball club of New York, the oldest, and generally accepted as best, and long-established champion, has issued, for the purpose of ratifying all rules, a call to an official baseball convention. Cards of invitation have already gone out to all eligible clubs—the Eagles, the Empires, the Gothams, of New York."

Chapter Thirty-one

I T WAS the second letter she had ever gotten from Larry, but it did not have the same flavor as the first. Out under the kitchen garden raspberry bushes, disturbed, she read it again:

> I said I would go back to New Bedford, but I decided I wouldn't go—not just yet. You're different, you can do things easier. If you only knew how it was about her. I'd like to talk to you sometime. And anyhow—the team needs me. We may get at the Knicks any day now.

Longing as she did for him to free himself, she supposed it must be his finding this fine handy excuse that worried her. Walt had told her she'd know how to help Larry. Yet, see, she had not. Maybe Walt, with his going in and going out of houses, his walking up and walking down on roads, and his long steady looks at the world, maybe he—

She was still, at every chance, buying songs at Firth and Pond's—fingering out the notes and singing softly at the concert grand in the music room when she could—and now she decided on her next trip she would try and see Walt.

At the table in Pfaff's, Walt looked up as if he were pleased at the view of her, and shoved aside all his scribbly papers and asked her kindly what way she did, and if she were meeting with happiness at all.

" 'Tis me could be the happiest woman you would meet going up or down, except that—there is something—but I don't know if it's right I should speak of it!"

"Well, then," Walt smiled at her, "of course, it's about your boy!"

Po flashed him a grateful smile. Now wasn't that wonderful, the way he could grasp out of the sky a thing like that no one else would have thought of? Yet she hesitated. Chat was all right—but what she wanted to talk about! But always she had to go acting from what was inside her, and not from what people said was decent. "When we want to love each other, he breaks off that way you could think he was afraid to commit a crime! It is now maybe a froward girl you'll think me to sit here talking of such a thing!"

Walt looked at her now, a long gentle look. "That you and I—I, a man who has spent the last seven years thinking about men and women and America, and you, a girl with all the future in you, sons and daughters—that it should be new and strange that we talk of sex—that is the only froward thing."

She burst out then: "Why is it a man, and he brawny and with the great strength in him, isn't able to love, the way he seems tied to—someone—even though the someone be miles away?"

"His mother, you mean." Walt was calm.

Now think of that, and what a great one he was, to get right to the grain of it, without a hint from her! She nodded yes. She did not want him to think ill of Larry though, and said hastily, " 'Tis a sad and unfortunate devilipment, but the woman is low-built in stature as myself, and that way it is easy for him to confuse the two of us!"

"Maybe he wants to confuse the two of you!" Walt said calmly.

With Walt you had to pick out the sense from the nonsense. "Now, why would he want to do any such a thing!"

"Because then—you can't expect him to love you like a man, can you?"

"But he wants to love me! I feel it! I know it!" Po broke out. "He is struggling against this way he has of feeling ashamed and guilty!"

Walt looked pleased and happy then. "There's hope for you then, for both of you. You have—I've always felt it—the most valuable thing in the world—the beautiful possibilities of growth. There's danger, though. And you must watch out for it. It happens many a time. He may give up the struggle. Instead of a real relationship, he may fob off on himself a boy's prize!"

Po stared, puzzled.

"I mean, something that makes him feel big, gives him a big front."

It was, and no doubt of it, rocky going sometimes to understand Walt. But he seemed sunk in thought and when he did go on, you could think he was some place far off.

"Many have stopped so, and are still children. And being children, it's easy to get themselves in a fix. All through America, there are children trying to pretend they are men by playing with forces beyond them. But the huge dynamic forces, once touched, move on of their own volition, in no way concerned that it was but a boy who loosed them to make himself feel big. Then the great Hero, the Dominator, the Conqueror, cornered by the forces he has loosed, turns, crying out, 'Mother, help me!' "

Po sighed gently. If he would but get back to Larry now. She waited quietly, though. You had to let people find the way through the underbrush in their brains.

Walt went on, still as if from some faraway place. "Often enough, these Conquerors, these Dominators, they're not even man enough to have a true mate! It takes more courage, more creative energy, more honesty, to build up an equal, face-to-face relationship with a woman, a partner, than it does to build a ferry or a railroad, or lead a group of men to victory, to be champion of the world! What are these things but playing with building blocks, or a boy's foray on a neighboring gang?"

'Twas odd, but the same thought had occurred to Po as she sang about the old ballad heroes—that they were like children. 'Twas like they'd be off with their wolf hounds and their spears playing their games—and what were their women doing?

Walt sighed a little. "Maybe sometime we will get over being Heroes, and come to grips with relationships. For notice these Dominators. Take Hymes. What's he but a pursuer of young girls? Yes, and your boy Larry! I've seen him with Louise. What's that but stealing an easy apple over a fence? Are the Conquerors afraid of a real relationship? If they're confronted with a delicate think problem, a creative problem, a problem of working out a cooperative relationship with another human being—why, they want to run back to their mother; or build a higher building, or subjugate a few more people. Then they can say, 'Look! A hero! No one can expect anything more of me!' And the danger is they must keep proving it."

Po hunched down in her seat and sighed again. It was all very well for Walt to go destroying himself over Men—but it was Larry, Po wanted to understand.

"How is it then—and the letting out of your love such a fine simple thing—how is it he must make such a shamed, guilty thing of it?" She turned puzzled eyes to Walt.

He glanced at Po, with his serene, tender look; then he gazed at some distant spot. "If a mother is mixed up herself, she can mix her son up so in his functions as a man, that long after, even when she's dead, she holds him still with invisible cords. But you must not hate her," Walt said gently, "and you must teach him not to hate her—else he'll never free himself. Let him feel pity. His mother didn't make the forces that shaped that hard New England life, that jerked a man's soul out of his body and hung it in a cupboard for use on Sunday, that made him ashamed of his body, his sex. Is a locust blossom unclean, or an animal? It's like Larry had been split into parts. What you must do is help him put himself back together in one piece."

Po remembered how indignant and imposed upon she had been when Walt had assumed she must act like a woman grown. She realized with a little surprise, that she didn't feel that way any more—she only wanted to find out how to do.

"But how?" she asked frantically.

"Let your love tell you! Let your woman nature speak out."

As Po dropped off to sleep that night, with a worried sigh, she thought that that was the trouble with Walt. He was the kindly one in every way, and the great one for listening and talking, but what did he do in the end, but tie it all up in a neat bundle and hand it back to you, the way you had somehow or other to work it out yourself.

Chapter Thirty-two

Po READ the newspapers carefully. She wanted to learn how things were going for Larry and the Brooklyn men of the game, and now nearly every day, in the *Tribune*, the *Clipper* or the *Spirit*, a paragraph or two would appear. (Po could imagine Dave, running about, persuading, busily talking.) They poked sly fun at the "Champions by Proclamation."

This was all very well, and undoubtedly caused smiles from friend and foe, but Po had a feeling the pebbles from Dave's slingshot were but striking against a wall.

And the more Po saw Hymes closeted with Van Leyn, sometimes alone, sometimes with Fielding and Jenkins, the more she was sure the slingshot would never breach the wall.

Once, Po saw Hymes come in, but instead of going into the day room, he stood, waiting, in the front hall. Po saw Augusta's barouche, waiting outside. Hymes must have known she would be passing. Sure enough, she came, the diamond cross on her white bosom flaunting itself, and her knowing arrogant smile taking Hymes in, but never stopping to give more than a queen's nod, and he standing, looking after.

It was that day Po decided to listen, to learn if Dave's printed pebbles were bringing Brooklyn one inch nearer to becoming champions, or if they mattered at all. She discovered they mattered—to Nicholas Van Leyn. And she also discovered what she had begun to suspect, that now, that wasn't enough.

At first, as she listened, she could not make out their words, but after a while, Hymes and Van Leyn must have moved nearer to the window, for she heard Nicholas say, "—puts us in such an undignified position! I think the simplest thing is to just quietly play them. We're being made so ridiculous!"

Then Hymes said, but as if he weren't much interested, "Why don't you get Porter over at the *Spirit*, to stop printing them? You know him, don't you?"

"Of course I know him, and the man at the *Clipper*, too, though Greeley I wouldn't speak to! But Porter says the sporting crowd around the city has begun to enjoy the joke and are betting on it, and he isn't going to stop printing the jibes at us, because it's good for circulation. It's most awkward, and it will sort of change things, but I'm afraid we'll have to play those people over there!"

Po was surprised at how different Hymes's tone was now from when she had heard him talking to Van Leyn the first time. Now, he said flatly, "No, we won't play them." He wasn't arguing at all. "What good is the Knickerbockers, if it's just a baseball club, playing immigrants from Brooklyn? We stand"—Po's eyes widened at the "we"—"for a certain kind of thing. I want that. Especially now while we're getting the ferry company set up. Leave it alone!" It was then Po knew Dave's slingshot of ridicule was hopeless.

For Po knew it wasn't only because of the ferry company Hymes was blocking them. He was also carrying out a piece of justice, hurting someone who had hurt him. Maybe he would have opposed the Knickerbockers becoming a different kind of club even if Larry had not let him see it was important to him—but, that sealed the matter. He had decided.

And Po could see that his decision counted now. If Van Leyn, by virtue of social position and long-established custom, ran the Knicker-bockers, Hymes seemed now to be running Van Leyn, for Hymes said, in a business-like tone, "I took care of the Maine Lumber Company. But don't, please, contract any more debts without seeing me."

There was a little silence, then Po heard Van Leyn say nervously, "I'll be all right—if only the venture would come in! Any word?"

"Cleared Sierra Leone, all safe and sound. Too bad you weren't in with me on the *Tanager*. She's back, and I'm thinking of fitting her again. She might last through the Middle Passage for one more voyage."

After Hymes had gone, Po fell into a deep frowning concentration. Sierra Leone—wasn't that in Africa?

With all the poring over newspapers she'd been doing lately, she had seen certain news items that, at the time, had made her thoughtful, though she had shrugged them away. Now, she went to find the *Tribune* again. Yes, here was the item!

"The bark *Clementine,* suspected of being in slave trade, was boarded by Captain Miller of the revenue cutter *Jefferson* as she passed Sandy Hook. The supercargo of the *Clementine,* seeing the cutter coming near, threw overboard the ship's papers, and she could not be detained for lack of evidence."

Po had to go downstairs then, and hull the strawberries for cook, but all the time she worked, she kept going over some oddly jutting-out memories, some never-quite-understood small happenings. She remembered the supercargo meeting Hymes in the Gardens. The empty hold of the *Red Tanager.* But then, she stopped. Mr. Van Leyn? Impossible!

At her first free moment, she ran upstairs and looked back in the old newspapers, trying to find other items she had seen. Here was one:

"Yesterday, U. S. Marshall Robert Jones seized the schooner *Peacock* off Fire Island, as she was preparing to engage in the slave traffic. The ship's manifest showed R. W. Mudge, well-known merchant of New York, and his brother, to have fitted the vessel for the trade, and they have been taken into custody."

She hunted feverishly back into the papers now, trying to be sure. Ah, here was one, signed by Mr. Greeley himself, and he giving the back of his hand to them:

"In spite of the law, which brands it as piracy, large sums of northern capital are invested in the slave trade. The practice is to buy up old or condemned vessels, fit them up here, and on the return from Africa, the cargo is landed on some quiet stretch of southern coast. We know the harbor police must time the seizure of such vessels within the short space between completion of preparations here, and their getting to sea, and must make the seizure at risk of being held for libel in case the vessel is able to get rid of her incriminating papers, but the harbor police must exercise more vigilance!"

What if Hymes—? It hardly seemed possible. And yet—

All the rest of the day, as she hopped and skipped to Scoreby's tune, she was bemused, putting pieces together in her mind. But it was not until she went to bed that night, and she had time to search the newspapers some more, and found another piece, that she began to feel it possible. She read:

"It is known these vessels take on a few innocent-appearing stores at their berths in the East River, then cast off for some lonely stretch off Long Island, where arrangements have already been made for them to ship the numerous water casks, rice and other material, to

216

fit her for the traffic, and then, under cover of dark, they slip past the harbor police—"

Po, stood in the dark at the open window now, trying to think. Could the Ventures be—

But if so—what then?

Suddenly she remembered why it was she had listened in the first place to Hymes's talk of Ventures. It was because she was afraid he might injure Larry, and she wanted to have some weapon Larry might defend himself with. Well now, he wasn't attacking Larry physically, but he was blocking something that meant a lot not only to Larry, but all Brooklyn—and for a moment Po could see Brooklyn faces, and feel how it was when the Bull was at bat, and see again the special case Hans had carved to hold the ball when they were champions of the world.

But deeper than this, Po understood even more surely now, what winning the first small goal he had ever set himself as an independent person might mean to Larry. He'd be surer.

As she tumbled into bed, her mind kept working. If it were really so that Hymes was engaged in something illegal—if they could some way use it to get Hymes out of the Knickerbockers— But no, that was no good. Van Leyn was in it too! Still Van Leyn had not been in on the *Tanager*.

She thought again of Hymes meeting Rimshaw in Brooklyn. Then she remembered that seafaring men flowed in and out of Dent's, and that Juba was there. Couldn't it be that Juba might overhear many a snatch of talk that would be dropped, and they paying no attention to such as him. Juba might know about Hymes. At last, she fell asleep.

Dent's was not a family place like Brady's, and Po was glad she found Juba in the street, and did not have to go inside. She walked along with him as he cried his oysters.

"Yes!" Juba's eyes flashed as he answered her question. "I hear! I know that's what Rimshaw is! I don't know Hymes. But Rimshaw. I heard him enough! I know!"

"Thank you for telling me, Juba!" Po was about to run off to try to find Larry, but Juba caught her sleeve.

"I needs a letter writ! I wuz lookin' for you. I knows you'd do it and keep silent lips! De letter gotta go back thru de underground!"

"Of course, I'll do it, Juba, and wasn't it the lucky day they taught me to write, though at the time the usefulness of it escaped me!"

In the Gardens then, Po sat down and wrote to a John Hicks. "He sent word," Juba said, "that my woman and baby was at Potters. I search up and down, can't find no Potters ever hear of dem! Put in de letter 'Where is dese Potters'?"

Po wrote it off, and so Juba would get an answer more quickly, she asked a reply be sent to her in care of Brian's.

Pleased, Juba put the letter inside his shirt, and went out quickly, to start it forward on its journey.

But by this time, Po had to return to Van Leyn's and it was too late to find Larry.

When she returned to New York, though, she kept thinking of how sure Juba had been that Rimshaw was a slaver, and she decided to write Larry a letter. For wasn't he the great one for contriving, and carrying out a plan? She did not ask him about his failing himself in not going back to New Bedford, but instead told him all she had pieced together in her mind about the slavers. For she kept thinking of all the possibilities if Hymes were in something illegal, and how it might be used to unblock the team. Maybe Larry would think of a way.

Chapter Thirty-three

PO HAD three days off, the Van Leyns having gone up to Saratoga for the holiday. Monday was Declaration of Independence Day, the great celebration here, when they'd told the king to quit off his nagging and they'd do to suit themselves and a pity there was no such holiday in Innis Fail.

Outside Brady's Gardens in Brooklyn, four bunting-decked stagecoaches waited, and the four horses drawing each stage made the flags on their harness twinkle as they switched about impatiently. The gathering picnickers hurrying toward the stagecoaches shouted at one another, blew horns and exploded firecrackers. Upstairs in Brian's flat, Po was enjoying even the haste of getting ready.

She brushed her hair till it shone and tied it back with a new blue ribbon she had bought. It had come to her she would feel right and good to wear her Irish clothes to the pic-nic, and she took them out of the bottom drawer, loving the feel of the rough blue skirt and the cool linen blouse, and put them on. Then, she pinched her cheeks until they were scarlet. She wasn't going to show herself dull against the fine women in Brooklyn and Larry there to look over them all.

Po suddenly realized, as she ran down the steps from the third floor, that she had known the greenhorn clothing would displease

Mamie. But Mamie would be wrong, and Po had not retreated into silent resentment, but gone ahead calmly and put it on. Well, now think of that! It was maybe in such little bits and pieces being a woman grown came to you.

Brian, his hat cocked over one eye, a blanket-roll slung over a shoulder, a bung starter in one hand and a covered basket of something in the other, had started down the outside steps, his friends in the coaches calling to him.

Po saw Mamie standing there, looking after him, and the expression in her eyes gave Po a sudden insight. Mamie's mouth was set in a straight pink line, as though she must disapprove of this common pic-nic, with beer and vulgar immigrants from the streets. But her eyes looked after Brian wistfully, like a little girl who wished she could have gone too, but who could not bend the bars on the bleak sterile prison she had made for herself. Something held her back. On no account must she ever be common or less than perfect. The instant lightning flash illuminating Mamie was gone, but Po had a sudden feeling of compassion for Mamie. Po came down the stairs, put her arms around Mamie and kissed her on the cheek. Then she ran down the outside stairs after Brian.

Beside the first stagecoach stood Larry, and he looking so handsome, with his reddy-gold hair gleaming out above his open blue shirt, your heart could burn up in a minute looking at him. Brian got tamely in below, but Larry caught Po around the waist and swung her on top. And there was Dave, softly fingering an accordion, and Po not even knowing he played one.

There were at least fifteen people packed into this stage, above and below, and as many in each of the three others. But now, off they went, galloping up Fulton Street amid cheers from the inhabitants, with Walt riding with Mr. Johnson, the driver, up front in the high driver's seat, and the Bull below, roaring out a song in a bass voice. From below rose jibes and jokes, from above, laughter.

As soon as they crossed the steam railway track they were in open country, and as they rumbled along, the man gathering early apples waved from his ladder, the reaper cutting the clover raised his scythe a moment in greeting.

It was nearly eight miles, and by the time they arrived, the sun was high and beat down on the picnic spot. A lovely long stretch of white deserted beach it was, at a place called Coney Island.

Quickly, driftwood was sought for fires, boards went up on barrels for tables, and, with a fiddler and an accordion, it was not long until, on a stretch of hard packed sand, dancing began. It was a figure like the Lancers, and Po thought she would just try her foot at it. Ah, it was a right day, what with salt breeze, music and peals of laughter. To have the Bull seize your hand, and whirl you down the figure was an electrifying experience you would not soon forget.

There was a Scot there with a bagpipes, and his wife and brother danced a fling while he played, and it was fine and scary to hear the pipes floating out over the waves.

And there was a boy named Thomsy Devlin, with bright red hair and a divil in his eye, who squeezed Po's hand and whispered, "Be my partner!" Then he called to the fiddler for "Rory's Comin'," and the fiddler, whose name was Dugan, after only a short stop for a toss of whiskey, broke out with the tune, and, on the clean hard sand, Thomsy and Po footed it to the planxty.

You could think you'd be back in Ballyhouna, but in Ireland, all had been confined, small, folded back in on itself, and under the mirth—the bitterness and hunger. Here, it was not so close-packed, so intense, so deeply felt, but—there was more room for dancing.

Larry had stayed at one side. As soon as she finished the dance, he took her arm almost roughly, and said, "Come on, we're going clamming," for there was to be roasted clams later, and other couples had already wandered away to dig the clams.

"You're a very pretty girl," Larry said crossly, as if she shouldn't have been making so free with herself.

Most of the clammers went off to where the beach was wide and flat, but Larry and Po, in bare feet, he with a short shovel and a pail, went in the other direction, where the beach was narrower and rocks jutted up, backed by sand dunes.

But as she walked along with him, Po picked up a scallop shell thoughtfully. She did not like to have him notice she was pleasing because he was jealous (what kind of a thing would that be after?), but because she was herself, the way she loved him because he was himself. Like you found a wonderful shell, you didn't set value on it because someone tried to take it away from you.

It was the first time they had been alone together since the day under the crabapple tree when he had promised to go back and face his mother. And now, underneath, every minute, as they walked along, were words, questions, shaping themselves in Po's mind. "Why didn't you go? Did you lose courage? What happened?" But she didn't ask. He must tell her himself. She could see that it was on his mind too, but he said nothing. Then Po stepped on a broken conch and sat down on a driftwood log to nurse her bare foot.

Larry sat down on the sand close to her. She looked at him then, and the question, "Why didn't you go?" rose into her mouth in spite of herself, but he put his arms around her waist, and like an ingratiating small boy fastened a big hand tightly in her skirt like he would never let go, and looked at her, and grinned. "What would I do without you?" Ah, he could be the oul' charmer could Larry, and affectionate and dear, till you were fair distracted. And so, she forgot, for the moment, her question at his not going back to New Bedford.

Po looked at the silvery sky, then, and out at the rhythmic water. But Larry didn't want her to get wondering again, for he said, "Look at me!" He tugged her skirt playfully. "What's out there?"

"It was the waves I was looking at, and thinking how they must feel."

He turned, astonished.

"I was feeling what it would be like maybe, stroking the cheek of the land!"

He stared, puzzled. "I never can see where people get all these feelings!"

Po turned, wide-eyed at him, then. "But, doesn't it make you think of something when you look at it!"

He looked a few moments. "Yes. A bunch of water!"

"But, no!" She was a little impatient. "I mean, can't you imagine what it would be like if you were a wave!"

Now he was irritated. "How could I do that!"

She stared, incredulous. "You mean, you can't imagine you're something else, a wave, or another person maybe?"

He stared indignant. "What would I want to for?"

Po was bewildered. How could you love anyone then, or even like them? She got up restlessly and started to walk on down the beach. The sound of the pipes from the picnic sounded faintly, far back.

Piles of rock jutted out of the beach here, and spray struck thunderously and glittered in the air. They turned inland to skirt around, so they would not have to climb up over the rocks in their bare feet.

As they rounded the jutting rocks at the top of the beach, Po saw them, the party of young fellows from the picnic. Six or eight of them they were, and too far from where Po and Larry were at the top of the beach, to see who they were, but only their joyful naked bodies leaping and curving like porpoises in the blue-green sea.

The swimmers came out then and ran along the liquid edge of the world, their feet springing away from each touch of sand. Watching them race back toward the picnic, against the deep blue-green, Po thought of the great vase in the entrance hall at Lough.

The afternoon light was softening into pearl, and the water into translucent green, and Po breathed evenly and happily, as she and Larry walked on up the beach through wet shells and seaweed. How fresh and wonderful the curved bodies had looked in the summer sea! Suddenly a mood of exhilaration seized her.

"How happy they looked—those swimmers! Let's go in!"

He glanced at her quickly, flushing a little and frowning. "You mean—?"

But Po, who had been standing, lips parted in excitement, happened to glance at his face, and the bubbles of her mood began to wink out.

" 'Twas only a thought," she said, her exhilaration evaporating.

He frowned, flushing a little. "Well, I only was thinking of—" He stopped then, but Po thought his face had a little of the shamed guilty look she'd seen on it once before. The last bubble winked out. She walked on quickly.

With his long strides he caught up with her, but he looked miserable and angry. They went on then for a long time in silence. Po picked up a curved shell, hard and smooth as Larry's body. The shell wound back in on itself in a stony labyrinth, and inside were walls of calcium the animal had erected against discovery.

"Larry," Po said suddenly, "why didn't you go back and have it out with your mother that way you were saying you would?"

He looked as if she had said the one thing he didn't want her to. He flung the clam shovel down resentfully.

"Why! I told you in the letter!"

Po felt as if he had vanished back into a labyrinth.

"Oh, Larry! Isn't it the more important thing to go back, than to stay with the team?" She wanted to say, "For us!" but she was afraid to. Instead she heard herself say stubbornly, "It's harder maybe!"

He stared at her coldly. "I know what I'm doing!" He walked on angrily then. After a bit she followed.

They were far away from the picnic by this time.

The beach was crossed by an inlet, and they turned up its bank. It opened into a good-sized bay, dotted with small pine and brush covered islands.

They had just passed one of these islands, when they both stopped. Beyond, at anchor, a ship came into view. A bark it was, dirty, and gray, with salt-worn planks. They stood and stared.

They turned then and looked at each other, then back, wide-eyed at the bark. You could think—and the sun shone clear and plain—you could think it was the *Red Tanager*.

She was anchored a fair distance out, with her stern to them. They could not see her name or figurehead, but Po remembered too sharply the moment in New Bedford when she was watching the ship, trying to get courage to stow on it. Every detail had scratched itself on some tablet in her mind. She glanced at Larry. She was startled by the look on his face.

It was almost savage with release. But, even as she stood, staring and startled at his look, out on the bark, the anchor was lifted, one sail run up.

But it did not seem they were making ready for sea, only maneuvering. The sail flapped in the light breeze, and the ship started to move. It swung around, the sail bellied out, and the bark beat slowly out through the inlet. Po and Larry dropped flat on the sand as she came near them. Two or three swarthy sailors moved on the deck. And, there was the figurehead! It was the two-faced Janus. It was the *Red Tanager*. She hove to some distance out and dropped anchor again. For some reason, she had wished to change her anchorage.

Larry stood up suddenly. "If she's in the slave traffic, and if Hymes's name is on any of her papers, I'll fix it!" he said aggressively. "Everyone in Brooklyn's going to be glad a man came to town! Did you ever hear of blackmail? If I can get the manifests or the clearance papers"—and Po noticed he didn't say we, but I—"and if they show fine citizen Hymes is in the traffic, well then! I'll pull it off! I'll show you! Why, do you know they can hang someone for piracy? It's not a thing to fool with!"

"But what can we do?"

"I know what to do!" he said impatiently. "Leave it to me!"

"But, I only—"

"You're always trying to—" He broke off, then, and looked at her angrily. "Like back there on the beach! You're always doing it!"

He grabbed her arm roughly then. "Come on, let's get back to the picnic! I'll take care of this later!" And he walked back hurriedly, in silence, as if, suddenly, he could not be bothered to talk to a girl.

By the time they got back to the picnic, the afternoon was fading. No one had missed them, though. Other sunburned half-smiling couples kept wandering in. A baseball game was just ending, with Brian as pitcher and Walt at first base, and now, races and feats began. A mark was set on the sand for jumping and all the lads must try.

Larry flung himself into this jumping as though something final depended on it, and at the foot-racing he ran as if, instead of a cheer, he was out to win a crown in heaven. He won the wrestling too, and watching him, Po had an odd little feeling of disquietude. Part of Larry's dearness had been that he did these easy strong things carelessly as if they were nothing. She had an odd little jolt when she saw him glance at her, unsmiling afterward, the way you could think he was saying, "Look! Not only a man. But the biggest, the best man!"

Larry was agile, but for strength, no one could match the Bull. Amid cheers, the Bull lifted a beer keg and drank from the bung.

Now came the feast, and the fragrance of clams and chickens

roasted, and great pots of coffee mingled with the salt air. By the time dusk brushed gray velvet fingers along the wave tops, the feasters had gotten to the chocolate cakes and the rhubarb pie.

And then around great driftwood fires, came stories and jokes and songs. And as the tales went around, Po thought of story tellers and poets around fires in Donegal or Limerick. It was the same but different, oh, different.

Walt said for them a poem he was making up which went:

"It seems to me, as I sit here, there are other men in other lands,
      yearning and thoughtful,
It seems to me I can look over and behold them in Germany,
      Italy, France, Spain,
Or far, far away, in China, or in Russia, or Japan, talking other
      dialects,
And it seems to me if I could know those men I should become
      attached to them as I do to men in my own land.
Oh, I know we should be brethren and lovers!
I know I should be happy with them!"

This one they liked better than some of his others, but the tales moved on and the Bull told one about his friend Johnny, in Trenton, who had fallen into the molten iron in a foundry there and been rolled out into the iron plate, and now every time he saw an iron ship he wondered if its sides were made of Johnny.

Stars were out glittery now, in a dark blue sky, and the man with the bagpipes played his clan march, and Dave played an overture from an opera on his accordion. Then it was Po's turn and she sang.

Maybe the song had been waiting below in her mind to tell her something, for she sang, her dark voice moving out above the sparks from the fire, across the shingle, toward the sounding waves, about the ancient heroes:

"Long, long ago, beyond the misty space
      Of twice a thousand years,
In Erin old there dwelt a mighty race
      Taller than Roman spears,
Like oaks and towers they had a giant grace,
      Were fleet as deers,
With wind and waves they made their biding place—"

She kept on, but her mind was not on it. For, singing about the old heroes, she began to understand better her disquietude about Larry. She could hardly finish the song. And after, as the stories and music went on, she wasn't listening. She was hearing Walt's earnest words: "There's danger though! And you must watch out for it!"

Chapter Thirty-four

"WHY," he shouted at her, "did you stay?"

The night was silent and dark and the stars trembled. Po cowered before his towering rage, but she stood doggedly looking at him. She had watched him steal some horse blankets from one of the stages, and disappear silently into the dark, and it had not been hard for her to get lost in the outer ring of dark when the coaches left. Then, seeing him go down the beach to where the *Tanager* lay beyond at anchor, her mooring lights riding up and down in the slow swells, she had followed him.

How could she tell him now the real reason she had stayed— how make him understand—when he was so angry?

"Be easy, now! It's me could maybe cause confusion to your inimies," she began ingratiatingly.

"You go on back to the fire and sit down!" he stormed.

He stopped to draw in a breath in rage, and as they stood regarding each other, they heard a sound coming along the bay side in back of them.

Creaking and sluffing over the sand came cart wheels. Stars shone, but no moon, and only the breakers made white gashes in the dark, as they stood listening. Then they could make out two dim moving things. They stood motionless. You could guess now they were two slowly moving, heavily laden carts.

What carts would be here on this lonely beach at night unless they were part of the *Tanager*'s business? Larry's fingers closed on her arm warningly for silence, and they moved back into the darkness, crouched down and listened. The carts passed on and stopped on the beach opposite the *Tanager*.

The driver of the first cart lifted from the seat beside him a lighted lantern, turned the flame up, and, standing up in the cart, swung the lantern in a wide circle two or three times.

In a few minutes, out on the *Tanager*, Po saw a light move in a similar circle. Then the cart drivers were silent, as if waiting, and there was only the sound of the horses chomping into the sand, or the harness jangling. Then, after a while, through the surf, coming toward them, Po saw a rowboat lifting with the billows, falling and rising. It came in then on a big wave, and a sailor, breeches rolled up above bare feet, jumped out, pulled the flat rowboat up on the shingle. Another stowed his oars and jumped over the gunwale. Then, puffing and panting, over the gunwale came the supercargo of the *Red Tanager*, Mr. Rimshaw, holding a lantern up to peer at the driver.

The sailors moved toward the carts, and as nearly as Po could tell in the dark it seemed as if they and the second cart driver were unloading something heavy. But Rimshaw puffed importantly over to the first cart driver. At his voice Po felt a reminiscent shiver of terror.

"What's the idea," Rimshaw snarled, viciously, "holding us up this way?"

"We couldn't take no chances!" the driver growled back.

"You take chances! Hell, didn't I tell you this morning that treasury boat's cruisin' around!"

"Yeah, you can make a run for it, but we're caught dead as pigeons here on the shore!"

"You was paid for seventy-five barrels! If you was going to stop at fifty, you shouldn't have taken the money!"

"What are you yellin' for? We got the rest here now, ain't we?"

"You got paid enough for it to deliver on time!"

"You ain't paying for the water, but for the risk, and you know it! I wasn't goin' to take no chances with them damn pic-nickers maybe watchin'!"

"Ha! You scared of a bunch of pic-nickers! Make us run the risk of gittin' picked up by that cutter!"

"Don't worry! That treasury boat won't be cruisin' tonight! It's a holiday! Them boys'll be gittin' drunk in Brooklyn!"

Now the sailors were rolling something down toward the rowboat. Po saw it was casks. They loaded six or eight into the boat, and started with a load through the surf toward the *Tanager*.

Rimshaw and the cart driver moved back toward the second cart, quarreling bitterly now over the number of casks.

Po knew this was the moment to get out there to the *Tanager*, for the crewmen would likely make a couple more trips. Perhaps there would be a ladder down, too, with Rimshaw on shore, and maybe the cabin empty. Larry went quickly and silently down the beach to the picnic fires, and she followed him. He ran off then. Near the surf, he threw off some of his clothing, plunged into the water, and headed for the *Tanager*.

She looked after him anxiously. It could be dangerous out there, but she knew that was not why she had stayed, or why she was going out there with him. It was a more important reason for both of them.

She stripped off her skirt and blouse and anchored them with a stone. The picnic embers would mark the spot. In her underthings, she raced down the shingle, plunged into the surf and started for the *Tanager*. By the time she had cleared the second row of combers, it seemed to her she could see Larry ahead. The water was invigorating, and the ship seemed not too far away. She was not worried about making it; but Larry had a longer stroke, and she did not actually see him until she was at the *Tanager*.

Yes, a rope ladder dangled over the side. A lantern swung above where the ladder came over the rail. The sailors had evidently just taken up the last two casks from the first load, for the empty rowboat bobbed up and down below. She knew Larry would have to wait, and she was afraid he would see her. She dived under, and swam a little way off. By the time she came back, the sailors had come down the ladder, gotten in the boat and started off for another load.

Larry grasped the ladder to pull himself out of the water.

At that moment, at the head of the ladder, one of the crew peered over, not at Larry, but at the boat going toward the shore. After a bit, the crewman moved away and Larry, who had waited, again started up the ladder.

Po followed.

Halfway up, he glanced back, and seeing her follow, whispered back fiercely, "No! Go on back to shore!"

He was so fierce, Po's heart failed her a moment. But it mattered— it mattered such a lot. She kept on going.

On deck it was dark. None of the crew moved about. Larry slid along, crouched down, and she followed. He saw her, but he could do nothing about it. Ahead, a square of light fell through a porthole to the deck. That must be the cabin. They crept up, not meeting anyone, and peered in. But—Po's heart sank. The cabin was not, as she'd hoped, empty. A squat man, heavy-set, with black whiskers and an evil-looking face, worked under a whale oil lamp. He wasn't loading his pistol though, or scouring up his Sunday knife. He was sewing a button on his coat.

They crouched, silent, intently watching. Po was hoping that when the squat man had finished, he might go out. But Larry would not wait. She could feel him tensing his muscles, planning an attack.

But the attack came against them, and from the rear.

One of the crew had come up behind them. He hurled himself at Larry. Po heard the thud of their bodies. In the dark she could only see them swaying and reeling and swinging, trying to grapple with each other. But, at the sound of the scuffle, the man in the cabin dropped his coat and ran out. "What's the matter? Is it the cutter?" And then he lunged at Larry, trying to grab his arm, and the three of them swayed back and forth, grunting and swinging blindly.

The cabin door was open. Po slipped inside. A neat place it was, with everything in order, and not so much as a scrap of paper careless-like about. The tiny desk, with pigeon holes, was bare.

Outside the cabin door, more of the crew came pounding along the deck, and Po heard blows and yells in guttural voices. She knew she must move quickly. She banged open every desk drawer. Tobacco pipes—brandy bottles. She tore around the cabin, jerking open cupboards, pulling out drawers.

"Po!" she heard Larry cry, but could not tell if it was warning or what. Frantically, she lifted up covers, turned over blankets on the little bunk. There, under a pillow, she saw a tarpaulin-wrapped bundle, a heavy piece of metal with a hole in it, lashed to it. She didn't know what it was, but it must be something. She snatched it up. But why, why, were there no papers about at all, at all? Nothing!

Then it seemed to her she heard the packeta-packeta of a steam vessel, coming closer it was.

Larry yelled then. "Po! Rimshaw's coming back! Get out of there!" Po ran out of the cabin, tripping over two men who lay tumbled on the deck, darted around Larry who was struggling with another, and got to the rail.

Back along the deck she could see lights. Rimshaw must be coming up the ladder. Her heart pounded wildly. She clambered up on the rail and went over.

The water felt colder, and her clothes seemed to hold her back now. Was Larry all right? She knew, chilled as she was, she had better strike out quickly, but she did not want to leave until she was sure he had gotten away. Then, just as she was about to go back toward the ladder, she saw him dive. She struck out quickly.

It was easy to spot the picnic fire embers on the beach, and she headed for them in the long slow swells.

She guessed it was because she had not been swimming lately. She could barely crawl up on the beach. She crept toward the fire embers gratefully. Once or twice, in the water, she had been tempted to call out to Larry, swimming near her, for help, but she did not. Now she stretched out, face down, head on arms, breathing in tortured gasps. After a bit, Larry came up and threw himself down, panting. They were too exhausted to talk.

They could still hear the packeta-packeta sound of the treasury boat circling about, and once it swooped in close to the shore. The

Tanager had put out all her lights, and moved away as fast as she could get up sails.

Finally, the sound of the treasury boat faded. They could not tell whether or not she had picked up the *Tanager*'s wake. Now they had the stars and the ocean and that portion of the universe to themselves.

After a bit, Larry's breath came quieter, and he got up and went to find driftwood. Po sat up too. She was cold. She found her skirt and blouse, took off her wet underthings, got into her dry top clothes. Then she came back to the fire embers and tried to fan them up. After a while, Larry came back with wood and built up the fire.

They sat then, knees drawn up, head on arms, still too exhausted to talk. After a long time, when the fire had warmed them, Larry exclaimed with sharp chagrin, "Dubbed it! Chance of a lifetime! Gone!"

Po sighed a long trembling sigh. "That cabin was bare of papers like a wind had struck it. Nothing! Only a bundle I found they had hidden—'tis maybe only the captain's laundry, but it was put away so neat I thought it might be something and brought it!" She kicked the tarpaulin-wrapped bundle with the iron weight tied to it, which she had towed all the way with her, over toward the fire.

Larry looked at it dully. After a while, he began to struggle with the wet cord, but it wouldn't untie. He kicked the bundle aside with his foot then and they sat there in silence, until they were breathing at a regular rate. Then he took out his pocketknife and slashed the hemp. He had to wind and unwind the large tarpaulin.

Inside was a bundle of letters and documents. The top ones were water smeared. Underneath they were dry. Larry fanned up the fire excitedly. They leaned down, intent, peering, as the driftwood flared up. The first one seemed to be a letter, addressed to a Gama DeCastro, in Havana, Cuba. Po squinted at the writing:

The bearer of this letter, Supercargo Rimshaw, has been engaged to take the bark *Red Tanager* to the Congo. He understands the trade thoroughly, and you need have no fear to put into his hands the rest of the promised money. He is promised on this voyage one in every thirty he lands alive. We have contracted to land in the usual place in Georgia, where we can get in and out on one tide, and where we are known, and where we have a doctor waiting to care for ones that can be saved.

W. R. Hymes

There were more letters, and a stiff paper with a legal-looking stamp, and in heavy black script, "*Red Tanager*, W. E. Hymes, Owner, in ballast, out of New York, for Havana and ports beyond."

There were other papers and letters, difficult to read in the flaring fire. But it didn't matter. They had what they wanted.

"I've got them!" Larry stood up and shouted exultantly. "Now, I'll show you!"

She couldn't talk to him before because he was angry, and now she watched him, worried. Would he ever listen to words of hers this night, and he like the cock crowing? But she knew she must try.

"Larry, why do you have to show me anything? Isn't it me knows you can run fast as the east wind, jump over mountains, play ball, and swim out and front those dark men beyond? But it's me," her voice trembled a little with excitement, "it's me also says—'tis not so much to do!"

"So," he broke in savagely, "that's why you stayed!"

"I'm only saying there are maybe brawnier deeds, things inside a person maybe, would take more courage! And if he can front them, why then, a man doesn't have to hide behind any little thing like this!"

"What do you mean, little!" Larry broke in roughly. "This'll unblock the Brooklyn championship!"

"Ah, I'm glad you spoke of that, Larry boy! Glad I am it's but the championship you're thinking of! Because then you must see 'twould be better if someone that Hymes bears no grudge against should face him down. Brian maybe!"

Larry glared at her, disturbed. "Why do you have to go and spoil everything?"

Po's breath came hard, and her heart was pounding as if she were in a physical battle, a fight with some demon, and she losing. Maybe it was better for her to be silent.

She stole a frightened glance at Larry. He frowned into the fire, but it seemed to her some battle was going on in him, too. Maybe he was struggling to accept what she was saying! Ah, if she had but the crystal words of wisdom of some bright angel! She wished she could remember Walt's words. Maybe that would show Larry what he was doing, to himself, to them.

"Larry," she began, earnestly, "would you unstop your inside ears for a moment only and let me tell you a thing Walt is saying to me? For 'twas that made me stay!"

"Well"—Larry did not look at her—"I'd sure like to know why in hell you took it on yourself to stay!"

"I'll give you the man's exact words, and he the weighty one in every way. He said—'tis an easy outside kind of thing, and you with the great fists nature gave you, to go strutting the world with a black-thorn stick on your shoulder, bashing in the heads of your inimies, and shouting out to the populace what a great boy-o you are! And the

230

whole landscape knee-deep in these heroes—building their ten-story castles, and their shiny rails with the cars whizzing by on them! But these are nothing but boys' games!" She stood up, now, intent, peering at him. "This swimming to boats, and facing down Hymes, and shouting 'Big Me! I made Brooklyn champion'!"

Larry glared at her, and switched impatiently. "Walt never said that!"

"Maybe a wee word could be twisted a twig or two, but, oh Larry"—she went to him swiftly, anxiously—"listen, for I'm trying that hard to tell you something"—she was trying to recall Walt's words— "'tis a boy thing to be this outside kind of hero!" She furrowed her brow trying to remember the words. "It takes more courage to make a face-to-face relationship, he said, with a woman—that could be a real mate—"

"That's got nothing to do with it!" he broke out, impatiently, now, and got up from the fire, and walked away with a sullen look.

"Yes, it has!" She followed him a step or two. She wanted to say, "What's going to happen to us, if you don't go back and fight it out in New Bedford, but hide behind this instead?" Ah, but what if he didn't care about that? Well, she cared!

She saw him looking at the tarpaulin bundle.

It would be better indeed, if Brian got the papers.

"Now, what are you doing?" he broke out furiously.

For Po had stooped down quickly, wrapped the papers in the tarpaulin and picked them up.

"'Twas me hauled them in, and 'tis me will say what to do with them!" She looked back at him stubbornly before moving off swiftly into the dark.

"Where are you going?" he shouted after her angrily, but didn't move.

She ran back of the dunes till she found some flat rocks. She piled them securely on the bundle. He'd never find them in the dark. Then she hurried back to the fire.

When she got back, though, she was scared. He looked at her, drew in a sharp breath, and clenched his fists. She ducked involuntarily, for she could see by his face he was having a hard time to keep from clouting her. But he pounded his fists on his thighs, and said, "Sometimes . . . sometimes, I hate you!" He swung away from the fire then, and paced about in the dark.

Po sat down, miserable. It wasn't working out at all, at all, the way she'd hoped. Maybe she had done the wrong thing to stay.

After a bit he came back and sat down, looking at her from across the fire. It seemed to her his eyes were like someone staring from the back of a labyrinth at a deadly pursuer.

Po was frightened. They sat silent for a long time, and after a while, he got up, and his voice sounded flat and tired. "I'll fix the fire. We'll have to wait till daylight for a lift back!"

He brought wood then, and mended the fire skillfully. He brought the blankets he'd taken from the stage, and when she wanted him to take one, he rejected it savagely, as though she should know a man could sleep without a blanket.

Po was exhausted, not only from the swim, but the struggle between them. As she dozed off, worried, she could see him sitting there, crossed arms on his knees, staring broodingly into the fire. Maybe she had only driven the demon deeper into the labyrinth.

Po woke. She sat up and pushed away the blankets and raised her arms in a long stretch. Dawn skimmed across the sea and tenderly touched the cloudless sky to luminous blue-green. Larry, his long form stretched out rigidly, was asleep by the fire embers.

Po stood up. She breathed deep breaths of the salt midsummer air. The world seemed as tremulous and fresh as if it had just been born and she the first to see it.

The sea shimmered like wet fire. She ran up behind the sand dunes, dropped off all her clothes and raced down the beach to where the combers beckoned. The sun showed a tip over the rim of the world and sent a silvery track to her feet. She ran down it and into the summer sea. She dived through the surf and came up, striking out in voluptuous easy strokes, diving under or over a wave, like a rolling silver fish.

The water and air and midsummer sea were all one, and she was all one with them. Oh, if only Larry were not split up, divided against himself! After a while, she swam in with joyful easy strokes, and raced for the sand dunes. Ah, did she feel good! She dried herself on her underclothes.

She put her hands under her small round breasts and lifted them, she spanned her waist with her hands, and stroked down a thigh. She had never felt herself with sensuous pleasure before. "Ah, now, I'm just seeing if I'm ripe at all!"

She shivered a little then in the morning air, dressed quickly, and went back to where Larry still slept as the sun spilled over the sand. She sat down beside him and looked at him, and a deep well of tenderness seemed to brim up and flow over in her.

Just then, he woke. He smiled, seeing her—a happy, boyish smile. He sat up. Then he kissed her, warmly, tenderly.

Po wished it would keep on forever and forever. And when it stopped, she said, "Oh, Larry! If only you were like this always! If only you could be different—"

But she felt him draw away from her sharply, and an irritated look came on his face.

Oh, she thought, in a panic, she had only wanted . . . He got up, and walked toward the fire and kicked the embers. She went to him swiftly and threw her arms around his waist urgently, looking up at him pleadingly.

"Oh, Larry, I only meant, that if you were—if you would—"

Suddenly he grabbed her roughly, and then he deliberately kissed her, savagely, so it hurt.

She had longed to be kissed so, but now, but now—you could almost think he were saying, "I'll keep you quiet!"

He picked her up off her feet then and started to carry her back toward the dunes. A warm feeling mounted in her.

Then she saw his face. She knew from the look on it, that if she did not fight herself now to keep from surrendering, things were finished for them forever. For he looked exultant, as if he meant to punish her.

"Put me down now."

But he kept on.

She struggled now. "Larry, put me down!" She pushed at him.

She knew he was stronger, she could only sting him with words, with little dagger words, to confuse him. But she had to! For them!

"So," she said, scornfully, "what kind of a hero are you trying to be now?"

He set her down then, and she stared at him. He was like someone she'd never seen before.

"Larry! It's no good if you don't love me!"

For answer he jerked her toward him roughly, and anger finally mounted in her. Didn't he think she wanted him, too? Didn't he care what happened to them? Why did he make it harder?

" 'Tis only because I want for us, maybe, to be happy some day, always," she said, controlling herself with an effort.

"Ha!" He looked at her grimly. "One thing I'm sure of, the man that marries you 'll have his hands full! You'll be telling him what to do all the time!"

Now her anger flared up in a searing flame.

"Arrah, the man marries me will have himself straightened out beforehand, I can tell you! And he won't be running away from himself and hiding behind some big hero false face! I want no heroes or children in my bed, but a man!"

He looked again as if he would like to strike her. He got very white instead, and turned on his heel and walked away down the beach. She watched him go until he was a small moving figure.

She sat for a long time, aching with pent-up, turned back feelings, and the impossibleness of life. The tide came up to her feet. She didn't care. Let it carry her out. Nothing mattered. He didn't *want* to be any different. He didn't care then, if they were finally a man grown, and a woman grown.

Away off in the distance, she could see his figure on the lonely beach. She walked along the sand dunes, hunting. At first she could not find the tarpaulin-wrapped bundle. When she did, she brought it back to the circle of embers. She got two stones to anchor it, and propped up the package, so he'd be sure to see it, when he came back to find her and take her home.

Let him be a hero.

Suddenly, she wanted to get away from there quickly before he came back. She wiped her eyes on her sleeve. She had failed. She had not had the wit on her to find the words that might have been like little lights for him. She took off, then, almost running, across the sand dunes.

Chapter Thirty-five

PO WAS not surprised to read in the next afternoon's *Herald,* as she carried it from the entrance hall to Nicholas Van Leyn's day room, a news item of the kind for which her eye had become alert:

> "Captain Ellit of the revenue cutter *Washington* succeeded, after a chase down the Lower Bay, in seizing off Atlantic Highlands, the bark *Red Tanager,* suspected of intent to engage in slave traffic. As all papers had evidently been thrown overboard during the pursuit, her owner is at present not known. Evidence that she was being fitted for the slave traffic was found on board and she was taken into custody."

And after reading that, Po kept watch for another bit of news she felt sure would follow. She kept seeing the little stories and jokes about those mind-made champions, the Knickerbockers, for everyone had joined in the fun now, and soon there began to be letters from readers in the *Spirit of the Times,* with a match being called for, and people lining up on sides and taunting each other. But it was not until the end of the week she found what she was waiting for.

She knew the owner of the *Red Tanager* was sought, she knew Larry had the manifests showing Hymes as owner. She was aware that Hymes seemed now to control Nicholas Van Leyn. And so she was not surprised to find, in the *Clipper,* the news she had been watching for.

"Only a bit of inky print," she thought exultantly, "sitting there quiet on the page, but won't the view of it send shiny bells ringing in every breathing heart in Brooklyn!" She read:

"A series of baseball matches has been arranged between a team representing New York, selected from the four officially recognized teams here, and a team representing Brooklyn, selected from the newer clubs in that vicinity. Widespread interest is shown in both cities, and we will keep our readers informed of details of time and place."

By the time Po got back to Brooklyn, the town was in a ferment of dedicated preparation. Brooklyn was going to show New York they knew how a high-class sporting event should be conducted. The series was to be played on Brooklyn grounds. Brooklyn knew that of the six hundred thousand people in New York not one could play ball as well as any half-grown boy in Brooklyn, so it was not their baseball prowess they were worried about. It was the amenities. Everything must be sportsman-like, polite, gentlemanly. Fines had even been instituted to break the players of the natural habit of cursing. There was to be nothing rough in any way, the crowds were warned, even expressions of feeling were to be as mild as possible.

And you did not suppose for a moment that a vacant lot with a cow running across it was going to do? Councilman Clancy said he could get the Fashion Race Course out on Long Island. The grounds would have to be fixed for a baseball match, however, and that would be expensive.

In Brady's Gardens, where the Brooklyn high command met in daily council, with the results quickly known and debated over the town—the reasoning went like this:

From the Brooklyn population of well over a hundred thousand, you would have to subtract, say, a thousand—people like nuns, infants in arms, men confined in the cells, some people on the Heights, and the dying. That would leave about ninety-nine thousand who would wish to go. Of those there would be a considerable percentage who not only would be willing to pay money to go, but had the money to pay. The high command took, therefore, a daring step. They decided to sell tickets to a baseball match.

The tickets were printed at Rome's and, even at the fancy price of fifty cents, melted away. Because of the newspaper jibing, the sporting element in New York demanded tickets, too, and it was not long until the high command had the necessary, and went ahead with happy feverishness to ready the Fashion Race Course.

It was known the New York teams were in the habit of banqueting each other after a match, and soon printed invitations began to appear about the town:

The Brooklyn All Stars
invites yourself and lady friend
to a Social Party
after the game
At Brady's Gardens.
Entertainment on the house.
Carriages by Rooney's Hack Service.
Floor Committee:
TONY ZAMBRINI, LARCOM WAINWRIGHT, THOMAS O'HANLON.

And now that the series was actually scheduled, Po began to listen shamelessly to any conversations in the day room. You could spy on an enemy in time of war. But she heard little until one day the Knickerbockers had a meeting there. And didn't she listen avidly! Maybe they would discuss strategy, or who was to pitch! But all she could pick up was dull talk about how the country was so prosperous. At last, they got to the series with Brooklyn.

"They play a different style game!" Jenkins complained.

"D'you remember the size of that one came here to our meeting?" Granger said.

"It's our game." Shelton sounded sour. "Why don't they leave us alone?"

"Gentlemen," Nicholas said, "we are to send a delegation to the other New York clubs for the purpose of selecting a team."

Then Po heard Hymes's flat voice for the first time. "I wouldn't mind going for you! After all, I'm accustomed to dealing with those people over there!"

Jenkins spoke up then. "I think that's a splendid idea! I'll be glad to go with him if you wish me to!"

"The rest of you won't have to bother any more about it!" Hymes added.

It came to a vote, and Hymes and Jenkins were delegated. The Knickerbockers quickly got back to gossiping about their merchanting, the way you'd think it more important in every way.

Then came the day, surely marked with a ring around it on the calendars of heaven, a day when justice would be ladled out with a big spoon, when the withered crowns on the balding heads of the Knickerbockers would be snatched off, and new laurels, bursting with green life, would be placed (for who could conceive of anything but victory?) on the heads of the fine roaring lads who could enjoy them.

And on that day, Scoreby, that serpent in plum-colored livery, denied Po leave to have time off. There was to be a party. Po was needed. Unless it was very important.

Scoreby knew Po was an orphan. She could not, therefore, tell him her mother was at death's door, or her father was being tried for murder. She could only say, tensely, " 'Tis a baseball match I must see!" But even as she brought out the words, she knew that Scoreby, a man of limited vision and no feeling, would not be able to grasp what that could mean. Permission denied.

"Is it a villain the like of him can keep me from Brooklyn this day?" Po glowered to herself. "Niver!"

But as she went through the hall, preparing to slip out, she saw Coventry Van Leyn come from the day room, his usually pleasant face red with anger as he talked to Jenkins, who was leaving.

"But shooting stars," she heard Coventry say, "that's too much!"

"Why, it's the best joke I've heard in a long time!" Jenkins cackled merrily. "Maybe they'll not be crying for matches with us after this!" He laughed again. "Where's your sense of humor?"

Po had to leave quickly then, for Scoreby was coming, but as she hastily crossed the avenue, she was worried. "Shooting stars, is it? Now, for the love of hivven, what could that be? A way of playing? It's these American jokes would bewilder a saint, with their queer style of humor!"

Perhaps it meant nothing, but Po was in a fever to get to Brooklyn in time to ask Brian, just to be sure. She was held up, though, at the ferry.

A great crowd waited to cross for the game! People who might have gone to see the horse racing, talking of this new game everyone was beginning to play. People who were in on all the details of the contest, from having read the *Clipper*, people who talked of playing the game themselves in back lots, and even some loud-talking men who looked like waterfront rowdies, drawn perhaps by newspaper and saloon talk of a sporting contest.

Po reached the Gardens, just in time to see a special stagecoach with the team and Brian rolling away. The watching crowd gave no cheers. It was more as if valiant trusted men were being seen off on a holy mission, and confident faces watched them go.

The stagecoach was to stop at City Hall, where the Mayor and Common Council would make speeches, and Father Genski, Reverend Myers and Pastor Werner offer short prayers.

"Shooting stars!" Po said the words over, wishing she had seen Brian.

It was difficult to get out to the converted race course, but that did not seem to keep any one at home. That small part of the population who owned carriages drove out Fulton past the old Dutch farm houses with gambrel roofs. Those who owned horses rode horseback, galloping along the plank road. Many went by small steamer from Fulton Ferry to Hunter's Point, transferring there to the steam cars on the Flushing railroad.

But at 26 Fulton Street, outside the American Hotel, Po was delayed again, for a great crowd waited to board the stagecoaches. Sailors from the Navy Yard, mothers with children, seamen from Clipper ships, women from brothels, ministers in kindly black, men from the East River shipyards, doctors, shopkeepers from Myrtle Avenue. There were old derelicts from the river front, laughing young girls, a handsome colored woman with her half-grown son, a father, mother and children who seemed to speak only Spanish.

There was a man in a tail coat, with a long tripod over his shoulder and a great leather knapsack over his back, and a strange square box in his hands. It was a camera, he told Po when she asked. Next him an old Irish woman with no teeth laughed with her neighbor, a man with a terrible twitch, supported on crutches. And then there was a horde of ragged eager boys from Battle Row, watching, shining-eyed, hoping by some miracle of justice they could get to go.

It was a good hot midsummer day, and when the stages got to the race course, there was the smell of dry, baked earth and green luxuriant vegetation. Po arrived just in time to see the players run onto the field, and she was so excited watching them, she forgot her little worry about shooting stars. For now at last the time had come. Brooklyn was playing New York!

It was a moving moment when the team, in uniforms with the wide belts marked Brooklyn, came running lightly from the dressing tent. There was such a focus of hope on them from that mass of people who loved them. As if to give the expectant hearts a full measure of happiness, they ran out singly. And when the Bull and Larry and Tony and Bushel Basket, and all those other brave and nimble men came onto the field, who could not feel that all injustices, all degradations, all frustrations in other departments of life, were about to be, for this little time, wiped out.

Then from the other dressing tent came the New York team. Po looked for Nicholas Van Leyn, or Coventry, but did not see them. But neither did she see Granger, or Shelton or Fielding. She looked for Quimby or Haviland. They were not there. These players looked younger, bigger, and moved faster than any New York players she had seen so far.

The Brooklyn team stood smiling politely. Even the crowd looked pleasant. It was customary to have police at any game in Brooklyn, but for this occasion it was thought it might not look well. Everyone in Brooklyn was determined to be sportsman-like and gentlemanly if it killed him, and it was known the New Yorkers were not apt at their games to indulge in any fits of temper. So now, the Brooklyn team stood, looking pleasant, the perfect sporting hosts.

Both teams had referees present—only now, Po remembered, they had begun to call them umpires. A toss was to decide which umpire should officiate. New York won, and even though it was not the same as having a Brooklyn man everyone knew, Brooklyn smiled with impeccable sportsmanship.

And now at last, the picture long visioned in the hearts of Brooklyn appeared before their eyes. The Bull, swinging his bat—their bat —stood there, confident, facing New York.

He had to take his chances out there on the field like everyone else, subject to good or bad luck—but he was the Bull, strong, skillful, cunning. He would not be downed by life's petty mishaps as they often were. A great roar and hum of pleasure rose and hung over the field. The moment was here.

Then came the absolute saturation of satisfaction. An electrifying crack shivered the air. The Bull started off the series between Brooklyn and New York by knocking a home run! There was, after all, justice in the universe.

And then there came the moment, which Po thought came rarely enough in life, when you burst your little isolated walls, for, looking into the face next yours, even though you did not know its nationality or disposition—you shared exactly its surge of triumph, its gleam of rejoicing or hope, and sometimes its bitter disappointment. Maybe it was this gave some of the delight she had in the men out there on the field and the joyous game.

The play rolled ahead, and then Po knew what she had been waiting for. Larry was up to strike, and she had heart and eyes only for that.

It had come to be known somehow that Larry had, in a manner unknown, brought about the scheduling of the series, and he was cheered as a hero. Yet he stood there, unsmiling, waiting for the ball.

He connected with it solidly to center. "Ah, now, 'tis second base he'll land on, with that fine crack!" Po exulted, as she saw him flashing toward her down the line. He rounded first, went on a few yards, passing the New York first baseman, who was standing a little toward second. Then—Larry fell headlong on his face. The crowd gave a disappointed cry. By the time Larry got up, and ran, chagrined, back to first base, the ball had come to second and been relayed to first. The first baseman was waiting for him with a grin. Larry, tagged out, looked at him levelly, then shrugged and walked off.

Po guessed she must have been mistaken, but, for just a second, she had imagined the New York first baseman's foot had come out a little, enough to trip Larry. She worried again, just a little. Was this what they meant by shooting stars? Ought she to try to speak to one of the Brooklyn men? "Still and all," she thought, "what kind of a thing would it be for me to curdle the air, and me maybe imagining only?"

Brooklyn, playing the game so long hoped for, quickly ran the score three to nothing. The Bull's underarm pitches were hard and fast, and even the sight of him was intimidating to the striker, though the players facing Brooklyn seemed quite good, and were powerful hitters. It was nearly the end of the first inning when Po heard a rather troubled voice say to another, "Joe, that New York striker! Looks sort of like a fellow I seen playing up in Newburgh!"

"A New York team all right! York State, huh?"

"Shooting stars, maybe!"

"What is this shooting stars, sir?" Po asked.

"Why, that's like a revolver. A fellow that revolves around from team to team, wherever he can get some money."

But just then something happened which caused Brooklyn smiles to become a little forced. A New York striker knocked one down to the shortstop, who picked it up like lightning and fired it in to Hans Schmidt at first. Was it on time—or not? It was a hairline decision. The umpire declared the New York player safe on first.

It was the first test of Brooklyn's temper, and their smiles looked a little strained, but they kept them. And after a bit the Bull was up to strike again, and Brooklyn was happy. The Bull swung, but instead of the cold chill down the spine that came with one of the Bull's electrifying cracks, there came only a disappointing f-l-umph, and the ball trickled down toward first. The Bull was out.

But Brooklyn was rich in other players. What if the Bull did get put out once? Brooklyn kept its pleasant manners.

And then, with New York up to strike, with two players out and three on bases, a big rangy New York player came to bat. He knocked a long ball toward left, but Brooklyn wasn't worried. In the left field, Brooklyn had Death-to-Flying-Things, who could catch anything moving in the air. But as Death-to-Flying-Things moved swiftly back to get the ball, he was jostled and interfered with by some of the crowd. Po wondered if it were not by some of the loud-talking water-front rowdies she had seen on the ferry. Whoever it was, the ball was missed, the bases unloaded. And Brooklyn, with glassy smiles glued to stiff faces, accepted the rule that the home team took the penalty for interference from the crowd. The score was four to three, favor of New York.

Never mind, as more innings passed, here was the Bull, that stalwart mountain. But again, the Bull hit a disappointing little dribble and was out. Po saw his great lower lip come out, his great black brows draw down in a frown as he started out after the ball to look at it. Some of the other Brooklyn players caught his arms and dissuaded him, and he went glowering off the field. And the next time he came up, the ball behaved as it usually did when it came near his bat. It went off in a long soaring arc, and Brooklyn hearts soared up with it.

The game went on, a hard, close contest. By this time the glassy smiles on Brooklyn faces had vanished. A questioning whisper was going around. The New York team had a starry look! Shooting stars? Brooklyn was sober, but watchful.

Then the Brooklyn right fielder brought shame and disgrace on himself and his descendants for ever, by failing to field a ball, the consequence of which was that two runs came in for New York. The score stood eighteen to eighteen. It was too close, too close. Twenty-one runs was the fatal number.

There were no Brooklyn runs in the next innings, and New York came up to strike. They got a man on every base, and no one was out. Then the rangy New Yorker came up to strike. He hit one that the third baseman quickly got, but then something happened. It was over so quickly no one could be quite sure how it happened. In his zeal to get away, the New York striker had swung his bat backwards, tossing it away. It hit Bushel Basket, the catcher, in the head, and knocked him unconscious. The Brooklyn men started for their injured teammate, but the New York base runners kept going, and three runs came in. While the Brooklyn men still clustered around Bushel Basket, the umpire called the score: New York 21, Brooklyn 18!

With murder in their hearts, the Brooklyn crowd let out a maddened roar. The Brooklyn men around Bushel Basket glanced back, worried. Po saw them conferring hastily. Then Larry, substituting for Bushel Basket as captain, walked quickly toward the center of the field and handed the ball to the New York pitcher, admitting defeat.

It was the only way they could see to prevent bloodshed.

Chapter Thirty-six

NOW that it was too late, Po understood the wonderful joke Jenkins had been laughing at. But if Brooklyn, in this matter, had no sense of humor, at least, with outrage came release. It was as if a boxer, bothered by a tricky shifty fouling opponent, at last could get at him with gloves off and hit him hard with bare fists. Brooklyn had tried to be gentlemen and sportsmen. If New York wished to play rough—well, now!

When all the bits of knowledge, surmise and memory were put together, it became clear that Jersey, near-by Connecticut and upstate New York as far as Albany, had been combed to put together a team of shooting stars. It was guessed that the Knickerbockers and the other New York teams had known little of the sordid details. "Or of the tricky ways of them shootin' stars, either!" Brian glowered; for Po had told them, " 'Twas me heard them with my own ears, delegating it all to Hymes and Jenkins!"

And now Po learned all about shooting stars—hard-slugging players who picked up money by coming on a team during some bitter neighborhood contest and winning it, no matter how, for the team with the most money.

All night, the streets milled with clusters of men, arguing, discussing what had happened, what could be made to happen tomorrow. In Brady's Gardens, lights burned till morning. They were remembering those disappointing dribbles from the Bull's bat. A dead ball? Tony Zambrini worked till late. If Tony, that skilled sail-maker, was clever enough to wind a ball to make it perfectly round, he was clever enough also to make it just enough off center so it looked all right, but would behave oddly.

Cleats were fastened in shoe toes for defense against tripping. Pocket mirrors were provided for flashing into the eyes of a man up to strike. Six-shooters were ready for firing off in back of a fielder just as he was about to make a catch. Well-knit bands of Brooklyn men with good clean murder in their hearts were ready to stand back of their own fielders to protect them from jostling. This was what they could think of beforehand. But Brooklyn's true genius, they knew, could be counted on for ingenious stratagems in the heat of battle for the demoralization of a tricky enemy.

The Bull sat at a table, eyes glaring out from under his heavy brows, brooding. Finally, he announced: "They had it comin' a long time. I guess I finally got to go over there and beat the place up!"

"No, Bull," they dissuaded. "You can't!"

"I been over there." He looked ferocious. "I ain't seen nothing but a bunch of little snot-noses. I can beat them up in bunches of ten!"

"It's not that you couldn't," they pointed out. "It's just that they's so many of them it would take too long!"

But the Bull brooded. "I got a good notion to jerk the whole damned island up by the roots, tow it out beyond the Narrows and dunk it for good and all!"

But he was dissuaded. He'd have his chance at them tomorrow. . . .

On the stage going out to the field, everyone seemed quiet, but Po noticed an unusual number of weighty pic-nic baskets, neatly covered with a white cloth, carried by men with grim expressions.

At this game, Po saw Hymes and Jenkins, with a couple of other men she did not know. They all looked smug and smiling, as if they had come to enjoy the working-out of the elaborate joke, and to laugh at these cheeky arrogant people who had meant to humiliate them and had gotten more than they bargained for.

The second game began. The shooting stars were good ball players. But so were the Brooklyn men, and now, they didn't have to be polite. They were just playing ball! With terrible zest, Brooklyn shot the score up quickly to nineteen to eight.

And it was at that point it began to rain. It had been sprinkling for half an hour, yet at such a time, who even felt moisture? But now it began to rain heavily.

Po saw Jenkins speak to one of the men playing for New York, and that man speak to the New York catcher, and the catcher speak to the umpire. The umpire shook his head at first. Still, the rain was coming down steadily.

The umpire summoned Twinkle-Toes, Larry and the Bull, and as they stood discussing, it became clear to the Brooklyn crowd that now that they were about to be whupped, the New Yorkers were trying to get the game called on account of rain!

A deep welling-up, a roar so savage in its outraged intensity rose from the crowd; the umpire glanced back nervously over his shoulder. Even the shooting stars looked frightened. In the pouring rain, the game went on.

And then, as if to make the matter forever plain, Brooklyn got three men on, and brought them all in with a home run by Larcom Wainwright, by Larry himself, and the score stood twenty-four to eight, in favor of the fair, the decent, the honorable, the roaring brave darlings of the world, Brooklyn! At last, New York was in its proper place.

The series now stood one to one.

There was no roughing of the New York sympathizers. Brooklyn didn't need that. They had a victory, and a decisive one.

Larry and the Bull were too big to be carried off the field on boisterous shoulders. The roaring crowd had to content themselves with surrounding them and escorting them toward Brady's Gardens.

Larry, laughing and happy, did not even see Hymes as the triumphant crowd surged past him. But Po saw Hymes. His cold level stare at Larry made her uncomfortable.

"Be easy!" she told herself. "For what could he do? And why should I be worrying on this day, when Brooklyn wakes the world to its mighty doings!"

All the church bells and the fire bells and the school bells and the bells on the ships in the river pealed out. Brooklyn had trounced the smug, the pompous, the undeserving! Up Brooklyn!

Of course there was a parade, with Restored Jones's old granddaddy, the Revolutionary War drummer boy, at the head, carried on shoulders, wearing his Continental uniform, and carrying his drum. There were the fire companies, the target companies, the Brooklyn teams. If you could move you were welcome, and it all ended up at the social party at Brady's Gardens.

The Brooklyn All Stars did not appear till later, and when they did, each man was cheered and toasted, and kissed by all the girls. Not a heart in Brooklyn but leaped with joy and laughter. Brooklyn had come into its own. There was one more game, but who was worried?

And Brooklyn, like a big jovial fellow, confident of his own strength, and so, willing to forgive his enemies, even served New Yorkers in the lager-beer saloons. And there were only good-natured taunts for them and no fighting.

Po could not bear to leave. "And what would I be doing in New York, gazing into the sour face of Scoreby, on a night like this, with joy raging in the streets of Brooklyn?"

She noticed one group of five or six men, rough-looking, the kind who usually hung about Dent's or the Brooklyn river front rather than in Brady's, who seemed to take no part in the celebration, but sat in a small tight group. But no one paid any attention to them, though, what with the fine dancing going on and the roaring songs the like could be heard over in Manhattan.

The Brooklyn team did not stay too long at the merry-making. They wanted to get a good night's sleep to be fit and ready for the final match tomorrow. They began to drift off early, one at a time and quietly, so as not to spoil the fun. Po saw Tony leave, and after a bit, Bushel Basket, then Larry.

As Larry went out the front door, the rough-looking gang got up quietly and slipped out through the side gate. Po was a little disturbed. "Whist with your worries! For who would harm a gleamy hair on his head, and he the fine towering hero this night?" Why, no one —except Hymes. But—if Larry had the papers from the *Red Tanager*, how would he dare?

On a sudden impulse, Po went out the side gate into Fulton. She crossed Fulton, for Larry lived now in a boarding house on Sands Street, and she knew he would cut across vacant lots to get there. As the sound of music and cheers rocked from the Gardens, Po started across the lots.

It was as she had feared. There was no moon, but from a gas lamp shining between the houses, she could see a milling gang in the vacant lot, hear grunts and the sound of heavy blows. She turned and ran back swiftly to the Gardens for help.

As she ran up Fulton, she almost collided with the Bull, who had just left the celebration. She seized his great hand with a sob of relief. "Bull! Run! A gang! And they're killing Larry! 'Twas Hymes did it, I'll wager! Come!" Fear gave Po's feet speed, but the Bull kept right behind her.

"Hunh!" The Bull gave a great grunt of satisfaction as they neared the struggling men, and dived into the middle of it.

Po stood scared, wondering what to do. Then in the narrow shafts of light from the gas lamp, she saw the Bull stand up a moment. Holding one of his opponents by the ankles, he whirled him around his head and the man came hurtling through the air and landed on the other side of a tall fence. Po saw another one, whirled and thrown. Then the gang began to flee, down Fulton Street toward the ferry. Po heard the Bull's heavy boots pounding after them.

She ran into the lot. Larry was on the ground.

Brooklyn went to bed that night happy, but woke up stunned. The gang, which it was conjectured Hymes had set on Larry, had decided after their encounter with the Bull, that they had their own grudge to settle. They had come back with a larger gang, vicious toughs from the low dives along the Brooklyn waterfront. They had found the Bull in bed. It had been a bitter cruel savage battle. The next morning, the Bull could not at first even get up.

On top of that it was learned that Death-to-Flying-Things Collins had been arrested and placed in the cells. Someone had unearthed an old warrant charging him with horse stealing, some months back, from his employer Simon Quimby. Frantic people flew to Boss Hughie McLaughlain, who said he'd work on it, but evidently other powers were at work and, for the time being, Death-to-Flying-Things was in jail.

But when the Bull learned that Larry could not play, and that Death-to-Flying-Things was in the cells, he shoved aside the doctor, who suspected internal injuries, and got up on his feet. Once up, who could stop him? He was going to play. "Why, this here is just how you tell a man from a boy," he growled, and went on out to the field.

Brooklyn and New York were no longer speaking. Signs appeared in lager-beer saloons, "No one from New York served here," and the people from New York soon learned to cheer in silence or walk away on a stretcher.

Hymes, nor any one of the Knickerbockers, appeared at the third match, and it was just as well. Brooklyn was in an ugly mood. If any little thing, no matter how small, of a crooked nature happened at this final game, there would certainly be murder.

In spite of the absence of two of their brilliant stars, Larry and Death-to-Flying-Things, the Bull was in there pitching, wasn't he? And as long as the Bull was there, a symbol in everyone's heart of triumph—they'd come through all right. Thomsy O'Brien was at center for Larry and Brian Brady at left field for Death-to-Flying-Things.

The Bull was not in form, though; his pitching was off. He grimaced at each pitch, and allowed New York to score eight runs in the first four innings, while Brooklyn, even with nimble playing, could only get six.

And then, at the beginning of the fifth innings, the Bull came up to strike. He swung the bat a mighty stroke, and came the sound that made all Brooklyn hearts glad—the electrifying crack of the ball on his bat. The ball soared far over the field. But it had no runner to match its splendid flight. For the Bull seemed to crumble in on himself. He fell heavily to the ground.

It took eight men to carry the mighty Bull from the field. A doctor was summoned from the crowd.

And when finally the game went on, something had happened to Brooklyn. The Bull stood for something. He was their native strength, their belief that they could lick anything. He was out of the fight.

Tony Zambrini came in to pitch now in the Bull's place, and he pitched well, but Brooklyn acted as if it had received a stunning blow and was dazed. Before they could get over it, the score had run up to eighteen to eleven.

"D'yuh concede?" The New York pitcher yelled tauntingly at Tony.

"No! No! Never!" The Brooklyn crowd had heard this, and

screamed back. Brooklyn rallied itself desperately. As if maddened by the idea of conceding, Restored Jones delivered the mighty blow of a stout rally that brought in a full eight runs. The tally was nineteen to eighteen, in favor of Brooklyn.

But now word came from the dressing tent where the Bull had been carried that he was in a serious state. Tony, pitching nervously, with a worried frown on his face, let three New York men get on bases. Brooklyn, its heart in the dressing tent, was aware of the precarious situation, but could not seem to react to it. Then a New York player made a lucky hit, which Rooster Hanlon tried, with every ounce of heart and muscle straining, to reach in time, but failed. The score was twenty-one to nineteen in favor of New York.

With sound judgment, the New York players and the New York crowd left quickly, and without uttering one single cheer, as if they were glad to get out alive. As for Brooklyn, they surged onto the field, and stood about the dressing tent where the Bull lay. They were silent, stunned.

The Bull died at ten minutes after five of a clear summer afternoon on a baseball field on Long Island. His last act had been to swing a bat for Brooklyn. The ball he had sent flying over the crowd seemed to be sailing yet. Maybe it would never come down.

There was a funeral in Brooklyn.

The funeral was not only in the black crepe on the outdoor gardens at Brady's where the Bull lay in state, or the procession that carried him forth later. It was in the hearts of the people.

The series had been lost. That was a blot they could remove. But this was something vanished forever. It was as though every man and every woman, covering eyes with their hands, turned away, sorrowful without quite understanding why. Maybe they sensed dimly something miraculous, alive, buoyant, cunning and sportive was being carried away from them forever.

Po wished her father were here. He could make a mighty poem, a song they could sing that would ease their hearts and keep the Bull with them forever. If she could only make one up for them! She tried.

"This is a song about an oak tree on a mountain,
A song about the Bull, who could knock a ball across the East River,
A fiery man who never stayed with dull truth if a lie was more uproarious—"

But she could not go on. It was only a singer she was, and she hadn't the poetry in her like her father had. She could make no song, though all the people's hearts were engaged and a mighty hero fallen.

She guessed even if she could make up no song, the Bull would remain, though, like the ancient Irish heroes. There would always be an echo, a trace of him, left in the hearts of the people, like an enormous footprint on a strand crowded with pygmies.

And when at last the Bull was carried forth, through an arch of crossed bat sticks, held aloft by sorrowing players who had loved him, Brooklyn hurried away and tried to get back to its everyday business —so it could cover with a thick layer of everyday things the knowledge that something precious had ended.

When people have taken a beating, that's when, Po knew, you understood what they were like. You came to despise, or love, or despair of them. Seeing Brooklyn and the men in Brady's Gardens now, Po loved them. None of those fine roaring hearts could stay conquered, and none would be bowed down.

For even on the next day after the Bull was carried forth, as eyes still gazed off into the distance, in Brady's Gardens they counted gains and discounted losses.

"Well, now," Brian said, polishing glasses behind the bar, "'tis way ahead we are from before! For what is one little child of a series? Haven't we got those fine boy-o's over there to playing us anyway?"

"You couldn't have said a smarter word." Bushel Basket bumped his glass down, and looked around at the others. "We got that set anyway! All we got to do now is get ready for the series next year!"

"Next year, Thomsy O'Brien in right field," Twinkle-Toes said dreamily.

"Naw, Manini!" someone said hotly.

And Tony smiled, white teeth flashing, as he lifted his glass. "Next year! We play and we win!"

Chapter Thirty-seven

PO HESITATED, bonnet on, in the Gardens, rubbing a finger along the bar, as Brian leaned across looking at her.

It wasn't that she feared she'd lose her place at Van Leyn's because of her absence (though she suspected she might), that she was reluctant to go. She would not mention that to Brian anyhow, for he would insist on her coming back to stay with him, and she did not want to add to the tension upstairs caused by Brian's spending so much time and energy on the series. Mamie, impatient, had brought up the big guns of tight silence and frigid politeness, and Po would on no account add to Brian's difficulties at the moment. It was not her premonition of what would happen in New York that made her linger, as she stood, rubbing a finger along the bar.

"And how," she finally brought out, "are all the men on the team, Brian?"

Brian blinked his eyes once or twice, then said dryly, "They're all well!" Now wouldn't you think he would have the kindness to go on with a little chat of this one or that one, but no, he stopped.

"Even—all of them?"

"Well, now"—Brian turned and took the cork off a bottle of brandy and smelled it experimentally—"wouldn't you think a grown girl would have the sense to say out what she had on her mind, instead of flithering about like a broken-winged bird?"

"Well, then," Po broke out, bright-eyed, "how is he then?"

"Could it be Larry you are speaking of? 'Tis to the hospital on Portland Street they've taken him so he could be cared for. He has an arm broke, and his fingers hurt some, though all right otherwise."

Now how could she go across the river without so much as seeing him? But she remembered the night Larry had been hurt, how he had looked at her cold and distant, when they brought him to the Gardens. It was like he did not want her to see him when he was injured and fallen. She shifted from one foot to the other uneasily. She had done so many wrong things at the picnic, she had lost her confidence. If she went now, would he just be angry with her? She sighed. She had better leave him alone.

But even as the ferry crossed toward New York, her mind and heart seemed to be pulling the boat back in the other direction, and instead of worrying about Scoreby, she kept wondering about how it was Hymes had dared have Larry beaten, and if Larry still held the *Tanager* manifests.

When she finally got to the Van Leyn house, she did not forget about Larry—but she had something else to think about. She had lost her place. But not because she had taken time off. For while Brooklyn was having a joke they could not appreciate played on them, mysterious forces had been playing a grisly joke on New York.

From what Po could snatch from the scurrying frightened staff, something had happened called a Panic. The Panic made everyone look like a famine did in Ireland, but a famine meant no food. The Panic seemed to mean no money, no gold, and it was that everyone wanted frantically, at once. The household had a stricken, anxious air. The entire staff, except Scoreby and Van Leyn's personal driver, had been given two weeks' notice.

Augusta Van Leyn, with many of her friends, was in Saratoga, and Coventry was at his rooms at the Astor. Po felt sorry for Nicholas Van Leyn. His pleasant face looked frightened and confused, and he spent a great deal of time alone in the day room. He would sometimes ring for a drink, then act bewildered when it came. At meals he stared distrait at a wall in the dining room, and did not eat.

Po wished Coventry would come up from the Astor to look after his father. She wondered if she should not go and find him. The rest of the staff seemed absorbed in their own worries, and Po did not know what to do. None of Nicholas' friends seemed to come either. Finally, however, Mr. Fielding, of the Bank of New York called, and even though he looked sour and grave, Po was glad to show him into the day room. She listened, too, for she wanted to see if Mr. Fielding would notice all was not well with Nicholas, and would perhaps send for Coventry.

But Mr. Fielding did not seem to be concerned about Nicholas. It seemed he had terrible worries of his own.

"I wouldn't dream of pressing you, Nicholas," Po heard him say, "but with Peyton Company failing, we *have* to keep open! Everything'll go!"

"You can sell the railroad stock," Nicholas said, worried. "That should cancel out the notes and more!"

"Nicholas, if you hadn't shut yourself up here the last days you wouldn't say a thing like that. Stocks are simply not salable!"

"But it's impossible. All that money I borrowed from the bank to buy the stock! It was you advised me to buy it!"

"You'd think this were all my fault. I'm not responsible!"

"No . . . No . . . I know." Nicholas sounded troubled. Then he broke out bewildered, indignant, confused— "But who is? What happened?"

"It's just the workings out of the law of supply and demand. It'll all right itself eventually."

"But in the meantime," Nicholas said desperately.

"In the meantime, I've got to call outstanding notes. What can I do? The depositors trust me."

"Is it the house here, then?"

"That was the security. Why don't you raise something on the yard?"

"It's already mortgaged."

"Oh. Well, I hear Hymes is in a sound cash position. Maybe from him?"

"It's Hymes holds the mortgage on the yard."

"Nicholas, put yourself in my place! What can I do?"

"Of course, of course. I'll manage somehow."

But after Fielding had gone, Nicholas paced the hall nervously for long. He ate no dinner that night, and the light was still burning in the day room when Po came past next morning.

Po wondered again if she should try to find Coventry.

But that day, Nicholas had two more callers, though neither made him look any happier. The first was Mr. Shelton, the Manager at Arnold Constable. Mr. Shelton knew that a woman of fashion required comforts and luxuries, but the bill was very large, and since they were friends, why Shelton hadn't let it go through the ordinary channels but come himself to mention it, knowing Nicholas would want to take care of it. And Nicholas assured him of course he would—in a few days—he was short—this Panic.

"Yes." Shelton sighed, and sounded bewildered and confused too. "It's sun spots, I guess. They say they come in cycles, and bring these things on. And then, of course, there was all that gold from California. With all that extra money, prices went up. Everybody speculated. And now—" He trailed off.

Scoreby had been sent to fetch the next caller. It was Mr. Jenkins, the lawyer, and Po was relieved to see him, the way one is when the doctor comes. But when Nicholas and Jenkins paced up and down on the flagstone terrace, Jenkins did not seem calm like a doctor. He seemed not only wildly worried and as confused as Nicholas, but angry, too. "It's all part of an international conspiracy, this panic!" He was vindictive. "Started in France, with that revolution. These workmen's combinations, where do they get ideas like that, raising prices! Why, do you know over nine hundred banks have closed already!"

Van Leyn asked if Jenkins thought he might be able to borrow money from Granger, or Blair, but Jenkins looked at him pityingly. "You haven't been in the city the last two days! Granger and Blair both failed. Credit overextended. Yessir, I tell you, it's an international conspiracy, aimed at private property!" Van Leyn shook his head, bewildered. "It wouldn't have worked. It wouldn't have happened," Jenkins said, "if it hadn't been for that California gold."

Nicholas stayed in the day room now, most of the time, and Po did not like the way he looked. She decided she must find Coventry. She thought of Carlotta Bradford, and how Coventry had seemed a familiar there. Maybe Mrs. Bradford would know where he could be found.

Then she remembered Carlotta had once promised to give her an introduction to the manager of Niblo's Gardens. Ah, wouldn't that be the handy thing at this moment? For Po was determined to find another place at once, before Brian even learned she had no job.

Since the staff, serving out their two weeks, came and went as they pleased, Po went off one day to the lower city to seek out Carlotta Bradford. But Carlotta did not know where Coventry was, and she herself was in a state of angry bewilderment. All the money her father and first husband had left her had been in railroad stocks, and something had happened, Carlotta didn't know what, for the stock exchange had closed, but they told her she had no money. She was brusque, and stared absently, and Po felt so sorry for her, she did not want to ask for the introduction at Niblo's and left.

As Po came back to the Van Leyn house, she saw waiting outside a private carriage, black and new and shiny. She hoped some of Nicholas' friends had come at last to give him heart. Passing the pantry, she stopped a moment to listen, to be sure it was well with him. Then she heard in the day room the flat voice of William Hymes.

She could not at first make out the words—the two of them must have been near the door—but remembering Nicholas' bewildered confused face, daily getting sicker and grayer-looking, she stayed to listen.

When Po heard Nicholas, she was glad to hear his voice rise sharply, he had looked so apathetic lately. "I should not have let it happen! You involved the good name of the Knickerbockers!" Po felt sorry for Nicholas. It was as if he had so many troubles, and this little one he would try to settle.

And Hymes, with a little apologetic laugh, said, "Well, I'll admit, I had a little personal grudge to settle. Just a joke! I settled it! We all have our little weaknesses. That's mine! I don't like anyone to think they can get the better of me. It was all a joke!"

"I feel responsible!" Nicholas was sharp. "I sponsored you!"

"It doesn't matter. I'd as soon resign. Jenkins has put me up at the City Club anyway. That's as well. For I'm going on with the ferry now. A good time, with prices so low. I had a feeling, not having seen you in Wall or in Brooklyn lately, you might be in a little difficulty, and I wanted to tell you about the ferry company. You might be able to recoup there."

"Thank you," Nicholas said stiffly. "I am in no position to—"

"Oh, I know, I know," Hymes said kindly. "But I got thinking of that beautiful wife of yours, your fine son. I figured I wanted to help you."

Van Leyn must have been facing away, for she could not hear what he replied, but then she heard Hymes go on: "That *Red Tanager* thing was a close call for me, too close for comfort. I don't dare buy up any ships, or man or fit them for a good long while. I wanted to let you in on the ferry company anyway, and it all pointed one way. I'll put up all the money; you buy the bottoms, fit, man and send out the ventures solely in your name, and I'll cut you in for ten per cent. How does that sound to you? Pretty good, eh?" Hymes sounded pleased, like a man doing a good deed.

"No. I won't do that." Van Leyn's voice sounded angry.

"Why not?" Hymes sounded surprised, a little hurt.

"In the first place, I need cash, gold, right now—not in six months."

"Oh, if that's all, we'll make the agreement now. You take it to certain men here we both know. They're still sound in spite of the panic. On a paper like that, they'll advance you money."

Van Leyn sounded tired, flat, dead. "And they'll know about me. Soon everyone'll know."

"What do you care? Your duty's to your wife and son, to yourself!"

"What would Pieter Van Leyn think of me?" Van Leyn sounded a little hysterical. "A failure!"

Hymes sounded stern. "Never say a thing like that! You got to keep strong in this world! It's the strong that keep the world running! I want to help you, if you'll just let me. Just move along with me, trust me, and you'll be back on your feet in no time!"

"I don't want to have any more to do with the business!" Van Leyn sounded desperate. "It's disreputable, ugly!"

"Oh, is that what it is?" Hymes sounded patient, kindly. "Now that's just foolish. Did we make the conditions? Did we set up the system? Good God, man, you're not responsible for it! I'm not responsible! There it is! You have to be realistic. And when you're in a tight place like you are now—it seems to me, if I had a beautiful wife like you, a fine son, I'd be thinking of them!"

Hearing Hymes talk of his grudge had made Po forget about poor Nicholas Van Leyn. She was suddenly flooded with thoughts of Larry, and would he, with his broken arm, be filling up again with hate?

She went, the next afternoon, back to Brooklyn. She must know if Larry was all right. At the Gardens she heard the news. His broken arm would mend, but his hands were worse than had been thought. Both the right and left hands had been smashed, and he would never again be a baseball pitcher. Po remembered Larry saying once, "The only way Hymes could hurt me is to break my pitching arm, and I'd like to see him try!"

Po remembered, then, Larry practicing in the April dusk; Larry building the field; Larry, smiling as he pitched, regarding guilefully the wary man with the bat stick, before the ball flew from fingers with art in them.

She went to the yellow frame hospital on Portland Street. Larry was up and about, but had to stay there while his hands were being pieced and patched. He did not look happy to see her. It was like when he had first been hurt and didn't want her to see him. His distant look froze her, made her unsure of herself, remembering she had made so many mistakes.

"Larry, I was only wondering— I want to help if I can," she ended lamely.

"I'm all right," he said quickly. "I'll be out of here in no time. And when I am"—he paced up and down the room—"when I get out! He thinks he got the better of me!" Disquietude filled her then, for she saw the look on his face.

"Plenty of things in this wide world a walking wonder the like of you can do," Po said with false cheerfulness.

"Yes," he said, "but some things I'm going to do right off! First"— and he sounded cold and steady—"I'm going to build up a team that will win a series from New York, or anyone! That's because I said I would, and nobody, least of all him, is going to keep me from it!"

But suddenly, Po felt miserable and strained. Louise had come in, her silk skirts rustling, her wide red mouth smiling, and she greeted them gaily. Larry didn't seem to mind Louise seeing him hurt. He looked as if he were glad she had come, and Louise patted his arm as if she owned him.

"He's going to mend up in no time! And then, watch out! He's going to give Hymes a beating he'll never forget! Right, Larry!"

"I got it all marked down," Larry said, and Po felt uneasy at his unsmiling look. "First, I win a series; second, I'll beat him till he's sorry he's alive!"

"And a fine way to spend your life," Po wanted to cry out bitterly, but she was so unsure of herself with him now, she was silent.

Going back to New York on the ferry, Po tried to keep her courage up by remembering happy times. She thought of how it had been in June, when they had talked under the crabapple tree. How sure she had been they would both quit off being green and misshapen. But what if a black blight stopped him? Ah, but wouldn't something in him push and insist, and go on? It must! She would believe it!

Chapter Thirty-eight

IN THE FLAT, Brian had, it seemed to Po, even more than usual, an air of walking on eggs, and as she recrossed the river she determined, again, to get a place—any kind of a place—at once, so as not to involve him. And as she rode up the Fifth Avenue, she was turning over in her head the possibilities. She'd begin at once to go about to the managers of the various gardens. She'd start now, today.

But when she arrived at Van Leyn's, where but a skeleton staff remained, she saw Nicholas Van Leyn, not sitting in the day room, but walking about the nearly empty house, his face lined as if he had not slept for long, his eyes with a vacant look, his usual gleaming neck cloth untied.

Po forgot her own plans. She must find Coventry.

She went first to the Astor. At the desk, the room clerk said, "Mr. Van Leyn has returned from Saratoga, but has gone out." Po stood troubled. Would he be at Pfaff's at this hour? As she stood trying to decide where to go, Coventry came in.

In spite of the August humidity, he looked fresh and handsome in white linen. He came over to her at once, smiling, pleasant, charming.

"Lady Violet-Blue-Eyes! In trouble again?"

" 'Tis not me this time!" Her errand was too urgent to soften it. " 'Tis your father!"

All the casual charm disappeared. "What happened?" He looked worried and intent. "Count Ossi?"

"No, 'tis this thing they are calling the Panic, and he that upset, and no one by to so much as say 'Be easy'! I thought you'd be wanting to know!"

He took her arm, walked her quickly outside, found a hansom cab and told the driver to hurry.

As they drove up the wide avenue, she stole a glance at him, and she saw under the pleasant casual charm, a great covered-up fear and worry.

"I should have been there!" he said. "I went away so as not to see, because I couldn't do anything for him!"

She wished she could find a word to ease him. After a bit she said, " 'Tis a thing I've learned lately from a bad experience I am having. Just say, 'No one is perfect! But I can try to do a little better!' "

When they arrived at the house, Nicholas Van Leyn was not in the day room, or the halls, or upstairs, or down. Coventry stood a moment, deeply troubled.

"Ah, now, himself may have gone to one of his friends to have a dish of wine and ease his heart. Belike to that Mr. Jenkins or some other!"

Coventry looked at her a moment, swallowed hard, seized her hand, pressed it a moment, then hurried away.

And Po had her own worries. She dressed carefully now, and went out to assail the wide world again.

Po stood on a dim dusty stage, shifting from one foot to the other anxiously, waiting to be "tried out."

It had not been easy to get thus far.

She had gone first to Niblo's, but the bill advertised a classical ballet with Mlle. Robert as *danseuse,* and Po knew there would be nothing for her there. She went on down to 472 Broadway then, where Christy was playing at the Marble Palace, but she could not even get past the stage door.

Then she had come here to Bryant's Minstrels, for the minstrels often used women singers before their main show. Billy Bryant had good-naturedly motioned her from his little cubby hole at one side of the stage, out here where a pianist sat.

From the battered piano came a flood of lovely melody, an intricate gavotte, and Po looked wonderingly at the pianist. Ghastly pale with feverishly bright eyes, he finished now, took a whiskey bottle from a back pocket, and as if fortifying himself for an ordeal, took a long swallow. Then he put it on the piano as if within easy reach in case of need, and motioned to Po with an air of weariness.

Po tried not to be nervous. She had gone as often as she could to hear American singing at the various gardens, and had listened to all the women singers. She had practiced in her room, singing in a low voice, exactly as she had heard the songs. She had carefully practiced too, the pronouncing of old and ever, so that she felt certain that in this song at least you could never tell her from an American singer.

She put her music sheet from Firth and Pond on the piano. The pianist stared as if in pain, but played. They had only gone as far as the first verse, however, when Po saw that something was wrong. The pianist stared at her wildly a moment. Then he dropped his head in his hands as if in nauseated despair. Po felt alarmed for the poor man, and was about to run for aid, when he straightened up and suddenly cried out, pounding the piano with maddened fists, "God send me strength!"

"Be easy now, what ails you?"

"All day I listen to women singing in a whining voice about a 'Rose Petal from Father's Grave.' My gorge rises, but I am patient. I bear it. I listen to men singing 'Found Dead in the Snow.' I am long

256

suffering. I hear caterwauls about 'A Lock of Mother's Hair.' I endure, I go on. I must eat!" He was tragic. Then suddenly he stared wildly at Po and broke out like a man pushed too far, "But that I should have to listen to 'Old Folks at Home' in an Irish brogue heavy enough to sweep the Liffey dry! Oh, God! No! No! It is too much! Too much!"

Po was about to tell the poor man to be easy, and she'd go quietly, when Billy Bryant and a man he had been chatting with in his office came out on to the dingy stage.

"No good, eh, Jimmy?" Bryant asked.

The pianist looked even paler than usual, and as if not trusting himself to speak, put one hand over his eyes and shook his head no.

"Say," Bryant addressed his friend, "she's little!"

The other man looked. "Yes! Say, sister, want a job?"

"If 'twill go with a whiff of an Irish accent I am fitted up with!" Po tried to sound dignified.

"Oh, it's just a walk on! No lines. For a couple of nights. Temporary. You're little is how I happened to think of it. Could you act like a drunkard's daughter? See, your old man hits the bottle. You go to the groggery, and stand there, looking like you ain't et. It's the temperance piece we put on before the main show. My regular gal's off on a drunk, and I need someone till she sobers up. Five dollars a week. Want to try?"

"That I do!"

"Fling her a shawl, Jimmy, something out of the prop room."

A musty-smelling old shawl was tossed at Po. She whisked off her bonnet. The man didn't know it, but he was looking at a woman who had seen many, many such children, on the streets and in shebeens in Ireland. She looked about for soot and found it on the tin shields in back of the gas footlights, and with a finger gave herself hunger shadows under the eyes, and a dirty face. She took off her shoes, and cringed under the shawl.

Mr. Bryant and his friend had gone down and were standing beside the first row of seats in the theater. Po came out and went toward Billy Bryant as though he were her drunken father, and think shame to him!

From the two men in front came a roar of laughter.

Po flung down the shawl in a rage. This was too much! She had been meek about the wee bit of a brogue that no one would ever notice who wasn't picayunish, but when it came to telling her she didn't know how such a child looked or acted! She was summoning up a few plain words from the rough side of her tongue, when Bryant's friend spoke up, still laughing.

"It's all right, sister! We're just laughing at the cheek of you!

Pulling our leg like that! Why, you nearly had me puttin' my hand in my pocket to give you a quarter!" They laughed again. "It's all right. If we laugh, they'll cry!" He was trying to mollify her now.

Po learned then, it was not in this theater she was wanted, but over at the Bowery Theater, where *Kit Carson* was the main piece, and *The Drunkard's Daughter* was played as a curtain raiser, and that Bryant's friend was named George Gillis, and that he was stage manager and doubled as an Indian on the main bill.

Gillis and Po got in a hack then, and he took her over to the Bowery Theater. "I just want you to run through it for places. All you got to remember is to keep out of the way of Mervin Fairfield, the drunkard, for he often has a load on."

Mr. Gillis found her quick and nimble, and when they had run through it, he asked her to go on for the evening performance.

He took her along with him then when he went to supper at the boarding house on Houston Street, where many of the theater people lived.

Po learned that she could get a small room there, cheaply, and decided to take it. It would be convenient to stay in now, and later, too, after the regular drunkard's daughter sobered up, when Po must look for a new place.

At the evening performance, Po found being the drunkard's daughter was easy. In fact, she enjoyed it. And didn't she lay it on thick, looking hungry and pitiful and put-upon, until she heard someone in the gallery call down, berating the drunkard, "You ought to be ashamed, and that child starving!" Then Po felt very good.

She had thought about Coventry and hoped that he had found his father, but there was a matinee the next day, and what with trying to get acquainted with this new life, and one thing and another, it was four days later before she went back to Van Leyn's to get her clothes.

It was from Scoreby she heard all the sad way it had been.

Coventry had hunted for his father all over the city. Nicholas' friends had joined in the hunt then, too. But so many other bad things were happening, banks crashing, business failings, men doing away with themselves, that even when Nicholas' body was found, it seemed only one more incident added to the confused bewildered nightmare the city was going through.

Nicholas, as if trying to hide himself, had gone to an old tavern on South Street, where, in earlier days, Dutch merchants had awaited their incoming ships. There, he had shot himself. He had been buried the day before Po came back.

And Po found, now that it was too late, his friends had come. Some of them were gathered in the day room now, trying to piece together his affairs, to save something for his estate. But they had a bewildered confused air. Jenkins kept repeating that it was caused by an international conspiracy, and the others said some other thing, and they kept repeating their words as if they were a ritual to scare bad spirits away. But whether sun spots or conspiracy, on one thing they all agreed—the whole nightmare had been set off because of all that gold discovered in California.

But for days, Po thought, she'd heard them all desperately crying for gold! Sure, they must all be daft, she thought. They acted rather like scared children, who had somehow broken up their world, and had no idea how to put it back together again. And these were the jackeens, too, Po thought, who had let all the lovely things—the lights, the cars running on rails, the open fields, the canals—all be thranced into money. And now it was as if the great pile of money had suddenly become a grinning berserk genie, out of control, that had turned on them.

Walt's words came back to her: "—children, pretending to be men, playing with forces beyond them. But the huge forces once touched, move on of their own volition—"

And Po thought about Coventry, too. He would be sorrowful and guilty-feeling. She hoped he had someone by to comfort him.

The other men in the day room left then, and Jenkins rang the bell for Scoreby. But Scoreby had gone out on some business of his own, and Po answered the bell.

"Will you find young Mr. Van Leyn and ask him to come here?"

Po finally found Coventry, pacing up and down wearily, in the back garden. He looked pale in his dark clothes, but he smiled as if he were glad to see her.

"Ah, 'twas a fine sweet man he was, and happy now without a doubt, and he above teaching that game of base to George Washington and"—she tried to think of an American saint—"Christopher Columbus!"

Coventry did not speak, but patted her arm as if to thank her.

"You've the look of a hollow man has not eaten for long! I'll bring you in some food from the pantry!"

She found cheese and cold meat and biscuits and wine, put them on a tray, and took them into the day room where Coventry sat now with Jenkins.

Somehow she did not like the look of things when she went in quietly, and she made excuse to linger, silently setting the food out. Jenkins was sitting at the heavy black walnut lowboy with the brass claw feet that Nicholas had used as a desk. Coventry looked confused

259

and badgered, as Jenkins said in his precise fussy voice, "If you'll just hand me the key, maybe I'll find some additional papers here that will help me to straighten out your affairs!"

Coventry looked bothered, but tossed out a key, and Jenkins briskly opened the lowboy drawers, and began to pick out bundles of papers and letters and, without examining them, put them into his capacious portfolio. Just then, from the hall, Augusta Van Leyn, even her mourning robe having a rich black glisten, came in. Her strong brows drew together. She crossed swiftly and laid a white hand with great rings shining from it on the portfolio.

"What is this?" she demanded.

"Nothing you need bother about," Jenkins said quickly. "I am just taking these to sort them, to see if there is anything—"

"Precisely"—Augusta looked at him levelly—"to see if there is anything! These are Nicholas' private effects. Leave them!"

"But I am his attorney!"

"And I am his widow! If there is anything to concern you, I will inform you!" She lifted the bundles and packs of papers, put them back, closed the drawers, and locked the lowboy decisively.

But even as she was handling the papers, Coventry, a white angry look on his face, had crossed and confronted her. If he had been apathetic before, he was not now. It was as if he did not mind too much Jenkins taking his father's things, but he could not bear to have Augusta touch them.

"Give me the key!" He confronted her.

She stared back at him, contemptuously, it seemed to Po.

Then Augusta became aware of Po. "You may go!" she said curtly.

Po left reluctantly, for some reason feeling she ought to stay and help Coventry. Shortly after, though, she saw Jenkins leave, his portfolio flat, and then she saw Augusta go through the hall, her black dress rustling, and go upstairs.

Po had meant, when she came, to get her things and leave at once, for she must be in the lower city in time for the curtain riser at seven-thirty. But somehow, she kept thinking of Coventry's face. He seemed so alone.

With all her things packed, ready to go, she hesitated. Then, she went into the day room. Coventry, sitting in a green leather chair, was hunched over, staring into space.

Po went over and stood beside him. Somehow, since she had made so many mistakes with Larry, she was not so sure that she could find the right word with people. She saw then that he had not touched anything on the tray. She wanted him to feel she was his friend, and she poured out a glass of wine and handed it to him. He took it, looking up at her, and said, "Thank you." Then, as if trying to rally himself and recapture his usual easy charm, "Lady Violet-Blue-Eyes!"

"Slean Leat!" she said softly.

"What does that mean?"

"It means, 'May the angels keep an eye on you and the saints a hand under your elbow, through all the blue bright days and the shadow dark nights in this wide and wonderful world.'"

Coventry did smile a little then, as she left.

Chapter Thirty-nine

By THE TIME Po got back to Brooklyn, a strange sight met her eyes. Right in the middle of a work-day morning, nearly every vacant lot had a baseball game going, and with a ring of spectators, too, calling out excited praise or blame.

The Panic had crossed the river. She noticed immediately the deserted streets, and going along, saw the white piece of paper rustling a little in the breeze, where it was fastened on the closed gate of the Van Leyn shipyard.

In the nearly empty street, one man idled along. He stared at the notice, but as if he knew what it said. She saw him stop outside the fence, where the half-finished work had broken off. He stared moodily in, then his hands came out of his pockets, and made an absent gesture in the air, as if he were holding a nail and pounding it into a plank— finishing the siding. There was a fence around the ship though, and he couldn't.

Po walked on then, past a little cluster of people, gloomily staring at the imitation marble Greek pillars on either side of the closed door of the bank.

"Better to have hid it in the earth, like my pap did," she heard one man mutter to another, "this way, you don't know nothing, can't do nothing! It's all out of your control!"

And Po discovered, as she moved on, that if, on the Fifth Avenue in New York, the Panic was a matter of gold and men doing away with themselves, and on Fulton Street, a matter of idleness—in Battle Row, it was already a matter of bread and meat. She saw on some faces here, peering from doors, the look she'd seen in Ireland, the fear of famine.

The unskilled, who sold their backs for lifting, the fingers which knew no craft, the sick, the lately come immigrants—people who had never had sufficient to accumulate layers of fat, the people whom two or three weeks' idleness put at rock bottom—these had already gotten the famine look. And—just as she would have seen in Bethel Court—the musicians in Battle Row were playing in the courtyard, with some taking a dance, or singing. What did you expect—they were going to sit down and cry?

And then, because not only the shipyard, and the Lead Works and the Cotton Wadding Mill were closed, and the Iron Works open only two days a week, Po saw all over the town—the baseball games. It was only August, and if on a few faces in the streets, or in grocery shops trying to get credit, there was a tightness, a held-back fear—the men on the fields acted like it was an unexpected holiday. Everyone would be working again in a few weeks. Now they played baseball through long hot sunny days.

And Po knew, as she walked on, that what she was really looking for was a sight of Larry. Here, but the short while ago, she had been hoping with all her strength he would have courage to go back and have it out with his mother. Now she hoped with equal intensity he would not. If he went now, it would be a running back to bury his face in his mother's lap. Po had worried about him, but so many things had been happening to her in New York she could not come before.

When she saw a big crowd with a great deal of shouting and excitement, she knew she had arrived at the Atlantic-Excelsior game. Larry had not run home with his troubles. She saw his big form standing on the side lines with a group of non-players. His arm was still in a sling, his hands bandaged. It was curious to see him, just a bystander, down on a level with John and George and William. He had never had to make a face-to-face relationship with them. His strength and cunning skill had always lifted him above them. She was looking at Larry with all the bright look gone. He seemed morose, and did not talk to those near him. His mouth always ready to burst into a great laugh—so sure he was he could never lose the game—now was set and cold and withdrawn.

She wanted to go to him and speak to him, but remembering how he had looked at her in the hospital, as if he did not want her to see him except when he towered above all, she went away.

But a wishful guess rose in her, just the same. A seed looked dead. It wasn't, though. . . . And Po went on to the Gardens, to tell Brian her good news.

Even though it was noon, a time the Gardens had been most

bustling, they were nearly deserted now, and Brian himself was upstairs in the flat.

"'Tis quit off I am being a butler's assistant," she told Brian and Mamie proudly. "I am now a drunkard's daughter!"

"Well, now," Brian looked amazed. "Isn't that the profession for you!" But Mamie's mouth drew thin and she looked hurt and scandalized.

"First I had the place but temporary," Po rushed on, trying to show Mamie it was really a fine grand job, "but the girl who had the part, God rest her, she was overcome with delirium tremens, so that they took her off to a place called Bellevue, and myself being at hand, why who is it they give the place to but me! So I am now fitted up with the steady job, and the lovely fine people to work with!"

"Fine people!" Mamie looked incredulously at Po. Mamie sighed a little, and looked around at the silver cake basket and the plush chairs, and back at Po, as if she could not understand her, who might have had the same if she had put her mind to it.

Po thought suddenly of the tea for Mrs. Selfridge in Mamie's parlor. Then Po thought of making tea backstage over a gas flame with Fifi, the wizened wardrobe mistress. Fifi, with gay relish, would relate scandal, known or invented, of the theater, and those who were married and oughtn't to be, and those who weren't but should be. Po guessed she had never been cut out to be a lady, for she liked the tea with Fifi better. . . .

But after that, Po did not get back to Brooklyn as often as she would have liked. The poplar trees were already twinkling yellow in early September haze when she walked up Fulton again. The worse times got in the city, the more crowded the theater became. They played matinees now three or four days a week. People were avid about sports, too. Indeed, it was because of that, and a line she had seen in the *Clipper,* she had come hurrying across the river. In the *Clipper,* that morning, she had read: "In order that our readers may be posted on this sport baseball, we have decided to appoint a reporter to cover the matches!" And Dave Posen working only at odd times, and wouldn't he be the mighty one for that job! And what if he missed seeing the item?

As Po walked up Fulton, she sensed at once a changed feeling. From people who spoke to her, she learned that another bank had failed. Families were losing small frame houses on Myrtle Avenue. Stores had begun to fail. And there was now the beginning of a helpless anger. What if the Yard, or Iron Works, or Mill never opened? What had closed them anyway? Some mysterious unfathomable force, something gotten too big for them, out of their control. And winter was coming.

And when she got to the Excelsior practice, with men in shirt sleeves standing about under the warm September sun, the first person she saw was Louise, in a red dress, moving through the crowd, calling to all the boys, greeted by all the men.

Po found Dave, hands in pockets, idle, watching the practice.

He read the news item she gave him. His face lit. He could not speak. He grasped her hand, and was off in an instant. Then, Po saw Larry. But he was standing with such a black scowl, she shrank back into the crowd. His arm was still in a sling, but the bandages were off his big hands. He was watching, with an impatient sneer, a boy who was pitching. Larry would glance away as if he could not bear to look at such bungling, then glance back quickly, with disgust, as the boy tossed underarm throws to a batter. Suddenly, as if he could stand it no longer, Larry yelled tauntingly, "Why don't you get a boy to carry the ball to the plate for you? It'd get there faster."

The pitcher turned, angry, red-faced, lashing back. "Think you can do better?"

Larry started out toward him. "Yes, even with my arm in a— Listen, why I can *tell* you better than you can do it!" He grabbed the boy's hand, and with insulting patience, curved it over the ball. But the boy, scared and nettled at Larry's caustic sarcastic manner, bumbled it.

Larry sneered at him. "Nah. Nah." Then, as if explaining to an idiot, "Try your fingers!" But Bushel Basket stepped between Larry and the angry, humiliated boy.

Bushel Basket, wide and steady as a rock, looked levelly at Larry. "Leave him be, Larry."

"Yeah!" Larry glared back. "You think you'll ever win a series with that kind of play?"

Bushel Basket stared angrily a moment—then walked away.

Larry spat disgustedly and turned back to the side lines. But now, Po noticed, the men did not talk to him. Po looked at Larry unhappily. He was not dead and inert now. He'd started to move. But, maybe he was moving in the wrong direction!

Now she would speak to him. She must! She went up and greeted him then, and he spoke to her, looking a little surprised, as if wondering how long she had been there.

" 'Tis glad I am to see you with no bandages!"

"Oh, I'm all right," he said almost gruffly. "I'll be back in there playing most any day!"

Then Po saw Louise start toward them.

Ah, if she had but the words on her now, Po thought, to make it plain, quickly, before Louise came, how a person could grow into the ground maybe, instead of up into the air! She didn't know what to say. She tried making a joke. "Ah, that lad pitching hasn't the wit in his fingers you have, and what little he has scared away!"

Larry frowned and drew back. And Po could only stand dumb as Louise came up to them, calling a rollicking greeting. And Larry greeted her heartily, as if to say, "Some one think's I'm big Larry!"

Po went away then, without saying good-by. She walked along Marcy Street very fast, trying to get away from her thoughts, but they kept pace with her. "You may leave off your mooning and your yearning, Po O'Reilly. And he thinking all hours in the daytime and the nighttime only how to be the big boy-o that can slay dead his enemies. And while 'tis so, he'll not love anyone at all, at all!"

When she got back to Manhattan, she hurried along Bleecker, wanting to get a bite of lunch before the matinee. She found Pfaff's almost deserted at this hour, only one or two men sitting about. She had nearly finished before she recognized one of the men sitting in a far-off corner, alone, with his head leaning on his hand, as Coventry Van Leyn.

Glancing over, as she finished, she became aware that at this early hour Coventry had been drinking. From his rumpled hair, disheveled clothes, she guessed it had been a long bout. He looked pale and gloomy, and sat, staring with a frown at the tablecloth.

Po remembered, suddenly, a night months ago. She had come in here, feeling lost and friendless. How wonderful it had been to see Coventry's kindly face then. She glanced over at him again. It was odd he had none of his friends by him. Might it be that he was in some kind of a predicament now, and if she went over and talked to him, he would be as glad to see her as she had been to see him? When she finished, she crossed and sat down at his table.

"Could it be Your Grace of Kilmally would like to pass a friendly word with a well-wishing acquaintance?"

He looked up and his eyes were bloodshot. In his face, she thought she saw confused bewilderment. Yes, he needed to talk to someone.

He tried, then, just as she had that night months ago, to summon raillery. "Why, Lady Violet-Blue-Eyes!"

She knew from the newspapers Van Leyn had died bankrupt, and that the house and its contents had been taken over by the bank. But somehow, even though Coventry was without means, she did not believe that was why he was disturbed now; she guessed, knowing how he had felt about his father, it would be something about him.

But it was part of Coventry's courtesy, that, in trouble himself, he asked about her. "And are you all right? Did you find another place?"

"Indeed, and a fine one. At the Bowery Theater! And yourself? What way are you at all?"

He grinned ruefully. "Stony."

"But your father had friends, and business acquaintances. They'll be reaching out the hand to you!"

Coventry glanced at her quickly, then stared moodily at the table-cloth. Finally, he said, "One of them has!" He sighed and went on after a bit. "I've been trying to make up my mind to accept his offer!"

" 'Tis a poor one?"

"No, a good one." He frowned, and moved uneasily in his chair. "That's why I've been trying to drown myself in a brandy bottle. You see—" He hesitated then a long time, his eyes on the tablecloth. "My father left a lot of debts."

"Arrah!" Po broke in warmly. "The poor man!" She was thinking of Augusta. " 'Twas not of his doing!"

"But he'd want me to pay them!" He looked at her then, and she saw his confused unhappiness. "If I took this offer, why I could begin to pay them!"

"Is it a hard job it is, then, or what?"

"Oh, no! I'd act as an agent, going about buying up ships." Suddenly Po had a sharp foreboding. Coventry went on. "It's just, well . . . I'm worried."

Po leaned forward now, intent. "I've not many years on me, still I had me wits with me the while I been walking the world. Could you tell me now—what you worry of?"

"Well"—Coventry stopped with a puzzled frown—"the one who offers says he wants to help me because he admired my father, and yet —and yet, for some reason, I don't trust him."

"Tell me—" Po leaned forward. "Is the one who offers—William Hymes?"

"Why, yes!" He looked up surprised. "Oh! You knew him in Brooklyn?"

"That I did!" Now Po looked into Coventry's face earnestly. "You must make up your mind in one way. No! Do not act as his agent!"

"Why do you say that?"

Suddenly Po sat back and bit her lip. For how could she tell Coventry that his dad, he thought so fine, had been mixed up in something illegal? "You must not!"

"But I owe it to my father!"

"No!" she said vehemently. "Your father would not want you to."

"But—why are you so sure?"

" 'Tis my Irish intuition tells me, and me first cousin to a lepre-chaun. Promise me you'll tell him no!" In her earnestness she leaned over and grasped his sleeve. "Promise me!"

"Well, all right." Coventry seemed to look a little relieved, but he was puzzled, too.

Po knew she must go at once to be on time for the matinee. Somehow, though, she did not want to leave Coventry there alone, with sorrow and regrets. He might begin drinking again, and goodness knows what to happen after.

"Come on along with me now, and watch the show at the theater. 'Twill do you good, and we can have a great dish of talk after!"

Coventry looked at her gratefully, as if it eased his mind he had someone to talk to who had understood his father. He rose. "At your command, Lady Violet-Blue-Eyes!"

Chapter Forty

OFTEN, then, Coventry would come to her boarding house or the theater. Always Po felt a kind of responsibility to talk to him, for he was much depressed. He had not accepted Hymes's offer, but taken a place as clerk, beginning at the bottom, at Quimby's. And when Coventry came, she would go with him to Pfaff's or some near-by café, and let him tell her his troubles.

But one brisk October afternoon, when Coventry appeared, she failed him. For she was just about to start out from the boarding house with Dave Posen, and Rory McCracken, the fiddler from the theater.

Po introduced her friends. "This is Rory McCracken, a great man with a fiddle! And this is Dave Posen, and he, mind you, a reporter of baseball for the *Clipper*! 'Tis to a baseball match we are going, this minute of the world, to see the great exhibition game between the Excelsiors and a team from New Jersey!"

Coventry, who still looked the elegant beau, bowed gracefully, but he looked a little crestfallen, and Po felt a twinge of conscience. Still and all it was a bright October afternoon, and how could she stay away from the game?

As a sop to her conscience then, she promised Coventry to look him up when she returned, and off they went, she and Dave and Rory. "And aren't we the queer-looking lot." Po smiled, looking at the three of them. Dave, thin and intense, darting bright glances every way, Po in a new plaid dress, and Rory, a gangling high-shouldered man with pale freckles running right up to his fringe of sandy hair.

Rory played the fiddle in the orchestra pit, and Po, discovering he knew lots of old Scotch and Irish tunes, would get him, many a time, after the final curtain, to cut loose on the empty stage, and while he fiddled, she would sing or dance. Rory was a great man for a joke too, and often, during the temperance piece, while playing his fiddle to wring tears from a stony rock, he would be making comic faces at her, while she was trying to be pitiful.

Po had taken him with her to Brooklyn, and Rory and Brian were friends while they were still ten feet apart. But, now, as she and Dave and Rory walked along the street she felt a little guilty. For even though she felt fairly secure in her job—the theaters were packed as times got worse—more and more men and women, vacant, workless, stood on street corners, with a growing look of helpless anger. To-day, as they moved along the street, there seemed even more than the usual number.

They were pulled into a stream of men and women with faces set and grim, all walking in one direction. Pulled along in this crowd, Po and the other two found themselves in a kind of park called Tompkins Square.

Thousands and thousands of men and women stood silently facing a little pavilion in the center. A man was speaking and from what he said, Po gathered these people were willing to work, but idle. They were here to ask for work and food.

"Funny!" Dave's eyebrows drew together puzzled. "We got a big wheat crop! Biggest in history! Of course it takes it awhile to get here!" Dave and Rory gazed at the people, troubled.

Po, thinking of Dave's words, could see open sunny fields stretching away in long beautiful vistas from this eastern rim, and the fields overflowing with golden wheat, so there were not enough bins, enough bags, enough mills to hold it.

And she seemed to see this golden flood moving through great forests, over mountains, down little stretches of new railroads, by barges, on rivers, before it could finally get to these men and women standing here with the angry helpless look. She wished it would hurry.

A plump little man was speaking now, the Mayor. Po guessed he must have heard of the wheat on its way, for he was calm and cheerful. "Time will remedy all evils," he said. "Confidence like the genial sun, confidence in America is what you need! That is my reply to you. Have confidence!" This did not seem to fill the crowd with enthusiasm. They just stood, silent, grim.

Now, as Dave and Rory and she moved toward the river, Po thought uncomfortably how odd the world was, that here, they should be jouncing off to a ball match, when all these people stood there troubled. She hoped the wheat would come soon.

But the wind was fresh on the river, and Po soon began to think excitedly of seeing Larry, and the new Excelsior team. For now that Dave was in Manhattan every day, he brought her all the gossip. The Panic had scattered some of the old team. Jim Tash's ship chandlery shop had failed, and Jim gone to the Ohio country to start over. Tony Zambrini, maker of sails and baseballs, had moved to Philadelphia, where he had heard Cramp's Yard was still open. Of the men who still had their jobs—Rooster on the ferry, Death-to-Flying-Things at Quimby's—none dared take time off for baseball, with lines waiting for every job.

But Larry had pounded together a new team. Larry himself wasn't pitching yet. Of course, he would be most any day now, as soon as the stiffness went out of his fingers. But in the meantime, Larry, burned up with caustic sarcasm, full of impatient sneering, hammered the new team together. "You could think," Dave said, as they crossed on the ferry, "if you listened to him coaching them, he is so nasty at failures, so brutal at little mistakes, that he was trying to make the whole team serve as his fingers!"

But, Dave had to admit, the new Excelsiors were good. Dave, who, as *Clipper* reporter, knew all the clubs around, had arranged this Exhibition Match. A purse of fifty dollars had been raised for the winner.

When they got to the game, Po could see how Brooklyn loved the new Excelsiors. The jobless men watching them seemed to attach themselves to them in spirit. And, not only in the men watching, but in the men playing their hearts out, Po felt the terrible hunger in their absorbed faces and bodies, for a team to belong to, something to lose oneself in.

Rory, before he met Brian, had been an ignorant fellow, who had actually, in the late series, thought New York should win. But he was now as enlightened a man as you could wish to meet. As Brian and Rory stood, arms over each other's shoulders, Rory cried out in delight, "Ah, and aren't they the lovely boys!"

And after the game was over, with the Jersey men beaten so badly it was hardly a contest, Brian must have Rory back to the Gardens for a drap.

They arrived there before the crowd, and while Rory was telling Brian stories about the theater, and about Bernard St. Croix, the actor who played Kit Carson, and how he had stood last week in a tailor's window as a dummy to pay a debt and keep from going to jail, why Brian remembered a letter had come for Po and handed it to her.

It was from a man named John Hicks of New Canaan, Connecticut, Po saw, but she had only time to wonder about it, when the team, surrounded by their followers, came in. Clarabel and Louise were there, and Po could not keep her eyes away from Larry.

The winner's purse, stuffed with ten five-dollar gold pieces, had been given to Bushel Basket as captain, by the committee. Now, while the others watched but pretended to make talk, Bushel Basket took Hans by the arm kindly, and started out with him.

Larry, at the bar, shouted, "Hey, Bush, throw out the purse on the bar! Say, girls, what will you have? The Excelsiors are going to have them a party! Brian, ale! The best Scotch ale! That's just to begin with. And any food that's fancy!"

Bushel Basket reddened and frowned, but kept going toward the door, as if wanting to get Hans outside quickly. Ansel Dop caught Larry's arm and said in a low voice, "Let him go, Larry."

But the new domineering Larry reddened belligerently. "I will not. Throw out the purse, Bush. We're going to drink it up!"

Hans got very pale and cried out suddenly in a terrible shamed voice, "Let him have it," and went out quickly.

Bushel Basket turned on Larry, fists clenched, but Brian spoke to Bushel Basket in a low voice, and Bushel Basket threw the purse down on the bar then. "I'll take care of this boy! You go after Hans, Bush!" Bushel Basket went.

Larry did not like being called "this boy." He glared at Brian. "I say we're having a party! Who earned it? Who's been slaving their guts out coaching that team?"

"Why, you have, Larry boy." Brian looked at him levelly.

"So what complaint have you got? It's a good team! Better than the old Excelsiors!"

"Yes, a good team, and you did a good job"—Brian looked at him unsmiling—"only the team you're working for is called 'Big Larry!' "

"What d'you mean?" Larry glowered. "I'm trying to make a team to win!"

"Or are you trying to work off a grudge?"

Louise cried out then, indignantly, "The boy can't pitch, so you all jump on him!"

"Keep out!" Larry said to her savagely. "Now," he glared at Brian, "I say, we're having a party!"

Brian handed Larry the purse, kindly. "All right, Larry, there it is. Now what was that you wanted to drink—Scotch ale? The best? All right. I'll get it for you."

"For me?" growled Larry. "Get it for everybody!"

Brian was gentle. "Well, you see, Larry, some of these boys been out of work three months now, and things is getting a little tough. But Hans, he's been out a long, long time, and now he's not even able to get odd jobs. His family are being evicted out of their house tomorrow. The boys had the idea the purse might come in handy. Now—Scotch ale, is it? I'll have it for you in but the moment!"

Larry turned a slow red. He dropped the purse as if it were hot. Then he looked around from under frowning, lowered brows, as if he could burst out crying he was so angry. Angry at himself and at them for making him be.

"Why didn't you tell me?"

"Well, now, Larry boy, we figure it's natural, you being footloose, with no responsibilities—but it is a fact you just don't seem to pay any attention to anyone's troubles. Now, who is joining Larry in some ale?"

Larry glared around, and Louise moved over a step toward him, but he flung himself out of the bar, red-faced, angry.

And so it was not until she got back to Manhattan that Po read the letter from New Canaan, Connecticut.

Chapter Forty-one

M OVING hurriedly along toward Dent's to find Juba, the letter held close under her shawl in the brisk wind—Po stopped suddenly in the middle of the pavement, unwilling to go on.

The letter was an answer to the one sent through the underground months ago. How could she tell Juba? Maybe Brian would do it for her. He was older. Yes, he ought to relieve her of the responsibility. She changed direction and moved on toward the Gardens.

Going along, she saw the Hymes plant was closed tight. The streets had a stricken air, but even now, because the weather was still mild, some ball games were going. And the men in Brady's talked with strangely passionate absorption about just who would make up the team, come spring.

Po found Brian behind the bar, but she decided not to bother him with her problem of Juba. For Brian was in a state. "I said, and I say it again"—he was full of angry determination as if Po had been arguing with him—"let there never come a day when in my place, a ball player has to go without his beer! Pay or not!" And Po remembered that in Ireland it was a poet that was never let parch, whether he had a copper to ring on the counter or not.

"As long as I can turn a tap"—Brian was vehement—"it's going to be so if it ruins me! And I don't care what Mamie says!" It did not seem the moment to ask Brian to take over Po's problem.

Before she left, though, Po stood, searching the crowd hopefully.

"He's not here!" Brian said a little disgustedly. "And I tell you where he is! He's scrounging and scurrying around in all the near-by towns and cities, trying to arrange these here exhibition games for money! He's trying to get in as many as he can before the winter closes in for good. And what with his haggling and bargaining, he's got all thinking Brooklyn is a race of misers! Of course, the purses go to the players, and times being what they are, the boys are glad to get the money! But that Larry! You'd think now he was trying to show what a great generous man he is with them! Always trying to prove something!" Brian said impatiently.

But going home on the ferry, Po defended Larry to herself against Brian's impatience. "With all his troubles, Larry's not run home to New Bedford." Something in him must still be wanting and trying to push outward! How could you ever be scornful or disgusted at anyone, as if to say, "He is finished, that's the way he'll always be, and what a misshapen, green, lop-sided job he did on himself!"

Who could say they were that wise as to know exactly what would happen to anyone? For as the ferry bumped in on the Manhattan side, Po knew that was true of herself. Didn't she feel differently now, for instance, from the way she had four days ago, before she had seen that man fall in the street?

And that was curious, too. She and Dave Posen often wandered about the city, dropping in at lectures, or listening to outdoor meetings. And there were many such, for the Panic, like a creeping vast glacier, was freezing the city, and the meetings were involved with ways to unfreeze the glacier.

They had heard a woman named Susan Anthony trying to form a league for the Protection of Working Women; they went to a meeting where a new political group was forming called the Communist Club; and once, they went to a meeting, with Dave's press card, of a group trying to elect a president of the United States, called the Know Nothings. And Po read the newspapers, now, too. At first, to see Dave's little inch or two of type about baseball matches. And then because she was puzzled, and wanted to understand what was happening.

She knew the men who had gone west were drifting back, because the glacier had reached there, too. Banks all over the country had failed, five thousand of them. In New York, fifteen thousand were idle, in Brooklyn, ten thousand, and in Tompkins Square, thousands and thousands gathered every day, no longer silent, but demanding now the work and bread which unfathomable forces had mysteriously taken from them.

She knew that, and yet she could not say she had been changed in any way. Then, walking along East Tenth Street that day, she had seen, in new shining America, open with miles of grainy fields, a man collapsed with hunger. Seeing him fall, she thought him sick, but in trying to help, she grasped his thin arm and looked into his face and saw the famine look of Ballyhouna. She took him to a place called a soup kitchen.

Now, moving along the street, she brought herself abruptly back to the present. She still had the problem of Juba and the letter. When she had to decide something she liked to go and stand beside a moving ripple of water—ocean or river. It soothed her. She went to the river now. And as she walked toward the Elephant Wharf at the foot of Dover Street, where she had come often before to see the ships in and out, she passed through a little park where evicted people were stretched out, sleeping and hungry.

And now, standing on the Elephant Wharf, she saw the wheat arrive! A stream of great drays, with piled sacks. It had come from the open sunny fields down the Erie Canal, and now it was piled mountain high along the wharf.

And then—stevedores began to load it into waiting ships.

"Where's that ship bound?" she worriedly called to a stevedore.

"Lisbon!" he called back, as a great bulging sack was lifted aboard.

Maybe the people in the country stretching back of Lisbon were hungry too. Anyway, with all this great crop she had been hearing of, there must be plenty left. She walked on then, but still she had not decided what to do about the letter.

Worrying about it, she suddenly thought of Walt. Ah! She knew the answer would come to her here! She would let Walt tell Juba! It was too hard and delicate a thing for her to take responsibility for.

But she could never find Walt at Pfaff's, and always, when she inquired at the newspaper office in Brooklyn, he had just gone out. Then, one day, crossing to Brooklyn on the ferry, she met him. His face lit seeing her, and he was pleased and amused to hear of her job.

Then Po told him of Juba, and his seeking for his wife Hannah and the child, and the letter she had sent and the answer.

" 'Tis not at a family named Potter Mr. Hicks left them, but at

Potter's Field, where they are buried. And if I'm not the fearful woman these times, destroying myself thinking, 'Is it well to give Juba this bad word? Or say nothing, but let him go walking the world with the hope on him?' "

Walt was silent a long time, as if thinking. Then he turned and looked down at her a few moments, as they leaned on the rail. "You"—his seer-like pale blue eyes seemed to go through her—"must tell him!"

This was not the answer Po wanted. Then she smiled ingratiatingly at Walt. " 'Twould come better, maybe, from a man like you!"

He was silent, still gazing back at the wake. Then he said, "Why?"

"Ah," she said, "and aren't you the one with the words in you could slay a man or make him rise up dancing?" And then she added with guile, "And besides, it's you have the knowing, the understanding!"

"Don't you?"

That was Walt for you. He was the great one for pretending not to know she was but a girl, and lately come.

"You have a mind," he said, "and eyes, and ears, as good as mine, as anyone. If you can't know and understand, who else? Remember, it's taken the world a long time to get to you! Why should you be excused from relating yourself to others?"

Po was aggravated. It was all right, and she had taken responsibility for herself. But, she thought, nettled, he ought not to expect her to go taking responsibility for things outside herself, too!

If he saw her disturbed hesitation, he did not rise to it, and they were both silent a long time. Finally, when he spoke, it was as if from some place far off.

"Perhaps, one day, there'll be a bridge across this river. Strong, so that men and horses and wagons can cross over. The bridge will make a relationship between the two cities. A wonderful feat to throw a bridge across a river! No living thing but man can do it! It's a mastering of the earth's materials—wood, and iron, and stone! It's a figuring out how to use them! But—against this other thing we are talking of—it is a boy's feat. To throw a bridge across to another, a different spirit! To discern what he is like! To anchor a bridgehead of imagination! And then, to build a bridge, light but strong, that thoughts can walk across!"

Po stood, trying to understand him, a little disturbed. Did he mean, then, she was to do it all herself?

"But," she said finally, a little angry, "I don't know what to do!"

The ferry was coming in on the Brooklyn side now. "Come on along with me, then!" Walt said. "Maybe it'll help you! I've just been to Federal Court getting a story. Now I'm going to the scene of the crime. Come on now!"

It was to the Brooklyn Navy Yard he took her.

Walt showed his press card, but the man at the gate knew him and nodded him in, though he looked doubtfully at Po. Walt offered no explanation, just walked her serenely through the gate and across to the dry dock.

A ship was warped in there, a schooner, named *John B. Green*, New London.

It was old and wormy-looking, just about the size and age of the *Red Tanager*. Suddenly Po wished she had not come.

Walt started up the ladder. "Come on." He motioned Po to follow.

On the deck, the first thing Po noticed were the muskets stacked on deck, then, a long row of casks, sixty or seventy lined along a rail, and in front of them were scattered a dozen or so large flat pans like troughs.

Walt opened a hatch, and started down into the hold. "Come on," he motioned to her.

Po, for some reason, didn't want to go. She wanted to go home.

"Come along," Walt called. She went, reluctantly.

Light from the open hatch fell into the dark, evil-smelling hold. They had to crouch down, because the hold had been filled up with light decks, layer on layer, so close together a person could not have stood, or even sat up, between them. And looking, she felt a little sick, for she suddenly knew what the pile of lumber in the *Red Tanager* hold had been used for.

"How do you like it?" Walt asked, his voice matter-of-fact.

Po's mouth was dry, and she licked her lips. " 'Tis like—" she faltered finally, "shelves to stow goods on!"

"Yes. On the manifest the cargo was referred to as bales of goods." His voice kept flat and calm as if he were simply noticing facts. "Each bale, if they can get it over here, through six or eight weeks of tropic storms and fevers, is worth six hundred and fifty dollars!"

Po felt scared of something suddenly. She wanted to get out of here.

"That's why they build the shelves so close together!" Walt seemed to be paying no attention to her. "More bales! In this space, which I guess is about forty by twenty, three hundred and thirty-five men, women, and children, lived for eight weeks. There were four hundred and twenty when the ship left the Congo River, but they figure three to one usually. If they can land three out of four alive, they're in the clear. If there are bad storms and the hatches must be kept closed, a lot suffocate. Many die of thirst and hunger, too, for it's a problem to carry enough food and water. Sometimes the cargo stampedes, too, and they hate that, for then they have to fire the muskets down here, and always lose a lot."

Po felt very sick. It was just the closeness of the hold, the stench, she guessed.

"There is a stench, isn't there," Walt said, as if noticing for the first time her trembling sick look. "Sometimes they can't get at the dead to throw them overboard."

Po knew it was not the stench that nauseated her.

She was seeing herself and Larry, on the beach. They had known it was this the *Tanager* was busy with! How could they have done it? All they had thought of was using the knowledge to bring about some little thing that was dear to them—the triumph of the team!

"They captured this ship," Walt went on, matter-of-factly, "because the owner and captain got in a quarrel, the owner saying the captain was dishonest. According to agreement, he was to pay him thirty dollars a head for all he landed alive—which he did, and then a lot of them died immediately. But—due to the argument, they caught this one! A lot of them got away!"

"That's it," Po thought angrily, unable to accept and face certain thoughts. "This thing is going on all the time!" She couldn't help it! Suddenly a chilling memory froze her. Words came to her—Hymes's words, as he scolded Nicholas Van Leyn righteously, "You're not responsible, I'm not responsible! We didn't create conditions!"

She had to get out of there or she was going to be good and sick. Walt started up the ladder then. On the deck, though, he stopped. They stood there a moment. Then, he looked back into the hold, and now his voice was no longer calm and matter-of-fact.

He suddenly broke out, terrible as thunder, "It's enough to make you ashamed of the human race!"

They walked along the waterfront then, Po pale and silent. Walt seemed lost in some sad trend, too. They loitered, stopping occasionally, saying nothing, absent, sober.

They stopped at one pier, and Po sat down a moment. She felt a way she had not ever remembered feeling before, and she guessed the blackness inside her was a feeling of guilt.

Along the pier where she sat, a big gray ship was anchored, a side-wheeler. And even as she looked, she saw a dreadful, horrifying sight. Two sailors lifted from the hold a great bulging sack. They slit it open, held it up to the rail, and over the side into the dull green river, something yellow flowed. It was wheat!

Po stared a moment wildly. They must be mad! Then she turned to Walt, but he too was staring moodily, frowning, silent.

More sailors brought more sacks; the grain disappeared in a steady stream now. No one stopped them! All the world must be mad! Po wanted to stop the stream of wheat, hold it back with her two hands! But what good would a few handfuls of wheat, unground, unbaked, do the people in Tompkins Square?

"Why?" she demanded fiercely of Walt. "Why?"

He spoke, still frowning, but calmly enough, as if this grotesque thing were not happening before their eyes. "That's the second ship I've seen dumped this week! News has come that they have one of the biggest wheat crops in Europe, too, and they can't sell it there. They have to clear the ships already loaded! If they throw it on the market here, prices will go even lower, and the men who handle it and grow it will suffer. The crop was too big this year."

They were mad, mad, mad! Too much wheat? Too much gold? How could there be?

Then she was, suddenly, in a fierce and terrible rage. Maybe her own guilty feelings about the *Tanager* made her anger deeper and fiercer. "It's mad they are, or children," she cried, turning on Walt, eyes blazing. "Sure," she raged scornfully, "and they growing wheat a couple of thousand years in the world! Why can't they do better? They ought to be ashamed!" she said, passionately angry.

Walt looked at her, then he said frowning, but calm. "Who's they?"

"Now how can I, who am nothing but a girl standing here on the rim of America, know who 'they' are! But whoever they are, the old jackeens"—her eyes blazed—"they must learn to manage better!"

But looking at Walt staring down the river toward the ocean, she knew she'd get no help from him! He just threw everything back at her. She sat down suddenly, and broke into sobs.

"There, there," Walt comforted her now. "Never, never give way to despair!"

"I'm never a one," she stifled her sobbing, "to sit and drop down tears . . . though it's many a time I could have reason to, what with the dogs of fear chasing me, and the ugly Eaters do be walking in the world, ready to have me murdered and slain—" Then from deep inside her, a great bitter accumulation floated to the surface.

" 'Tis this thing of America and how 'twas to be! Not only the ship back there, but seeing the men with the life of them used up with the long hours in the dreary mills, and the children living in the rot of Battle Row, and men hungry, and people with the hopeless fear on them!" She turned, frowning, wide-eyed, dismayed. "If it isn't good here, where then? What else?"

Walt was sober still, but he was untroubled. "Oh, but America isn't finished. We're working on it! And after I'm gone, you'll work on it!"

Yes, Walt always threw it back at you.

Then Po realized a frightening, a bitter thing. She and Larry must, somehow, try to undo what they had done!

But how? Had Larry destroyed the *Tanager* manifests? And Larry, and he so filled up with proving things, was it likely he would listen to Po if she tried to explain?

Suddenly, she grasped the sleeve of Walt's shabby gray coat and looked up at him with intense earnestness. "Will you do a thing for me?"

Walt looked down at her, and then nodded slowly.

"Go to Larcom Wainwright! Take him into the hold of that ship back there!" She was ashamed, then, in front of Walt. "I can't tell you why! But you must tell him Po gave him the message, '*The Red Tanager*'!"

Walt regarded her a moment, then he said, "Why is this?"

"You once said the words to me that I must be far seeing for him; you said Larry was a one might take any road! Will you do it? It's a terrible, terrible, important thing!"

"I'll try!"

Po and Juba stood looking at a plain green field in Joralemon Street, in back of Fulton. This was the Potter's Field.

She had brought him here.

"Juba," Po began finally, "the letter from Mr. Hicks is after coming to me now about Hannah!"

Juba turned slowly and looked into her face. He knew, if the news were good, she would have been rejoicing. His look was one that stayed with Po and came back at moments all through her life. And it was always mixed up in her mind with herself and Larry, at the happy pic-nic, and they so busy about getting the slaver papers and letting the ship go, to further their own ends, unregarding, unmindful.

Juba stood steadily, a man who had been mutilated of any means of fighting back at vindictive forces too huge for him. He could be plucked from a forest, thrust into a slave ship, shoved hither and there, worked like a horse, his wife and child gone so that he didn't even know where they were buried, and he—a strong brave man—was helpless, and it was that Po saw was the bitterest thing.

" 'Twas a fine letter, and he after telling me what a great woman she was. For in the large building with many families where she was lodged, waiting for Mr. Hicks to come and pass them northward, a sickness broke out—a terrible disease they are having here called the White Evil, which deadens all who touch it. But Hannah, feeling to show her love for the town and people who harbored her, nursed them, warning all from the door. And she running night times and day times with the water and food the populace set before the door. In that house some died, but many lived, thanks to her. But that woman who showed herself strong, that bright and radiant heart, she died, and her little infant child died."

Juba stood motionless, silent.

"Then the town was after making a procession would take a day to tell of, with the mayor in a black and silver coach, and the children and mothers and loving husbands walking after. But they did not keen, for a mighty woman was being carried, and they were that honored she had stopped with them. They put no head marker on that grave for that would seem to make her little and like everyone else. 'This woman belongs to all,' they said, 'to every heart. We lay her here in this place unmarked that all may know she was larger than any small grave. She is in the soil, in the air now—the remembrance of nobility.'"

Po looked anxiously at Juba.

Maybe in his heart he was glad at last to have a sad peace.

"And that John Hicks, in Connecticut, Juba, he is after saying you could come there and stay with him, if 'twould suit you."

Juba turned then, surprised. "Leave here now? Oh, no! This is my town now. You belong where your folks is in the soil! And what's that they say—she in the soil, and"—he looked around—"in the air."

The little dressing room was deserted, for those who shared it with Po had changed their clothes and gone, but Po still sat, Mr. Hicks's letter propped up against the mirror, considering her reply. She read the letter again:

New Canaan, Conn. Tenth month, 1857—I remember this family well. The woman Hannah and her child ran into cholera in Brooklyn and died and are buried in Potter's Field. I would be glad to know of the fate of this man, for I have a concern for him.

Well, that Walt was the one that had made her take the responsibility of Juba, and she had done it in her own way, and if that way was only a pack of Irish lies, why whist! then with any complaints. It was the best she could do.

But as she changed into her street dress, she pondered many things. Had Walt found Larry, and taken him to see the slave ship? And had that sight fallen on him in the same way it had her? Did Larry still have the manifests?

She remembered Juba's face and sighed. The *Tanager,* no thanks to her, had been stopped. But the cast pebble of the slave ship she would have let go, could have washed rings of misery up on a distant continent. Yet that little thing she and Larry had been trying to accomplish had been good—for their team. And maybe the "they" who emptied the grain into the harbor had been accomplishing something too—for their team.

She stopped, her dress half-hooked, troubled. You had to be so alert all the time you didn't hurt something bigger. The world widened around her dismayingly.

She went on and finished hooking her dress, but she thought, "The world is not an easy place to live in. Sure, you but get somewhere, and are feeling good with yourself for making it, when something begins prodding and insisting at you to start off again!"

She began to put on her shoes then. But all this about the wasted grain, and the slavers, how could she be expected to know anything about that, or to do anything about it? It was all too big for her! Then she sat up, one shoe off, and one on, as a thought came nipping and barking at her. Maybe now, she was supposed to learn!

She put on her other shoe and stood up, knowing now, that whether Larry was moved or not, whether he had destroyed the manifests or not—she herself, Po O'Reilly, must do something to stop Hymes. For how could she know but what he might be going on in the same way?

She sat down, suddenly, weak. Why, he *was* going on! Hadn't he tried to get Coventry to act as his agent? And if Coventry had not, someone else probably had! Now, she knew she must do something, and at once!

She thought then of Coventry. What if she told Coventry all about it, and he went far enough as Hymes's agent to incriminate him?

"Ah," and Po got up then and walked around uneasily, "but that would mean I must tell Coventry about his father!"

She chewed her thumb, disturbed.

But, wasn't this other thing more important? Yes, it was!

She sat down then to answer Mr. Hicks's letter. Suddenly, from its page, a sentence burned up at her so that she became motionless, hand in air. Words seemed to stand away from the rest of the letter as if with a light around them. "I have a concern—"

Chapter Forty-two

P O WAITED a week. Larry did not come. Walt would surely have kept his word. But what if, seeing the slave ship, Larry did not feel as she did?

Well, then, she ought to go ahead herself. But she would pause then, thinking of how it would seem to Coventry, knowing his father had been mixed up in a dishonorable thing.

"Tis a rocky word to tell the lad and he no giant," she thought. "Maybe Larry will come tomorrow, and with the manifests in his back pocket, that way I'll never have to tell Coventry."

But Larry did not come, and the problem stayed with her. She thought of it on the street, passing groups of idle men shivering on corners. She thought of it in the theater as she went through the temperance piece.

A strange ugly thing was happening in the theater these days. It did not occur every performance, but often enough to be dreaded. A band of three or four, not always the same, but always staying together, sometimes old, sometimes well dressed, sometimes young, sometimes poorly dressed—would single out someone in the audience, and then, standing in their places, cry out, "Down with the dirty foreigners! America for the Americans!" Usually the person they had singled out to humiliate would try to leave quietly, only to be followed into the street.

The performers in the theater were always worried about it, and always glad when the disturbance moved into the street, for they feared something bad might happen.

Po learned these hecklers were the group called Know Nothings. Silent behind her shawl, as the drunkard's daughter, watching them operate, she tired to puzzle out what made them do it. As times got worse—they got worse and noisier, more quarrelsome and ugly. Maybe, she wondered, they shouted and humiliated others because they didn't know what to do about what was happening around them, and it was a relief to stand up and shout at someone, "It's your fault!"

At one performance, she saw a group of nice enough looking young men drive from the theater a Jew who went scurrying frightened away. Watching the Know Nothings, Po suddenly thought of the Excelsiors and how the men attached themselves to them, as with a terrific hunger to belong to something. "Arrah, it's kind of an upside down team they belong to, these Know Nothings! But maybe they feel what they do is right, for their team!"

Suddenly, she felt the blood flush up into her face under her shawl. And wasn't that what she was doing again, sheltering Coventry and his memory of his father, excusing herself that way from going ahead?

That night, she wrote Coventry, and asked him, if he received the note in time, to come to her boarding house before the next evening's performance.

The next evening, she had scarcely finished her supper when she was told someone wished to see her in the boarding-house parlor. But it was not Coventry. It was Larry.

He was standing at the fireplace with his back to her, warming his hands from the coals in the grate, his bigness dwarfing the stiff little parlor. He turned then, and she knew from his face he had seen the slaver, and that he felt as she did.

It was the first time they had been alone since the day in the hospital, and Po came toward him, feeling shy, not knowing how to act, how he felt about her. He took her hand, but people were passing every minute in the hall, and she did not know what was in his heart.

"Walt gave me your message!" he said, looking down at her.

"We made a mistake, and it's us must right it!"

"Yes." He let go her hand then and paced around a few moments, as if not wanting to bring something out. Then he said, "I gave Hymes the manifests."

"Oh!" She could not keep the disappointment out of her voice.

Larry frowned. "Hymes drives a hard bargain!" Then Larry's hand came out as if trying to explain. "And I didn't care! All that mattered was—was to win!"

Po sat down on one of the horsehair chairs, frowning thoughtfully. "If we went to the peelers—?"

"They wouldn't believe us, without evidence!"

Po sighed. "And me thinking day times and night times of what way it is for those souls on the ships!"

Larry walked around a little, then he stopped. "In the hospital, and after that, for a long time, I used to plan the horrible beating I was going to give him." And he spoke as if he had made his mind up to something. "I've gotten over that!"

Po felt a surge of hope.

"What good would it do? I beat him, I land in jail! No! I'm going to use my head!"

Po came over toward him with warm impulse. "A better word was never spoke!"

"Those ships—" Larry began, frowning.

" 'Tis that matters, not who wins, you or Hymes."

"What do you mean? You think I like him now?"

Po did not feel so sure and happy.

"I got a plan. Maybe no good, but it's a beginning. I know every boat dealer, every captain, around New Bedford. Hymes bought the *Tanager* there. If he's buying more, I'm going to find out. I know that won't be enough—it'll take real evidence—" Suddenly he broke off, pounded his fist into his hand. "When I think how I let those manifests go!"

"We both did it!" Po tried to comfort him.

Larry turned around and looked at her then, and his eyes were kind and warm, so she wished he would speak out the thought behind them.

They looked at each other silently a moment, then he said, "I'm going back to New England! I guess Dave told you what we're trying to do!"

"Niver a word!"

"We're going to take the Excelsiors on a tour in the spring! Dave's trying to get the *Clipper* to send him along, he to send back stories!"

"Well, aren't you the great one to plan out such a fine and daring scheme."

"It is risky, for we'll have expenses. But, if haggling will do it, I'll see the men come out all right." Then he stopped and looked at her soberly as though it were a thing might never have occurred to her. "Some of the men need the money!"

Po nodded. "Yes."

Larry went on then earnestly. "It isn't only the money, either. When we were playing ball, fighting with the Atlantics and all, everyone was happy. With everything closed down now, they feel sort of helpless. This is something we can do ourselves, all together!"

Po nodded.

He was silent a few moments, then he came over near her. "And, now, I'm going back to New Bedford!"

Questions trembled up into her throat, but she did not have a chance to ask them, for just then Coventry came in.

His crisp blond hair gleamed with snow crystals, and he shook snow from his caped coat, as he hung it in the hall, and came in, greeting Po gaily.

"Ah, Lady Violet-Blue-Eyes. I came just as soon as I got your note! I hope I didn't keep you waiting!"

Then Coventry, who always made a great game of things, kissed her hand gallantly, and it seemed to Po, his eyes darted amused toward Larry and back again, as if he were enjoying doing a little teasing.

Even when Po introduced them, Coventry did not let go her hand, and it seemed to Po that Larry looked a little distant.

"Sorry! I didn't know you were expecting someone! I'll be moving on!" He went toward the door then, and Po went with him. He held out his hand. "Good-by!"

"Good-by!" And as Po watched his big form go out the door, she thought ruefully, "Ah, my guardian angel must have been out to the corner having a drap, not to have spread things around better for me!"

Po stood bemused as Coventry chatted on, recounting with gay mockery some doing at Quimby's. "I suspected from the first," he was saying, "that Agatha, that's old Simon's thin daughter, went with the job—"

But Po hardly heard. She was thinking, "Larry does not have the manifests." And his plan of talking to the people in New Bedford was not evidence. Po knew now, she must get Coventry to help.

After a bit, she broke into his talk, her voice sober. "Have you seen that William Hymes lately?"

"Why, yes, as a matter of fact." Coventry looked surprised. "He came looking me up at Quimby's last week!"

"What was he wanting now?"

"He reminded me"—Coventry smiled grimly—"I'd be a long time paying my father's debts with what Quimby pays me as clerk."

"Did he ask you to be his agent again?"

"Why, yes he did!"

"It might be a good thing!" Po frowned.

"But you," Coventry said, astonished, "were the one told me—"

"What if now, I told you, he wants you to go out buying ships and getting crews—for the African slave traffic?"

Coventry sat up straight, a black frown on his face. "So, that's it! But why do you tell me to go in with him?"

"Ah," Po thought, "here it comes!"

She went over to Coventry, and looked at him kindly. " 'Tis not a guess, or an idle rumor I speak now, but things I know from seeing with my own eyes. He got your father in debt to him, then involved him in this slave traffic!"

"My father!" He stared at her as if she were daft.

"He got him so mixed up in it he could not get out, even though he wanted to."

Coventry stood up, with a terrible look on his face. He could not speak at first, and then he broke out passionately, "So that was it! Of course! How else could he even have associated with him! My father didn't—do what he did, because of the debts then! It was this!" Coventry got white then, and stood rigid, as if all the implications were seeping into his mind. Then he broke out. "Why, Hymes as good

284

as killed him! As much as if he used a gun!" Suddenly Coventry trembled and his hands clenched. "Why—I ought to kill him!"

"No, listen to me," Po said anxiously. "Would your father want that? There's more in it than Hymes! There's Spanish and Cubans and other people here! Your father would want you to break it up if you could!"

But Coventry stood rigid and white, his eyes staring, as if he didn't hear a word she said. "I'll get my pistol!"

Po tried frantically to say a word to distract him. She tried to remember Larry's words. "Don't you see all that'd happen would be you'd land in jail, and what would be changed? Is Hymes the only one with a skull crammed with thinking?"

But Coventry was sullen now, and white.

"If you go as his agent, and stay long enough to get evidence, that would more likely be what your father would want. We must use what wit we have on us!"

Coventry stood rigid, silent. It was late, but she could not leave him here so.

"Coventry, will you come now, while I go to the theater, and then, when I'm through, I'll tell you all I know. Please, please."

"Oh." Coventry still looked sullen. "So you know more! All right, I'll come and wait for you."

The theater was crowded, but Po managed it so Coventry had a seat down front. She wanted to keep an eye on him while he had the sullenness in him and the urge to do violence to Hymes. And even when the temperance piece got under way, Po watched him worriedly.

After a bit, when the piece had gotten started, she saw a group of Irish countrymen come in, eight or ten, and sit together in the center, well down front. Their faces were red and shiny as if they had just come from celebrating something. Through the sad wails of Rory McCracken's fiddle in the pit, as the temperance piece proceeded, Po listened to the soft slurred voices. She guessed the men were newly come, and that this was some society of Irish county or district met to dine together in some beer cellar and come now to the show.

But after the temperance piece had been running on for a little while, a group of Know Nothings made their presence noisily known. There were three of them, off at one side down front, and one after another, they stood up and yelled, "Down with the dirty Micks!" The newly arrived Irish looked astonished, then scowled, but, feeling good after their dinner, went on talking again.

Then the second Know Nothing got up to heckle and insult them. It was no good trying to eject the Know Nothings, the theaters had learned, for it was always discovered they had plenty of sympathizers in the audience, and a free-for-all would ensue.

Now, Po sensed bad trouble in the making. For this time, it was not a single Jew the Know Nothings ridiculed, but a group of country men, who would stand together, and if there would be plenty of Know Nothings in the theater, there would be plenty of Irish too. Po could see the drunkard, Mervin Fairfield, was nervous, and Rory, the fiddler, and the pianist in the pit, looked worried. In the wings, she could see George Gillis and some of the players for the next piece looking tense and frightened.

The third Know Nothing stood up then and called out sneeringly, "America for the Americans! No Jews or Catholics wanted! Kick out the Irish!" Po could see two of the Irishmen were taking off their coats. Something must be done quickly or the lot of them tomorrow would have broken heads or be in jail, and what way was this for them to taste their new country? It seemed to her from their voices maybe they were from Tipperary. Then she heard one cry out, "Are we Kilkenny men, or are we cowards?"

Po moved quickly to the gas footlights and spoke urgently to the worried fiddler. "Rory! Play 'Kilkenny Men!' Fast and loud!"

The fiddle left off its sad wails and began to lilt and dance. Po threw off her shawl, and right down front, in a jolly loud voice, singing right at the men so as to drown everything out, she sang while Rory's fiddle hopped along with her:

"Oh, the boys of Kilkenny,
Are stout roving blades!
Whenever they meet with
The nice little maids!
They kiss them and coax them,
And spend their money free,
Of all towns in Ireland,
It's Kilkenny for me!"

Po shouted gaily.

If she could, even for a few minutes, take their mind off fighting, maybe someone else would think of something to do about the Know Nothings. She swung along in the second verse, as Rory fiddled, fast and gay.

The group of countrymen turned away from the Know Nothings and looked delighted and astonished. They clapped, and one or two joined in a line.

As to the rest of the audience, they were in gales of laughter. They had been bored at the sad little temperance piece, and to suddenly

286

have the starving child throw off her shawl and begin to sing a loud jolly song, struck them as a good joke. They joined the clapping and called for more.

Po could see the Know Nothings still standing glowering, an ugly look on them. She had stopped the trouble so far—now she had to keep on. If she could just keep everyone laughing, especially the Irish, until the fighting mood was gone!

She stepped down to the footlights, rolled up her sleeves rowdily, put one foot up on the footlights, and sang out in a hoarse voice:

> "It's me can make the valley
> And the tavern to roar!
> But without a drap of whiskey,
> I can sing no more!"

At once, there were shouts of laughter, and willing hands handed up bottles square and round. Po took one. She made believe then she had a thirst on her had taken a month to raise, and threw her head far back, and pretended to drain the bottle dry with gusto. Then she wiped her mouth heartily with the back of her hand.

The audience resented the temperance piece anyway, and now they felt things were going in the right direction, and began to call out for a song. Po sang out a line to the fiddler, he picked it up, and they were off:

> "My name is Cash the Piper,
> I'm seen at race and fair!
> I'm known to all the jolly souls,
> From Wicklow to Kildare,
> I play at dance and wedding,
> From Bray to Clonegal,
> But the cream of intertainment,
> Was at Mick the Dalty's ball—"

Po stopped now and danced a jig, and she did it to tease. She knew the Kilkenny men would know there were a lot of bawdy verses to the song. She wanted them to keep calling for another verse in the hopes she'd sing them, and the longer she could keep their minds on the bawdy verses of a song, and off avenging insults, the better.

She began another verse, saucily winking at them:

> "There was Jenny and Nancy and Mary,
> And Micky and Mike and Fin—"

Now when she would finish a verse, the rest of the audience would join in the clapping for her to go on.

With great relief she saw the actors—dear hearts—and the stage manager, scurrying backstage, and knew they meant to help her out by beginning the Kit Carson piece quickly, and with a bang of shots and Indian yells which would seize attention. She kept singing, until she could see they were all in their places ready to rush on. Then she kissed her hands to the boys from Kilkenny and ran off.

Sure enough, with a whoop and a yell, the settlers came on, pursued by the Indians, and there was enough gore, and feathers flying, and shooting, for the next hour on stage to keep things peaceful in the audience.

As Po ran off, the people standing about backstage shook her hand, or kissed her. George Gillis, waiting to go on, tomahawk raised, patted her shoulder with approval. "Good gal!" Then with a blood-curdling war whoop he rushed on stage.

But Po, thinking of Coventry, hurriedly changed her clothes.

When she came from the dressing room he was waiting. He said not a word, but took her arm firmly and walked out. He seemed grim, but the sullen look had gone.

In the café, it was he, now, who questioned her. And even though he looked pale, he had a determined look.

"If I did go as his agent, it's unlikely he'd let me get hold of anything that could be used as evidence."

"'Twill not be easy," Po said, troubled.

"No, it will not be easy!" Then he leaned over, and even smiled at her a little sadly. "But, Pocahontas, maybe I can use what wit I have on me, too!"

Chapter Forty-three

"HYMES SAYS this shipping business is just a sideline with him," Coventry told her at a table at Pfaff's. "He was thinking of closing it out, but from respect for my father, he was glad to have me take over as his agent!"

"But did he tell you to do anything yet?"

"No, not yet." Coventry frowned. "We talked terms. It seems a lot of my father's debts were to him. He suggested ten per cent commission, to be deposited against the debts."

"He doesn't want you to get away, for some reason. Now don't forget, we'll use our wits together! Let me know what happens!"

A few days later, Coventry was waiting outside the theater. They walked down Broadway together, picking their way through January slush. "He's given me my first job." Coventry was still tense and grim when he talked to Hymes. "Buying up some ship's stores in Newark!"

But the next time Coventry talked to her he had been sent to acquire a barge load of barrel staves and hoops. "All the business is done by cash," Coventry said, "in my name. It's going to be difficult."

"Never mind! Just you go along with him easy and quiet. One of these days, it'll maybe be a ship he is asking you to buy!"

And Po left him, patting his arm encouragingly, before she hurried to get into her shawl as the drunkard's daughter. But Po forgot all about Coventry and Hymes that evening, for Mr. Gillis brought a friend of his, Harry Sweet, around to talk to Po.

Mr. Sweet, a man with a broad red face, who kept his high beaver hat on as he talked, managed a noisy crowded concert saloon on the Broadway. He had been backstage the night when Po sang for the Kilkenny men.

"D'you know any more good loud jolly songs?" Mr. Sweet grinned at her.

"Many a one."

"With all these here hard times, folks like 'em funny! Now my place ain't exactly Niblo's, you understand, but I'll pay ten a week, two matinees. Like to try?"

Would she though! Gillis was happy for her and let her go at once, and Po started at Sweet's the next night.

Sweet's, she found, was smoky and noisy, used to singers known as female baritones, but Po did the best she could. Sometimes a few people sitting close by would say "Hush!" to the crowd angrily, and want her to go on, but usually they were drowned out by the general hubbub.

The second night after she had gone to Sweet's, Coventry met her as she came into the street.

He grasped her hand as if he did not want to let it go. "I went to the Bowery and you weren't there. I had the strangest feeling. As though I'd lost you! I heard you tonight. Why, you're good!"

And the next afternoon, Coventry was waiting, with a friend, a quiet, dark man, named Durston.

"Coventry thought I should hear you sing and I'm glad I did." Mr. Durston smiled at her. "I enjoyed it!"

"Thank you, sir." In all the smoke and rattle of beer mugs, it was not easy to know when she pleased, for Mr. Sweet's only requirement was that her songs be loud and jolly.

Mr. Durston bowed. "I'll see you again." And he left them then.

Coventry beamed and said, "A decent chap. I knew he'd like you. He owns Durston's Gardens!"

Durston's Gardens! Why, that was one of the best entertainment places in the city! Po was glad she hadn't known who he was.

"Come on along with me. I'm going out of the city and I want to tell you something!" And as soon as they were in the cab, Coventry went on, "I think I've got the chance I've been waiting for!" His voice sounded different now when he spoke of Hymes—not so tense, and more as if he knew what to do. "I'm going to Baltimore!"

"For a ship?"

"Yes. In the Chesapeake area. Old. Bark or schooner. But it's to be bought in my name. Cash, of course."

"That'll be hard then, to tie him in with it!"

"Yes—but I have a plan."

"Ah, you're using your wit now!"

He smiled down at her then, and leaned over and Po thought he was going to kiss her, but he stopped and patted her cheek. "I'll be gone three of four weeks, maybe. I'll see you when I come back."

And he boarded the ferry then, smiling and waving good-by.

A few days later, Mr. Durston reappeared at Sweet's.

"My dear, how would you like to sing in a quieter place? It would better suit your style."

Blood rushed up into Po's face. Did he mean—

"Why, sir, any complaints I'd raise could be beat down easy by a ten-year-old boy with a straw and it broken!" she managed to get out.

"Well, then," he smiled, "how would forty dollars a week do?"

Forty do—!

"Any objections I could have thought of, Mr. Durston, have been washed away in the flood of your eloquence!"

"I wouldn't be surprised if you have a great many songs you haven't sung!"

"Why, Mr. Durston, sir, it would surprise you to know how many songs can be crammed into a girl as small as me!" Then she thought of Rory, and what a great thing it would be if she had a natural-born fiddler. She looked at Mr. Durston, and somehow he seemed like a man that would appreciate Rory. She told him about him, and Mr. Durston nodded and said he'd look into it.

A chance to sing, in a decent place, and at the fine great salary, and with a real Irish fiddler! Up O'Reillys!

It was no wonder she forgot about Hymes and Coventry.

But when Po came out into the February snow on the Broadway

that night, she drew her new long cloak with its furred hood tight around her. She suddenly understood what loneliness was. It wasn't being alone when you were in trouble. If was when you had something to celebrate and no one to celebrate with.

She remembered when she first came to Brooklyn and discovered the ball game, and how she hoped then she would find a pair of eyes to dance in joy with. If only Larry— "But he's forgtten I'm walking in this wide and windy world."

She might find Dave at the *Clipper*. But she was chary of seeking him out. His feelings radiated from him so plainly, it was not fair to hurt him.

Coventry. But Coventry was in Baltimore.

Po could hardly wait till Sunday came to get to Brooklyn and tell Brian her good news.

As she went up the outside stairs to the flat she thought, "Maybe it's some word of Larry, Brian will shed in an unbeknownst way!"

But she got no word of Larry on Sunday, and even her own news fell a little flat, for the glacier Panic had finally spread into Brady's Gardens. More and more men had not been able to pay, but Brian kept his word, that no ball player should go thirsty.

Now, Brian himself could not pay the brewer.

He owned the building though, and, Mamie went on to Po, "The Brewery has offered to rent the Gardens from him, they to take them over and run them. But no, he doesn't want to!"

Brian looked stubborn. "I tell you, Po, even if the beer taps are dry, I want to keep it open. It's a kind of clubhouse for the boys!"

"I can't understand how you can be so weak!" Mamie broke in. "I've learned of a fine position Brian could get! A fine respectable position! In Mr. Selfridge's office!"

"Yes," Brian glowered, "and what do you think I'd be doing? Collecting back taxes! Why, I'd as soon spend me days slappin' little children!"

Now Mamie turned to Po for support. "If he'd take the job, I know of a house we could rent—on the Heights!"

"Yes, the house of someone who got flying too high, and lost it in the Panic," Brian threw out angrily.

"We may as well have it as anyone else," Mamie broke in. "It will get us out of here, at least!"

"I don't like any of it!" Brian said, sullen.

"Oh," Mamie said, "he's not only weak, but stubborn! Tell him how wrong he is!"

Brian, in an office! Po was dismayed. But— "Never mix in a quarrel between a husband and wife," she told herself hastily. She'd been walking the world long enough to know that, anyway. And then she heard herself saying, "Well, Mamie, it's the truth if I die for it— Brian needs the Gardens and the Gardens need him!"

Mamie flushed hotly as she turned on Po. "Oh! You!" she said furiously. "You've always managed to set him against me!"

"Now," Brian interposed quickly. "Now, Mamie!"

And Po knew then she had finally made the mistake she had always been afraid of making. "I disremembered something I must do in Manhattan."

In the door, she looked back at Brian, wishing she could make him a sign saying, "Courage!"

And so, Po did not celebrate in Brooklyn. And soon the mood of celebrating was past. Now she was absorbed with little cares, studying out, with Rory, how to make what they had to give fit this new place. Looking out at all those faces gazing up at her from the small tables in Durston's, Po had a curious yearning over them. They wanted something, straining to get away from all the hard times and trouble outside. She wanted to make them happy.

So mornings, she and Rory practiced, prodding each other's memory, piecing out the other's knowing, recalling every rowdy comic song they'd ever heard at feis or cattle fair, sifting the best.

And in the evening, it seemed to Po the faces out there, straining up at them, did look gayer, when she sang and when they clapped for more, Rory and she, brimming with plenty, would sing again. And when they came off, with gales of laughter in their ears, Mr. Durston would often pat her shoulder silently, and once he said, "They love you!"

And then one day around noon, Coventry appeared at her boarding house. In the gray February light filtering into the ugly little parlor, she saw him, sitting hunched over in his overcoat, and it reminded her of how he had looked, puzzled and discouraged, the day she first found him in Pfaff's.

"Now, lad," she said briskly and cheerfully, "tell me what happened."

"The ship got away," he frowned. "Right under my nose. I'd an idea if he fitted her there, I'd manage at the last minute to let the authorities know. I bought her, a bark, on the lower Chesapeake, had her brought into the port at Baltimore, paid the cash, and was waiting to get money and orders to fit her. Next morning, comes a man, one of his agents, with a captain, a crew—Cubans, I think. The agent put the crew aboard at once and she left without being fitted."

"Did you hear that other agent's name?" Po asked, tense.

"Yes, a man named Rimshaw. You see how Hymes works—a ship here, crew from another place, stores another. This could go on and on." Coventry walked around impatiently. "We're getting no place!" He stopped then and looked grim and discouraged. "He's clever!"

"And so are we," Po broke in. "It's just that he's been at the diviltry longer!"

And then, it was like Coventry that when he learned of her good news, he put aside his own disappointment, and was pleased and happy for her.

At last Po's good news did get celebrated, for that evening after the performance, Coventry was waiting for her, and declaring ordinances had been passed in the city that no problems or disappointments were to be discussed for the balance of the evening while happy events were celebrated, he put her in a hansom cab.

At Pfaff's a table had been reserved, and at her place, though it was midwinter, there were violets. Everything had been arranged. The delicious food, the best wine from the cellar. Coventry was without means now—but his credit was good everywhere. He had never really assimilated the fact that it was actually possible he must deny himself anything he wanted.

He went chatting on, charming, gay. Suddenly Po remembered the first time they had sat thus at a table here, and how he had looked at her, smiling, but with speculation. Now he looked at her, but differently. Her name had always amused him, and he said it over, "Pocahontas!" smiling with delighted fondness.

He picked up her hand and kissed it then. And wasn't he the one could make you feel like a princess, with a purple train studded with diamonds?

"But, ah, then," Po thought even as she smiled back at him, enjoying it all, "isn't he easy with his soothering because he's practiced on the girls in their hundreds!"

"Tell me," Coventry's manner was bantering, as he leaned toward her, "something." He still had his handsome wardrobe, and always looked the great beau. "Are you engaged to that big chap I met at the boarding house?"

Po dropped her eyes a moment, and a flush came into her face. "No."

And Coventry said her name over again, smiling, enjoying it. "Pocahontas!"

When Po went into her room that night, full of Coventry's gay compliments, she found a letter under her door. It had been forwarded from the Bowery Theater. It was postmarked Binghamton, N. Y. The writing looked like—Larry was out, arranging the tour! Her hand trembled and she tore the envelope clumsily in her haste. Holding it under the lamp she read:

February, 1858

Dear Po:

Friends in New Bedford promised to keep in touch with me. The schooner *Fair Hope* was bought in New Bedford by Hymes's agent. Keep an eye out for it.

Faithfully yours,
Larry Wainwright

That was all. Not a word of soothering. Not a bit of wishing her well, and never asking her if she were alive or dead.

Then she remembered the letter she had written Larry about the Knickerbocker meeting. *That* had been a love letter. If you took this one, and read between, and over and around, and above the lines, why— Maybe. Po sighed. Faithfully yours!

But, then, when she got over her mooning, she suddenly realized that this might be the chance she and Coventry had been waiting for. The schooner *Fair Hope!*

Po hurried, for she was to meet Coventry in Brooklyn outside Dent's at three, and she wanted to have time to stop in at the Gardens first.

She had known how things were going in the Gardens, but even so—it seemed strange not to see Brian.

The brewing company's man was behind the bar, looking around the almost empty place as if he would be grateful for a kind word, but one or two men who sat about ignored him. Po recognized Twinkle-Toes and spoke to him. "It's not the same." He stared sourly at his empty glass. "You come in and pay your four cents and drink your beer and go out with as big a grouch as you come in with."

Po went up the stairs then, with some uneasiness, but Mamie smiled as she said, "Well, come in!" With Mamie, though, you could not be sure what a smile meant.

"Brian's so much better off!" Mamie said. It seemed there was in her voice a shade of defiance. "It's all new to him, but he'll get used to it. And after a while, he'll come around to the idea of moving away from here, too!"

Po swallowed hard, but said nothing to this. She was trying to imagine Brian behind a desk, Brian in a high narrow house on the Heights.

"I must go now." It was nearly three. "Give him my love and kindly wishes."

And going down the steps, Po felt unhappy somehow, and decided she would come again when she could see Brian and make sure he was all right.

Po hurried to Dent's. Coventry was already waiting outside the door.

She was hoping Juba would come out, selling oysters. After a bit, when he did not come, she decided to go in and find him.

She stepped inside the rather dim room, crowded with sailors and roustabouts, ships' crews and officers, drinking and noisy with loud talk. Then she stopped and all the breath seemed to be blown out of her body. Across a table, leaning forward, staring at her, was Rimshaw.

By the time her breath came back, she would have turned to run. Then she saw that he did not recognize her. In her furred hooded cloak she did not look like any little raggle-taggle out of the hold of a ship. Po decided not to retreat and moved on quickly. She saw him turn to stare after her, but she stepped into the kitchen.

Juba was filling his basket with oysters from a great cask.

"Juba," Po said hurriedly. "I must see you. Watch for me down the street!" And she left quickly by the kitchen door.

She and Coventry moved down the street and waited. When Juba met them, they were nearly a block away.

"I want you two to take a good look at each other!" Po told Coventry and Juba. "For Juba, it's maybe you can help us in something we must do! We're trying to stop Hymes from sending out ships to steal away the people from Africa. I know in Dent's you must hear lots of talk of ships and when they come and go."

"Deed, deed I do!" Juba nodded his head.

"The ship we want to get word about is a schooner, the schooner *Fair Hope*," Coventry said.

Juba nodded and repeated, "The *Fair Hope*."

"I'll come back to find out if you've picked up anything," Coventry said. "But we must know at once, Juba, if you hear of her! Where she is, when she's sailing!"

"You tell me where I can find you." Juba looked at Po. "And I'll come day or night and bring word."

Chapter Forty-four

Po DID not see Juba again until nearly the middle of March. She was standing outside the American Hotel in lower Fulton Street in Brooklyn. The men in the little crowd gathered there had to hold onto their hats in the fresh March wind. Some of them were still grimy from work, they having stopped to learn how the Excelsiors were doing before they went home. Now the hotel clerk came out, and pasted up a sheet of paper, painted in a brush with ink. It read, "The Excelsiors won!" The crowd cheered. "Three thousand people attended the game today!"

"They're sure going to make expenses all right! They take the gate if they win!" one man said jubilantly.

"Sure, they'll make out! Didn't you read Dave's dispatch yesterday in the *Clipper?* Says when the Excelsiors come to town, business stops—everyone goes to the game!"

Now the clerk pasted up an additional sheet, and Po read, "The hometown cranks at the game nearly had the satisfaction of seeing their club defeat the unbeaten Excelsiors when George Hertz, Excelsior second baseman, came down with grippe. As the team is carrying only nine men, the Manager, Larcom Wainwright, had to step in and substitute, and the Excelsiors squeezed by on the narrow margin of 21 to 20!"

Po's eyes widened in joyful amazement. Larry had played! Maybe he would not pitch again, but he could hit and run, and in a pinch, casually, when he was needed, he had played again! He must have been exercising his fingers all the while!

It was then that Po felt a tug at her sleeve and, turning, saw Juba. He moved away from the crowd, and she followed him swiftly.

Po knew that Coventry had kept in touch with Juba at Dent's, but that Juba had heard nothing of the *Fair Hope.* Now, she followed him swiftly up Fulton Street.

"That ship you ask about!" he said in a low voice as soon as she caught up with him. "I hear talk of her."

That the word should have come just now! Po knew Coventry was in Philadelphia on an errand for Hymes and she did not know when he would return. Larry was in far-off Baltimore. Maybe Brian—!

"Juba, come with me! I want to get help!"

Po meant to run upstairs to the flat, but as she started to climb the steps, she glanced into the bar. She saw Brian sitting at a table. She went in quickly, but then slowed down, her heart sinking as she crossed the long room toward him.

His shoulders hunched forward, his face sullen, immobile, he sat staring at a half-empty bottle of whiskey before him. Brian, who never drank; Brian, who always greeted her with a warm smile, looked at her in morose silence.

"How are you, Brian?" she faltered.

He was silent a moment; then he said in a surly voice, "I'm fine now. I wasn't. But now, I am just fine."

She hesitated a moment, deeply troubled. Then she saw Twinkle-Toes, near the bar, watching her. She stopped close to him.

"He's been sittin' there," Twinkle-Toes said in a low voice, "for days! Won't go to that there office! Won't talk! Won't do nothin'! I guess he was just druv too far!"

Disturbed, Po did not know what to do.

Juba was waiting for her. At least she could try to find something to do about that. She went out swiftly then, resolving to return as soon as she could get in touch with Coventry.

"Thank you, Juba," Po said. "I'll walk along with you back toward Dent's. Has it been long since you heard of the ship being here?"

"This afternoon. Rimshaw's here. He wuz talkin' to a man!"

Then, outside Dent's, who should be waiting, watching for Juba, but Coventry. He had just returned from Philadelphia. The three of them moved away from there then, so that if Rimshaw came out, he would not see them.

Dusk was falling as Coventry asked, "Have you any idea where the ship is?"

"I think he say a place called Fishkill Inlet," Juba said.

Po had to leave, or be late for the evening performance, but before they parted from Juba, Coventry said, "I'll come tomorrow to find out if you've learned any more!"

Going back on the ferry, as lights twinkled on in Manhattan, the two of them stood close together at the rail, as if to stand up to the wind.

"Maybe this time," and Coventry's voice sounded firm, "I'll get him! I've been hoping for this for months. I have it all planned. The police are careful of arresting on this charge; I have to time it all carefully. Just when she's ready to go! Not before, not after! Oh, if only he uses me to fit her out!"

The wind coming up from the sea billowed Po's cloak out behind her. The ferry was nearly in. "If I'm able to pull it off, and Hymes is stopped—I have been thinking of going away from here—making a new start! Couple hundred years ago"—Coventry was light and pleasant again—"old Pieter Van Leyn made a new start! I'm thinking of going to California!"

" 'Tis a fine place, I am hearing." Then she stopped, realizing she was a little sad. "But—a long way off!"

"Yes, but a marvelous country. Why, they tell me—" he was Coventry, the charming, again now—"there's a tree there called a shamrock tree, and in autumn it bears seeds shaped like harps, and the wind through them plays old Irish airs. In southern California, the airs are in the key of C, but in northern California in the key of G." His hand touched hers for a moment. "Which key would you prefer?"

Po was glad it was dark now so that he could not see her flush. The ferry boat bumped in then, and she said hurriedly, "I must run for it or I'll be late, for we're early on the bill, and Rory'll have me destroyed.

"Let me know how things go with the *Fair Hope?*" she called as she jumped into a hansom cab.

But things did not go well with the *Fair Hope*. And a week later, when Coventry knocked at the little dressing room, and she opened the door, she knew as soon as she saw his frowning face that it was not all as easy as he had hoped.

"At first," Coventry said with troubled disappointment, "I was sure I'd get him this time. I was sent to New London to gather ship's stores, cash. These I was ordered to load on a tender, and bring to Fishkill Inlet. She's there all right. I saw her! Nothing in Hymes's name—the clearance papers in Rimshaw's name, and the manifests are with one of his agents in Georgia. But what I planned to do was wait until the ship was unmistakably fitted as a slaver, then to plant evidence! I was going to leave there Hymes's message to me, with the instructions about the ship's stores, and the unloading. Certain other similar messages, also. The messages alone aren't enough, but found on the ship they would have been evidence."

"Why, 'tis a fine plan!"

"Yes, but now, he sent me away. I'm to go to Philadelphia at once. I don't think he suspects me—he's just careful."

"And then another ship will go!"

"Yes, and he still walks free." Coventry was bitter. "Oh, he's flying high these days. He's seen everywhere with Augusta. When I think of my father—" Coventry clenched his hands.

Suddenly he said, "I see now what to do! I'll go to his office, get the orders he wants me to carry out in Philadelphia. Then I'll notify the harbor police, and instead of going to Philadelphia I'll slip out to Fishkill Inlet after nightfall, and see what I can do!"

"Luck walk with you and fill your brain with tricks and guile!" Po patted his arm.

When Coventry had gone, Po thought, "I wish Larry were here! For he has the wit and the size on him!" What a wonderful thing it would be if Larry suddenly arrived in Brooklyn to help them.

But when she got back to her boarding house, she found a letter from him, and she knew it was in no way likely. The letter was from Washington, D. C. It contained a bank draft for forty dollars and he asked her to see it got to George Hertz's wife, who had just had a baby. The money was Larry's share of the last game, but, the letter said, "George's just a youngster and doesn't know how to take care of himself. I should have been looking after him, and now he's sick and I'm worried about the wife and baby. I feel kind of responsible."

Reading this, Po felt herself fill up with a warm feeling. She almost laughed aloud happily. "Why, Larry has a concern for them!" She read on, "We play Wilmington, then Cumberland, and on north to New England. Were you able to get track of the *Fair Hope?*"

So she knew there'd be no help from Larry, but when she read the *Tribune* the next morning, she knew they didn't need him. Reading, Po thought to herself, "With all his light ways, Coventry has the courage on him, too!" The story read, "The Schooner *Fair Hope* was apprehended in Fishkill Inlet, preparing to engage in slave traffic. It is said that incriminating papers were found aboard, and William E. Hymes has been taken to the Federal Court for questioning."

Po could hardly keep her mind on the "Pat Shinahan's Cow" song, during the matinee. She kept thinking of how happy Coventry would be, and she hoped he would come to see her soon so that she could rejoice with him. He did not come to the theater, though, and Po had gone into Pfaff's for some supper before he found her.

His face was set and angry-looking. And as soon as he sat down opposite her, he broke out, "I've just come up from the Federal Court Building! Do you know what happened?" He tried to control his rage. "That Jenkins! I can hardly talk of it! Jenkins made the court believe that Hymes was an upstanding substantial citizen being persecuted by his enemies! Said the papers had been deliberately planted by Hymes's enemies in the rival ferry company!" Coventry dropped his head in his hands for a moment, then raised it, and went on, angrily— "And they believed him! It was only letters with his name on them. Not manifests!"

"A sorry thing," Po said, "but the ship was stopped anyway!"

"And Hymes still walking high and wide! But he's not going to be for long." He broke off then, and looked at her for a moment. After a while he said, "I was going to talk to you, but now there's no point in it. I won't be going to California for a while!"

Chapter Forty-five

As PO HURRIED up Fulton Street from the ferry that afternoon, she was still worried about Brian. Every time she'd been back since she'd found him three weeks ago sitting in the bar, he had seemed more sullen and morose. He wouldn't go to that office any more. He wouldn't talk; he wouldn't do anything. He just sat there in the bar. Maybe today, Po thought, he'd be different.

As she hurried along in the April sunshine, she sensed a change in the air. There were more people in the street, and they walked along briskly. The grocer shop was open, and the shoe store opposite. And across the sky, she saw rising from the stack at Hymes's, a drift of smoke.

The plant gate stood open! At one side, a notice was posted. She stopped to read it.

> Because of the needs of my employees, I have decided in spite of the panic, to take a chance and begin manufacture again. I have confidence in the country. If we all work together, everything will right itself soon.
>
> William Hymes

And as Po came up the street, it seemed to her she could almost feel the ripple of hope. Why, Bushel Basket and Twinkle-Toes would have their jobs back! Suddenly she stopped in the street, frowning and troubled. She, and Coventry, and Larry too, meant to do everything they could to inform on Hymes, get him into trouble. And if they did, and he was apprehended, and as a result the plant closed again— How could they do that? Yet, maybe Hymes was able to take a chance, to manufacture goods, to have confidence, because he had cash from the slave traffic!

" 'Twould be so much easier," Po thought, frowning, "if a thing were black, or white, instead—of plaid!"

In the Gardens, Brian still sat at the little side table, and he still had whiskey before him. He had a companion now however— Clarabel. And today he was talking. But he was not kindly, or easygoing. He was harsh and quarrelsome.

Po sat down at the table with them, and she tried to make small talk, to get him into a kindlier mood.

"Did you know that William Hymes was married yesterday in the fashionable wedding to Augusta Van Leyn? 'Twas in the papers. They have gone off to a place called White Sulphur on a honeymoon." Po went chattering on, hoping to bring him to easiness.

But Brian seemed not to listen to her.

"I got the chance to get the Gardens back. The brewing company never made it pay! I can get it back! And I'm going to!"

"That's what you ought to do, honey." Clarabel patted him on the shoulder. "You're the best man ever walked in shoe leather. I told you that last night; I tell you now. Don't let anyone tell you different!"

Watching Clarabel, as she put an arm around Brian, looking at Brian's changed, defiant face, with an unaccustomed ugly look, Po suddenly wondered about Mamie. What was happening upstairs?

As soon as Mamie opened the door of the flat for her, Po could see she had been crying. And she had a peculiar air, as if she were grateful Po had come. Po tried to make small chat, and told her about Hymes and Augusta Van Leyn being married, and Mamie tried to answer. But her voice had a kind of fright behind it.

And finally, as if she did not mean the words to come out, she said, "He didn't come home last night. Nor the night before."

Po did not know how to comfort her. Looking at Mamie, bewildered, terrified, Po remembered how she used to think life was like people crossing the bog. Some walked surefooted, but some were carried. Being carried, it was easy to believe you were a queen, and to get dictatorial and haughty. But if the one carrying you stumbled, or sat down and refused to go on, you found you weren't a queen and strong, but a helpless child.

"And," Po thought, "she's got nothing stored inside herself, like food on cupboard shelves, to tide her over a lean winter!"

"He's just downstairs, sitting in the Gardens," Po said comfortingly.

"Is—Clarabel there?"

Maybe it would be good for Mamie to get a hard knock once in a way.

"Yes, she is."

Mamie's face seemed to disintegrate. "He has a comfortable home here. What would he get from her that he doesn't get here?"

Po remembered that she had spoken out to Mamie once before, and it had been a mistake. Instead, she said, gently, "Mamie, he wants to open the Gardens again."

Mamie's words came in an urgent panic. "Why, I don't care. It's all right. Anything, anything at all!"

"Mamie is not a bright woman or a clever one," Po thought, "but she has been terribly strong in her weakness. Brian's not clever either, but he is so much stronger, that in his anxiety not to hurt her, he was weak—and giving in to her gave her a contempt for him. She thought she was the strong one—until she was thrown down to walk alone."

"Mamie, do you know what I would do if I were you?"

"What?" Mamie looked anxious and pathetic, as if wanting direction.

"I'd go downstairs this minute, if not sooner, and I would go soothering him, and I'd let him know how you feel about the Gardens!"

Mamie looked taken aback for a moment, as if she could not bring herself to do this. She cried a little. Then she went and got her shawl.

Even Brian looked up, taken aback, at seeing Mamie in the Gardens. The barroom was nearly deserted, but she looked around almost placatingly, as if she wanted to make friends. Then she saw Brian and Clarabel. She stopped, rigid and white. Almost timidly, she crossed and sat down at the table.

The three sat there, silent, Clarabel looking angry and contemptuous, Brian staring at Mamie, and Mamie looking at him pleadingly. Finally Brian broke out, "It's as well you came down. It'll save me coming up to tell you. I'm taking the Gardens over again, to run. I'm not going to do anything else, ever, but be a saloon keeper. That's what I'm going to be—always." He glared at her defiantly.

"If that's what you want to do," Mamie said, in a frightened tone.

"If—" Clarabel burst out at her. "If! You heard him say. And if you were a whole woman instead of a half, you'd not have driven him to misery! You ought to be ashamed of yourself! You ain't deserving him! Why, I give him more happiness in one night than you could give him in five years! You ain't a woman. You're a child—"

Mamie began to cry, and suddenly Brian intervened. "Stop, and leave her be, Clarabel!"

Mamie spoke through tears. "Brian, you ought to run the Gardens if you like it! Anything! It's all right with me!"

"All right, Mamie, all right." Brian patted her arm. "Stop crying now!"

Clarabel got up, angry. "Well, I'll be damned. In a week she'll have you miserable as you were!"

But Brian looked up, suddenly calm and strong. "In a week, I'll have the Gardens back!"

As Po went back down Fulton to the ferry, she was seeing Mamie's face, her supplicating look turned toward Brian. Walking along, the air felt fresh and stinging, and Po thought of how, when she had come a year ago, she had been frightened of Mamie. Thinking now of

Mamie being carried across the bog forever, Po planted her feet firmly on the ground at each step. The pavement felt solid and hard, and it was a good feeling.

She remembered the Irish tale which ended, "Life says, 'Take me and pay for me.'" The pay you gave, she guessed, was snatched out of the inside of you when you fronted danger. It was taking your chances, deciding quicksand or not, having to think all the time and to take blame—and responsibility. It was "having a concern." Suddenly, she stopped. She was just passing the open Hymes plant.

She had walked on down the block and stood waiting for the ferry to come in, before she allowed herself to finish the thought. It was saying, "My friends Bushel Basket and Twinkle-Toes, and all those men, lose their jobs—if the plant closes—and so . . . I let the ships go?"

When Po got back to her room, she sat down and wrote a letter to Larry

> Dear Larry: We found the *Fair Hope,* but Hymes was not arrested, or stopped in any way. Without fail, when you pass through going to New England, come to see me, for we must do something more.

She was just going out to post the letter, when a man came to the door of the house with a large brown parcel for her. The man said he was a stage driver in from the Cumberland mountains. She unwrapped great wads of damp cloth and wet newspapers, and then, out came a flood of lovely fragrance, from a mass of tiny star-like pale pink flowers in dark green foliage. The landlady said it was a mountain flower, called trailing arbutus. Po knew the Excelsiors would be playing about there now, and that Dave was out with the team. What a sweet kindly thing it was for him to send those flowers all the way from the high mountains, like a cool fragrant breath of spring, to the girl in the city!

She ran upstairs, to write him a letter, too. "'Twas a beautiful thing to think of sending me those twiny little arbutus all the way from the high mountains . . ." and she mailed it with the letter to Larry.

Chapter Forty-six

DID YOU THINK then that Brooklyn was going to let the Excelsiors, their own shining darlings, slip through town without so much as a clap on the back? On all the Excelsior tour—in Troy, Binghamton, Syracuse, Rochester, Albany, Wilmington, Washington, Baltimore, and many another town, not once had they been beaten. Dave's stories in the *Clipper* had sent all the loving details. And didn't the proud name "Excelsior," standing in front of the words "of Brooklyn" ring out like a great bell in the air so that the vibrations remained, for where they had played, teams came into being all across the landscape?

They'd have them for one game anyhow, on their way to New England. A picked team of Atlantics, Putnams and Eckfords, would play them at Wheat Hill.

There was a matinee at Durston's, but Po was determined to go to the game, even though she could stay but a little while. She was wistful though, that May afternoon, as she got ready. She was a wealthy woman now, who could not only take the old wardrobe mistress at the Bowery out for a good dinner, but could buy herself bonnets trimmed with lavendry-blue lilacs. But even as she tied the wide blue ribbons under her chin, she looked ruefully into the mirror.

"I take no pleasure in it at all, at all. Here am I, running with my heart lepping out of the eyes, to catch a glimpse of Larry, and he never so much as squiggling a word on a scrap of paper to me these months!"

And she bragging to Coventry what a help Larry would be! For two weeks ago, when Hymes, after questioning, had gone free, Coventry had been black discouraged. To cheer him, Po told him she'd written Larry, and that Larry might—by something he remembered from the *Tanager* manifests, or from a bit of a word picked up in New Bedford —be able to help them when he came to town. Po sighed then, thinking that not only had she had no answer to her letter—she'd had no message from him for these long months.

When she got to Brooklyn, Po could feel the warm life pulsing up Fulton Street again. The glacier was melting. Other plants were opening, men were getting their jobs back. And out at Wheat Hill, under the cloudless spring sky, Po stood a moment, watching the nimble men flashing about the field, beautiful in the easy flow of their skilled precision now.

304

"It shows you," a man said admiringly, "how good a team can be that don't do nothing but play ball!"

Po stood on tiptoe, straining for a first glimpse of Larry.

Ah, there he was, moving along near the first base line!

At first, Po wanted to cry out in shock, he looked so much older and thinner. All the bright look was gone now. He looked dusty; even his hair seemed less bright. His hands were thrust into an old jacket, as if he hardly knew what he had on. He was completely absorbed in his men. He did not, though, yell caustic and insulting sarcasms as he had when Po had first seen him with this team. If he spoke at all, it was in a low voice, a word or two, and the men moved quickly, without even answering, as if they understood and respected each other. Po knew, watching him, Larry had found out that a team was made up of men.

But now the Excelsior pitcher was in. Why, it was the very young lad Larry had been cruel to. As the boy pitched now, a half-smile came on Larry's face. He looked like a proud father who cannot repress his satisfaction at a clever son.

Larry wasn't out there any more, knocking the most powerful ball, making the best pitch—big Larry. He just stood there, concentrating, absorbed, half frowning, half smiling. Watching this Larry, with the kindly half-frown, absorbed in his men, Po felt he would not have forgotten about the slave ship either. He must still want to right that if he could.

Maybe her letter had never come to him, and he moving around? Or maybe she had not gotten his reply, what with her leaving the Bowery Theater. She'd go up to him now. She started forward impulsively, then stopped. He was busy with the game. Besides, she did not like to go tugging at his sleeve in what way you could think she was begging him to cast a look at her. And she could not wait—she must return to Durston's!

"I'll leave him word then, where he can find me, and that it's important. That way he can come or not, whatever is in his heart."

By six o'clock of that day, Po and Larry and Coventry were sitting at a table in Pfaff's.

Po had left the message with Brian, asking Larry to come here right after the game when she would be through at Durston's. What if he did not come? Well, there he was, sitting across from her.

Coventry ordered the dinner expertly. Po looked from the face of one young man to the other, from Coventry with his light easy charm to Larry. He was the same—but not the same, older somehow. A grim little line seemed to stay between his brows, but his mouth looked kindly. His gray eyes searched her face, it seemed to her—though she could not be sure—with a warm light. Problems or no problems, they were young, and when delicious potato soup was put before them, they ate.

"When I agreed to go as Hymes's agent," Coventry was explaining to Larry, "well" —he turned to smile fondly at Po, and Po saw Larry glance quickly from her face to Coventry's and back again—"we thought we'd be able to get him that way! But even with your telling us about the *Fair Hope,* why, he's still free as air—"

"Up to now!" Larry said grimly.

"With the three of us making our plots and our schemes," Po broke in, "maybe he won't be." She turned to smile at Larry. "We thought maybe you'd have the great idea of what we could do."

"I could try to get more information in New Bedford." Larry frowned thoughtfully. "And you should keep on acting as agent. Try and get him on the next move!"

"Oh, but I can't," Coventry said, chagrined. "I'm through, though I don't think he suspects me. He never asked how those papers got on the *Fair Hope.* He's closing out his shipping sideline, he told me. Offered me a place in his new ferry company instead. You know he's married to my—my—" Coventry's nostrils quivered in distaste—"my former step-mother. He's trying to be the gentleman now." Coventry turned to Po. "He's taken over my father's house on the Fifth Avenue. Oh, he's going to be the fine citizen from now on!"

"Until he needs cash for some deal," Larry broke in angrily.

"Then he'll be sending out the black ships again," Po said.

"Yes. Sometimes I think I should just have gotten a gun. What other language can you use?"

But Larry said calmly, "No. A year ago, I'd have gone over and beaten him up. But you know—I passed him on the street today in Brooklyn. I clenched my fists; I remembered certain things and I thought—What then? What's better?"

But Coventry frowned blackly. "What can we do?"

They sat a moment; then Larry said thoughtfully, "How was it you knew about your father?"

"From Po."

"Oh, I thought he might have left some papers!"

"Of course he did!" Coventry broke out in a rage. "But—Jenkins, who was my father's lawyer, took them all before I suspected anything!"

But as Coventry talked on, Po was suddenly remembering something. She was seeing a picture in her mind. It was the night after Nicholas' funeral, in the day room of the mansion. She could see Coventry, pale and sad, and remembered how sorry she had felt. Then she saw Jenkins motion for the key to the lowboy, and Augusta, in majestic black, come into the room imperiously. Suddenly Po interrupted Coventry, urgently.

"Did you get the key from Augusta for that lowboy of your father's?"

"What?" Coventry blinked, not knowing what she meant. "Oh—you mean—my father's. Yes, I did. I couldn't bear to have her touch his private mementoes."

But Po said, excited and intent, "After, did you look to see what was there?"

"Yes, I did," Coventry said. "But to tell the truth—I—well, it was old souvenirs, and letters of my father's. It was so soon after he—well, I couldn't bring myself to sift it all through or destroy anything. I just left them."

They sat silently a bit. Then Larry said, "Do you think there could be anything there."

Coventry sat, his brown knit, as if trying to recall. "You know, there might be. Packets—some ledgers . . . You see I wasn't suspecting anything then—" Suddenly Coventry gripped the table hard, so that his knuckles showed white as the cloth.

"What's the matter?" Po asked.

"Hymes and Augusta are moving into the Van Leyn house. They're already there. They moved in two days ago. They were at the St. Denis. I had a notice from the bank to come and remove my private effects and I paid no attention."

"Is it too late it is now, do you think?"

"No, it's not too late!" Larry cried out.

"But with Augusta and Hymes there, don't you think they'd have them by now?" Po asked.

Coventry was tense now, and frowning. "No! Hymes will have them soon, I'm sure of that, when he begins to take possession of the place, really. But now, he wouldn't know there was anything there."

"But Augusta. She lived in the house," Po cried, "until the bank took it over and closed it up!"

"Augusta," Coventry said sarcastically, "is a stupid woman. A lusty woman, but stupid. She wanted to get them away from Jenkins just out of acquisitiveness. She glanced in and saw old love letters, my mother's miniature. I got the key from her then. And the more I think of it—" Coventry was pale with excitement now. "I remember —I think—some heavy papers. I paid no attention!"

"Can we get them?" Larry asked.

Coventry stood up.

Po said at once, "Maybe I could slip in, me knowing that house, and if you could give me the key, why—"

"No," Coventry said, "I'll do it. I have a right to my father's private effects, I guess!"

"I could go along," Larry said. "If there's any trouble—"He clenched his fist.

"It won't be necessary!" Coventry replied, a little stiffly.

"Arrah, you'd be wise to take a girl my size, Coventry, that can squiggle in and out, and is that full of tricks and guile as would confuse any three sensible people, if it's needful."

They both looked at her, frowning. Finally, Larry grinned a little—but out of the one side of his mouth only, Po noticed.

"Well"—he looked at Coventry—"she's not bad."

It was dark by the time the hansom cab stopped in front of the Van Leyn house. They had stopped at Coventry's rooms and he had found the letter from the bank and a large empty portmanteau.

Now, they asked the hansom to wait and crossed the street. There was no light in the day room, but Po saw that the library on the ground floor was lit, and upstairs too, there were lights in Augusta's suite.

Larry waited in the shadows. Po and Coventry went to the door. The butler was new, but he was a man who had served in the house of one of Coventry's friends, and Coventry had no difficulty being admitted.

They were shown then—not into the day room where Nicholas used to sit, but into the library with its red plush and brass chandeliers.

"Well, Coventry." Hymes stood rigid behind a desk, but he extended a hand. "Well, Coventry!" And she could see he was making an effort to be the gentleman. "Do sit down."

When Coventry spoke, Po suddenly seemed to hear his father—Coventry was so pleasant and smooth.

"Thank you, sir. But as a matter of fact, I came to say good-by. I'm going to California. This is Miss O'Reilly . . . she may go to California too!"

Po gasped. But Coventry went on, pleasant and oh, so very casual.

"The bank asked me to pick up my private effects. They're mostly in the day room. I don't want to trouble you with them any longer."

"Oh, no trouble at all! Leave them."

"Well, there are some things of my father's I'd like to get. I'm sure they mean nothing to you."

"Why," Hymes protested, "all his things mean a great deal to me. A great deal!"

"Well"—Coventry was smooth, but biting—"you can hardly have formed any warm attachment as yet for the Van Leyn ship models! I'll just step in and get them."

"I'll come with you." Hymes moved.

"Oh, don't bother," Coventry said, and walked quickly out and toward the day room.

Po, wishing she could think of some deviltry, watched Coventry pick up the portmanteau, and saw Hymes start at this. Then Hymes, in his heavy rigid way, moved across the room after Coventry. But just then, the door bell rang. The butler answered.

By the time Hymes had reached the library door, the caller had come into the hall. In the long mirror across the hall from the library door, Po saw a man smoothing his beautiful black mustaches. It was Count Ossi. Hymes stopped and a kind of heavy shudder went through him, his massive shoulders seeming to hunch up as if he were getting ready for a spring. The Count bowed mockingly, and was shown upstairs to Augusta's sitting room.

In the library, Po sat, small and still in the red plush sofa, as Hymes turned toward the day room, irresolute. Then she saw him looking up the stairs. A terrible sad look came on his face. He looked stunned, a man used to feeling only blunt emotions—lust, hate or greed—and suddenly a situation of complex feeling had descended on him with which he could not cope. He could kill Count Ossi, but all his carefully built up dream of himself, The Conqueror, in a castle, reigning with a queen—how could that be if it were spoiled with a sordid crime? What else then? Was he to live here like this, a constant fool in his own house! That was the trouble, Po thought. When you got to knowing people, you couldn't hate them so easily. If only Hymes would go upstairs, then she would run back to the day room and help Coventry, and they would be out of there in a flash. But Hymes stood, rigid.

He did not go upstairs. He did not go back to the day room, either; he stood, watching the stairs. Then, as though dressed for the opera, Augusta appeared at the stair head and began to descend, her apricot satin gown rippling behind her. Hymes had started and turned away, as if not willing to be caught in so undignified a position, and turned into the library.

The Count and Augusta came down then, and stopped in the library door. "Good-night." Augusta smiled brilliantly, as the diamond cross on her bosom glittered. "Don't wait up for me. We're going on to a party afterward." And she waved her hand as she moved off smoothly. A heavy perfume hung in the air where she had passed.

Hymes's back was to Po now, and she could only see his face in the mirror across the hall, but it frightened her, and at the same time she felt pity for him, too. But now Coventry appeared in the doorway. He had several pictures under his arm, and Po sprang up, and took a ship model from him. He had left the portmanteau at the library door.

"Good-night, sir! I hope I see you before I leave."

By the time Hymes had managed a thick "Good-night" Po was already in the hall, skimming toward the door, opening it. She looked back. Hymes had come to the library door, frowned and started to say something, as he saw the portmanteau, but Coventry was at the front door now, and in a moment they were outside.

They walked quickly to the hansom and climbed in. Then they waited for Larry.

"Drive downtown quickly," Coventry told the driver, as Larry climbed in.

In Coventry's room at the Astor, he turned up the gaslight. Larry put down the portmanteau, Po carefully deposited the ship model on the mantel. Coventry had laid the pictures across the bed, and Po, turning, saw staring up at her the framed photo-graph of the Knicker-bocker baseball team in uniform.

They stood there then, looking at the closed portmanteau.

"Well, let's open it!" Larry said. "Might as well see."

Coventry lifted out some miniatures, one of him as a baby, and packets of old letters in faded feminine handwriting, tied in faded ribbon. There were old cotillion programs.

Po thought, "What a feeling thing it is to touch the little scraps of paper a person stores up to remember." Then she saw tears glistening in Coventry's eyes. He held in his hand a packet of old Knickerbocker baseball scores. There was a big menu card for a Knickerbocker annual banquet. There were some ledgers with clasps on them. There were folded papers, and many, many letters.

Po suddenly came to with a start, and remembered she must get to Durston's Gardens for the evening performance by nine o'clock. It was the first time she had ever been so forgetful. As she dashed off, they promised to meet her afterward, when they would know what was in the mass of papers.

Rory had to play a melody twice before she began and when she did sing, it was absent and thin, and Mr. Durston looked at her question-ingly. Po tried to put her heart and mind into singing "Down by the Sally Gardens," but she didn't fool anyone, least of all the audience, which clapped perfunctorily. At last she was through, dashed into her street clothes, and hurried toward the street.

They were waiting, Coventry and Larry, and seeing them she tried to tell from their faces if they had found anything.

"Is it news you have or not?" she burst out in sudden temper. "And standing there like two stony statues."

"We found something!" Larry said.

They went to Pfaff's then, and Po saw that Coventry looked pale and unhappy.

They ordered oysters but Coventry shoved his aside. He could not eat, and sat staring into space.

"What is it?" Po asked gently.

"We found enough, Po, to incriminate Hymes. This time he could not get away. It's manifests and a clearance paper which, for some reason, my father saved, and the whole story of voyages, with names and places. In the ledgers there was a great deal of information, too, not only about Hymes, but Jenkins and the Spanish and Cuban people."

"Well, then—"

"If I turn it in, it's a kind of betrayal of my father! He'll be blackened, too—and he's not here to defend himself. His name meant such a lot to him. He was so proud of it. How can I—" Coventry ended miserably.

They sat stricken silent then for a long time.

Finally Coventry broke out. "The slave traffic'll go on anyway. We're not responsible for it. Everyone is!"

They sat silent then, but finally Larry said, frowning, as if it had just occurred to him, "But we're everyone."

"It's easy indeed," Po thought, "to tell someone else to be noble and self-sacrificing. He must make up his own mind!" And so she was silent.

She looked at Larry's face then. He looked older, and he spoke in a kind of rambly voice, like he could be thinking out loud. "Today, when I walked past Hymes on the street, I thought to myself that that gang he loosed on me went on and killed Bull Bender. Hymes didn't mean them to, but he loosed them—so I guess he was responsible. But then—we loosed the slavers, too, and let the *Tanager* go, so I guess we're responsible for that!"

"And a strange thing to think of," Po said. "If Hymes had not hired the shooting stars, the games would not have gone just so, and the Bull likely not been killed!"

Coventry was staring at her suddenly. "You know, I remember the meeting when we delegated the responsibility to Hymes. We didn't know what he'd do—but maybe we didn't much care!"

The waiter came then and asked if they'd have anything more, and they shook their heads no, and left.

One week later, after Larry had gone with the Excelsiors into New England, Po read in the *Tribune* that Hymes had been arrested. He was out on bail at once, but this time, there was such a weight of evidence, it would take more than Jenkins to free him.

Chapter Forty-seven

A SOOTHERING soft air, that May night, wandered even into the little dressing room at Durston's and Po stopped, the make-up half off her face, for just a moment, as the May night touched her. Springtime was a bad time for being alone. Last winter she'd felt alone, too, but she'd thrown her whole spirit into the singing at Durston's, and she knew too from the look on the people's faces, that in those hard days, she had warmed them. But now that the glacier ice was melting outside, things were different inside the theater, too. One night, on impulse, Po had sung, instead of a rowdy comic song:

> "The Minstrel boy to the war is gone,
> In the ranks of death you'll find him.
> His father's sword he has girded on,
> And his wild harp slung behind him."

And they had not seemed to mind it. And then one night, and it spring, she had sung not for them, but for herself, a song of longing, "My Love is a Red Red Rose," and Mr. Durston had seemed moved and patted her shoulder and said, "Do it again, my dear."

And when she did, and other such songs, she saw the couples in front kiss in the half dark, and go out after in the May night to make love—but Po was alone.

Why was she clinging to hope about Larry? She'd had no word or message since he'd gone to New England . . . and before that, all last winter—nothing but a letter signed, "Faithfully yours." When she had seen him, he had only looked at her and said nothing!

Outside, the May night waited for her, but now, she looked in the little mirror dismally. "My youth is slippy-slipping away from me," she thought. "I'll never see seventeen again. A woman could go on this way and get old and never know a day of happiness." She sighed then, and tied on the bonnet with the lavendry-blue lilacs and went out into the street.

She no longer lived at the boarding house, but had rooms of her own—not so elegant as Carlotta Bradford's, only a furnished sitting room and bedroom in an old house near Durston's. But Po was in no hurry to get home, for nothing was waiting for her there. At least, here in the street, people walked. And going along through the spring dark, she felt as if she were the only woman in the whole world who did not have a man to love her.

For the May night surrounded everyone with its coaxing warm air, and in front of her a couple walked, swinging clasped hands, and laughing at some joke. Everywhere, young, middle-aged, old couples walked together, talking, silent or laughing—but together. It was quieter and darker here in this block. Under a little tree whose thin spring leaves did not shadow them, a couple stood melted into one.

Po hurried on. She did not feel bitter. She was glad everyone had a mate—but she felt queer, as if she had not been admitted to the human race. She was nearly home when she heard footsteps running behind her, a hand clasped her arm and held it and she felt for a moment a slender hard body against hers. It was Coventry, looking down at her, smiling, eager, breathless.

"Po, I missed you at Durston's. I was kept talking at Mr. Fielding's house. Something wonderful! Fielding's bank is opening a branch in California—San Francisco—he's offered me a job, managing it!"

Impulsively, Po reached up and patted his cheek. "Coventry! I'm that happy for you!"

"Are you, Po?" he said tenderly.

Then Po realized he'd be going away for good, and she felt lost.

"You know, sometimes"—Coventry took her other hand and held it firmly—"sometimes it's fine and exciting and right to do things on the spur of the moment! To put everything behind you, to say I'm making a fresh beginning! Without thinking, without weighing, just trust your heart—and go ahead." He stopped then, and pressed both her hands. "Don't you agree?"

"Well," Po faltered, "yes, sometimes."

"It might not be much of a life at first but"—he was warm and eager—"I could make it so . . . if I—had you there!" He put an arm around her then, so tenderly, and stooped down and kissed her.

Po wanted to cry. It was not the same. It was not the same as Larry; she could not pretend to herself. But it was May, it was love, and she needed love.

Coventry held her off then for a moment, and said "Pocahontas" fondly, the way he had. Ah, he was so deft, so knowing in the ways of women. He knew when not to urge, when not to go too fast. "It's all right. Don't be troubled, darling. You don't have to tell me now. I'm not going for two days!" He kissed her lightly then, as he started to go. "I'm rushing off now to see a man about steamship accommodations. I'm going by way of the Isthmus. Do you mind—oh, just in case—if I make it for two? I'll come to see you, then, tomorrow night —to know."

Next day was a fragrant late May Sunday. Po tried to do things that needed doing. Usually she cleaned and dusted the rooms on Sunday, her free day. But as she worked, she would suddenly remember, "Coventry will be here tonight!" And she would find herself ten minutes later, standing dreamily staring into space, wondering, "What will I say?"

Her rooms, facing a small open square, were on the second floor of an old red brick Georgian house. Po loved the house with its white mantels, high windows, and tarnished brass wall candle sconces. It was a house of cheerful ghosts, departed gentility, memories of happy parties and pleasant faces.

She ran down now into the little square, where children rolled hoops and crossed to the stand the farm woman always set up, to sell garden flowers on summer Sundays to passing churchgoers. Everyone else seemed sleepy, calm. Only to Po it seemed a matter of moment whether to select purple irises bearded like imperious kings, or peonies, white with scarlet hearts. A girl does not get engaged every Sunday.

Back in her rooms, she started energetically to arrange the iris in the tall vase on the floor by the mantel, but, kneeling there, the rich honey smell set her off musing. Where was Larry now, and was he different? She remembered his face at the field when she had last seen him with the team, and he smiling proudly at his protégé, the young pitcher. She sighed. He might be different with the men, but with that other part of him, he might still. . . .

She thought of Coventry then, his crisp blond head as he bent solicitously, putting on her cloak, or Coventry and she laughing at some piece of raillery. Yes, the Duke of Kilmally was the wonderful one to laugh and no mistake. And then there would be the mad excitement, the fine hair-raising things that could happen any day and twice on Sundays in a place like that California!

She started gaily to finish her work. She had been able to buy the piano she wanted. Old and battered it was, with one leg wobbly if you touched it. As she arranged the flowers on it, her hands, touching the soft silkiness of the petals, sent her off dreaming again.

She was fond of Coventry. Fond enough? Was there a way to measure?

By six o'clock, she had bathed and washed her hair. She sat at the piano a moment, her bare feet thrust into slippers, a towel wrapped around her wet hair, her body, in its thin shift, still cool and damp. She struck the keys, and remembered, in a gathering dusk like this, in April, in a little glen, she had sung a song once:

"Put your head, darling, darling, darling,
  Your darling black head, my heart above!
Oh, mouth of honey, with the thyme for fragrance,
  Who with heart in breast, could deny you love—"

She stopped then, and suddenly buried her face in her hands and cried.

But after a bit, she shook off her tears. It was fragrant May. She was loved. Coventry loved her. In the little bed chamber, there was no mirror, and she came back to the sitting room and lit the candles in the tarnished sconces on either side of the tall streaked glass.

She took the dress out of its excitingly rustling tissue paper, and the odor of the rose sachet it had been in drifted off into the air.

Seeing the dress, she felt sad again. It had been acquired long ago, for the day—a day that had only been a fantasy. Some day, she had dreamed, Larry would come back. He would come up those stairs. Some day, he would see her in this dress, and would think, "How could I do without her!" But the dream had been as insubstantial and crackly as the tissue paper.

The white dress had been purchased in Brodie's, the expensive shop on the Broadway, where Po had once been refused a job as clerk. She regarded it a moment, in delight at its fragility. Then she slipped it on over her head, its skirt folds smothering her a moment until she emerged, a pale bud. It left her rather thin shoulders bare, but it was of sheerest white mull, laced with eyelet embroidery, and glowed over a pink taffeta slip, the bodice clustered with moss rose buds. The little flat-heeled slippers were of green the color of the moss rose stems, and fastened on with rose colored ribbons.

She looked at herself breathlessly. She was pale, but her eyes sparkled like blue fire, and her lips were parted, but with only a half smile, almost as if she could burst into tears. In sudden mood, she wished she had on her old blue skirt and blouse. But then, she moved, and the white mull skirt made charming little sounds over the slip . . . and besides, the dress was guileful and made her look exquisite, when really she was only pretty, and full of infinite possibilities.

The candles guttered as the air stirred the long chintz curtain. She blew the candles out, for it was hardly dark. She stood then, by the tall windows in the dusk, looking down. California was a long way. Once there, you did not return easily, perhaps never. She would never see Brian, again, or the men of the game. Or Brooklyn.

And she would never see Larry again.

Across the little square, she saw in the deepening dusk, a party of young men, six or eight, well dressed in their tail coats and white stocks, gathered in front of a house where a popular young girl lived. They must be serenading, a custom of the place. Then she heard the young men's voices, poignant, floating scross the square in the May dusk.

"Come where my love lies dreaming, is sweetly dreaming, the
happy hours away,
Come with the lute, come with the lay, my own love is sweetly
dreaming, her beauty beaming—"

The world was very beautiful. If only . . . If only . . .

She heard someone on the stair. It must be Rory the fiddler, who
often dropped in at odd hours when he had quarreled with his wife
and needed a refuge. She opened the door. But it was Dave Posen,
and he looking rich and important in a dark suit, and standing, pretending to be awe-struck at her appearance.

"I just got in from being with the team on tour!" he rushed on
gaily. "The team still has another game to play!"

Then she asked about how everything had gone on the trip, wanting to ask only of Larry, but not quite daring to.

And he went on, full of fine stories of the team's victories and all
their doings.

"You know," Dave threw in then, "I often meant to ask you about
it. When we were traveling in Maryland, I had a letter from you. I
could never make any sense of it. Something about 'twiny arbutus.'
What was it all about?"

"But was it never you sent me those little blossoms from the high
mountains?"

"No," Dave frowned. "Should I have?"

Suddenly Po felt all warm inside as if fires had flamed up radiantly.

"Why do you look so happy?" Dave asked, bewildered. "Did I say
something?"

Po's cheeks flooded scarlet. That was the trouble with her. Her
feelings always showed as plain as flower stems through a clear vase.

Dave looked at her, a sad little smile on his face. "Well, I'll move
on. You're expecting someone. Whoever he is—he is a lucky fellow!"

Then he left.

If Dave had not sent the arbutus, then—!

That Larry would think of sending those shy little flowers wrapped
in wet newspapers, all the way down from the mountains! Then—even
if he had only written her once, and signed it "Faithfully yours—"

A great buoyant surge of hope lifted her up as if she were floating
on a cloud.

When Coventry came, he found tears in her eyes, tears of mixed-
up happiness, and sadness too.

It would not have been Coventry if he had not brought a bouquet,
in lace paper, tiny hard curled little pink rosebuds for her; and he
looked at her in the dress, just like you would want a man to look at
you. Only . . . only.

"I'm glad I saw you, once, looking so enchanting. In California it will be rough for a while!"

How could she tell him?

"For I won't be going alone, will I?"

It was almost as hard as telling him about his father. But that had been the right thing, and now better to tell him straight out than to say she would be here waiting. But it was hard. She couldn't say, "I'm engaged to another." She had to say, "No, it is not you!"

Then, after all the easy, kindly ways that had come into her head, in the end she heard herself saying, "I'll not be going, Coventry!"

The serenaders had finished now and gone away, and the candle-light wavered over the fragile white dress, over Coventry's blond hair. He picked up the nosegay of rosebuds and handed it to her as if he were making a little offering of devotion. "I was always afraid you wouldn't. But you know, Pocahontas, even though I don't have you with me, I have a feeling a little of your flavor will always stay with me."

He kissed her tenderly, goodby.

Chapter Forty-eight

IT WAS early June when the Excelsiors returned. Po heard the news through Dave. And now, even in Manhattan, Po's heart acted oddly every time she saw a big form on the street; her breath stopped every time her dressing room door opened. But Larry did not come to see her.

The team had returned on Thursday, and on Friday, she asked Dave, "How is Larry?" "Fine!" said Dave, noncommittally. But Larry did not come.

On Saturday, she met Dave on the Broadway, as he was rushing to the *Clipper* office, and he told her, "One of the men on the team, Barney Wright, is in trouble, and Larry's been trying to get him fixed up. Barney never sent money home like he should have, his wife left, and now his goods are up with the sheriff. Larry's been working on it for him!"

Po turned this over thoughtfully. Wasn't that what a grown man would do—take care of responsibilities before he rushed off for a fling of talk with his friends? Ah, but wouldn't he want to see his girl right away? If he loved her? If he had a girl?

He did not come on Saturday either. He would surely have taken care of everything by now. Maybe Larry didn't have a girl.

By Sunday, she guessed she had built too airy a castle on the foundation of some arbutus sent from the high mountains. But that Sunday in early June was the kind to tear your heart out, what with its fragrance, and its mild bright sun, and Po felt unbearably lonely. She put on her new blue dress and went to see Brian.

In the flat, all was somnolent and peaceful and sunny and relaxed. Yes, Larry had been around the Gardens. Seemed fine. And wasn't it a wonderful tour? And wasn't it fine all the boys were home again? He had not even left word for her, then.

Out on Prospect Hill on that June Sunday, Po looked across the little glen. The crabapple tree had long since dropped its white petals and looked bare and vulnerable with all its work of growing before it. She had come back here because she remembered the surge of hope she felt at this place the day Larry seemed trying to struggle free of the cords—the day she had seen the green crabapples clinging to the broken branch.

She looked for the branch. And now again! She felt the same surge of hope! From the broken branch, new leaves had sprung, and yes, there had been blossoms! Every day these miracles happened with no one to celebrate! She wondered if the green crabapples she had seen last year had made themselves round with black glisteny seed, and been carried off, to grow perhaps, in some distant place, a new tree! She thought it unlikely, for at any time they had been here they had never seen a living soul. Maybe they had fallen, still green and misshapen, to rot into the ground? She would never know.

And then—she looked up, and her heart broke into a loud pæan of joy. Coming across the open green space—was Larry.

He raised an arm in greeting. Then he began to run. She, as if pulled by some force beyond herself, began to run too.

And when they came together, he picked her up, and held her, his face alight with more than June sun. The busy trees and hurrying grass went on about their affairs, as if this were only another miracle, and who had time to stop and shout, "Look, we have come through!"

He put her down then, and they stood a long, long moment, looking at each other hungrily, as if wanting fully to realize the moment. Then his arms, steady and sure, were around her and he kissed her. They stood there then, with the fragrant June sun falling on them, close and warm, for a long, long time. Po did not feel the way she had on the beach, wanting him. She was just filled with a great peaceful warm feeling that the loved one was near, and she could actually touch him.

They stood so, holding the precious moment, Po did not know how long. She lost track of time. Larry did not draw back now. After a long time, she suddenly felt his body arch hard against hers as if at last to come forward, body to body, to be one with her.

But—something was stopping Po now.

It was as if a force beyond her kept her from letting herself go. Something which seemed to have nothing to do with any activity of her mind or heart. Some deep feminine wiliness, it was, maybe, that nature had planted in her seed long before Po existed, to make her be sure the mate was strong, a possible father to children. She hardly knew what she was doing, she did not consciously think, "This is too fast!" But she pulled back.

For—what had been happening to him all this time? Was he just the same as before? Or was it that she was just a girl, any girl, met after a long time away from girls, and actually he was the same—not able to be open and free, unashamed, not guilty!

She walked away a little bit then, and looked back at him. And suddenly they were awkward and shy. They had been separated for months, and who knows what changes had moved them? They were in some ways like strangers. They looked at each other curiously and hungrily. She saw that he looked handsome, but older—years and years older—than the boy, dressed just as he was now, who had jumped into the hold of the *Red Tanager*.

Po had a need to keep away from him now, and suddenly, they were constrained, and talked of surface things. She asked about the team, and he said the tour was a success, everything easy and fine. Looking at him, though, Po guessed maybe it had not been so easy as he made it out. He seemed to have a permanent line between his brows, even though his mouth looked smiling. And, as he talked of the team, he said earnestly, as though he'd discovered a personal truth not before known, "Just because you see the men out there playing and running, it all looks easy and carefree. But every one of those fellows," he said seriously, "have problems, terrible problems. They're worried about money, or their wives aren't true to them, or they have sick babies, or—" he looked at Po straight and steady now— "they have mothers that need to run them."

Maybe something in Larry knew, too, that nature was making Po be sure he was strong, for he went on, calm and steady, as if she had a right to know.

"You know, it's a funny thing, my pitching hand going bad. That seemed like miserable luck when it happened and yet—if it hadn't, I might not have been able to do like I did. For the minute I got home in New Bedford, I saw it. I guess she didn't know how plain her feelings showed—maybe didn't even know she had them—but she had a look of victory! Now I'd stay home!

"It wasn't at all like you said—my being able to be nice to her and walk away. I left with a terrible quarrel. That was better than the first time, when I'd sneaked away.

"This spring, the team played in New Bedford. And my mother came! For her, that was something! She was ashamed of what I was doing, but she came. She had had to accept that in spite of my broken hand, in spite of everything, I'd gone on and done what I meant to do, apart from her! And she treated me now like I was a grown son, and she my mother, getting a little old. And then, it was like you said. I began to feel sorry for her."

Po wanted to go to him, she felt so buoyant and hopeful, but she waited.

"I guess, too, she wasn't the only one bent around and headed in a different direction. I'm not quite sure how it happened, but I guess it was me getting to like the men did it. I never knew I didn't like them, that I was just using them, the game, the team. They were just a way for me to be big, I guess. Don't get the idea I'm any reformed character, or anything like that. I guess I still use them—but in a different way.

"I don't know—it's hard to explain—it's like they were my children. I'm responsible for them, sort of, and when things go right with them and their families, and they're winning, and so making money, why I feel good. Better, much better than when I had to get all the applause. You'd be surprised how much you like people when you don't feel you have to be biggest, and best!"

Po felt a strong surge of hope rise now. She could see the calm set of his chin, his mouth not laughing, but not grim either. And then, suddenly, as she watched him, she knew what had happened. He liked himself!

After all, you knew yourself down deep where no one else could see, better than anyone could know you, and if you liked yourself, why everything was probably all right down there. Po stood beside the little bush that had been in early spring covered with tight furled bronze spikes. It was a syringa bush, and now its cloud of white waxy petals strained out, blooming to their uttermost peak, around the yellow hearts furred with pollen. The bush assailed her senses with its spicy fragrance.

Suddenly Larry came over to her and pulled her to him, facing him. His hands were urgent. "And now—I think we better get married—right away!"

Her heart gave a great pound, and her breath came so rapidly she

got no good from it, but finally, she brought out faintly, "Tis a thing
—needs—considering."

"Certainly. I don't expect you take me on faith. Don't think I
forgot what you told me on the beach last summer. That you'd have
no heroes or children in your bed! That you'd never marry me until
I was straightened out! Well, Miss O'Reilly—" with a firm, authorita-
tive hand, he grasped her around the waist and pulled her steadily
toward him— "I have come to show you you have got yourself a man!"

Now! This minute? Oh, no! Impossible!

She was panic-stricken with delight. Her mouth opened and her
breath came fast, but she could only look at him, fascinated, terrified.
Yes, she had been right about what made the difference in him. He
liked himself, and he was in no mood to punish himself or deny himself anything he wanted.

She slipped out of his grasp, and retreated behind the bush, and
looked back, imploring, her face burning. Suddenly, as she brushed
against it, all the petals on the bush, as if too full of love, bloomed
out to the fullest reach, and fell in a shower.

He was beside her again, sure, not hurried. "You see," he nodded
to the fallen petals, "that's what happens when you wait too long!"

Now she tried to sound calm, sensible, grown, and dignified, to
put him back in his place as a little boy. To do it, she had to move
away again, and face him, separate. "Maybe," she began, though her
breath and her voice was not very even, "I did things—said things—
was ready to do things—" she was flurried and scared now—"last summer. But it was because I meant to help you!"

"And now"—he refused to reduce his stature—"I'm going to help
us!"

"But"—she got a little angry—"it was different then!" She moved
away a frightened step.

"No."

"The entire matter is now a rose of a different color!" If she could
just breathe more evenly, she'd sound firmer.

"Same rose, same color!" He advanced toward her.

"No!" she said, holding up an imploring hand to ward him off.
"No!" Oh, the wonderful feminine luxury of saying "No!" and stamp-
ing her foot, and shaking her head, and saying, "No! No! Never!"
and being confident and easy that he would pay no attention to her.

Suddenly he crossed under the tree and picked up his coat from
where he had thrown it on the grass.

Was it possible he believed her?

But, no—he was only tossing it out of his way. Now he advanced
toward her again. If she could only have cried and laughed both at

the same time, she would not have felt so frightened. But he paid no attention to her. Sure and unhurried, he came toward her decisively.

Now? This second? Oh, no, no, no!

He picked her up as easily as if she were a petal. Suddenly Po remembered before how his love play had been that of a little boy, tugging at his mother's dress. Now it wasn't. It was wonderful to be carried. Po sighed a little. Their relationship had changed. What a luxury not to have to plan, to think.

He sat down with her on the grass.

"It's a shame to spoil that pretty dress. I think we better take it off!"

At this she jerked away from his arms and sat up in outraged dignity. "No! No!" she said wildly. "No!"

"No?" he said, unflurried.

The deep feminine wiliness seemed to take possession of her again. She hardly knew what she said, what tone she used. She sounded positive, withering, indignant. It was as if the feminine wiliness had to be sure he was not only strong enough to stand up to men, strong enough to stand up to his mother, but strong enough to stand up against her!

"This has gone far enough. We will stop here, I'm thinking! And it would be best maybe if you took yourself off from this place before harm is done!"

He held her just as firmly and steadily and warmly as before. "Ah," he said lightly, "the Irish are charming people, witty and gay, but it's my observation they are a race of cowardly braggarts!"

And she knew with breath coming faster, and he knew she knew, that it was she who had dared him to swim naked to the summer air and sea.

The dress came off.

Gently, oh, so tenderly at first . . . But then at last it was as if they both raced hand in hand far far out into the slow voluptuous swells of a warm summer sea. Somewhere in the air above the slow waves burst a brilliant glittering chord of music—as though the taut strings on the harp, on which only partial melodies had been played, now resolved with deep release into a magically satisfying chord.

Chapter Forty-nine

PO STOOD with her hand in Larry's, that hot July night, in the side gate leading to Brady's outdoor gardens. The baseball men of Brooklyn were having A Great Big Party. How else could they gather together the town's feelings and let them go in one great shout—seeing the banner stretched across the gardens, above the swaying red and yellow Chinese lanterns? The banner read:

CHAMPIONS OF THE KNOWN WORLD
Second World Series, Elysian Fields

July 6	July 8
Brooklyn 21	Brooklyn 23
New York 13	New York 18

Brian stood, red-faced, beaming, in the door from the bar. "First time I had her open out here since I took over again," he told Tony, who had come all the way from Philadelphia for the celebration. "Knew I'd have to, for the crowd!"

The dancers swung, and the fiddle rippled its gay ribbon of sound, and children darted and called, and every once in a while from inside the barroom a shout or cheer rang out as some darling, who had lent glory to his clan forever by nimble catch or mighty throw, came in.

Po and Larry crossed to greet Tony, who had brought his wife and children too, that they might not forget there was joy in the world.

"So, when the boys got back from the tour, you understand," Brian was telling Tony, "with everyone knowing we had a team no one could beat—" he reached up an arm over Larry's shoulder—"did we have to go crying around, and stammering, and standing on one foot? We says, polite, but firm-like, 'Will yez call a convention now, or will we do it ourselves?' "

"They called it quick enough then," Larry put in, while Tony's eyes gleamed.

"And would you believe it, if those boy-os over the river," Brian recaptured his story, "them Gothams and Eagles and Empires and Knickerbockers—if they didn't try to say no one under twenty-one could belong to an official club! And they wanted a big annual dues from everyone too!"

"But you licked 'em on that?" Tony enjoyed it all in retrospect.

'You bet!" Larry said, laughing. "And now we got it official the game's to be nine innings instead of twenty-one runs!"

"Ah, good," Tony put in. "That way you can finish a game after work, sometimes, before it gets dark! But didja make 'em change about a ball caught on the first bound being good?"

"Don't worry," Larry said, "we'll take care of that next year. Big thing, Tony, is, we know there'll *be* a convention next year. We don't have to go whining around, trying to get the Knickerbockers to call it."

"No, sir! We got a real organization!" And Brian said the words over proudly, "The National Association of Baseball Clubs!" Then he leaned over and grabbed Tony's arm, to be sure he wouldn't miss the point. "And when we come to the electing officers, Tony, why there are the Knickerbockers sitting there with their mouths open, waiting to be asked—but not one of them was elected to office! It was pitiful!" And Brian let out a roar of laughter.

"And when they tumbled off their high and mighty throne," Larry said, "they didn't make anything but a light, puffy crash!"

Then Larry and Brian began to give Tony a loving second-by-second account of the series at Elysian Fields, and Po decided to slip upstairs to see Mamie.

It was a hot night. Mamie, closing the oven door, straightened up, turning a flushed face to Po.

"I know this celebration means a lot to him, so I'm making some extra food to send down."

Po regarded the two cakes piled high with icing, and sniffed the delicate odor from the oven. She knew Mamie was an excellent cook.

"I'm just finishing the gooseberry pies. They taste better when they're still warm. I'll have the chicken salad ready in a little while. Maybe you will come back up and carry it down for me when it's ready."

"But, Mamie," Po said, "aren't you coming down to the party?"

"Oh, no!" Mamie said quickly. "What would I do down there?" She shook her head positively. "I'd be out of place!"

"Well, I'll be back." Po ran down to where the air vibrated with music and laughter and talk.

And standing at the crowd edge, Po took a long breath enjoying it. "You could walk long years in the world, going in the high places and the low, and it's rarely you'd see happiness an inch thick shiny on every countenance!"

And then she saw a little ways off, Walt, standing near the door, regarding her with his serene tender smile, and she went over to him.

"I'm just leaving," Walt said. "I have to get back to the newspaper office, but I'm glad I saw you. Congratulations! I hear you are going to change your name!" Po nodded, smiling happily, and Walt said it over, as if trying it out, "Pocahontas O'Reilly Wainwright!"

"Sure, it's a terror of a name, I don't deny it," Po laughed, "but in America they don't mind a name going this way and that and jumping a fence or a great wall, and walking on for itself!" Walt laughed then, and patted her shoulder, and turned away, and she saw him looking at the crowd a moment, as if he wished he could stay. Then he slipped off into the outer dark.

Po would like to have danced, but she could see Brian and Larry still playing the series for Tony. As she stood hesitating, wondering whether it was time to go back for the food, Louise in a bright pink dress danced past, smiling up into the face of a big Eckford named Charlie. As she passed, Louise reached over and touched Po's arm. "You're not woman enough for him," she cried out jokingly. "Besides, you got a temper, and you're bossy!" And Louise rolled her eyes warningly and laughed. "So, watch out!"

Po smiled stiffly.

Bossy, is it? Louise was jealous. She decided to go upstairs. The pies ranged on the table, aromatic, enticing; the chicken salad ready in a great bowl; and Mamie looking flushed and excited with this offering of love.

Suddenly Po was struck with a bit of guile. She picked up the salad, and the two cakes. "Mamie, it's a shame—the pies'll be cold by the time I get down and back, what with people stopping me to talk and to chat, and asking who made this delicious food and all. You bring down the pies!"

Mamie looked a little hesitant. Then she picked them up. "Well— it is a shame for them to get cold!"

Po led the way quickly and took the food out to a long table in the outer gardens, then she darted away in the crowd, looking every which way. She was remembering how wonderful it had been when Tony had seized her long ago and danced with her, and how she had felt one with the crowd. She found him standing alone.

"Tony! Ask me no questions! Go there where Mamie stands setting out the pies. Take her around the waist, and get her into the figure." For the couples were stomping feet and clapping hands and twirling and stepping along. Tony flashed a gleaming smile, said not a word, and was off.

Po saw Mamie's astonished face, as Tony grabbed her. But Tony wasn't talking; he was dancing. If only the music didn't stop now! It didn't. It kept on. And then Po saw Bushel Basket get Mamie as she came whirling down the figure. Mamie looked a little breathless—and yes, a little pleased, too. The dance kept on. Why, Mamie was smiling now! Then the music stopped.

Would she go upstairs and freeze up again?

Po sped toward her. "Mamie, I guess it's me should be behind that table, handing out that cake and pie, but now, I'm longing to take a dance. Couldn't you stay but the little while only, just to help?"

Mamie was flushed, but she was smiling a little. "Well, I guess—Yes, I'll do it!"

And there stood Mamie Brady, handing out gooseberry pie at the Great Big Party, a little self-conscious, but still stealing a smile around every once in a while. And Po saw Brian pat her on the shoulder and Mamie trying to look as if she had only come down to help.

Po could not find Larry then. What if that Louise—

But after a bit, Brian found Po, and took her arm firmly. "Will you come over here a minute, darlint. I would like to talk to you!" He did not look very jolly though, but as if he had some kind of a grim duty to perform.

He guided her to a table at the edge of the gardens where it was quieter and sat her down. He swallowed once or twice, cleared his throat, and pulled his whiskers, and frowning portentously, began, "Now, Po, me girl, you are going to be married—" He stopped then and cleared his throat again nervously. He shoved aside some glasses on the table in front of him, as if clearing the way. "You got no mother." He stopped again and clawed his whiskers, and screwed up his face.

Po squirmed, in a panic.

"You got no father to talk to you either." He fiddled with some silver on the table, and finally burst out, "You only got me!"

"Whist, now!" Po twisted uncomfortably. "Is he going to tell me about Things?"

But finally, as if he were going to say it though the heavens fell, Brian plunged in. "You'll never remember the great horse fair at Kilcrae, but at one end of the place was a fenced-off pen, and a big sign in front saying 'As Is.' Inside were horses—maybe something wrong with them, maybe not—but you looked them over, you paid your price. If you got to your own glen with the animal and discovered it was spavined, or had a way of whinnying you didn't like, or a way of jogging along when you wanted to gallop—it was no use screaming to the high saints you'd been robbed, and black injustice done! You had taken it 'as is.' " Brian was not nervous now, but vehement. "Men are mostly a little spavined, or have a bad gait, or a blind eye or something. What he is now—that's what you got. If you don't like it, don't take him! I notice you kind of like to tell him what to do. So every once in a while, on the third Thursday of the month, maybe, 'tis well to say to yourself the words, 'as is.' "

He patted her shoulder then, and went away into the crowd, and Po sat blinking a little.

Then she smiled. Whist, then! When people gave you advice, it was usually their own troubles speaking. If it fitted in with your needs, fine, but in any case, 'twas a great comfort to the giver.

She went on from there then and spoke to Tony's wife, but, even as she was talking, a thought opened its petals in her mind.

"What'd they mean, Louise with her 'bossy' and Brian with his 'as is'? Me, is it?" Po thought in consternation. But—what if she were? They must have been trying to tell her something.

Then she saw Larry coming toward her, and felt comforted. "Ah!" She smiled at him. "Wasn't I shot through and loaded down with a weight of luck to find this great laddo with the gleamy hair on him!" He picked her up then and whirled her into the dance. But as the fiddle rippled out, Po put into her memory, on an easy low shelf where they'd be quickly come by, the words, "as is."

Chapter Fifty

ALL THAT SUMMER, Larry toiled like a man possessed. He was trying to make real a new dream. Baseball was his life. Was it possible for a man to make a living at it?

What if he built a baseball field—huge, where thousands could watch easily, which he would keep in prime condition at all times, where the best teams would play, where you didn't have to chase the geese and chickens off, or ask old man Green if he would pasture his horse somewhere else for the afternoon? A field big enough for a decent space between spectators and players, so in case, as often happened now, natural feelings overcame a spectator, and he was tempted to help out his team or a favorite player by interfering with the play, it was not easy for him to do so.

Larry had tremendous energy; it was released into building this field. By August, the dream had become reality. It was on a small truck farm to whose edges the city had crept. On one side, a new row of three story flats had recently been built. On the other side, a new brick building with two great smokestacks stood. There, instead of in back of your own fireplace, or in your own smoke house, thousands of hams and bacon slabs were cured at once. But on the other two sides, open fields and small farms still stretched away.

The glacier ice had nearly melted, and most of the men had their jobs back. Things were not quite the same though. For one thing, the

Van Leyn ship yard sign was gone. No more Clipper ships would float from Van Leyn ways out on the East River and so to the seven seas, for though the yard was open again, it was being reorganized to make iron ships. It had been combined with the Hymes Iron Works, and another plant across the river that made marine engines. The same company owned part of the new ferry line, too, but it had all become sort of vague in people's minds—just what was made where, and who, exactly, owned what. It had become sort of impersonal, like the new name—The Continental Corporation.

Now that everyone was working, baseball had become again something you threw yourself into passionately after work or on Sundays. On the tour, everyone knew and understood the men had to live and pay their expenses, and was glad they were paid. But now, things were back to normal. And although "shooting stars," and occasionally some others, took money for playing, it was considered not quite sporting.

But, on the new field, admission was to be charged. Part of the gate would go to the clubs to pay their expenses. The rest, to the ball park. In winter, the field could be flooded for ice skating, and that would help financing. All these details were known and discussed and approved, for every baseball man in Brooklyn had worried with Larry over raising the money, knew when he had half the amount, three quarters—worried with him over the interest on the debt. The bank had finally gotten six or eight men who, observing the crowds attracted on the tour, had formed an investment pool.

All the baseball men were concerned with Larry, too, when rain fell and held back the work. Many of them even lent a hand on the leveling of the field, in building the high board fence, and the other buildings. Larry, however, had done most of it himself. He had one pair of paid hands. Po had found Juba in straits, for Dent's had closed temporarily in the Panic, and Juba had become Larry's first employee.

It was hot the August Saturday the "Atlantics were to play the Excelsiors to inaugurate the opening of the new Grand Union Ball Park, owner, Larry Wainwright."

Po waited at Brady's Gardens. Larry had said he would pick her up early, for he still had many things to look after at the field. Brian did not play on the new Excelsior team—it was a younger and faster team —but he and Mamie were coming later.

Po waited, but Larry did not come. She began to wonder then if he had said he would see her at the field. She knew he had many things to do. She had just decided to start by herself when Larry, panting and red from hurrying, arrived.

Po blinked her eyes. In his hat was a large bunch of—something green. She looked, wide-eyed. It was a large bunch of real, quivery, nodding, delicate little shamrocks!

Larry looked at her, a happy grin on his face, as she stood, staring, mouth open. Then sudden tears came swimming up toward her eyes. It was so foolish and gay, and, in a way—unlike Larry.

"Larry!" Her voice sounded quivery as the plants. "You—wearing the green!"

"And what a time I had finding them! That's why I'm late!" She held her brimming eyes steady.

"But . . . 'tis never St. Patrick's Day, or near it!"

"Who said it was! It's Po O'Reilly day I'm celebrating!"

Po's tears suddenly brimmed over. "And why," he demanded, "are you crying in the middle of my celebration?" She didn't know why. Maybe because what he had done was so—childish, sentimental, crazy —why—it was almost Irish! Then he kissed her hastily, for they must set out at once.

As they walked toward the corner, with people staring and smiling at the large bunch of shamrocks in Larry's hat, it came to her why she cried. He was busy today, with many worrisome things on his mind. It had not been a casual, easy thing for him to find the green. He had had to take thought and trouble—but it was not that that moved her. He must—to have done this particular thing—have had to imagine what it was like to be her, what would make her gay and happy! She remembered the day of the pic-nic on the beach, and she could hear Larry saying, "I don't see where people get all these feelings," and his saying he had never, and didn't want to imagine what it was like to be someone else. Now, he had.

They went out on the Putnam Avenue horsecar line, and Larry worried on the way about whether the field was too far out, whether having to pay the car fare would keep people away. Whether charging twenty-five cents was too much. If they got a crowd of three thousand, he'd be in the clear for this game; four thousand, fine; five thousand, a big success.

But when they got there, they could not repress excited smiles. Only a few people had arrived, as they stood for a moment, looking at the field.

At the gate of the high board fence, surrounding the entire huge field, was the little wooden office and ticket window. There were, instead of tents, little wooden dressing rooms for the men. In back of the office was a little restaurant, where Juba was already busily arranging his wares, for he was going to sell oysters and beer, and run it like a little business for himself. Beyond that was a Chinese pagoda, with seats around it, for ladies who might get tired standing, or who wished to protect their hats in case of rain. Larry thought, sometime, he might even put seats around the field for the spectators.

Po had brought along the *Clipper,* so they could see if Dave had gotten in the story about the opening of the new grounds. Yes, there it was! Trust Dave!

Larry already had his mind on other things.

"It's those shadows on that field that bother me!" For the tall smokestacks of the packing plant, when the sun reached a certain height, cast streaks of dark across the white sunshine on the field.

But then, the crowds began to arrive, many carrying black cotton umbrellas against the brilliant sun. The trickle became a heavy stream. Pouring past the little ticket office manned by Ansel Dop, and on around the field, standing on the new clipped grass, staring about at the new fence, the new field, the dressing shacks, laughing, and happy.

Soon Po could see Larry had nothing to worry about. The crowd was huge. Larry was in the little office behind the ticket window now, frowning, busy, responsible, getting change to Ansel, keeping track of the crowd tally.

Po was happy for Larry that his long tension in building the field, in risking his all in it, seemed over. It was strange, though—the few minutes before an Atlantic-Excelsior game, to be counting, anxiously, money in a little office. Well, Po sighed, they were older now.

It had been wonderful being sixteen, seventeen, eighteen. Everything had seemed possible, like when you waked up on a fresh morning, glisteny with dew. But you could not stay sixteen, any more than the dew could remain. Whether you liked it or not, you got to be seventeen, and eighteen and twenty, even thirty. The excitement, the unknown, was gone. Now you knew you'd run a ball park. You couldn't just play ball on sunny afternoons. You had to count the gate, and worry, with little new lines on your face, whether you could pay taxes and interest on the debt.

Now the players walked out to the new pine dressing shacks. Twinkle-Toes, Death-to-Flying-Things, Bushel Basket, Rooster Hanlon, Restored Jones, and all the others, and as each was recognized, he received a welcoming cheer.

Then, in the office, Larry yelled at Po, "Five thousand three!" The crowds were still pouring in, but Larry wanted to get this news to Bushel Basket, the captain, who would spread it to the men, for they would share in this success.

As Larry ran across the field, a sudden thunderous roar of joyful welcome rose and trembled in the air. Why, it was like they were cheering for the Bull! Po saw that they were beginning to substitute Larry for the Bull. He was not the same; he could not do things with the same effortless power. His forehead, like theirs, was lined with problems and scurrying. He was different from the Bull, too, for he used his mind now instead of his hands. Nevertheless, and another thunderous cheer rose, this was the man who had planned the tour, and made the name of the Excelsiors ring out in the land. This was the man who, in spite of his injured hand, insisted on playing, and often did as substitute. This was the man who dared to try to make a living at baseball. They cheered again, clasping him to their hearts. He was nearly as big as the Bull, and he was all that was left to them.

As he came back, Po greeted him, excited, with the new tally. "Larry! Five thousand three hundred and eight!"

They clasped hands, looking at each other with triumphant smiles. Then they went out beyond the gate to judge how many were still coming up from the car line, for the crowd inside was getting restless, waiting for the magic, "Pl-a-y Ba-a-wl!"

From the crowds hurrying to get in, Larry decided to wait five more minutes. A shining-eyed, eager boy, about twelve, with muddy shirt hanging out, one trouser leg rolled up, his face glowing with excitement, came hurrying up, then, panting.

"Is this it?" he demanded eagerly. "This where the Atlantics is playing the Excelsiors?"

"This is it," Larry smiled.

"Gripes!" The boy breathed a long panting sigh. "I made it!" He stood then, panting.

"Is it a way you've come?" Po asked, seeing the mud on his bare legs.

"Sure is! I been travelin' since dawn! I lit out 'fore Paw put me to sortin' the onions for market! I swum the crik, walked some, got a ride, walked some more—"

"Where'd you come from?" asked Larry.

"Out on Long Island. Three Corners is where our farm is!"

"Why, that's ten miles," Larry said.

"Yup"—the boy started toward the gate, eyes shining—"but I made it!"

The crowds were thinning now. They had better begin. But at the ticket window, a disturbance had broken out. Larry and Po moved quickly through the crowd.

The boy from Three Corners stood, fists doubled up, chin set belligerently, the shine gone from his eyes, and instead, angry sparks darting.

"What's the matter?" Larry said quickly to Ansel.

"Nothing! I jus' told him it was twenty-five cents!"

"What's goin' on here?" the boy demanded fiercely, squared away for a fight.

"It's only twenty-five cents," Ansel said patiently.

The boy stood glaring in fierce outrage. "You mean you got to *pay* to see the Excelsiors now?"

"That's right!"

The boy swung around, fists clenched, brows drawn down indignantly, squaring away at Larry, at everyone now. "Who says?"

"It's only twenty-five cents," Ansel repeated wearily.

"I ain't got twenty-five cents." The boy was outraged.

"Here." Larry stepped up. "Go in, son." His voice was brusque. To Ansel he said, "It's all right. Let him in."

Then Larry walked away quickly, frowning.

The game began then, but as Larry, crouched down near third base, watched the play, with Po standing beside him, she could see he had a troubled look.

Everything went smoothly. In a way—almost too smoothly. No cow wandered across, mooing angrily, no spectator grabbed a ball and threw it in to home in excess of zeal for his team. And the two teams played with beautiful precision.

The crowd seemed a little subdued, too. As they watched the eighteen excellent players, it was as if they sensed something slipping away; the bat sticks were slipping out of their hands. Soon they might hold them only through proxies, in their imagination.

She remembered the day she had first seen the joyous leaping game, the Sunday she arrived in Brooklyn, the terrifying zest, the mad exuberance. Maybe it was only the boy's angry outcry had troubled her, and she only imagined it. But it seemed that a certain shimmering glisten in the air had gone. Something seemed subtly different. Was it because now the field had a fence around it, with a ticket window?

But the day was a great success. The Excelsiors won, 23 to 20, everybody congratulated Larry on the fine arrangement of the field, and the crowd went home happy. Even Juba had had a success, with a fine profitable day at the oyster bar. Yes, it was a great triumph.

Po and Larry were almost the last to leave. As was his habit, Larry crouched down at the first base line, squinting at the shadows cast by the stacks, as the waning sun turned the grass a brilliant green. Po wondered if he was bemused about the shadows on the playing field from the smokestacks. He had foreseen them, they troubled him, but he did not know what to do about them.

But it was not the shadows from the stacks that made him look troubled and musing.

"I wish we could have kept it for free, but"—the troubled puzzled look came again—"I didn't see just how to!" Then he looked around the field, almost bewildered. "I built the fence!"

Po put her hand on his shoulder.

But to herself she reflected that you had to be so careful all the time. It was like when they let the *Red Tanager* go about its slave business, or like the grain ship dumping its cargo in the harbor within the cry of hungry people. You had to watch out all the time, take responsibility for things. The field was a great success, a personal success. You wouldn't think that what you did could change things—but it could.

"I wish it were for free again," Larry repeated.

He got up and they started off across the field.

"Po, how?"

Everyone was always thrusting responsibility at her. But—as they walked off toward the car line, she began to wonder if, maybe, there was a way it could all be like before, open and wide and free. She had a concern about it.

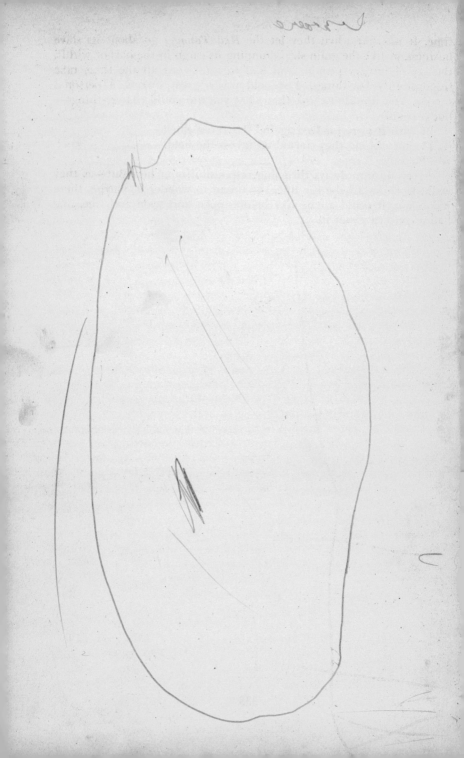

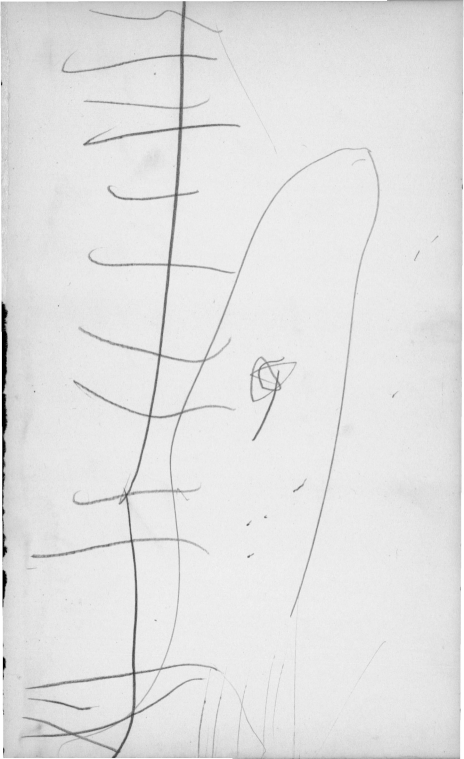

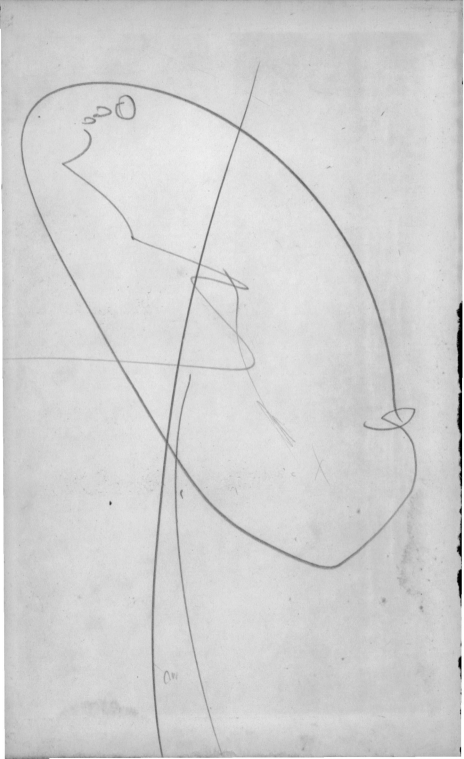